Praise for *Black Thunder*

"Satisfying . . . [an] insightful portrait of a native culture still evolving between tradition and modernity."

—*Publishers Weekly*

"The authors' intimate knowledge of the ways of life, culture, and mores of the Navajos shows in their writing. *Black Thunder* can be read as a stand-alone [but] is a must-read for fans of the Ella Clah mysteries. [It] is a novel anyone who loves great mysteries will enjoy reading."

—*Mysteries Galore*

"Without ever reading any of the previous books, I was able to enjoy Ella's adventures and not feel at all lost."

—*When Falls the Coliseum*

BLACK THUNDER

Also by Aimée & David Thurlo

Ella Clah Novels

Blackening Song
Death Walker
Bad Medicine
Enemy Way
Shooting Chant
Red Mesa
Changing Woman
Tracking Bear
Wind Spirit
White Thunder
Mourning Dove
Turquoise Girl
Coyote's Wife
Earthway
Never-ending Snake

Plant Them Deep

Lee Nez Novels

Second Sunrise
Blood Retribution
Pale Death
Surrogate Evil

Sister Agatha Novels

Bad Faith
Thief in Retreat
Prey for a Miracle
False Witness
Prodigal Nun
The Bad Samaritan

BLACK THUNDER

✖ ✖ ✖ ✖ ✖

AN ELLA CLAH NOVEL

AIMÉE & DAVID THURLO

A Tom Doherty Associates Book
New York

BLACK THUNDER

Copyright © 2011 by Aimée and David Thurlo

A Forge Book
Published by Tom Doherty Associates, LLC
175 Fifth Avenue
New York, NY 10010

www.tor-forge.com

Forge® is a registered trademark of Tom Doherty Associates, LLC.

The Library of Congress has cataloged the hardcover edition as follows:

Thurlo, Aimée.
    Black thunder : an Ella Clah novel / Aimée Thurlo and David Thurlo.
        p. cm.
    "A Tom Doherty Associates book."
    ISBN 978-0-7653-2451-1 (hardback)
    1. Clah, Ella (fictitious character)—Fiction.   2. Police—New Mexico—
Fiction.   3. Navajo Indians—Fiction.   4. Navajo women—Fiction.
5. Policewomen—Fiction.   6. Mothers and daughters—Fiction.
7. New Mexico—Fiction.   I. Thurlo, David.   II. Title.

PS3570.H82B57 2011
813'.54—dc22
                                                                                    2011021585

ISBN 978-0-7653-2454-2 (trade paperback)

First Edition: November 2011
First Trade Paperback Edition: October 2012

Printed in the United States of America

0 9 8 7 6 5 4 3 2 1

To Melissa Singer,
our editor, who believed in us from day one.
And to Sydney Abernathy—may you always
walk with beauty before you.

ACKNOWLEDGMENTS

With our special thanks to:
Steve Henry, Attorney at Law, Corrales
Bill Ellis, Professor of Law, Emeritus
Sergeant Ryan Tafoya, Bernalillo County Sheriff's
Department

ONE
✖ ✖ ✖

Tribal Police Investigator Ella Clah stood next to her department's cruiser, a dusty, white SUV that had more miles on it than a Two Grey Hills sheepdog. As she stood beneath the shade of the Quick Mart station's island, watching the dollar amount shoot past fifty as the pump fed regular into the tank, her second cousin and partner, Justine Goodluck, was busy cleaning the windshield.

"It's been so quiet lately," Justine said. "I hate slow days. I'd rather be up to my ears in an investigation than catching up with paperwork. It's nine in the morning and it already feels like we've been on duty all day."

"I hear you," Ella answered. "At least we're not behind a desk."

Justine stopped working on the windshield and looked directly at Ella. Although among Traditionalists that would have been considered extremely rude, tribal cops had learned to walk the line between the old and the new, adapting to a reservation in transition.

"What's eating you, partner?" Justine asked. Seeing Ella shrug, Justine added, "Don't try to tell me it's nothing. We've known each other too long."

There were many advantages to working with a close partner but the ability to second-guess each other was often a two-edged sword. With some partnerships, familiarity bred contempt, as the old saying warned. Yet Justine and she had found a middle ground. Though they weren't what Ella's daughter would have termed BFFs, they'd become attuned to each other in a way that gave them a distinct advantage out in the field.

Ella was still thinking of how to answer that when a call came over their radio. "S.I. Unit One, see the clerk at the First United Bank on Highway 64, east of the bridge. He reports a man posing as Chester Kelewood is trying to cash a two-hundred-dollar check. The clerk will try to stall the subject until you arrive."

Ella hung the gas nozzle back onto the pump and reached inside the open window to pick up the mike. "Unit One responding," Ella said as Justine paid the bill.

"We're less than a mile from there," Justine said, slipping behind the wheel. "How do you want to handle this?"

Ella began accessing information on the MDT, Mobile Dispatch Terminal. As her partner eased out into downtown Shiprock traffic, she answered, "Chester Kelewood has been on our missing person's list since last June second, and in these situations the bank always flags their accounts. Let's go in silent and try to get next to this scam artist before he catches on."

A few minutes later, Justine dropped Ella off near the bank's front door, then headed for the closest parking slot. As Ella approached the entrance, an anxious-looking man stepped outside—not Kelewood, judging from the image she'd just viewed on the terminal. She hesitated, wondering if this was the suspect or just another patron.

His gaze shifted to the badge clipped to her belt and a second later, he spun around and bolted down the sidewalk.

"That's him!" a man in the foyer yelled.

Ella raced after the man, who darted around the corner of the building.

Although he'd only had a slight lead, the man moved like the wind, fear of arrest undoubtedly motivating him. He reached the back corner of the bank, then disappeared down the alley to his left.

Just as Ella appeared in the alley, he reached a six-foot cinder-block wall. Seeing her closing in, he scrambled clumsily over the top.

Ella followed, jumping up, then over. This was a lot easier than the ten-foot barrier at the county police academy's obstacle course. Dropping to her knees to absorb the shock of landing, she searched the perimeter and quickly spotted the suspect. The Navajo man was hightailing it down a dirt road.

She hit Justine's speed-dial number on her cell phone, slowing just enough to make the call. "Justine, I'm in pursuit. Drive down the ditch road and try to cut him off. He's heading north through the brush."

"Roger that," Justine replied, then hung up.

Ella continued pursuit into the *bosque*, the wooded area that lined the riverbanks. She knew she couldn't match his sprint speed in a 440 or less, but she was sure she could wear him down cross-country, providing she could keep him within sight or track him. Even as she processed this thought, the man raced fifty yards down the road, then cut right and disappeared into a clump of twelve-foot-high willows, red and gray-green from their early summer growth.

Less than ten seconds behind, she ducked in after him. Ella could hear his labored breathing and the thump of his boots on the sand as he ran parallel to the San Juan River, here only about a hundred yards wide. Although there were steep bluffs on the opposite shore, on this side there were many possible exits back along the north bank. She'd have to be careful he didn't slip back into town. Hopefully, Justine would see him if he crossed the ditch road.

The path the suspect had chosen kept him close to the river. The chase required constant swerving and twisting to avoid getting whipped by the long willow branches or tripping on a tuft of salt grass. Ella found herself constantly ducking and throwing up her right or left arm to avoid being, literally, bush whacked.

She'd already eased into her long-distance running rhythm: two strides, inhale, two strides, exhale. She knew from her regular conditioning runs that she'd be able to keep up this pace for miles. Even with the heavy ballistic vest she always wore under her shirt, she'd catch up sooner or later. Unfortunately, the moment he realized that, he might turn on her, so she'd have to be ready.

Still on his tail, she remained alert, forcing herself to keep her breathing smooth and regular. Even if she hadn't been able to hear him crashing through the brush like an enraged bull, his tracks were easy to follow. Soon she noticed that he was angling steadily toward the river. The bluffs a quarter mile farther down were lower and receded from the banks, leaving easier access to the shore and possible escape. Maybe he'd decided to swim for it next—though it was probably more of a deep wade or wallow unless he dropped into a pool or undercut in the bank.

Suddenly Ella stopped hearing his footsteps. She slowed to a brisk walk and listened carefully. Almost instinctively, she reached up to touch the turquoise badger fetish hanging from a leather strap around her neck.

Her brother, Clifford, a medicine man, or *hataalii* as they were known to the *Diné*, the Navajo People, had given her the Zuni-made fetish years ago as a gift. Since that time, she'd noticed that the small carving invariably became hot whenever danger was near. Right now it felt uncomfortably warm. Though she'd never been able to explain it, she suspected that the heat it emitted might have something to do with her own rising body temperature in times of crisis. Either way, she'd learned to trust the warning.

Ella stopped and slowly turned around in a circle, detecting the acrid scent of sweat—not her own. Before she could pinpoint it more accurately, a man burst out from behind a salt cedar, yelling as he swung a big chunk of driftwood like a baseball bat.

Ella ducked and the wood whooshed over her head, missing her skull by inches. Before he could take another swing, Ella drew her weapon and aimed it at her assailant.

"Drop the stick, buddy, now!" she ordered.

The man dropped the branch, but dove to his right, rolling into some tall grass. Then, leaping back to his feet, he sprinted away.

"Crap!" Ella holstered her gun and took off after him again. No way this jackrabbit was going to get away from her.

Running out of steam, the panting suspect tried to leap a fallen cottonwood branch, but caught his toe, or misjudged the jump. He fell to the sand, face-first.

Ella caught up to him a second later, but he swung around, still on his knees, and dove for her feet. He grabbed her boot and twisted her leg, trying to knock her down. Ella broke free and recaptured her balance just as the guy leaped up and lunged.

Ella kicked him in the chest with her heavy boot.

The impact stopped him in his tracks, and he gasped. He was wobbling back and forth, but somehow he stayed on his feet. He took a step back, then held up his fists, waving them to and fro like a fighter working out in a gym as he took a bob-and-weave defense.

Ella kept her fighting stance. "Stop. I'm a cop. Don't fight me. You'll go down."

"You wish," the Navajo man yelled, his face beet red from exertion.

"Have it your way," Ella said, and reached for the canister of Mace on her duty belt. She had it halfway up before his fists suddenly opened up. Showing his palms and outspread fingers, he took a step back.

"No, stop! I'm allergic to that stuff. Really. I give up."

Ella immediately spun him around and cuffed him. "If you run for it again, I'll Taser your ass."

Taking him by the arm, she informed him of his rights as she guided him east toward the dirt road that paralleled the *bosque* along the irrigation ditch. As he stumbled along she asked him for his name, but all she got was a request for an attorney.

By the time they reached the road, a patrol cruiser was waiting, having come from the north. Justine was inching up from the south in her unit, less than fifty yards away. Ella looked at the uniformed officer climbing out of the cruiser. She recognized Mark Lujan, a young cop with about four years on the tribal force. "Thanks, Lujan, but I've got him now. My partner and I will take him in," she said, seeing Justine climbing out of the SUV.

"Let the officer take him, boss," Justine said, leaning her head out of the SUV. "We've got another call."

"What's happening, partner?" Ella asked, climbing into the vehicle.

Justine turned the SUV around, then spoke as they drove toward the highway. "A Navajo crew was replacing fence posts on the Navajo Nation side of the border, just the other side of Hogback, when they found a body."

"On tribal land—they're sure of that?" Ella reached for a tissue from the glove box, then wiped away the perspiration from her brow with one hand and redirected the air-conditioning vent toward her face and neck.

"Yeah, from what I was told. They called 911 and dispatch called us immediately."

There was no direct route to the site. When they passed

through the wide, river-cut gap in the Hogback, the long, steep-sided outcrop towering above the desert for miles, Justine had to continue east off the Rez. Their intended route required them to circle back to the northwest along the old highway, which came much closer to the spinelike ridge.

There was a dirt track that ran along the north-south fence line through an old field and former marsh, and the ride was extra rough. Trees and brush dotted the area, thickly in some places, and it took a while to spot the tribal truck, which was in a low spot. The tailgate of the oversized pickup was down and the bed filled with coils of wire and fence posts.

"Where's the crew?" Ella asked, looking around.

"Way over there," Justine said, gesturing with her chin, Navajo-style, toward a shady spot beneath an old cotton-wood at least a hundred feet northwest of the pickup.

Ella wasn't surprised. As a detective on the Navajo Rez, she usually didn't have to worry that a murder scene would be contaminated by the Navajo public. Whether they were Traditionalists, New Traditionalists, or Modernists, fear of the *chindi* was a fact of life here.

The *chindi*, the evil in a man, was said to remain earth-bound waiting for a chance to create problems for the living. Contact with the dead, or their possessions, was a sure way to summon it to you, so avoidance was the usual strategy.

The foreman, a short, muscular Navajo in jeans and a pale blue tribal-issue shirt, came to meet them as they parked and stepped out of the SUV. His yellow straw cowboy hat was stained with dust and sweat. It was getting hot already here in northwest New Mexico. "We called you as soon as we realized what we were digging up. You can see what's left of a human hand down there. It's over by that spot where we were taking out some fill dirt."

"Thanks. We'll handle it from here," Ella said.

Justine joined Ella and they approached the location he'd pointed out. A shovel had been left beside the area where sand had been scooped out, probably to fill around a newly planted fence post about ten feet away. The original ground had been eroded by heavy rain and the old post still lay nearby, the wood badly rotted.

Ella and Justine moved carefully, stepping only in the fresh shoe and boot prints left by the work crew and making sure no other potential evidence was disturbed.

"Our crime scene team is on the way," Justine said, looking down at the dark, leathery-looking, dried out remnants of what was clearly a human's right hand. "Benny's driving the van. Ralph Tache wants in on this, too. He said he can't dig—doctor's orders—but he can collect evidence and document the scene."

"I don't know about that," Ella said, giving Justine a look of concern. "I'm not sure Ralph's ready. This could be labor intensive, and we'll have to do it all by hand. We can't bring in a backhoe, and all that bending over . . ."

"Ralph's had a lot to deal with after all those surgeries. That pipe bomb incident at the college did more than just put him in the hospital. But he's spent months in rehab, and needs to get back to work, Ella. His doctor's given permission for him to resume field duty, and the chief agreed. Let him have this assignment. He's not cut out for a desk job, and we need our best personnel on this."

Ella nodded. Although Ralph had already made it clear he wasn't ready to take up his bomb squad work again, he wanted to get out of the station and take part in fieldwork.

"After all those months of recovery and therapy, I thought for a while he'd just take an early retirement and go on to consulting work," Ella said. "He was a veteran cop when I joined the department."

"I think police work's in his blood, Ella, and he needs to reconnect." Justine glanced down at the missing joint on her index finger, recalling the brutality of her kidnappers years ago. "We all pay a price for what we do, but police work's a calling. That's why we're drawn to it so much."

Ella said nothing. Justine was a devout Christian and her religious beliefs shaped her views. Yet no matter how Justine defined it, she lived and breathed the job, too. It was that dedication to the tribe and the department that made all of them overlook the downside—like the crappy pay and long hours.

"I'll start with photos," Justine said. "I want shots of the tire tracks on the dirt trail leading in. I saw two distinct, fresh sets as we were coming in, and there's only one tribal vehicle here."

"Good eye. I'll get statements from the crew," Ella said.

As she walked over to the men clustered in the shade of the cottonwood, Ella understood the wariness in their eyes. She spoke to the foreman first and he pointed out the two men who'd found the body. One of them, a stocky Navajo in his early twenties wearing a turquoise and black Shiprock High School Chieftains tee-shirt and worn jeans, stood fingering the leather pouch at his waist.

Recognizing the medicine bag for what it was, an essential personal item for Traditionalists, Ella decided to speak to him first.

She introduced herself without using names. Traditionalists believed that a name had power. To use it needlessly deprived its owner of a personal asset that was his or hers to use in times of trouble. Asking to see his driver's license, she took the necessary information off that.

"I got too close to that body," he said, explaining that he was the first to uncover the still-attached hand, and that the shovel left at the location was his. "I'm going to have a Sing done. Your brother's the *hataalii* who lives on the other side of Shiprock, off the Gallup highway, isn't he?"

"Yes, he is," Ella answered, not surprised he'd made the

connection. Despite the vastness of the Navajo Nation, theirs was a small community, and she'd been part of the tribal police department in this area for nearly fifteen years.

"I came ready for work, but this . . ." He shook his head, then kicked at a clump of dry grass with the toe of his worn lace-up work boot.

"Why did you happen to dig at that particular spot?" Ella said.

"I needed fill dirt so I picked a spot where there wasn't much brush. It was pretty loose and easy to scoop out, so I dug deeper. Then the shovel snagged on something that looked like a leather glove." He swallowed hard. "I reached down to pull it out when I saw that it was a hand—still at-tached to an arm. I backed off, fast." He avoided eye contact with Ella out of respect for Navajo ways. "Do you think the whole body is down there?" he asked in a strangled voice.

"We'll know in a bit."

"Do we have to stay around while you . . . dig it up?"

"Not for that long. I'll need to take statements from everyone and make sure I know where to find each of you in case we need to talk again. Once that's done, you'll all be free to leave."

"Good. I don't want to stick around."

Ella couldn't help but notice that the entire crew seemed anxious to leave, even those who appeared to be Modernists—their curiosity, their more relaxed expres-sions, and the absence of medicine pouches at their belt or in hand easily identified the Modernists.

Going about her business, she spoke to the other men, but nothing new came to light. Nobody seemed to know anything about the extra set of vehicle tracks. The foreman also made it clear that he didn't think any other tribal em-ployees had visited the site before them. Their job here to-day had been part of regular maintenance and scheduled months ago.

Shortly after the crew left, her team arrived. Ella watched Ralph Tache climb out of the van. Though he still moved slowly despite having lost at least thirty pounds in the last year, determination was etched in his deep-set eyes.

She knew that look. The need to restore order so all could walk in beauty was more than just a concept. It was the way of life on the *Diné Bikéyah*, Navajo country.

The crime scene team quickly cordoned off the area, using the boundary fence as the eastern perimeter. They each had specialized jobs, but no one would touch the ground around the hand until every square inch had been photographed from all possible angles.

While Ralph helped Justine take photos, Sergeant Joe Neskahi brought out two shovels and stood them against the van for future use.

Soon afterwards, Benny Pete and Joe surveyed the ground outside the yellow tape looking for tracks, trash, or anything out of the ordinary. If the scene needed to be expanded, they would be the first to make that determination.

Joe was a longtime member of the team, but Benny, their newest member, had fit in almost instantly. He'd come to them as a temporary transfer, then had opted to remain with their team. They'd all welcomed him after seeing his skills, particularly when it came to spotting even minute details.

"What's the M.E.'s ETA?" Ella called out to Justine.

"Ten minutes," Justine called back, not looking up from her work.

Looking over at Ralph, Ella saw him taking a photo of something off in the direction of the highway. "What'd you see, Ralph?" she asked, walking over.

He shrugged. "Someone was over there, standing by a white sedan, watching us through binoculars. I saw his reflection off the glass and it caught my eye. It was probably just a curious motorist, but you know what they say in Crime Scene 101."

"Yeah, sometimes perps hang around to watch the police work the scene—might even volunteer to help," Ella
said.

"I'll also be taking shots of every car that stops to check
us out. You never know," he said.

"Sure would be nice to get lucky," Ella said, "investigation-
wise," she added quickly, seeing Ralph's eyebrows rise.

Hearing someone clear their throat directly behind her,
Ella spun around. "You don't make a lot of noise when you
walk, do you?" she said, glaring at Benny.

"Sorry about that, boss," he said. "We looked around for
footprints connected to that extra set of tire tracks, but there
isn't anything fresh. The driver must not have exited the
vehicle. We did find something interesting—another set of
fresh prints that clearly belong to a child. They're along the
fence line and elsewhere, but not close enough to the tire
impressions for the child to have been the driver or a passenger."

"So the only adult prints belong to the work crew?"

"That's right," Benny said.

"The next thing we'll need to do is check on kids who
live in this area. Anything else?" Ella asked him.

"So far we've found the usual windblown debris of candy
and food wrappers, paper cups, and the kind of stuff we'd
normally find alongside the highway. But something struck
me as particularly odd."

"What is it?" she pressed.

"I'd rather show you," he said.

"Lead the way." This was going to be one of those cases
where nothing fit the norm. She could feel it in her gut.

TWO

—— ✗ ✗ ✗ ——

Benny Pete came to a stop at the western edge of the crime scene tape line and looked back to where the hand had been uncovered. "Notice anything?"

Ella studied the area but nothing struck her as particularly noteworthy. Then, as she widened her focus, she saw what Benny was talking about. "The surface of the ground doesn't look quite right."

"Exactly," Benny said. "I'd say someone did a lot of digging, then spent time reshaping and smoothing everything over. It's such a large section, too. Makes you wonder just how big the body beneath there is . . . or if we've stumbled onto some kind of graveyard."

"It's also been replanted with vegetation, and at different times, too," Ella said after a beat. "The section closest to the hand is covered with tumbleweeds and goatheads. Those are the first type of plants to appear in soil that has been disturbed. That should give us a rough idea of when the grave was dug."

"All the plants in that location seem younger and smaller than the ones farther out, too," Benny said. "We'll need a plant expert to help us with the time line."

"I know just the person," Ella said, thinking of her mother, Rose Destea, a prominent member of the Plant Watchers.

She reached for her phone, then saw Dr. Carolyn Roanhorse's van coming up the dirt trail. Ella put the phone away and went to meet her. Carolyn stepped down out of the van easily and without all the mobility problems she'd had in the past. It was clear that her long-term diet was working. Her old friend looked like a new woman.

"We're still working the scene," Ella told her. "We haven't even begun digging up the body yet. You're going to have to wait a bit."

Carolyn smirked. "Terrific. I postponed my lunch just so I can sit here?" She exhaled softly. "What's kept me on this diet all these months is making sure I don't go hungry."

"It's sure working for you, though. You look great. How much more do you want to lose?"

"Another ten pounds, then I'll switch to a maintenance diet. It was never my goal to look like a model. As far as I'm concerned, real women jiggle and come with curves."

"I agree with you," Ella said.

As Ella and Carolyn watched, Neskahi and Benny began uncovering the body using the hand and the emerging arm of the victim to guide their progress. They placed the dirt removed on a ground cloth. Later, they'd sift through that soil, searching for evidence. Any uncovered foreign objects would be carefully recorded.

The first several inches of surface material was more dirt than soil and had clearly been mixed and disturbed by previous digging, which made the exhumation easier. Within fifteen minutes the men had removed enough earth to reveal the remains of a naked adult human body buried facedown.

Ella and Justine came forward to help. From what Ella could see, most of the closely cropped hair was still attached to the dried out, dark brown, leathery skin on the skull. In the back of the head and slightly higher than ear level were two nickel-sized holes. The size and shape immediately suggested bullet wounds, and from their location, she thought of an execution-style murder. This person didn't die an accidental death.

Ella stood. "People, work *very* carefully," she announced, looking into every face to make her point clear. "We're dealing with a murder here, and I don't want to lose a single piece of possible evidence."

After the body was completely uncovered, still intact, Justine took another series of photographs. They carefully widened the excavation so they could place a thirty-inch-wide piece of plywood next to the body. Then, working together, the four team members slid the body onto the board and lifted it to the ground beside a stretcher.

The M.E. came up, bag in hand, and while everyone watched, she examined the body for several minutes, concentrating on the skull. Then she looked up. "Help me turn the body over, people, then give me some more room to work."

Benny and Joe assisted, working carefully to ensure the body remained intact, then moved out of the way to let Justine take more photographs of what was clearly a male.

Ella stared at what had once been a living, breathing human being. There was no way anyone would be able to make an ID without forensics now. Even if the body hadn't been decomposed, the destruction caused by two exiting bullets would have made facial recognition nearly impossible.

Ella moved away and watched her friend work. As she did, she caught the appreciative looks Benny and Joseph gave Carolyn as she knelt down beside the body. Ella bit back a smile. Her friend had always been a beautiful woman, but was even more so now. There was a new grace to her movements.

"The victim was shot twice," Carolyn said, speaking

into her digital recorder and confirming Ella's earlier and obvious assessment.

Justine came up and stood beside Ella. "The body was buried deep enough to keep scavengers from uncovering the body and to prevent it from being washed out in anything less than a flood," she said.

"That means the grave took some time to dig," Ella said. "I noticed that some of the harder-packed sediment was broken apart in big chunks. To get through that layer the digger must have used a pick. He came prepared."

Ella told Justine about the plants around the crime scene. "I'm going to call Mom and see what she can tell us about this."

The phone rang several times before her mother finally picked up. Rose sounded winded.

"You okay, Mom?" Ella asked quickly.

"Yes, I was just trying out a new, whole-wheat bread recipe. I wanted to give your daughter something more nutritious than store-bought."

"She doesn't really mind the regular stuff, Mom."

"Well, I do," Rose snapped, then with a sigh, continued. "I'm sorry. I'm just trying to get this right. Was there something you needed?"

Ella wasn't sure what had been bothering Rose lately, but her mom simply hadn't been able to relax. Although Rose no longer worked for the tribe surveying native plants, she hadn't followed through with her initial plan to just take it easy and enjoy her retirement. Ella suspected part of it was due to the fact she'd been laid off so abruptly. Tribal funds were so tight that even the police department was operating on an austerity budget.

"I'd like to run something past you, Mom," Ella said. "It concerns the Plant People." Ella described the plants she could see closest to the grave site. "So how long ago would you say the ground here was disturbed?"

"It sounds like you've got a crop of second-generation tumbleweeds sprouting up, so I'd say last summer," she said. "Snakeweed comes afterwards, and grasses are usually the last to appear."

"Thanks, Mom."

"If you need more specific information, bring me some photos and I'll see what I can do for you."

"I will, Mom." Ella hung up, then stared at the phone for a moment, lost in thought.

"Something wrong?" Justine asked, coming over.

"Mom hasn't been acting right lately," Ella said, then shook her head, brushing aside the distraction. "That's for another time. Right now I need to focus."

Justine nodded, then called Ella's attention to the general layout of the site. "This spot is hidden from the highway and that old secondary road that curves around close to the Hogback," Justine said. "That means the suspect had time to work, even in the daytime."

"All the brush between here and the roads also gave him a sound buffer. No one driving by would have been able to see that the ground had been disturbed, either, not unless they happened to stop and then go walking through this area. All things considered, the suspect chose a good place to do their dirty work."

"The victim was shot twice in the head, and maybe elsewhere. We may be talking about more than one suspect."

"That's certainly a possibility." Ella saw Carolyn rise to her feet and pick up her gear. The next step, getting the body into a bag and placed inside the van, usually sent everyone running for cover, but not today.

"Look at that," Ella said in a hushed whisper. "Both Benny and Joe *want* to help her."

"I heard Joe say that Carolyn's looking hot. And he wasn't referring to the temperature."

"He's lucky she didn't hear him. Otherwise, he would have been leaving here in a second body bag," Ella said.

While Benny and Joe carried the body to the wagon, Carolyn walked over and gave Ella a wan smile. "They used to turn tail when I asked for help. Now I get volunteers."

"Men are taking notice of our slimmed-down M.E.," Ella said.

Carolyn sighed. "Suddenly less is more . . . appealing. But I'm still me. Nothing's changed on the inside."

"Packaging matters. It shouldn't be that way, but it is."

Carolyn nodded. "Did I tell you that the new Anglo doctor has asked me out—twice."

Ella smiled. "The tall blond with the big shoulders and killer smile?"

"Yeah," Carolyn said with a tiny grin. "Imagine that, huh?"

"You going to take him up on the offer?"

"I don't know. I've been down that road before," she said, making a veiled reference to her former husband. "Some of these Anglo doctors come to the area filled with ideals, but seldom stick around."

"So what's one date? You don't have to marry the guy. Just go have fun."

"Maybe you're right."

"How are things with you and Ford going?" Carolyn asked.

"We're still dating, and I care about him a lot, but . . . ," Ella responded.

"Let me guess. You're not sure if you want to become a conservative preacher's wife," Carolyn answered, lowering her voice. "And that's what he requires? Reverend Tome's got a domineering personality."

"And I know what I want."

"Is it the religion, him, or just uncertainty in general?"

Seeing Joe and Benny closing up the van, Ella decided

to use the opportunity to duck the question. She didn't really know how to answer it anyway. Quickly she focused back on the case. "Anything preliminary you can tell me?"

"He was shot twice, that I know about, in the back of the skull. I recovered two jacketed hollow-point bullets just beneath the body, so the vic was killed where he lay."

"That's cold. Being forced to lay down in your own grave," Ella replied.

"Exactly. The exit wounds confirm the paths of the bullets. This was an execution, not a crime committed in the heat of passion," Carolyn said.

"That should help us get into the mind of the killer. Any idea how long the body has been there? Months, years?"

"Judging from the soil and climate, and what I've learned from studies done at some body farms, I'd say it has been there around a year, give or take. I'll have to do more tests and confirm the research, but I think my estimate will be close. Of course if we knew the name of the victim and when they went missing . . ."

"No chance of fingerprints?"

Carolyn shook her head. "Nope, the usual gang of decomposition critters pretty much consumed the friction ridges and smoothed everything out. But I'll get DNA samples once I start my autopsy."

While Ella walked with her friend to the van, Ralph and Justine finished taking photographs and set up wood-framed wire screens to sort through the loose earth that had surrounded the body.

Ella held the van door open for Carolyn while she stowed her medical bag. "Go out and have some fun with the new doc. Then you can tell me all about it."

As Carolyn drove off, Benny came up to Ella. "Maybe she should have stuck around. I've taken another look at the ground and I have a sinking feeling that there are more bodies here—maybe three or four."

"Because so much ground has been disturbed?" Ella said.

"Yeah. I also did a little probing with a screwdriver and noticed that some spots seem to be undisturbed, hard packed. Those lie between the three or four softer, worked-over places. Like squares on a checkerboard," Benny said. "Some hard, some soft, but in a pattern."

"Any additional digging is going to be a hit or miss proposition—that is, unless there are bodies in each soft spot," she said.

"I spoke to Joe about it and he brought a metal detector from the van that'll pick up dense metal three feet down," he said, gesturing to the sergeant. "That might help us locate the presence of bullets—if other vics were killed here in the same way."

Ella watched as Neskahi searched the ground, sweeping the loop of the long-handled device back and forth like a weed cutter.

"He's going to find bottle caps and all kinds of trash, so we'll still have to do a lot of careful exploratory digging," Benny said.

"We need more technology," Ella said. "I have an idea that may speed things up."

Ella made a call to the station and put in a request for a ground-penetrating radar device. Although their department didn't have one, county did, and an official request would soon go out.

"Do you think we'll get to use the new unit county recently purchased?" Benny asked, looking over to Neskahi, who had just unearthed a beer can.

"I'm hoping. I've heard it's state-of-the-art. Their tech could save us a week's worth of digging, and in this heat I'm all for quick answers," Ella answered.

"I'd like to get a better overview of the scene," Benny said, "I'm going to climb up the Hogback a ways, then look back in this direction. Maybe I can spot some features we just can't see from ground level. Unless you can call up a helicopter?"

"That'll never happen, but I'll go with you. Two pairs of eyes and all that. Let me find some privacy so I can shed this ballistic vest. No sense in climbing with all that extra weight in this heat."

The steep, slippery climb up the essentially bare-faced, spinelike ridge was even harder than Ella had expected. Although they'd chosen the lateral route with the most footholds and handholds instead of going straight up, the climb was still precarious. The nearly sixty-degree outcrop was solid sandstone broken into large and small slabs, and extended for miles north and south, undulating like a dragon's tail.

The cracks were far apart, and often the bedrock was covered with loose material and windblown dust that made each footstep slippery and dangerous. Rocks continually shifted under her boots. After sliding downward a few feet across naked rock, twice in a row, she decided not to go any higher.

Keeping the tips of her boots firmly lodged in a narrow joint and leaning into the cliff, she turned her body around as much as possible and looked to the east. She could see up the valley for miles from here. Spotting Joe still sweeping the ground with the metal detector, she oriented herself further by finding the fence line and posts.

From where she was, Ella could see three other areas that were a shade lighter than the surrounding topsoil. The former marsh to the south toward the river had been dried up for years. Yet change had come slowly and the darker sediment was contrasted by three roughly rectangular lighter spots around the uncovered grave. The vegetation was also a little out of phase, as they'd noticed before, though at this distance that was apparent only in color shifts.

"Tell me what you see, Benny," Ella said, turning her head. Never a fan of heights, staring down a nearly vertical drop was making her dizzy.

"I see three other spots that look suspicious, two farther south of the grave, and one almost due east, just across the fence," Benny called out, clinging to the rocks a few feet below and behind her.

"Yeah, that's what I saw, too. One of those is on the county's side, so that's going to bring us a brand-new set of problems."

Carefully retrieving her handheld from her jacket pocket, Ella directed Justine to the various sites so they could be marked with numbered flags. She then instructed her and the other officers to expand the crime scene to include the new areas, and to call the M.E. again.

"Let's get back down," Ella called out to Benny after he confirmed the placement.

They worked their way slowly, and there was a tendency to slide. The footing seemed even more precarious on the way down, but maybe that was only because they were both eager to finish their descent.

Ella breathed a sigh of relief the second she hit solid ground. Benny, who'd slid the last ten feet on his behind, landed a few steps away from her. Reaching for her cell phone as they walked back toward the site, Ella wasted no time calling FBI agent Dwayne Blalock and San Juan County Sheriff Paul Taylor to give them the news. Jurisdictional matters required special handling, though, for practical reasons, the officers present would have to pass back and forth over boundaries as needed.

Neskahi met them before they reached the yellow tape line and held up a plastic evidence pouch with another bullet. "Nine millimeter, probably from the same pistol as the other two. I found this about two feet down in the place

Justine marked next to the current grave. I also have some hits from other, deeper locations. I marked them."

"Good. We can start digging where you found the bullet, but we'll wait for radar on the rest. We don't want to risk tainting evidence if there are other bodies here."

Justine was at one of the sections they'd been able to identify from higher ground, the same spot where Neskahi had dug up the bullet. She pointed to six small yellow flag-tipped markers she'd placed in a crude rectangle about three by six feet. "I did some probing with a piece of wire, and outlined the area of soft ground. This is almost exactly the same size as the grave we dug up already."

"Body size," Ralph added, coming up with more markers.

"At least it's on our side of the county line. Let's get the tools."

As her team came over, she could sense their uneasiness. The possibility of mass graves could make even the staunchest Modernist edgy. Few Navajos willingly entered an area the *chindi* had claimed, but duty bound them now. They'd each battle their own demons and do what had to be done.

THREE

—— ✕ ✕ ✕ ——

The second grave was nearly a foot deeper than the first, but after an hour of slow, careful work another body was uncovered. At a glance, they could see this victim had been laid to rest far longer. Only a few traces of hair were left on the corpse, along with some dried sinews of muscle. As before, there were two holes in the back of the skull.

Two San Juan County officers, one of them Justine's roommate, Sergeant Emily Marquez, arrived on the scene, having come from the east down Highway 64. Accompanying Emily was a fit-looking thirtyish Navajo county plainclothes officer in slacks and a SJCSD jacket. Emily introduced him as Detective Dan Nez.

Nez gave Ella a nod, but didn't offer to shake hands out of respect for Navajo customs.

Ella filled them in, pointing to the staked-out rectangle on the county side, and identifying it as a potential grave. As she spoke, Ella also studied the county's new detective. He was tall, with classic Navajo high cheekbones. His features were too angular to be described as handsome, yet he had a certain presence about him. His hair was a little longer than most of the other male deputies, black and wavy rather than the army-recruit look so popular today, and maybe that was what made him distinctive. An inch shorter than her, Nez was still above average height for a Navajo. He was also less chunky—with a runner's build, not that of a barrel-chested wrestler like, for instance, Joe Neskahi.

"Any news on the ground-penetrating radar Chief Atcitty requested?" Ella asked, looking back and forth between the two county people.

"It's on its way, along with our techs, but I've got some bad news, too," Emily said. "The press picked up on the story and they're right behind us."

Ella looked toward the east and spotted two vans topped with satellite dishes approaching from Farmington. The vehicles slowed, then turned off the main highway farther east. "We'll have to keep the reporters back. We're no longer certain of the perimeter boundary, so we need to avoid con-taminating the scene."

"I'll find another route that leads directly into the county side, then instruct our crime scene van to join us over there," Emily said, then turning to Nez, added, "You're okay with that?"

"Yeah, Sergeant. I'll grab my camera and get started in the meantime," Nez said.

Ella knew that, though Emily technically outranked him, they worked in different divisions and this was his area of expertise.

As Emily drove away, Nez climbed over the fence at the closest post, then put on two sets of gloves before going any farther.

After Ella ordered Ralph Tache to keep the press back until more officers arrived, she took over his work helping Justine and Joe screen the debris from the first grave. As she worked, she looked over at Nez, wondering if he was a New Traditionalist or a Modernist. The very fact that he'd opted for two layers with his gloves didn't say much one way or another. Avoiding contact with anything that might have touched the dead was a common practice for most Navajos.

Dwayne Blalock pulled up next, on the tribe's side, and that brought Ella out of her musings. The seasoned FBI agent left his four-wheel-drive SUV well outside the crime scene and approached on foot. These days Dwayne seemed much more relaxed about everything. It undoubtedly had something to do with the fact that he and his ex-wife were back together again.

Ella left her work and gave him a quick rundown as they stood beside the grave of the second victim. Several feet away, Justine and Neskahi continued screening dirt.

"I knew something big was coming our way. Things have been too quiet lately," Blalock said, watching as Tache hustled away two reporters who were getting too close.

"Does that mean you welcome the change, or do you wish it could have stayed the way it was?"

"Funny you should ask, Clah. These days, I've discovered I enjoy going home at a decent hour. For the first time in umpteen years, I have a life outside the job."

"I thought you might say that."

"Hey, Clah, that doesn't mean I'm losing my edge."

"It never even occurred to me," she said, biting back a smile.

More county deputies in tan uniforms soon arrived and took on the job of removing members of the press who'd pushed in too close to the scene. Their number had grown quickly. Three vans and a cable station sedan were now parked beyond the perimeter, and satellite dishes were being positioned.

Part of the fence line was soon taken down to facilitate digging near the boundary, and everyone was able to move back and forth as needed. Emily oversaw the task, then joined Blalock and Ella. "Detective Nez got a call from Sheriff Taylor. I'm going to be directing crowd control and support, but he's responsible for the county's involvement in this investigation."

"Understood," Ella said.

Hearing another vehicle approaching, Ella turned her head and saw a second sheriff's department van pulling up. Two techs removed the portable ground-penetrating radar unit and began working the area of disturbed ground over on the county side.

Before long, one of the techs stopped work and went to speak to Nez while the other placed markers. "Readings indicate the presence of a body," the man said.

Less than ten minutes later, the presence of a third victim was confirmed. The body was facedown like the ones on the reservation side. "Two holes to the back of the skull— another execution," Nez muttered.

"Make sure county uses their ground-penetrating radar on the entire site, including tribal land," Blalock suggested to Nez.

"Copy that," Nez answered, "but if we've got more bodies farther east and south, radar might have a problem detecting those."

"Why's that?" Blalock asked.

"The ground we're checking now is relatively dry, but closer to the river, it'll contain a lot more moisture. Too much water and the radar won't penetrate. We may have to finish the job the old fashioned way—digging blind—if we find more disturbed ground."

"Without radar, working farther south and east could take weeks, months," Ella said.

"True, but I don't think the killer would have risked digging closer to the highway where he might have been seen," Nez said. "The three victims we've got appear to have been killed at different times and he took great care to hide the bodies. We're after someone who plans and thinks like a pro. He doesn't act on the spur of the moment."

"What's also strange is that he chose to bury his victims on both sides of the fence," Ella said.

"Maybe he knows the law and deliberately wanted to create jurisdictional issues," Nez said. "Or it could be his priority was finding areas where digging would be easier, and that would also keep him out of view while he worked."

Hearing a vehicle pull up and reporters shouting questions, Ella turned her head and saw the M.E.'s van passing through a temporary gap in the yellow perimeter tape. "Here comes Dr. Roanhorse, our M.E.," she said. "She might agree to process the deceased on both sides of the border. If she does, that would simplify the process."

Nez glanced at Ella. "Are you suggesting that we officially request her services?"

"It makes more sense to have our M.E. handle all the bodies. She won't have the backlog they have in Albuquerque, considering they handle autopsies for the entire state."

As Nez's expression hardened slightly, she knew what was on his mind. Jurisdictional issues invariably created problems. "It's just a suggestion. I'm not trying to tell you guys what to do. I just want to make sure we get answers quickly. Having only one M.E. involved will make it easier for her to spot links or commonalities in the M.O. that might otherwise be missed. And she's licensed at the same level as the medical examiners in Albuquerque."

"It's not my call," Nez said after a beat. "Let me check with Sheriff Taylor."

"I'll speed things up," Blalock said. "Tell Paul that I'm recommending we have Dr. Roanhorse perform all the autopsies. The slugs and all the other hard evidence found on your side will get processed by your people. Results will be shared equally, including testimony and paperwork. Combining forces and efforts is the only way to go here since we're all looking for the same killer."

Nez made a quick phone call to Sheriff Taylor, then gave them the nod. "It's a go."

Processing a crime scene was long, painstaking work, and theirs was extended even more when a fourth body was found, again on tribal land. By then, Ella's team was weary of digging and the county crime scene team helped with exhumation.

It was midafternoon and temperatures were in the low nineties now. Pizza had been provided via an arriving deputy, and officers were drinking bottled water by the case— supplied by a Kirtland grocery store owner who had a son serving as a county deputy. With the sun beating down, Ella was grateful she didn't have her ballistics vest on anymore as she moved from place to place, almost never in the shade.

Each piece of evidence was photographed, numbered, collected, and tagged, and a dozen officers went over every square foot of ground for a hundred yards in every direction.

Ella and Nez established a central processing area on a folding table surrounded by law enforcement vehicles. That allowed them to conceal much of their findings from the prying eyes of the media.

"A total of eight slugs were found in or around the victims," Neskahi said. "Six are nine-millimeter one-hundred-forty-seven-grain jacketed hollow-points. And here's a surprise, the slugs found beneath the oldest victim, the second body we found, are one-hundred-grain AP, armor piercing. They're barely deformed, but still nine millimeter. In doing an eyeball comparison of lands and grooves, they appear to have been fired from the same weapon as the hollow-points—though forensics will have to confirm that. Justine recognized the maker of the AP slugs. Those rounds are supposedly only sold to law enforcement."

"So, either those rounds got into the wrong hands or we might be dealing with a cop," Ella said.

"Or an ex-cop," Joe replied. "But that's the extent of the evidence we can link conclusively to the crimes. We haven't found any spent casings, which means the shooter gathered them up. Nine-millimeter revolvers are extremely rare, so we're almost certainly talking pistol here—and an evidence-wise shooter."

"Then there's the usual gazillion lift tabs from old beer and soda cans dating back to the seventies and before, empty booze bottles, soda, beer cans, and gum wrappers," Benny Pete said. "None of them appear to have been tossed recently."

Ella nodded. "There used to be a bar not far from here. The Turquoise Bar, I think it was called. But that closed down twenty years ago or more."

"Not counting those two AP rounds, there's one piece of evidence that struck me as unusual," Nez said, "or weirdly coincidental, depending on your point of view. On the ground directly over the body found on our side of the fence was a pair of dice. Facing up were two ones—snake-eyes."

"Interesting. Any idea what it means?" Ella asked.

Nez shook his head. "Maybe the killer was telling us that the vic was a real snake and deserved two bullets in the skull. Or maybe it's not connected at all. There are several casinos in the general area."

"Here's a likely connection. Children's board games often come with dice. Remember the child's shoe prints I found? A kid's been playing in this area recently," Benny said. "In a little smoothed-out spot on the tribal side—I marked it on my sketch of the scene—Officer Tache found the child's footprints. He also discovered a small red toy Jeep, several olive-drab plastic soldiers, and a doll's head—nothing else, just the head. There are no splatter marks or mud on any of them, so they were left here around the same time the kid was here, yesterday or last night."

"The kid may have seen something, though based on

the deterioration of the remains, he would have had to have been hanging around here for months," Ella said. "In any case, it's still worth looking into. Where's the closest residence?"

"There are houses scattered about north of here, and, of course there's the old, abandoned Hogback trading post." Justine pointed in the direction of an old white cinder-block building that butted up against the eastern wall of the Hogback formation.

"We need to check all those out, including the trading post. *Anaashii*, squatters, take up residence almost anywhere these days, so the old trading post's fair game," Ella said.

While her team cataloged the gathered evidence, Ella opened up her cell phone and called her brother, Clifford. His wife, Loretta, answered after several rings.

Hearing her voice, Ella stiffened, then forced herself to relax. Loretta and she had never found it easy to get along. "I need to speak to my brother," Ella said, wishing for the umpteenth time that Clifford would carry a cell phone.

"I'll go get him for you."

Moments later Clifford answered. "I heard there's a situation over by the Hogback and that there are officers everywhere. Are you okay?"

"Yes, but we've been around several bodies and my team will need a purification rite done right away. Otherwise it'll be nearly impossible for my officers to question other Navajos," she said, then gave him their precise location.

"I'll be there as soon as possible and bring what's needed. How many Navajo officers are with you?"

After Ella gave him the information, she saw Dan Nez standing behind her, holding up one hand.

"I'd like to be included in the rite," he whispered.

Ella nodded and counted him in.

"Thanks," Nez said after she hung up, but he didn't move away.

"Something else on your mind?" Ella asked.

He nodded. "Sharing jurisdiction is always tricky. You have your own ways of getting results, and I have mine."

"It's part of the job," Ella said. "We'll get it done."

"I was born on the Navajo Nation and I know that crime here weaves its own unique patterns. If I have to share jurisdiction, I'm glad to be working with someone who's practically a law enforcement legend."

Ella looked at Nez, trying to figure out if he was actually feeding her a compliment or giving her a hard time. She concluded he was either a great poker player or completely serious.

"I don't know what you've been told—"

"You've made the local papers even in my far corner of the Navajo Nation in Arizona, and my captain knows Chief Ed Atcitty. He apparently talks you up a lot—and justly so. You are what you are," he said flatly.

"Where exactly are you from in Arizona?"

"I grew up in Leupp, and eventually became an officer for the Winslow P.D., just off the Rez. I moved here in January when a detective's position opened up with the San Juan County department."

She wondered if he'd ever applied for a tribal job, but decided not to pry. Instead, she'd do a little background on *him* to see who she was going to be working alongside.

"Since we'll be together on this, maybe we should spell out some basic ground rules," Dan said. "If we settle some of those issues ahead of time, it'll avoid conflicts later."

Ella nodded, used to coordinating with county. "Let me offer a suggestion. You and your people take lead when interviews and operations are conducted off the Rez, and me and my team will call the shots with people and places on the Rez. We'll make it a point to brief each other daily, and whenever possible combine our efforts when making any arrests. If we have to meet, let's get together at the Shiprock tribal station. It's closer to the crime scene, and all but one of the bodies was buried on Navajo land."

"I'm okay with that."

"Good. I'll tell Agent Blalock what we've decided before he leaves today. He has a stake in this."

Nez walked off to assist the county team, and Ella found and told Blalock about the interagency strategy. Justine came up a while later. "I just spoke to Emily, and she said that Dan's a little dogmatic, the kind of guy you either like or hate, but he gets the job done."

"See if she'll give you more specifics. Unofficial stuff can be far more enlightening sometimes, and no sense in setting him off on some trivial differences."

"Okay."

Procedural issues demanded her attention and called her back to the crime scene. Unaware of the passage of time, Ella was surprised to see a familiar pickup at the turnoff. A county deputy was talking to the driver.

"That looks like my brother," Ella said. "I better go meet him."

Clifford was sorting through the contents of a cardboard box on the seat beside him as Ella and Justine came up. When Clifford stepped out of his truck, Ella noticed that her brother looked as formidable as ever. Although his clothes were casual—just jeans, boots, and a old chambray shirt—he was wearing the white sash of a medicine man tied around his head. That, and his tall, slender build, gave him an undeniable presence. She'd heard others describe it as *'álí'l*, an extraordinary supernatural power, a secret strength beyond what was seen, required to bring about successful cures.

"I can begin whenever you're ready," he said. "But if you find any more bodies, I'll have to come back and repeat the ceremony."

"I know. We've checked most of the area, and hopefully that won't be necessary. But I'm anxious to be able to offer some immediate protection to those working here now. I'll gather our people, and the Navajo detective from county I told you about."

"I brought additional pollen bags just in case, all with flint, so anyone is welcome to take part," he said, reaching for the box that rested on the passenger seat of his pickup.

"Good," Ella said. "There are a few uniforms who may want to be included." Ceremonies were about chasing evil away and attracting good. Pollen signified happiness and light, and was supposed to draw those blessings to the ones present. Flint was said to have power because of its hardness. The light that reflected off its shiny surface was also said to scare evil spirits away.

Ella, her team, Detective Nez, and two patrol officers gathered in the center of an area bordered by their parked vehicles. This would give them privacy from the curious eyes of the press. Several reporters had requested to join them and film the rite, but Clifford had turned them away.

Before he began, Clifford spoke to the group before him. "This chant's function is to purify, so I'm going to ask all of you to keep your thoughts centered on beauty and harmony. Those of you who speak Navajo will understand my words, but I need to ask everyone not to share details of these rituals with others. Knowledge is a living thing that needs to be protected."

Clifford gave each of them a medicine bag, then asked that they take out a pinch of pollen and hold it between their forefingers and thumbs. "That is your shield from evil," he said.

As her brother's voice rose in the air, Ella felt the power of the chant. With each note, uncertainty and fears were pushed back.

"Now reach for the turquoise bits inside the bags and throw those into the air," Clifford said.

The chant continued, and after several minutes, Clifford

asked them to repeat his words if they could, then throw bits of white shell from their pouches into the air three times.

When Clifford spoke the final words, *"hózhne háazdlíí*—it is beautiful all around me," the blessing became far more than just words. The power of the rite had united them and restored their harmony so they could walk in beauty once again.

Ella looked at the others around her and saw the relief and assurance the rite had inspired. After everyone had gone back to work, Ella approached Clifford. "Thank you, Brother."

"Let me know if there's anything else I can do to help," he said, putting away his ceremonial items.

Ella attached her medicine bag to her belt. This pouch, like the ones given to her team, would dispel Navajo fears about the *chindi* and allow them to continue their work with a renewed sense of peace.

FOUR

✖ ✖ ✖

As soon as the opportunity arose, Ella went with Justine to check out the old trading post. Ella was glad for the chance to sit down, if only for a few minutes inside the SUV. She'd put on her vest again, and it felt heavier than ever at the moment.

By now, the press had dwindled down to one newspaper reporter who was still taking photos of the site. That meant they didn't have to be concerned that they'd be followed and didn't worry about the solitary vehicle they passed.

As they circled, following the curve around the south end of Hogback, Ella spotted an old, apparently abandoned, wood and shingle house off to their left. The building was in a low spot and not visible from the crime scene. As they got closer, she could see a big hole punched into the north wall, a sign that a death had occurred there.

"Pull over a minute," Ella said, noting the mailbox still had the house address on it. Justine stopped, then parked on the shoulder of the road.

"Somebody took a pickax to the stucco," Justine said, pointing. "That's not vandalism. Somebody died there."

"That's what I was thinking, too. Let me run this address and see what turns up," Ella said. A moment later she

BLACK THUNDER ✻ 47

had the information she needed. "The Begaye family moved there in the 1970s, but over the years they each went their separate ways. Lucille Begaye was the last one to live there, but she had to move to a nursing home back in '95. Squatters apparently moved in after that. It's been occupied, unofficially, off and on, until last winter. According to an incident report, that's when an old man died there—natural causes. It's been empty ever since."

"I guess no one's been desperate enough to ignore the *chindi*," Justine said.

"There are lines even the *anaashii* don't like to cross. But since this place appears to be closest to the crime scene, it deserves a look," Ella said, reaching for the SUV's door handle.

They crossed the empty highway and walked down a weed-covered driveway. No tire tracks or footprints were present, and they checked all the way up to the entrance, which was missing its door. After noting the spiderwebs and the wrecked woodstove that had served as a nesting place for rodents, Ella turned to leave, but as she did, something caught her eye. Sitting on the window ledge was a small toy car with one wheel missing—another Jeep, this one blue instead of red.

"A child played here not too long ago. Look at the marks in the dust," Ella said, pointing out small tracks in the dust where the child had moved the toy back and forth.

"Maybe squatters took shelter here for a while, then moved on as soon as they could," Justine said.

"And the kid left his toy behind?" Ella picked up the tiny metal car and looked it over. Letters had been scratched on the bottom. "It's a name, Del, I think, unless that first letter is a badly formed A."

"Looks like a D to me," Justine said.

Ella put it in her pocket. "Let's ask the area residents and see if someone can give us a lead to the kid. There's no telling what he might have seen or picked up. If we find him,

I'll return his lost toy, too. That might help us get a conversation started."

Ella looked off into the distance toward the Rez boundary. "I wonder if Nez has found any leads."

Justine smiled but said nothing.

"What?" Ella pressed, having noticed it.

"You want to be the one who comes up with something first."

"I'm working a case, not keeping score," Ella said.

"Yeah, and when I grow up I'm going to be tall and blond like Emily."

Ella smirked. "You're being annoying. Focus."

Justine chuckled.

When they walked back up the driveway, Ella spotted a house a few hundred yards from the Hogback and farther to the north, in the opposite direction they were going. It was hidden beneath a cluster of cottonwoods, which explained why she hadn't noticed it before.

"Let's go there first. I can see a truck out front," Ella said.

Justine drove back east and they found a narrow gravel lane that led straight to the house. A minute later they pulled in front of a sand-colored stucco home and parked beside a blue pickup.

As Ella looked around she spotted a hogan constructed of pine logs out in the back.

"Do you think they're Traditionalists?" Ella asked.

Justine shrugged. "Call dispatch and see what you can get."

Since there were no street names out here and they hadn't seen a mailbox, Ella had to describe the location, which was situated right along the tribal–county border. "Is there a resident's name on record?"

"I know them," the dispatcher said without skipping a beat. "That's Jennifer and Billie Blackhat's home. They're in their late sixties, or maybe older. They've lived there forever. He used to work at one of the coal mines farther to the north."

"Are they Traditionalists?" Ella asked.

"Very much so."

"Thanks, Melanie," Ella said, then racked the mike. "We'll wait out here, Justine. They heard us pull up, I'm sure."

Ella rolled down the window on her side, and Justine did the same. It was late in the afternoon, and the heat was at its peak.

Several minutes passed, then a woman with white hair tied into a bun, a long broomstick skirt, and a loose white blouse opened the door. She stepped out onto the covered porch and waved an invitation for them to approach.

"I saw all the police over a ways when I was coming home from the grocery store in Waterflow," she said, walking into the small but cozy living room. "Please sit down, officers."

She motioned them to a well-worn sofa. Opposite that was a love seat with the same blue and yellow floral fabric. A large potbellied stove stood in one corner, and there was a small TV atop a plain wooden table. Yet what caught their attention and held it was the wonderful scent of freshly baked bread wafting in from the adjacent kitchen.

"What's the trouble? Is it those kids partying again?" the woman asked, easing into the love seat.

"What kids?" Ella asked instantly, reaching for her pocket notebook and pen.

"The high school kids. It happens every year at this time. Graduation's close, and they start to go a little crazy." She sighed and reached for a cushion for her back. "They usually leave beer bottles all up and down the highway, and sometimes even come up our driveway. We only call the police when they go completely wild, but since school isn't out yet they're still being careful."

"You say they go wild," Ella said. "How wild?"

"Parties, and fights, too. When I'm passing by in the

truck, I don't stop or say anything, I just keep my eyes on the road. If I see or hear a fight, I call the police."

"Have you ever heard gunshots?"

Her eyes grew wide. "No, not at all. The kids come to cut loose and celebrate, but it's mostly just drinking and loud music."

"Thanks. Is your husband here? If he is, we'd like to talk to him, too," Ella said, looking around.

"He's at work right now and won't be back till much later. He retired from the mine, but can't sit still. That's why he works till midnight at the Speedy Mart. I dropped him off, then did my shopping."

"One more thing. Have you seen anyone besides the kids hanging around the area—not a regular resident, maybe a transient?"

"There's *anaashii* living at the old trading post. I've seen a woman and her two kids, a boy and a girl. They've been there for a while. The school bus picks them up by the highway."

"Thanks," Ella said.

"The trading post, right?" Justine asked as they climbed back into the SUV.

"Yeah, let's go talk to them."

"That's assuming they'll even let us get close. It's more likely that they'll run and hide, especially after seeing all the police activity."

"It's also possible they've left already, but if not, we'll have to do our best not to scare them off," Ella said. "They've had the best view of the crime scene and we really do need to speak to them."

As they pulled up to the dilapidated trading post, they noted that the cinder blocks above the word Hogback painted on the upper wall had fallen or been broken off. All the windows had been broken out, but they'd been partially backed on the inside with plywood, providing some protection from the elements.

Justine parked about fifty yards to the north of the old store on the east side, closer to the imposing height of the giant rock formation. They were well into the shadows here, and it was noticeably cooler.

Walking up the side of the old road, the main highway of a previous generation, Justine silently pointed out recent tire tracks. The pattern left behind showed barely a tread mark. This was definitely not the same vehicle that had been driven near the unmarked grave sites.

As they approached the doorway, they could both see that sections of the ceiling inside had rotted away in places and the roof had fallen through in at least one spot. The boards from a porch overhang above the entrance also sagged down, and looked as if they'd break away in the next windstorm.

"The walls look sturdy enough, but the roof is going to give way once the summer monsoon kicks in. If anyone's still here, we need to persuade them to find another place to stay that's safer," Ella whispered.

"The problem is that they probably don't have anyplace else to go," Justine said.

"There are rescue missions and tribal agencies that'll help," Ella said, then peered through a gap between the board that covered the window and the framed edge. "Tribal police officers. Anyone here?"

In the darkened interior Ella could see clothing draped across packing crates that served as chairs. There were paper plates and several unopened cans of food on a circular wooden spool table, the kind used by the utility companies to hold rolled-up wire.

"We're not here to create problems for you," Ella said, raising her voice after seeing an old bed frame resting on six cinder blocks. There were evenly spaced boards across the top, and atop them a cardboard box with the word blankets written on the outside in pencil. Beside it, also on the bed, were two worn-looking book bags, one with a purple-and-white Kirtland High School sticker on it.

They listened, and looked from different angles without entering, but it was clear that the interior of the old trading post was unoccupied at the moment. Ella had a feeling the squatters had left when they'd pulled up and were probably nearby, hiding.

Ella then noticed a solid back door, half open, which faced the rock wall of the Hogback not ten feet beyond. Whoever had been inside had probably ducked out the back.

"You're in no danger from us. All we'd like to do is ask you a few questions. Won't you come talk to us?" Ella asked, trying again.

All they could hear was traffic on the highway to the south—and the creaking of wood. Ella pushed against the door. It was wedged shut from the inside by a board, but Ella knew she could easily reach down and remove it. Deciding against that for now, she called out again, but no one came forward or spoke.

The sound of an approaching vehicle drew her attention and Ella turned around. An old red sedan pulled to a stop, brakes squealing, leaving a pale cloud of blue smoke. The driver, a weary-looking Navajo woman in her mid-thirties, stepped out to meet them.

"I'm Lois Bitsillie, and those are my children inside. They're both going to school in Kirtland, and I'm now working at the Burger Haven, so I can provide for them," she said. "We were only going to stay here long enough for their uncle to get back from overseas. We'll be moving out of here tomorrow sometime, so leave me and my kids alone."

Ella recognized the cap and red-and-yellow uniform of the popular area fast-food restaurant. "We're not from CYF, ma'am, we're tribal police officers."

Ella opened her jacket slightly, showing the badge and

weapon on her belt, then turned to look over her shoulder as she heard footsteps from inside.

A teenage girl in faded jeans and a black tee-shirt had come in through the back, followed by a boy around eight wearing baggy chinos, a faded knit shirt, and worn sneakers. The girl looked more angry than frightened, but the boy was clearly scared and hesitant to come forward.

"Del?" Ella asked softly as they came out. "You left one of your cars in the house up the street. The blue Jeep. Would you like it back?"

The boy kept his head down, avoiding eye contact. "It can't be mine. I'm not allowed to play inside that haunted house. . . ."

"What's this all about?" Lois asked Ella, coming closer. "I saw all those police cars over by the fence line. Did somebody run off the highway? Are you two okay?" she added quickly, turning to look at her kids.

"We're fine, Mom," the girl said, and Del shrugged, his head still down.

"Can we come in for a bit, Lois?" Ella asked the mother. "We're investigating a crime and we'd like to talk to people from the area."

"Sure, but the place is a mess. Our housekeeper has the day off," Lois said with a quick half-smile.

Ella stepped through, followed by Justine, then reached into her pocket and brought out the toy Jeep. "I think this is yours."

Del started to reach for it, then pulled his hand back, and looked up at his mother.

"Go ahead, Son," Lois said with a sigh. "And thank the officer for finding it for you."

As Ella held the toy out in the palm of her hand, she saw the red dot of a laser gun sight appear in the center of Del's forehead.

FIVE
✖ ✖ ✖

Gun!" Ella yelled, lunging at the boy. There were two faint pops and a massive fist punched her twice in the back. The breath knocked out of her, Ella fell forward and crawled over to the boy, shielding him with her body.

"Stay down!" Justine ordered the others, her voice barely heard above Lois' screams and that of her daughter.

When no more shots sounded, Ella, nearly paralyzed with pain, rolled away from Del. The boy, whimpering, curled up in a fetal position on the worn tile floor.

As Del's family crawled toward him in the eerie stillness that followed, Ella sat up. Justine was crouched beside the doorjamb, pistol out. "I can't get a location."

"He's using a silencer. Where the hell is he?" Ella said, coming up next to the partially boarded north side window but keeping her body out of view.

"Across the road somewhere. Ella, I saw you get hit. I assume the vest held?" Justine said, still searching for the shooter.

"Yeah, I took two below my left shoulder blade. My back is killing me. I can barely move," Ella said, trying to steady her voice.

"Better soreness than a G.S.W.," Justine said.

"Did any of you see anyone?" Ella asked, turning her head toward the family. Lois had slid over and was covering Del with her body. The daughter was huddled beside them.

"There was a dark shape in the shade of that tree," Lois said, pointing across the road.

"Which tree? There are a half dozen over there," Ella said, peering around the window ledge opposite Justine.

"Kind of in the middle," Lois said. "Just this side of the falling rocks sign. I'll show you later—if we make it out of here."

"Cover me, partner," Justine said. "I'll duck out the back door and work my way down beside the cliff. If he goes south, you'll spot him."

"No. Call it in. There must be fifteen cops within a mile of here. They can close in from the east. He won't get away." Ella crawled on her knees over to the doorjamb. "And while you're calling, cover the back door—just in case he crossed the road."

"Roger that."

Backup arrived within a few minutes, but there was no sign of the shooter, or a vehicle, only adult-size shoe prints beside a tree about a hundred feet from the front of the building.

Neskahi and Officer Pete picked up the tracks on the east side of the road, where the shooter had crossed. From there, they followed the trail north along the base of the Hogback into a large grove of cottonwoods. They soon found tire tracks, which disappeared as they entered the asphalt. The tread pattern seemed to be a match for those they'd found near the graves. Yet the shooter and the vehicle had somehow vanished, driving right past the turnoff leading to the crime scene. No ATL, attempt to locate, was possible. They had no idea who or what they were looking for and since it was late afternoon, the highway was crowded with people going home from their nine-to-fives.

Ella, stiff and sore, took off her vest, which would have to go into evidence, and recovered the nine-millimeter bullets trapped in the fabric.

She handed them to Justine, who'd log them in as evidence as well. The jacketed, hollow-point rounds looked identical to the six of that type and weight found among the bodies, but only lab comparisons would be able to verify that they'd come from the killer's weapon.

Despite all her efforts questioning the family, especially the boy, Ella was unable to get any more information about the crimes or the possible shooter. Del's continued silence and refusal to even look at her made her suspect he knew something. More importantly, nothing else explained why he'd suddenly become a target.

Ella took Lois aside. "We need to find a way to get Del to open up. I have a feeling he may have seen something he wasn't supposed to see."

Lois used her hand to wipe the tears that fell down her cheeks. "I try my best, but when you're a single mom, every day is a fight to survive. The mortgage company took our house in Kirtland, and since then, we've been living anywhere that has a roof, including our car. All my clan members live way over in Arizona, and I'd go there if I knew I could get a job. Right now my daughter, Belara, has more responsibility on her shoulders than anyone her age should. She and her brother usually have to hide out so Child, Youth, and Family doesn't track us down. But I can't stop them from going out in the afternoons and playing games. They're just kids. If I could watch over them all the time, I would, but I need my job."

"I understand, but this place isn't safe for you anymore."

"We never planned on staying here long. My kids' uncle is in the New Mexico National Guard and his deployment is

finally over. I finally managed to contact him and found out
he has a house in Shiprock. He told us we could move in
with him, but we had to hold off until he returned because
his landlord might make trouble. I was hoping to drive over,
get the key he hid, and have the house cleaned and ready
for him when he arrives tomorrow evening."

"Leave right now. I'll get one of my officers to escort you
to his house and make sure you're not followed. If the landlord complains, we'll arrange for a safe house until the sol-
dier returns."

Her eyes grew wide. "You think this killer will still
come after us, don't you?"

"He might, which is why we need to make sure he can't
find you. Now start loading up your car."

Ella called Officer Marianna Talk and requested that
she escort the family. By the time they finished gathering
their few possessions and crammed them into the red sedan,
Marianna arrived.

Ella hurried Lois and the kids to the car. "I'll be in touch
soon." Stepping back, she signaled Marianna, then looked
back at Lois. "You'll be safe. Now go."

After they disappeared from view, Ella walked back to
the SUV with Justine.

"I want you to do something for me, Justine. Drive back
down the road to the Blackhat residence, advise Mrs. Blackhat to expect a test shot, then go back to the crime scene.
After you tell everyone what you're going to do, fire one
round into the ground. I'll stay here and listen. I need to
find out how far the sound of a nine-millimeter round carries, especially this close to the ridge. If I can hear it from this
location, the Blackhats, who are closer, would have heard it,
too."

Justine nodded. "That'll help us determine if the shooter
used a silencer when he killed the vics. If he did, then that
also suggests that he was the one who just shot you. It's not

likely to be a coincidence. There aren't many silencers in the hands of the public."

"That's what I was thinking, too."

"Luck was on your side today, Ella. It just occurred to me—those slugs . . ."

"Yeah. Good thing they weren't armor-piercing, like with the first victim. We wouldn't be having this conversation."

"Let's hope he switched ammo because he ran out," Justine said.

"I'm with you on that."

Ella started back to the abandoned trading post, now stripped of everything the Bitsillie family could load into their old car. Noticing a narrow trail, Ella climbed up the side of the cliff to a large rock even with the level of the trading post's roof. After checking for snakes underneath, she took a seat on the warm, flat surface. Her back still hurt, but Ella forced herself to shake off the discomfort, gave thanks for Kevlar, and tried to make herself comfortable.

From her position on the rock, she took the time to study the surrounding area. She quickly noticed a house almost due north, in the direction of the old coal mines. Like the trading post, it was nestled next to the cliffs of the Hogback, and, painted a pale green, was almost hidden from view. It was farther away from the crime scene than the Blackhat house, but it was possible that someone living there could have seen something.

As the minutes ticked by, she watched the vehicles pass by on the four-lane main highway to her right. Below, down the far side, lay irrigation canals and the San Juan River.

Her thoughts drifted before eventually settling on Rose. Something had been bothering her mom lately and that, in turn, had resulted in a cooking frenzy. The food was wonderful as usual, but Dawn had complained that Rose was packing huge lunches for her, enough to feed the five girls she hung out with at school. It was starting to make her feel like a walking cafeteria.

Ella wondered if the reason Rose was tense was because Dawn had decided she didn't want the traditional *kinaaldá*, a coming-of-age ceremony that usually took place when a Navajo girl had her first menstrual cycle. The ceremony required the girl to carry out a series of traditional tasks and chores, such as baking a cake over coals, grinding corn— and all that with no sleep through a night of prayer in a special hogan. It was very demanding, and lasted from two to four days.

The *kinaaldá* was meant to help young girls understand more about family responsibilities and the demands life would make on them in the future. Ella had left the decision whether to have the ceremony or not up to her daughter, just as her father had insisted that Ella be given the freedom to choose for herself when she'd been young.

Dawn had eventually decided that since none of her friends was going to be doing that, and even Ella had opted out at her age, there was no reason for her to go through the ceremony either. Certainly for most Navajos times had changed, along with the role of women in their families.

Ella hadn't pushed, but the news had clearly hit Rose hard. After convincing herself that her granddaughter would choose to follow tradition, she'd secretly preordered a ceremonial rug dress for Dawn, an essential ritual garment. When Ella had found out, she'd wanted to tell Dawn, but Rose had asked her not to do that. Ella knew that Rose was still hoping Dawn would change her mind on her own and have the ceremony.

As Ella continued to speculate about what was troubling Rose, a gunshot reverberated in the air. It was much louder than she'd expected. The Hogback had actually amplified the sound.

She now had her answer. The sound had been thunderous and unmistakable, and since no one had reported it, a silencer must have been used. The presence of the bullets adjacent to the wound sites contradicted the possibility that they could have been shot elsewhere.

Justine arrived a few minutes later, bringing a spare vest from the crime scene van. It was too big, but Ella put it on anyway and got into the SUV. They headed toward the house she'd noticed while waiting for the gunshot test. The access road ran east and west, not along the cliff, so it took a while to get there. Eventually, they found the right lane between two blue-green, knee-high alfalfa fields that looked ready to cut.

"Keep your eyes and ears open," Ella said. "Although this area has been searched already, we still don't have any idea where the shooter went."

On the way there, Ella called dispatch to see if they could ID the resident. The reply came in a matter of seconds. "Mr. Willard Pete lives there. He calls the station at least once a month to report skinwalkers."

Ella racked the mike then looked at Justine. "The patrolmen who responded probably concluded that he was a crackpot. But from what we've discovered today, I'm wondering if there might have been more to what he saw."

As they drove closer to the house, they noticed the hogan in the back. The path leading to it was cleared of weeds and grass. "It looks like Mr. Pete's a Traditionalist," Justine said.

"So we'd better wait in the car until we're invited in," Ella answered.

It took a full twenty minutes, and it was dark outside before an elderly man turned on his porch light and stepped out. He looked at the car, noting the antennae and lights, then waved for them to approach.

As they reached the door, Mr. Pete glanced at Justine and Ella's medicine pouches, then looked back at Ella. "I've seen your photo in the paper. You're the *hataalii's* sister."

"And this is our second cousin," Ella said, nodding toward Justine. "We need your help, Uncle," she added, using the term out of respect.

"Is this about the . . ." He peered into the shadows, searching for trouble. "Skinwalkers?" he finally whispered, knowing that to say the name too loud might summon the evil ones. "I've been watching the activity over there all day," he motioned with his hand toward the crime scene. "And a while ago deputies were driving up and down the roads, looking for somebody. One Navajo officer, a sergeant built like a bear, came up and asked me if I'd seen any strangers. Only cop cars, I said. Then I told him about the skinwalkers, and he left right after that. Then a little while ago I heard a gunshot."

"We're investigating several serious crimes, and I'd like to talk to you about the things you've seen and heard," Ella said.

He led them to the hogan, not the house, brushed aside the heavy blanket that covered the east-facing entrance, and reached for a battery-powered lantern. Once it was on, they could see the wood-and-coal stove in the center of the hexagonal room. The pipe extended through the log ceiling, but was well insulated to avoid a fire hazard. Although it was still warm outside, the interior was cool. Sheepskin rugs were scattered on the floor, and he gestured an invitation for them to sit.

As was customary, Ella stepped to the right and took the seat on the north side, reserved for women, married or not. Justine sat next to her. Mr. Pete sat on the south, which signified that he was unmarried. Heads of family usually sat to the west, facing the entrance.

Ella waited for him to begin.

"Some nights I hear wild animals roaming around outside near the house. We don't have bears and wolves this far from the mountains, so that means the evil ones have claimed this area."

He lapsed into a long silence, but Ella didn't interrupt. Long silences were commonplace among older Navajos.

"The police . . . they're mostly young Modernists, like that sergeant who came by earlier. They think I'm a crazy old man. But evil *is* out there," he said.

"I agree, and it's our job to deal with that. Tell me exactly what you've heard," Ella asked.

He shuddered. "It started about a year ago. I saw a figure all hunched over and making animal sounds—grunts and groans, mostly. It was digging up something, I think, because I could hear the regular thump of dirt hitting the ground. But I didn't stick around. I slipped away as fast as I could, then ran the rest of the way home. Since then, I haven't seen anything, but I hear them out there at night all the time. The police come, but they never find anything."

Ella glanced at Justine, then back at Mr. Pete. "Uncle, can you show me where you saw that figure you spoke about?"

He left the hogan, led them halfway to his home, then pointed down toward the generator-powered lights that now illuminated the crime scene. "There, down where those police cars are, next to the fence and under the lights. That's why I asked what was going on."

"Tell me again what you saw," Ella said, noting that the angle and elevation had given him a better view of the grave sites than she'd expected. "Try to remember everything, even little details that don't seem to matter much."

"I don't normally wander about after dark, but it was different that night," he answered. "We'd been having some bad lightning storms so I'd made myself a couple of cattail leaf mats to keep my home and hogan safe from lightning. My friends had seen them and asked that I make one for them. I'd just finished theirs that evening, and since it looked like we'd be in for another storm before morning, I decided to take it to them. On the way I saw . . . too much."

"We need to know exactly what you saw, sir," Ella insisted gently.

With a sigh of resignation, he answered. "My friends live on the east side, closer to the river where I gather the cattails. There's a dirt pathway along the reservation boundary, but the bushes along the trail are as tall as a man. That's why I didn't see it right away and got too close before I knew it." He shuddered, remembering. "It was big and hunched over, low to the ground, with arms and legs. All the stories I'd ever heard about skinwalkers came rushing back to me. I've never been more scared in my life."

"Was he wearing an animal skin?" Justine asked, trying to rule out coyotes or runaway livestock.

"I couldn't see clearly enough. The moon wasn't out and it was cloudy, but I heard the noises it made. What else could it have been? So I went back home. I didn't give my friends their mat until the next morning. Since then, I only go out during the day and I've kept a close eye on everything around here. No skinwalker's gonna catch me by surprise again." He gestured with his chin to the rifle propped against the hogan wall.

"You say you only saw one figure?" Ella asked.

He took an unsteady breath. "There might have been another one around there. I'm not sure," he said. "My eyes don't work so good these days. I saw shadows and I felt . . . evil."

"Have you ever heard gunshots around here before, like the one a while ago?"

He shook his head. "No, and I listen carefully. My eyes may not work so good, but my ears are fine. And I know guns. I used to hunt a lot when lived over by Shoe Game Wash—that's north of Beclabito."

Ella smiled, recalling the area from her father's tent revival days. He'd preached in that community on several occasions.

A few more minutes of silence went by, then he looked up at her. There were questions mirrored in his eyes, but instead of voicing them, he stood.

Ella knew then that the interview was over. "Thank you for your time, Uncle." Ella reached into her pocket for her business card. "Please call me if you hear, or see, anything unusual, or if you notice any strangers hanging around."

He took the card. "I will."

As they walked back toward their SUV, Ella could feel the man's eyes still on them. He had many questions but hadn't spoken up. Words had power, so fear and silence often became allies here in the *Diné Bikéyah*.

SIX
✖ ✖ ✖

Ella leaned back against the SUV's headrest, squirming slightly from the sore muscles in her back. She still ached from the bullet impacts and knew she'd have fist-sized bruises there tomorrow morning. "You've worked with the county's lab tech before haven't you?" Ella asked.

"Many times," Justine answered. "She's good and will share whatever she gets quickly."

"Good. Stay on things. Let me know if the bullets found at the scene match the ones meant to take out the Bitsillie boy."

"I'll handle it," Justine said. "Where to next?"

"I need to pay Carolyn a visit."

"I have an idea. Why don't I stay at the crime scene and help them wrap up while you take the SUV?"

"Sure, no problem," Ella said knowing how much Justine hated the morgue.

Once they reached the crime scene, Ella stepped out long enough to thank everyone still there for all their hard work. After bumming a couple of aspirins, she drove into town.

By the time she arrived at the hospital, it was dinnertime,

but there was no way she could take a break now. She'd called home while en route, but the family wasn't surprised she'd be late. Word of the grave sites had spread far and wide.

Ella parked in one of the police slots beside the emergency room doors, then rode the elevator down to the basement. The morgue was out of the way and easily ignored by a busy hospital staff focused on life, not death.

As she walked down the silent corridor, Ella was once again struck by the stark loneliness of Carolyn's job. The majority of Navajos avoided her because she had regular contact with the dead.

Seeing Ella, Carolyn smiled and set down her coffee cup. "Good timing. I'm taking a break." Carolyn went to her computer and called up the file she knew Ella wanted. "I've got preliminaries for you. The four victims were killed around a year apart. The most recent has been dead for about a year. The oldest, around four, naturally."

"That's a lot of time between killings," Ella said, lost in thought.

Carolyn nodded. "There's more. I'm still waiting for DNA, but the most recent victims were probably Native American, and the victim killed two years ago was female."

"So they're not being targeted by sex," Ella said, thinking out loud. "If it turns out that they're all Navajo, maybe we're dealing with a serial killer who's targeting members of our tribe."

"Most murders, statistically speaking, are committed by others of the same ethnic background," Carolyn said. "It's who they hang out with."

"Another interesting point," Ella said softly. "Could you check the most recent body and see if it might be Chester Kelewood's? It's a long shot, but worth a try. He disappeared about a year ago."

"I'll get on that. Hopefully, dental records will exist some-where," Carolyn said, writing down the name.

Ella's phone rang and from the ring tone she knew it was her daughter.

"Hi sweetie," Ella said, answering. "I'm busy right now. Is this important?"

"Kinda. *Shimasání* has made enough mutton stew for an army, Mom. She wants to know if you can bring your part-ner and a few others for a late supper." Dawn lowered her voice. "*Shimá*, please bring them. *Shimasání* won't throw any-thing out, and I don't want to be eating mutton stew for a week!"

Ella bit her lip to keep from laughing. Her daughter *hated* mutton stew. Ella suspected it was because she'd entered that rebellious stage when less nutritious meals like pizza tasted far better, even for breakfast.

"I probably won't get home for a while, kiddo, but I'll see what I can do." Folding up the phone, she looked back at Carolyn and filled her in.

"Mutton stew?" Carolyn asked, a dreamy smile on her face.

"Yeah. Apparently Mom's on another cooking binge. Dawn wants me to bring people over so there won't be any leftovers."

"I wish I wasn't on a diet. I'd kill for mutton stew," Caro-lyn said. "But what's with Rose?"

"I have no idea what's going on with Mom. She's been acting . . . weird."

"What's happening in her life—or not happening?"

"My daughter doesn't want a *kinaaldá*, but I don't think that's entirely it. There's something else. . . ." She shook her head and shrugged.

"Rose is an adult. Don't push her. She'll talk to you when she's ready." Carolyn watched Ella fidget in her chair for a moment. "What's up with you? You're not moving right. Did you hurt yourself?"

When Ella told her what had happened, Carolyn insisted on checking her over.

Ella left some time later, assured that she was fine, except for some bruising. As she drove back to the station, her thoughts remained centered on the case. A serial killer on the Rez . . . She didn't like this at all. Hard times lay ahead—for all of them.

Ella sat in her office, her team seated wherever they could find room. Dwayne Blalock had begged off, going instead to brief the Farmington Police Department's chief of detectives.

Despite the long day—it was nearly eleven—Ella wanted to pool information and talk strategy so they could start on the run tomorrow morning. Seeing Nez, wearing a visitor's ID around his neck, appear at the door, Ella gestured for him to come in.

The sheriff's detective glanced at the others. "If I'm interrupting, I can wait," he said.

"No, we're working together now, so you belong here." Ella told everyone what she'd learned about the victims from Carolyn.

"Sergeant Marquez and I interviewed most of the off-reservation residents within a mile of the fence line. They all agreed on one thing—the local high school kids love to go to the Hogback area to party and cut loose—Kirtland Central and Shiprock both," Dan said.

"I can't see these murders as something that was carried out by high-school-aged kids," Justine said. "They were premeditated, and we're talking about a span of years, too."

"But here's the thing," Ella said. "Any of the kids who party in that area could have witnessed something. Does anyone know a high school kid who'd talk freely to us?"

Ella asked, looking around. "Keep in mind that, judging from the tracks and other evidence, the killer has been in the area, maybe scouting out the place in preparation for his next victim."

"My nephew goes to Shiprock High and I've already given him a call," Dan said. "He told me that it's a regular hangout, but the only people he's ever seen there are kids his age. He's going to ask around and see what his friends have to say."

"Did you tell him what was going on?" Ella asked him.

"Not the particulars, no," Nez said, "but the story will be public knowledge soon enough. The networks carried it and there was Internet coverage."

Ella nodded, accepting the truth. These days news traveled at lightning speed. "We need to move quickly on this and get answers, people. These murders have been going on for years, so I don't think this is over yet. If this is a yearly thing for our suspect, he may already have his next victim in mind."

"What about that shooting incident at the abandoned trading post? There's no doubt the boy was the target?" Dan asked.

"None," Ella answered.

"I also saw the red spot on the boy's forehead just as my partner reacted," Justine said.

"Okay then. Does anyone know why the boy was attacked?"

"He wouldn't admit it, but evidence indicates that he's been playing near the grave sites," Ella said. "Maybe he saw something he shouldn't have. Our suspect doesn't strike me as the type to leave loose ends."

"Where's the kid now?" Dan asked.

"The family's staying with a relative," Ella said. "I've got an officer watching them now. Tomorrow, I'm going back to see if I can get him to loosen up a bit."

Ella turned to Sergeant Neskahi, who'd been silent up to now. "Any word on today's manhunt for the shooter?"

"We had a dozen officers combing the area, both tribal and county but, somehow, he slipped past all of us."

"I turned the rounds we retrieved from Ella's vest over to county because your department can handle things like that faster than we can," Justine said looking at Dan. "Have the bullets been processed?"

He nodded. "That's one of the things I came to tell you. I'm having the results e-mailed to your lab, but here's what it comes down to. All the bullets used on the vics and on Ella, including that pair of AP slugs, were fired by the *same* weapon—a nine-millimeter Glock. It looks to me that the snake-eyes killer was at the scene today."

"Snake-eyes killer?" Ella asked.

"One of our county techs suggested the tag. The roll of the dice found near the graves, two shots in each skull—you get the idea," Dan said, then shrugged.

"Any way of tracking who bought those AP rounds?" Joe asked. "Maybe we could narrow down which local agency may have purchased some for their department, or see if there are any reports of thefts of that type of ammunition."

"That particular round was discontinued about five years ago, and the manufacturer recalled all unsold inventory," Justine said. "Some kind of powder instability problem in a batch. But I'll see who ordered locally, and check the crime reports and see if we can get any hits on stolen ordnance."

"Do that, then. But let's also settle on a plan of action," Ella said. "Our first priority is identifying the victims. Justine, I want you to get the best description Carolyn can give you of each of the victims—size, weight, age, anything that'll narrow things down. Then I want you, Joe, and Benny to work together, and compare that to the list of missing whose

time frames match. Pay particular attention to Kelewood—
I've already suggested the name to Dr. Roanhorse."

"Not every Navajo who disappears is reported missing,"
Benny said. "Even before the economy went south, people
around here often dropped out of sight or drove off unan-
nounced."

"We'll have to work with what we have," Ella said.

When their meeting came to a close, Dan stepped out to
meet with Police Chief Big Ed Atcitty, who was still at the station despite the late hour. Ella was about to join them when
Justine approached.

"Earlier today I ran Chester Kelewood's height and time
of disappearance against that of the most recent murder victim," Justine said. "They're a match. Maybe we'll get lucky
and be able to make at least one positive ID."

"Do you think these people were killed so their identi-
ties could be stolen?" Ella asked her. "It sounds a little extreme, but that would fit with the check-cashing scam that
started our day."

"Yeah, but why wait a year to try and pass a bad check?"
Justine said.

"Patience, stupidity, who knows?"

"I'll look into it and see how far I get."

As Justine walked away, Ella glanced around. Dan was
gone now, but Big Ed had remained behind. "My office," he
said with a toss of his head.

Ella followed him down the hall. Over the years she'd
learned to read Big Ed, and right now, judging from his pur-
poseful strides despite the late hour, she knew that he had
an agenda. Their meeting wouldn't just be a request for an
update.

At his invitation, she took a seat across from his desk
and waited for him to begin.

"You were shot today—twice—and if you hadn't been

wearing a vest you'd either be in intensive care or one of Roanhorse's patients. I want you and your team to continue to play it smart. And speaking of that, did you have someone look at those injuries? I noticed you flinching when you sat down."

"Dr. Roanhorse looked me over," Ella said. "It's just bruising. I'll be sore for a few days."

He looked at her closely. "Take care of yourself, Shorty," he said, using the nickname he'd given Ella, though at five foot nine inches, she was taller than most other Navajo women. "And keep me updated on this case. I want you to make it your team's top priority. I'm in talks with the tribal president and the council. Any progress you make—or fail to make—will have an impact on those."

Ella looked at him, surprised. Big Ed wasn't the type who played politics, and this seemed out of character.

"I'll do the best I can, Chief. I've already pulled Marianna Talk for special duty, guarding the child who was targeted this afternoon, but we need more manpower. Even with county sharing the load, we're going to be handicapped working on a shoestring budget. Just today's overtime is going to cost us a bundle."

"I know, that's why I'm meeting with the president and the council. It's no secret that the tribal funds are tight, but I want them to know the pressure we're under, even though we can't expect much help from them." He leaned back in his chair, took a breath, then let it out slowly. "I've also spent the last few months working on a federal grant that, among other things, will give us the funds needed to upgrade the crime scene van. Let's face it, that old hand-me-down we got from the sheriff's department is barely adequate."

"It's been giving us problems, that's for sure," Ella said. "A few weeks ago the van refused to start. Then as soon as the engine was fixed, the refrigeration unit broke down. All in all, I'd say it's only a matter of time before evidence is compromised. Today it worked, but a month from now, when it really gets hot, we could have problems."

"This investigation is going to generate a lot of publicity, and our elected officials are going to want answers quickly. This is the perfect time for me to point out that we're currently working with insufficient resources. But I need you to give me something straight."

He paused, and as his silence stretched out, she waited. She'd learned the hard way never to interrupt the chief or try to press him.

"I know you hate speculating, but I need you to do just that. Are we really up against a serial killer, and is it likely he's going to strike again?"

Ella hesitated, then nodded. "Based on the little we know and today's incident, I'd say yes. He's also very smart, careful when it comes to leaving any evidence behind. None of the rounds collected match anything we can link to any other crimes, so until we find the weapon, we've got nothing except the bodies themselves."

"Those two AP rounds are available only to law enforcement. Someone in that career field knows about evidence collection—and how to minimize a trail." He added, "You think we might be dealing with a cop?"

"We can't rule that out, and it would explain how he managed to slip out of the area after the trading post incident. Nobody paid much attention to the other officers or their vehicles. But what would be the motive?" Ella asked.

"To a serial killer, just being in the wrong place at the wrong time is often enough, and police officers face a world of stress and tragedy that can turn them upside down. I just hope that's not the case. What do you think was going on today that led to the shooting?" Big Ed said, leaning forward in his chair.

"My guess is that he was scouting out the area, in preparation for his next hit, when he came across the boy. Once he realized he'd been seen, and we'd found the bodies, he tried to neutralize that witness—his first major mistake that we know about. Now that he's failed, he may go to ground, or at the very least, he's going to be more cautious next time. He'll probably scout out another burial site. With luck that'll set back his schedule and give us the opportunity to track him down before he can strike again."

"I hope so. The press is going to be all over this," he said.

"Yeah, I know. TV and the Internet already have the story and by tomorrow it'll also be the front page headline in all the local newspapers."

"What there are left of them," he said.

Ella nodded. The *Diné Times* had cut back to publishing only twice a week, and the statewide papers and the Farmington daily were clearly in trouble. The afternoon paper in Albuquerque, second largest in the state, had expired two years ago. These days, most newspapers seemed to be on life support. "They ran into problems when they could no longer compete with real-time news, and advertising revenue fell off due to the recession. Now their only salvation is to give readers more in-depth, local pieces that can't be found on the Internet or TV. That's why the reporters are getting so aggressive. They're fighting for their jobs."

"Watch your back on this one, Shorty—literally."

"Always."

Ella walked out of the chief's office, and hearing her stomach growl, checked the time. She hadn't eaten since noon, when an officer had brought pizza for the crime scene unit. Dinner at home had probably been consigned to the refrigerator by now, but her mother's leftovers were second to none. Looking forward to that, she got ready to leave.

Ella passed Justine in the hall and asked, "Are you on your way home?"

Her partner nodded. "You asked me to talk to Emily, and this is the best time to catch her. She should still be up, tending the plants in her greenhouse, and we can walk around and talk. It's how we both decompress at the end of the day."

"You like having her around, don't you?"

Justine nodded. "When I first moved into that house, I thought being alone was great. For the first time in my life I didn't have seven brothers and sisters in my face. For a while, I loved the silence," she said. "But as the months went by, I found the quiet . . . unnatural. I started to bring people over more often, but that's not the same thing as actually sharing a home."

Ella nodded. "It would take me a long time to get used to living alone again. I haven't done that since my years in the FBI. I thrived on action back then, and my apartment was just a place to sleep, shower, and change clothes."

"Have you ever wondered what it'll be like for you once Dawn goes away to college?"

"Are you kidding?" Ella laughed. "I'm still trying to figure out how I'm going to survive her high school years!"

They parted company in the parking lot and Ella drove the SUV home. Dawn might still be up, and if she was, Ella intended to spend some time with her. Although rigid bedtimes weren't really part of traditional Navajo culture, the Modernist in her insisted that Dawn be in her room no later than ten. Months ago, that had meant Dawn would be asleep, or nearly so, shortly thereafter. Now, more often than not, she'd find her twelve-year-old still on the computer. That was why Ella had implemented a new rule. No social networking after nine.

As Ella walked through the living room door, Rose, who'd been sitting in her chair reading, looked up from her book with a worried look on her weathered face. "Are you okay? I heard that there was a lot going on today."

Although that was all she'd said, Ella heard more in her mother's worried voice. Rose hated what Ella did for a living, though she understood the part it played in helping others walk in beauty. Hopefully, word about the shooting wouldn't reach her for at least a few more days.

"I'm glad you hired your brother to do a Sing for you and the others," Rose continued. "Under the circumstances, you all needed more protection than a gun could give you. And it seems to be working already. Your second cousin said your vest stopped a bullet this afternoon."

"I wish Justine hadn't told you."

"She wanted to make sure you made it home okay. Partners worry, you know," Rose said. "So do mothers." She stood there looking at Ella for a moment, tears welling in her eyes.

Ella smiled. "I'm fine now, Mom, really. I'm just a little sore. Actually, a lot sore."

She gave her mom's hand a gentle squeeze, then went into the kitchen, placed her weapon on top of the cabinet, and plopped down in the chair.

"You know that's no longer necessary, right? Your daughter could reach your gun no matter how high you put it," Rose said.

"I know, but I trust her to leave it alone. I just don't want to be looking at it continually because it's part of my work, not who or what I am when I'm home."

"Your daughter will probably be as tall as you are before long. She's already five-foot-six and growing like a weed."

Before Ella could answer, Rose placed a large bowl of mutton stew before her, then brought over some fry bread. "I put it into the microwave oven when I heard your car coming up the road. There's more in the freezer, for next week, perhaps. There was just too much for us, and I don't think your daughter is fond of stew anyway."

"She just doesn't like mutton. But *I* do. Thanks, Mom. I'm really hungry tonight."

"You don't eat enough. That's why you're as thin as a rail."

"The waistband of my jeans begs to differ," she said, chuckling.

"I took some to your brother's home, too. My son and his wife love my cooking," Rose said.

"You've been cooking almost nonstop lately, Mom. What's bothering you?"

"*Everyone* has to eat!" Rose countered, crossing her arms across her chest. "I'm just taking care of my family."

Before Ella could answer, Dawn came into the kitchen, gave her mother a hug from behind, and sat across the table from her, stifling a yawn.

Ella recognized the hopeful look on her daughter's face even before Dawn said a word. "Can I just save time and say no?"

"But you don't even know what I want!" she wailed.

Ella smiled. "I was just teasing. Relax."

"Mom, this is serious, okay? I want to start my own page on the NT4SKOOL site at Yahoo!, but I need your permission. Everyone's doing it, and—"

"*Stop*. You're not going into any social network where there are adults. We've had this talk already. There're too many predators out there, not to mention convicted felons who know you're the daughter of a cop and one of our tribe's top attorneys. That alone makes you a target."

"But, Mom, I would only allow kids I know on my page. You have to click to give anyone access and you can block out anyone you want, so it's not a big deal. Come on, Mom! *Please*? Rita's mom let her have a NT4SKOOL page."

"Look in the mirror. Do you see Rita?"

"But—"

"Why don't we look around for a network just for young people? I'm sure we can find one."

"Mom, I'm *not* a kid. I'll be in the eighth grade next year, and that's practically high school. My friends will laugh at me—or worse."

"Dawn, you have an e-mail account in your name and I let you text. You're not exactly stuck in the Stone Age. But what you're asking for now isn't going to happen. Your father doesn't want you on social networking sites, and he pays for your online stuff, both here and at his house."

"Yeah, but Dad's so old school, Mom, and you're not. You're cool, all my friends say that. Just let me try it for a week or two. You can watch me set it up, view my page whenever you want, and I promise not to let anyone 'friend' me unless you say it's okay. Rita doesn't have to know that part."

"I'll have to discuss this with your father first, Dawn."

"Yeah, and that means no. This summer is going to suck, really suck," she said, then stormed out of the kitchen.

Ella felt her temper rise. "Dawn, get back in here. *Now*."

Dawn did as she was asked. "Mom, I have to study for tomorrow's science quiz."

"It's late, and you should be in bed. Why on earth did you put it off this long?"

"It wasn't my fault. Wind needed me," Dawn said, speaking about her pony.

"What's wrong? Did he colic?" Ella asked quickly. She knew how much her daughter loved that pony. Though she'd been lobbying for a horse, Dawn hadn't wanted to sell Wind.

"No, he's just . . . old," she said. "He needs company. He and I went for a walk."

Ella sighed. "You should have taken your homework and studied outside beside him while there was still light. You used to do that all the time."

"But it was *earth science*."

"Meaning what—you're afraid of boring Wind?"

Dawn cracked a hesitant smile. "Mom, I *hate* science, especially earth science. How exciting is a sedimentary rock?"

"Hey, you love visiting the Bisti Wilderness, Angel Peak,

and all those sandstone formations. And what about Window Rock?"

"Yeah, but reading about sediment, silt, and weathering is like watching corn grow."

"Not everything in life is there for your entertainment. Sometimes when there's a job to be done, you just have to buckle down and work. You need to keep your grades up. Next year in the eighth grade, you'll have physical science, which is even harder, at least it was for me. Lots of math involved there."

"I get it. That's why I was going to go to my room to study."

Ella glanced at the clock. "It's too late now, close to midnight. Why don't we both get up early, say six, and I'll help you study for about an hour. It'll be fresher in your mind then."

"Okay," Dawn said. "But think about NT4SKOOL, okay?"

Dawn hurried out of the kitchen before Ella could reply.

Rose, who'd been cleaning the countertop, sat down beside Ella, then sighed. "It was so much easier when she was younger."

"Yes, it sure was," Ella said.

"In a lot of ways she reminds me of you at that age," Rose said.

"Me? Why?"

Rose smiled. "You were the queen of excuses back then. You'd put off everything to the last second. On weekends, you didn't even start your homework until Sunday night."

Ella laughed. "Guilty as charged."

Ella watched her mother water the three small pots of herbs on the windowsill. The kitchen was the center of their joint home now, culturally and literally, and was the furthest point east from her mom and husband Herman's sitting room that vegetation inside the house was certain to grow, aside from the mold in the refrigerator.

A few years ago, her mom and Herman had constructed a new wing for the two of them off the kitchen. This created nearly double the floor space, and allowed privacy for Ella and Dawn. This was a clear advantage for Herman as well, who was always in bed by nine these days. Rose, like Ella, tended to stay up late and rise early.

"What's been going on with the Plant Watchers lately?" Ella asked.

"There are only a few of us left. Some have passed away, and others have left the reservation to be closer to their families. We've tried to recruit new members so we can pass our knowledge on to another generation, but the younger ones barely have time for themselves these days."

"It's hard for families everywhere, Mom."

Rose nodded. "It used to be that all you really needed to do was take care of your sheep and tend your garden. They'd provide food, and wool for you to weave. Unlike bank accounts, these were investments you could really keep an eye on. But these days . . ." Rose shrugged, then without saying good night, ambled down the hall.

As her mother disappeared from view, Ella thought about what Rose had said. No matter how badly we might want things to remain the same, life was constantly evolving. She saw the proof of that every time she looked at her own near-teen daughter.

Too tired to think anymore, Ella wandered down the hall to her room and tossed back the covers. Her mother had given each of them a light blanket she'd woven in their favorite colors. Ella had earth tones, Dawn had an array of pinks, and Herman, turquoise.

Snuggled beneath her own, and wrapped in warmth and silence, she fell asleep immediately.

SEVEN

———— ✖ ✖ ✖ ————

The shrill ring of the alarm clock jolted Ella awake. She'd tried more soothing tones, but had learned the hard way that she often slept right past those. With a groan, she muted the sound but remained where she was, refusing to open her eyes.

Enjoying that blissful state of semialertness, time slipped away from her. When she finally forced one eye open and looked at the clock, she drew in a sharp breath and jumped out of bed. It was nearly seven.

Ella showered and dressed in a hurry. She'd promised Dawn she'd help her study.

By the time Ella reached the kitchen, there was a flurry of activity there already.

"Mom, there you are! I need to cram for my quiz, it's on sedimentary, igneous, and metamorphic rock—chapter seven," Dawn said, braiding her hair. It had grown to her waist, and she often worked it into a single braid that hung down her back.

"Why didn't you wake me earlier, Dawn?"

"Because she just woke up ten minutes ago herself—about the same time as me. Guess we all stayed up too late last night, Daughter," Rose responded.

"Sorry. I forgot to reset the alarm. I'm ready now, though." Ella sat down across the kitchen table from her daughter and found chapter seven. Then she began firing questions at her based on the highlighted vocabulary in the text, asking Dawn to explain or define the terms.

They'd barely discussed the principle of superposition when the phone in Ella's pocket began ringing. She braced herself. Early morning calls were never good news.

Ella identified herself and heard Big Ed's voice at the other end.

"Shorty, the bodies we found over by Hogback are now headline news. We've got reporters everywhere. A few even managed to track down Justine's home address. Once they found out Sergeant Marquez lived there, too, they all but beat down the door."

"Wonderful," she said acidly. "That means they're trying to find out where I live, too."

"That's the reason I'm calling. They know you're the tribe's lead detective on this case, so it won't be long before they succeed."

"Thanks for the heads-up, Chief."

Ella ended the call and jammed the phone back into her pocket. "I've got to get out of here before the reporters show up. I'll have more control over the situation if I'm at the station."

"But, Mom, you were going to help me study for my quiz," Dawn said.

"Your *shimasání* can do that," Ella said, then brushed a kiss on Dawn's forehead. "I'm sorry, Daughter. It's better for everyone if I leave now."

As Ella drove to the station, her thoughts remained on her family. Dawn was pushing the boundaries, but like it or not, that was all part of growing up. It was Rose who worried her the most. There was something troubling her, but in order to help, she needed to know what was going on.

Hearing the monotone beep that signaled a text message, Ella pulled out her cell phone and glanced down. The message was simple and to the point. It read, I'M WATCHING YOU.

Puzzled, Ella looked at the display, then checked the rearview mirror automatically. Nobody was in sight. Had it been meant for someone else? If not, who had her cell number? Remembering that it was printed on her business card, she muttered a soft curse. If she got another text along the same vein, she'd track it down, but acting now would be premature.

She pushed the entire thing out of her mind just as a call came over her phone. Ella answered and heard Justine's voice.

"Partner, when you arrive I recommend you come in through the door adjacent to the impound yard. There aren't any reporters around there, and I can unlock it for you."

"Things are that crazy?"

"You bet, but that's not the only reason I'm calling. Big Ed wants everyone in his office in another half hour."

"Anything I should know about?"

"One of the secretaries said that he's been fighting some higher-ups in the tribal council, but I'm not sure how reliable that information is."

"Have you heard anything about the watch placed on the Bitsillie family? I'm worried about their safety, especially the boy's."

"Officer Talk clocked out and turned her watch over to Philip Cloud. The mother's keeping both kids out of school today so she can keep an eye on them. That'll make it easier on the officers," Justine said.

Ten minutes later Ella arrived at the station. Getting inside the station turned out to be easier than she'd expected. She drove into the rear impound area past the security guard, then walked across the yard to the station's rear entrance.

"That wasn't so hard," she told Justine, who opened up as soon as she knocked. They immediately headed toward her office, taking another hallway to avoid the lobby.

"You got unexpected help. County Detective Nez got Big Ed's okay and is now giving the press a statement. I saw the text, and it's mostly sound bites. He's asking for their cooperation in helping keep the public alert, but warning them to be careful not to start a panic. Basically, he's repackaging what everyone already knows, and finishing by making a promise to leave no stone unturned. You know the drill."

Ella nodded, familiar with the technique. "What's Dan doing here so early? Did he turn up something?" They reached her door, and she opened it, then waved Justine inside.

"He found out about the man we've got in custody for impersonating Chester Kelewood, and came up with the same idea—that the deaths may be linked to identity theft."

"So he wants to interview the suspect?" Ella asked, taking a seat behind her desk.

"Yes, and I gather Big Ed is okay with that, if you are."

"No problem."

Before Ella could say anything else, Big Ed appeared at her door and motioned for them to follow. Once they reached his office, Ella saw that the rest of her team was already there. Agent Blalock and Detective Nez were also present.

Blalock spoke first. "After shooting an officer, then slipping past a dozen law enforcement officers, our suspect may be feeling cocky. We'll have to pick up the pace if we want to stop him before he kills again."

"I agree. So what have you got so far, people?" Big Ed asked, looking around the room.

Dan spoke. "John Curley, the man arrested while trying to assume Chester Kelewood's identity, is definitely a person of interest. Since he was in custody yesterday afternoon, he couldn't have been the perp who shot Investigator Clah, but it's possible he's working with the snake-eyes killer. That could explain how he ended up with Kelewood's checkbook. Of course, this is all just speculation until we can get ID's on the victims."

The theory didn't feel right to Ella. A lot had happened since she busted the guy, and the connection just didn't seem to be there except by coincidence. The murders were carried out by someone who was very careful to protect their own identity. Curley would have to be really stupid, at this late date, to pose as one of his own victims and finger himself as a suspect. Now, if Kelewood did turn out to be one of those buried beside Hogback, all that could change. She glanced at Justine and saw her partner shrug.

"We don't have much on Curley," Justine said. "We identified him after a fingerprint check. He has a record of assault on a police officer—stemming from a tribal fair disturbance where he ended up getting Maced. He received a suspended sentence, probably because the Mace put him in the hospital. After that, he's been clean. So far, he hasn't said a word to us directly. He speaks only through his attorney. He also hasn't been in contact with anyone else since his arrest."

"What else do we have?" Big Ed glanced around the room again.

"I've got a follow-up," Justine added. "Five state law enforcement departments made purchases of the brand and type of AP rounds used to kill the first victim, including FPD and the local sheriff's department. Most of that stock was returned to the manufacturer seven years ago, but hundreds of officers were issued those rounds, and some of those rounds were never returned, according to their armory records. There's no official report of thefts of any of that ammunition, either. We've got a boatload of possible suspects if we include cops in our investigation."

Benny spoke next. "I got more information from the M.E. this morning. The four victims, three male and one female, range in ages from their late twenties to their early sixties. We've compiled a list of area citizens reported missing during the years that correlate to the vics' deaths, but it's extensive, so narrowing things down is going to take time. And if any of the victims was passing through the state, an ID is going to be even more difficult."

Big Ed's phone began to ring, and he picked it up. A second later, he glanced up at them. "We're done here."

Ella looked at her team. "Let's move to my office," she said quietly. "Dan, I'd like you to come, too, if you can join us."

Ella had just stepped out into the hall when Big Ed called her back. "Hold it a moment, Shorty," he said, and came out to meet her. "You're putting in long hours, so it might help you to know that the council is starting to see how badly we need additional funding."

"Thanks, Chief."

As Ella walked down the hall, she thought of what her brother Clifford would have said. Navajo ways taught that everything had two sides, and this was a good example of that. From the apparent disharmony funding meetings created, harmony would come.

Ella entered her small office, full of officers now, most standing, and walked to her desk. "What is county doing to identify the vics?" Ella asked Dan.

"Our list of missing people is larger than the tribe's, so I've got every deputy I can beg, borrow, or steal, including our auxiliary people, running down names. We're going to be checking each person, ruling out those who don't fit the parameters right away, and updating each hour."

"I'm helping county narrow down the list, too," Blalock said. "I've got access to a variety of databases not available to Sheriff Taylor. I can speed things up a bit."

Ella looked at the members of her team. "Talk to the relatives of the missing people whose descriptions and time frames fit. Our first priority is to identify those victims."

"Many of our people won't want to speak of the dead, or those they think might be dead," Neskahi said.

"I know, but stay on it anyway," Ella answered.

As they streamed out, Dan lingered. "What do you say we both have a conversation with Mr. Curley and see what we get when we push him for answers."

Ella had Curley brought to one of the interview rooms, then led Dan there. As they went inside, Curley gave them a tired, bored look.

"Mr. Curley, we need to ask you some questions," Ella said, sitting down across the table from him.

"You'll have to wait. My tribal-appointed attorney is running late."

"Here I am now," a voice at the half-open door called.

As Ella turned her head, it took all she had not to cringe. Martin Tallman's reputation preceded him. The defense attorney was notorious in the Four Corners for doing whatever was necessary to get his clients off. Ella studied him as he strode into the room. He had the cool, calculating confidence of a seasoned trial lawyer. Some still referred to him privately as Hammerhead—a lawyer/shark analogy reinforced by his high forehead.

He nodded to Ella and Dan, then sat down beside his client. "Have you said anything at all to them, Mr. Curley?"

"They haven't asked me any questions yet."

Tallman gave Ella a flat, emotionless look. "I need five minutes to confer with my client."

Ella tried not to curse. She already knew what was going to happen. He'd advise his client not to say a word until he could negotiate a deal, and she'd waste half the morning playing games. Her hope of interviewing Del Bitsillie this morning was fading fast.

Ella gave Tallman a curt nod, then led the way out of the room, Dan a step behind her. As they waited just outside the door, Dan gave her a long look.

"I can tell this guy's been around the block. Should I assume from your reaction to him that we're all but screwed?" he asked.

"Tallman knows how the game's played," Ella said. "He pushes hard for his clients and never backs down. His usual strategy is to make his client look like a victim."

A moment later, Tallman opened the door. "Come in. Mr. Curley is ready to talk to you." As they each took a seat, Tallman continued. "In exchange for my client's cooperation, we'd like all the charges dropped."

"You've got to be kidding," Ella said after a beat.

Tallman said nothing and continued to stare back at her.

"I think you need a reality check, Mr. Tallman. We've got your client for assault on a police officer and identity theft. That's just for starters," Ella said.

"Maybe so, but that's not your real interest in my client. I know what you're investigating. Mr. Curley isn't involved in those murders, not in any way, but he has information that could help you find answers."

"If, as you say, he's not involved and has valuable information, we could subpoena him to testify before a grand jury," Ella said.

"True, but that could take weeks, and you might end up with a witness who's hostile or has memory problems."

"Only the US Attorney can grant your client immunity from prosecution on these charges, and he won't do that unless he knows that the information is worthwhile. Give us something to use," Ella said.

"Not without some assurances. We have every reason to believe the information might be very valuable. Just to prove we're willing to make a deal, we'll be happy to wait while you make the call."

Ella looked at Hammerhead, trying to decide if Curley really knew something or this was all a bluff. As it usually was with Tallman, she couldn't tell.

Ella nodded to Dan, then walked out of the room, the door automatically shutting behind them. Out of hearing range, Ella leaned against the wall, arms crossed. "We'll wait here for a bit."

"You're the officer Curley attacked, right?"

"Yeah. I could drop the charges and have the D.A. recommend lenience on the forgery part in exchange for cooperation, but I want Tallman to sweat it out. Do sharks sweat?"

Ella waited, deliberately biding her time. She bought herself and Dan a soda then drank it at leisure before going back inside.

When they entered the room, it was Tallman who looked bored this time. His client seemed to be on the edge of his chair.

"If the information's good enough, we'll water down the assault charge and recommend leniency in exchange for cooperation. Your client has a real chance of getting off with probation—if he cooperates fully."

Tallman sat back, apparently satisfied, then gave his client a nod.

"So what's your story? How did you end up with the checkbook?" Ella asked Curley.

"I found Kelewood's checkbook and wallet a little over a year ago, I think. I remember it was warm out by then, so I think it was the end of May or maybe a week or two into June," Curley said. "I was driving back from Farmington on Highway 64 when I started having some steering problems with my truck. Something always acts up on that piece of crap."

Ella and Dan waited.

"I took a left onto the old highway near Kirtland, then found a place to pull off the road. I wanted to take a look and see if I could fix whatever was wrong. Turns out I'd picked up a nail and my tire was going flat. When I was searching for a rock to put behind my tire to keep the truck from rolling, I spotted the wallet in the drainage ditch. A little farther down I saw the checkbook. Both were brown, almost the same color as ditch dirt, so I nearly missed them." He shrugged. "I tossed them onto the seat of my truck, changed the tire, then drove to the closest gas station to get the flat fixed. It was that Phillips 66 across from Flare Hill, I think."

"The wallet and checkbook—did you try to return them?" Ella asked.

He shook his head. "I meant to—at first. I asked around about Kelewood, did a search on my nephew's computer, and found out the guy had a real good job working for the state. He was some kind of mine inspector. Then I lost my job, and my life got complicated. I had to spend the money in the wallet, about some sixty dollars in cash, but I hung on to the wallet and checkbook. I kept looking in the newspaper, hoping he'd offer a reward, you know?

"Not long after that my wife ran out on me and I started drinking. I forgot all about the wallet and the checkbook until about a week ago. I found them at the bottom of a drawer while looking for a clean pair of socks."

"Was there anything else in the wallet—not counting the cash you'd already spent?" Dan asked.

"Yeah, his state ID, driver's license, a few credit cards, some receipts, family photos, stuff like that. I thought I should at least return the credit cards and the two ID's."

"Decent of you. So what happened next?" Ella said.

"I asked some friends about Kelewood, trying to come up with an address. The house listed on his driver's license was rented to someone else, so I called the number given on the Web site for his job description and asked for him. They said he no longer worked there. When I pushed for more info the secretary told me he'd gone missing a while back.

"That's when I decided to write myself a check to cash and sign Kelewood's name. He wasn't around, so I thought, what the hell? The photo on his driver's license was crappy, but the license was still good. I figured I could pass. Problem is, the clerk knew Kelewood. I'm telling you, I've had nothing but crappy luck lately."

"You want us to believe that you found Kelewood's checkbook and wallet by accident, then sat on it for a year? Give me a break," Dan said. "You killed him, found yourself low on cash, and decided to try and cash one of his checks."

"No way, man. I'll take a lie-detector test if you want, but what I've told you is the truth. I found that wallet and checkbook, but I have no idea what happened to Kelewood. I've never even seen the guy."

"Think back," Ella said, playing a hunch. "Once you found the wallet and checkbook, you probably kept looking, maybe for car keys, a cell phone, stuff like that. Did you see anything else there, something that caught your eye but wasn't worth picking up?"

Curley stared at his lap. "Like what?" he muttered.

"You tell me," Ella said. "If you want a deal then you've got to give me more than what we already know."

"Now that I think about it, I remember seeing a smashed-up cell phone," Curley said after a beat. "It looked to me like someone took a boot to it and stomped it pretty good. It was black, one of those flip-open kind. It was trashed, so I left it there."

"You never saw Kelewood's body, or some clothing, or maybe papers or a notebook?" Ella leaned back, her gaze still on him.

"There weren't any papers or stuff like that, and I'd definitely remember seeing a dead guy or bloody clothes. I'm not holding out on you. I took the wallet and checkbook, sure, but that's it."

"Tell me *exactly* where you found the checkbook and wallet, Mr. Curley," Ella said.

"About a mile before you pass the high school, on the

right, make that the north side of the road, about fifty feet before you get to the big casino billboard," Curley said. "I remember the billboard because of that blonde on the swing. You've seen the ads on TV, probably."

"There you have it, Inspector Clah. My client has cooperated and told you all he knows," Tallman said. "You've even brought out memories he didn't know he had, which is more than you could have hoped for. You have a relative date, time, and place to search for evidence. The locale Mr. Curley mentioned is miles east of Hogback, where you found all those bodies. Now it's time for you to hold up your end."

Ella nodded. "One more question, Mr. Curley. Do you own a rifle or handgun?"

"No, I don't. I had a hunting rifle years ago, but I hocked it and I guess it was sold to someone else. I never went back. It was a thirty-thirty lever-action Winchester."

"Thanks. We may call on you again, though," Ella said, still staring at Curley. "Especially if one of the dead turns out to be Chester Kelewood."

"Wait—call on me to do what?" Curley said. "I've told you everything I know. If you think you can pin those murders on me, you're nuts."

Tallman cleared his throat, caught Curley's eye, and shook his head. "No one will pin anything on you. Please relax."

Something about his tone made Curley grow silent.

"May we have a word?" Tallman said, looking at Ella, then headed out the door without waiting for an answer.

Ella and Dan followed the lawyer into the hall.

Tallman waited for the door behind them to close before speaking. "It's been a pleasure seeing you again, Investigator Clah. You may be interested to know that I'll be working for the prosecution in the near future. We'll be on the same team then."

"Now there's something I never expected to hear, Mr. Tallman," she said, surprised. "You could earn a lot more in private practice, particularly off the Rez. I always figured that would be your next step."

"That was part of my original career plan, but the tribe paid for my college, and I'm needed here."

As Tallman walked away, Ella tried to process the news. He'd be one heckuva prosecutor. Before she could give it any additional thought, her phone vibrated and she picked it up. Carolyn's voice greeted her.

"I've got a few more things for you, but I won't have time to fill out the official report anytime soon. Do you want to head over here or talk on the phone?"

Ella considered the phone, but the chances of being overheard here with the press lurking around every corner were better than average. "I'll come over."

After hanging up, she looked at Nez. "Dr. Roanhorse has some more information for us. Why don't you come with me so you can hear everything firsthand."

"Better not. I have a long list of people to interview," he said quickly. "You can catch me up to speed later by phone."

Ella watched him go, suspecting that, like many other Navajos, he wanted to avoid the morgue. She'd never been to Leupp, where Dan grew up, but she'd heard there were a lot of Traditionalists in that corner of the Rez. The influence would have been strong.

Blalock, who'd been coming down the hall, joined her. "Did I overhear you right? Dr. Roanhorse has information?"

"Yeah, you want to come along?"

"You bet."

"You might want to hold up on that," Justine said, hurrying down the hall toward them.

"What's up?" Ella asked quickly.

"The Bitsillies spent the night at their relative's house, but they're now leaving, according to Marianna. When she arrived to take over the protective detail, she saw them loading up their car again."

"Why? What's going on?" Ella asked.

"She's not sure. All Lois would say is that she knows what's best for her kids."

"I was planning to interview them again this morning and see if I can coax the boy into talking. We have to find out why he was targeted. Unless they're in immediate danger, have Marianna keep them there until we arrive."

Justine brought out her cell phone and stepped away to make the call.

Blalock looked at Ella. "Go take care of that. I'll meet you over at the morgue later."

EIGHT

✕ ✕ ✕

With Justine at the wheel, Ella was soon on the way to see the Bitsillies. The uncle's home was along the east side of the river past the old downtown area. "What else do we know about Lois Bitsillie and her children? Anything about the father?" Ella asked. "I haven't had time to do a background check."

"I took care of that for you. The husband worked construction, but was killed in an on-the-job accident near Bloomfield about eighteen months ago. Lois and the kids lived in Kirtland, off the Rez, got behind on their house payments, and were evicted. Since then, they've been run off a few other places for vagrancy, but she's stayed in the area and kept the kids in the same schools. Lois makes minimum wage at the fast-food place. She wants to work full time, but the company's policy is to limit everyone to under forty hours a week so they can avoid paying benefits."

"At least they're still together," Ella said, thinking of her own family and how lucky they all were to have each other.

Soon they arrived at a wood-and-stucco frame home, a pale green building with curling asphalt shingles that needed work. Ella spotted Lois Bitsillie and her two children right away. They were standing beside their red Ford sedan. Marianna Talk, in the tribal department's tan uniform, was a few feet away, next to her patrol unit, which was blocking the road.

"Keep an eye on the family," Ella told Justine as they stepped out of the SUV.

Ella went to speak to the young patrol officer. "What's the problem, Marianna? Mrs. Bitsillie said there might be a problem with the landlord."

"That's not a problem. Lois is worried the killer will track her son here since the uncle is also named Bitsillie. A male cousin volunteered to take them in for a while after Lois called and told him what's going on. The cousin lives in Farmington and has a different last name. Mrs. Bitsillie's convinced they'll be harder to find there."

"She was ready to stay here, and now all of a sudden she's changed her mind? What's really going on?" Ella asked.

"I asked her, but she wouldn't say. It's clear that the shooting really frightened her. She's determined to do whatever it takes to keep her kids safe," Marianna said. "I ran a background on the cousin before you got here, figuring you'd need it. He's legit."

"For this to happen, I'll have to check with the Farmington Police and see if they can keep an eye on them."

"Understood," Marianna said.

Ella walked over to join the family. "Good morning, Lois, Belara, Del."

"Are you feeling better?" Lois asked her.

"You were *shot*!" Del said, his eyes huge.

"Yes, twice, and that's why officers wear vests, to keep us safe," Ella said with a gentle smile. "Today I'm a little sore and bruised, but that's it."

"How big were the bullets?" Del asked.

"Son, that's *not* nice," Lois said, shaking her head at Del.

Ella took advantage of the question, reached into her

pocket, and brought out a spare, loaded magazine. She slipped out a nine-millimeter cartridge and placed it into her palm, holding it out for them to see. "They were just like this one."

"Wow. Just like on TV," he said, clearly impressed.

"You can hold it for a moment, Del." Ella placed the round into his hand.

"It's kinda heavy," he said, staring down at the cartridge.

"Del, I need your help to catch the man who tried to shoot us. Something bad happened over by the reservation fence line, and we need to know if you've seen or heard anything unusual going on near there. We know you like to play around in that area. If you can help us, we'll make sure that person can never hurt anyone again."

"It wasn't just me . . ." The boy's voice trailed off, and he stared at the ground. His sister, Belara, shifted nervously, and looked away from Ella.

"Neither one of you are in any trouble," Ella said.

"You say that," Belara said, "but if we talk to you, how do we know we'll be safe from . . . you know."

"We protected you once and we'll continue to do that," Ella said. "Officer Talk and others have been watching over you since yesterday."

"Being afraid isn't something you can run away from easily," Justine said softly. "Sometimes the only way to beat it is to face things head-on."

"Tell her what you told me earlier," Lois said, looking at her kids and giving them an encouraging nod. "She needs to know."

Ella looked back at the kids and waited. She'd had a feeling the sudden move had been prompted by something.

As Belara looked at Ella, her hand fisted into the fabric of her loose top. "Del went where he wasn't supposed to! Mom told us to stay inside until her shift was over."

"It wasn't just *my* fault! You went, too," he said.

"Yeah, but you started it. I just followed—to bring you back before Mom got home."

"Slow down," Ella said, looking at both of them. "Start at the beginning."

Del glanced at his mom, and seeing her nod, spoke. "I like to take my Jeeps and stuff over there to play in the sand. I set my soldiers up in foxholes, then blow them up with gravel and clods. I was just messing around. Belara came looking for me, I guess."

"You're not supposed to be that far away when it's dark outside," Belara said.

"The moon was really bright. I could see, and finally it wasn't so hot outside."

"So what happened that frightened you?" Ella asked, getting them back on track.

Del kicked the sand with his shoe, building up his courage as he spoke. "I was setting up my soldiers and Jeep again after knocking them down when I saw my sister looking for me. She didn't know where I was, so I decide to circle around and scare her. I was sneaking along that trail beside the fence when a car came right at me. I don't think the guy saw me at first because he had his headlights off."

"I *heard* the car, but I was coming from a different direction and couldn't really see it through the brush," Belara said before Ella could ask Del for more details. "I thought it might be some pervert, so I looked around for a stick or a rock."

Del nodded. "I ducked back off the trail against a bush, but the car came straight down the trail and almost ran me over. He must have seen me at the last minute, because he suddenly slammed on the brakes.

"I hid in the bushes," Del continued after taking a breath. "The driver had one of those spotlights, like the police do. He aimed it around, but I was lying flat on my stomach and he never saw me. After a while he turned off that light and backed out onto the highway. Then he took off. When he got to the main highway he turned on his headlights and drove toward Kirtland. I was running back when I caught up to Belara."

"I found *you*, and we went home," she argued.

"They didn't tell me about this until last night, and it scared me silly," Lois said. "Why would anyone be driving a car around there at night with its lights off? To me, it sounded like drug dealers."

Ella looked back at Del. "Were you able to see the driver at all?"

He shook his head. "I was too busy trying to get away."

"Maybe you saw his license plate when he drove off? Do you remember what color it was?"

He thought about it a moment, then nodded. "It was from New Mexico—yellow with red numbers and letters."

"Do you remember any of those numbers or letters?" Ella prodded gently. "Try to picture it in your mind."

"I remember it had a D. Like with Del."

"Any numbers?"

He shook his head. "No, sorry."

Ella looked at Belara. "How about you?"

The girl shook her head. "When he turned on that search-light thing all I was looking at was my idiot brother. The guy would have run him over if Del hadn't taken cover in the brush, I'm sure of it."

"What makes you think it was a guy?" Ella pressed.

Belara paused. "It was the kind of car guys drive . . . hot engine, squealing tires."

"What kind of car was it?" Ella asked.

"It was white, maybe cream-colored, kind of like one of those sheriff's department cars, except without the gold star on the side and the flashing lights on top."

"Is there anything else you might remember that might help me identify whoever was driving that car?"

Belara shook her head, and Del looked off into the distance.

Ella allowed the silence to stretch.

"He was a big man. His head was almost to the roof of the car," Del said at last. "As soon as he took off, I ran and didn't stop until Belara grabbed me over by that old dead-guy house."

"Did you leave anything else behind besides your soldiers and that toy Jeep?" Ella asked.

"Yeah, my dice, and an old doll head I stuck in the ground, like a monster attacking my squad," Del said. "I don't play with dolls, but can I have my other stuff back?"

"Probably later. Right now, it's evidence," Ella said, then turned to Lois. "Give me a minute to make sure the Farmington P.D. has officers who can watch your cousin's house while you're there."

Ella brought out her cell phone and walked away to keep her conversation private.

Five minutes later, she got a return call from Blalock. "It's all set. The Farmington P.D. has agreed to handle it."

Shortly thereafter, Lois and her children set out, heading east toward Farmington. Officer Marianna Talk followed several car lengths behind.

Justine walked back to the SUV with Ella. "Where to, boss?"

"The morgue. Blalock's meeting me there. Carolyn's got something new for us."

"So you want me to drop you off?"

Ella caught the hopeful lilt in Justine's voice. Her partner would do what was necessary, but a visit to the morgue required a strong stomach. Even if you didn't believe in the *chindi*—and Justine, a Christian, did not—a corpse's grayish pallor, or seeing what had once been a human being cut open on a table, could give anyone pause. She remembered her first time there. A burn victim had been brought in and the overpowering scent of something resembling pork rinds had almost made her throw up on the spot.

No one who'd ever seen a lifeless body in that state could doubt that a human being was more than the sum of his biological parts. Navajos believed in a "wind spirit" that defined each person, giving them life. Justine's faith termed it a soul, but no matter how you looked at it, a person had little in common with the shell it eventually left behind.

"I know I'm being a wuss, partner," Justine said quietly after a moment. "But it's not the bodies that get to me. It's the smell . . . like bad meat and disinfectant. Scents that come from nature don't bother me, not even a hog pen or a skunk. Mind you, that last one's the kind I'd rather avoid, but it's not . . . offensive . . . to me. When I go into the morgue, it's different. The scents there make me think of the word *natzee*, or maybe *niłtcxon*, something that's spoiled." She lowered her voice to a whisper. "It just makes me want to run out of there as fast as I can."

"I know. You have to spend a lot of time there to get used to it, and that's a level of conditioning I hope I never reach."

"How do you think she does it—Dr. Roanhorse, that is? She's Navajo."

"Carolyn is one of the strongest women I know. She's there because the tribe needs her to be, and she knows it," Ella said. "In that way, she's no different from you and me. Our jobs are different from hers, sure, but we each do what needs to be done."

NINE

✖ ✖ ✖

As Ella reached the basement and got out of the elevator, the funky odor of an old butcher shop hit her. She tried to take shallow breaths as she walked across the hall and entered the autopsy room where Carolyn was working. On the table before the white-clad M.E. was one of the skeletal remains they'd found at the Hogback. Ella was reminded of dried beef and leather, and that helped with the disassociation process that allowed her to cope with the demands of her job.

At the moment, Carolyn was measuring the entry wound on one of the skulls and comparing it to an x-ray attached to a screen on the north wall.

"I'm glad you're here," Carolyn said, glancing over at her. "I've got some interesting findings, and I thought you'd want a rundown as soon as possible."

"Sure do," Ella said, joining her. "Has Blalock come by yet?"

"Here I am," a familiar voice said as the tall agent in the light tan sports jacket joined them. "Sorry. My meeting with Big Ed took longer than expected."

"Shall we get started?" Carolyn asked. Then, seeing them nod, she continued. "You see these two entrance wounds?"

she said, pointing to the skull. "They're nearly an exact dupli-
cate of what I found on the other victims. What it tells me is
that both shots weren't fired in rapid succession. The angles
are different, and I estimate that the position of the weapon
shifted at least four or five feet between shots. Either wound
would have been fatal. There was no need for the second."

"Maybe he wanted to make sure," Blalock said.

"Or you've got two shooters taking turns, or one shooter
expressing cold, calculated anger," Ella said.

"I suspect all were Native American, probably Navajo,
but I'm still waiting for the DNA markers to confirm race,"
Carolyn said. "Two of these victims suffered broken bones
while alive. Those were set and healed normally. I'm in the
process of running that detail through tribal databases and
trying to find dental and medical records that match."

Ella nodded. "If the broken bones were set, that means
they got medical care. That should help. Many of our people
don't visit a doctor. Sometimes it's a matter of choice or access, but, either way, the fact remains."

"I'm also going to check off-Rez medical facilities within
fifty miles, starting with the regional medical center in Farmington, but that'll take time. The DNA is taking forever,
though. Any way either of you can speed it up?"

"I can get the Bureau lab in Albuquerque involved and
push that a bit," Blalock said. "Give me about a half hour to
make the call."

"Good. I've got samples of hair, skin, dried tissue, and
bone marrow ready to be sent in." Carolyn gestured to the
table. "I've also recorded the height, approximate weight, and
sex of each victim, and made a printout for you. In there
you'll also find an estimate of how long each has been dead.
I'll have the official report, minus toxicology, ready by the
end of tomorrow—maybe."

Ella took a deep breath. Death and police work went
hand in hand. Yet deep inside her, the little Navajo girl

who'd been taught never to wish anyone dead out loud because that could have the power to kill, and not to put her
shoes on the wrong feet because it could call death, still respected the old beliefs. They whispered a different set of
truths, but ones that were as much a part of her as the badge
she wore. For years she'd fought against that duality, but she
was a product of two cultures and both deserved respect.

Blalock made his call and got confirmation before they
left the hospital.

As they walked to the parking lot, Ella glanced at FB-
Eyes—his nickname among some Navajos because he had
one blue eye, one brown. "Since all the vics were Native
American, the Bureau can claim jurisdiction," she said.

"Yeah, but it's better if we continue to work together on
this and use local officers. Between county, the tribal P.D.,
and the Bureau, we're bound to get answers faster."

Halfway back to the station, Blalock glanced over at her.
"Spill it, Clah. You're too quiet, which means something's
eating you. What is it?"

"The details of this case don't make a lot of sense. For
example, these were execution-style killings, but why two
shots, when either one would have been a guaranteed kill,
even with AP rounds, which are less lethal? And there's no
obvious sexual link—victims were male and female. There's
also another oddity about our serial killer: Why so long between victims—a year each time? And did he show up the
other night to prepare the site for the next victim, or was
the body already in the car, ready to bury?"

"Del Bitsillie may have thrown off his plans," Blalock
said.

"I also keep thinking of what Mr. Pete told me about the
person he saw in the area. I can't figure out if we have someone trying to impersonate a skinwalker, or if that's just Mr.
Pete's interpretation of what he saw."

"That's why we need a Navajo officer leading the chase.

Issues like those need to be put in the right perspective. Obviously, there's still a lot we don't know, but we're barely out the starting gate, Ella," Blalock said. "I'll get the lab to push through the DNA results while you stay focused on what's happening out in the field."

Ella's phone beeped, signaling a text message, and she flipped it open with one hand. Her hand tightened as she read what was on the screen. "I've got a comedian-stalker," she commented, shaking her head.

"What's it say?"

"'You see dead people,'" she read aloud. "Looks like I was followed to the morgue." She looked back in the side mirror and checked the vehicles behind Blalock's car. "He's probably not there now, not after having made his point," she muttered, then tried to click on the options to find out who'd sent her the text message.

Ella told Blalock about the previous one as soon as she saw that the sender's number had been blocked. "I'm going to have to get a court order to find out who this guy is, but that's going to take time."

"Keep me updated on that," Blalock asked as he dropped her off at the station.

Halfway to the side entrance, Ella's phone rang and the display revealed an incoming call from Kevin Tolino, Dawn's father. She and Kevin had remained friends over the years, but their relationship wasn't without its rocky moments.

"I just spoke to our daughter," Kevin said, his words clipped and abrupt. "She said that you and she had talked about letting her have a NT4SKOOL account, but that she had to have my permission, too."

Ella paused for a moment. "Our daughter is starting to sound like a politician. She's cutting and pasting different parts of our conversation, trying to play us off each other. Or maybe she was just trying to change the subject. What were you talking about before she brought that up?"

"School and grades. I wanted to know how she'd done on her science quiz. She told me that you hadn't been able to help her study like you promised because you had to rush off. Then she went into the thing about NT4SKOOL."

"She's playing you, Kev. She's been slacking off in school these past few weeks and didn't want you to know. The fact is, she put off studying until late the night before. I sent her to bed, but when I had to leave early the next morning, it all became my fault."

"She's a smart kid, and has always worked hard at school. What's going on?" he said.

"She's growing up and deliberately breaking rules—testing us. We'll have to find a way to rein her in and demand she meet her responsibilities."

"At our last teacher conference, we talked about Dawn's study habits and class work. She was doing B-level work and Mr. Andrews thought she wasn't applying herself. I remember we talked to her about that. Has she dropped to a C? Is that why she switched the subject so quickly?"

"No, not yet, but her grades are slipping. She's pretending to be studying, that's my guess."

"How should we handle this? Any ideas?" he asked.

"She loves playing online. Let's take away that Internet privilege and make her earn it back in increments. If she meets her responsibilities, then that'll be her reward. If not, then she faces a consequence—no computer playtime. And her cell phone goes, too."

"I like it."

"And by the way, I'm definitely against the NT4SKOOL thing. It's an adult forum—or at least for much older teens. I'll try to find out if there's another site more suitable for someone Dawn's age. Having our daughter approached by an online predator is the stuff of nightmares for me."

"She's beautiful, and already turning heads," Kevin said

softly. "I'm dreading the time when she starts dating—or wants to go on Facebook."

Ella sighed. Dawn, with her long black hair and dark expressive eyes, was a stunner. She was tall and slender, and although only twelve, had a head start on physical maturity and looked more like a sixteen-year-old.

"I wish I could hold back the hands of time, Kev, but things are bound to get worse before they get better. High school's just around the corner."

"Just shoot me now," came the strangled response.

Ella smiled and put her phone away. As she walked through the front door, she saw Neskahi talking to Justine.

"What's the situation?" she asked, joining them.

"I remembered that my uncle and cousin had a friend by the last name of Kelewood, so I drove to Two Grey Hills to talk to them in person," Neskahi said. "My uncle's a Traditionalist, but my cousin's a Modernist, so I figured I'd talk mostly to him. But my uncle overheard me and burst into the room we were in. He said I'd come to talk about the dead and was inviting the *chindi* into his home. My cousin tried to calm him down, and I explained that all we really knew for sure was that Kelewood was missing, but I still got kicked out. I wasted an hour getting there, and got nothing."

Justine looked at Ella and filled in the gaps. "Word's out that Kelewood's dead because Curley got caught with his wallet and checkbook."

"But there's no shred of evidence that indicates anything more than the obvious—he's missing," Ella protested. "We haven't identified those four bodies."

"I know, but gossip on the Rez runs wild, particularly when someone finds a body, much less four at the same time."

Ella knew Justine was right. "I've got some additional information on the victims that'll help us narrow the possibilities. We need everyone working on this. Maybe we can make some progress today and start pairing up names with bodies. Then we can focus on those names."

"We're down a man. Tache had an emergency dental visit," Justine said.

"What happened?"

"He broke a tooth cracking piñon nuts," she answered.

"So he'll be out for the rest of today," Ella said, knowing how dental visits often worked. "We'll have to double up." Yet even as she said it, she knew that the interviews they had to conduct couldn't be rushed. Being one person short would set them back a day or more.

Justine plugged the information Carolyn had given them into the computer. By the time comparisons were made, they had a three-page, single-spaced list with the best matches underlined.

"Here one missing person with a time frame and body type that fits. Betty Eltsosie reported her dad missing about three years ago," Justine said, starting at the top. "She apparently found out weeks after the fact, but phoned us as soon as she knew. She'd been deployed overseas so her mom hadn't wanted to upset her. She waited until Betty was stateside to tell her."

"Her mother never called the police?" Ella asked, trying to understand.

Justine nodded. "Ronald Eltsosie had been sick for months—cancer—and then one January morning, he walked away. Although an extensive search was conducted as soon as Betty called the department, the body was never found."

"Her mother just assumed that Ronald went into the desert to die and respected his decision," Ella said with a nod. "It's the way of The People," she added, though she didn't agree with that method at all.

They e-mailed Joe and Benny a revised copy of the list with their share of names to pursue based on particular communities. Once that was done, Ella and Justine left to track down either Betty Eltsosie or her mother.

As they drove down the highway, heading south on Highway 491 toward Gallup, Ella's phone rang. Seeing it was Rose, she picked it up immediately.

"Would you like to bring your cousin and partner home for dinner tonight?" her mother asked. "I'm making a new recipe, but as I experimented with different ingredients I realized I'd made too much. It all started as a special treat for your daughter, who has now decided she loves red but not green chile."

Ella bit back a sigh. "I'll ask her, Mom. Hang on." Ella glanced at Justine and repeated the invitation.

"Absolutely," Justine said with a happy smile. "And if there are leftovers, I could take some to my roommate," she said, loud enough for Rose to hear.

Ella closed up the phone moments later. "There'll be lots of leftovers, so bring a large container."

"I don't get it. Why are you upset? If Rose wants to cook all day long, and it makes her happy, what's the big deal?"

"It's not her cooking. It's the reason for this new hobby of hers and its frantic pace that worries me, partner."

"Have you tried talking to her?"

"I brought it up a few times, but she doesn't want to discuss it."

"I remember when my aunt retired after thirty years at the post office," Justine said after a moment. "She thought she'd love having all that free time, but after a while she nearly went nuts. It took her a while to finally find a hobby she enjoyed. Do you think your mom's just missing her work as a consultant for the tribe and trying to stay busy?"

"I have a feeling it's more than that."

"If I were you I wouldn't push her into talking. Just look for an opening and take advantage of it if it comes."

"Yeah, that might work." She'd have a talk with Clifford, too, he might know something. Although she hated to admit it, in a lot of ways Rose was closer to Clifford than to her.

After about thirty miles, Justine pulled off the highway and, along with Ella, checked for names along a row of rural mailboxes.

"This is the right road," Ella said, pointing west toward the Chuska Mountains. She looked up at the anvil-shaped cumulonimbus cloud forming above the foothills. "We might get lucky and run into some rain."

Justine turned onto the dirt road. "Yeah, well, if it does rain, I hope we don't get stuck. This road looks like it could get iffy in a downpour."

The clouds continued to build and darken as they drove west, but the temperature was still rising when they arrived at the Eltsosies' old faded white stucco house. Here the grass and shrubs were about a foot taller than back by the highway, and there were a couple of hardy apple trees. The branches were tipped with green, grape-sized future apples. Even here, so much closer to the mountains and usually too cold for dependable peaches to set, it was still an upland desert.

Out back they could see a big, hexagonal pine-log hogan among a stand of low junipers.

"A medicine hogan," Ella commented. "Assume they're Traditionalists and keep your medicine pouch where it's easily seen."

They parked within view of the front windows, then waited. Before long the winds started to pick up, a sure sign of an imminent thunderstorm. The car rocked with each gust, and dust flew around them in thick sheets.

"I hate these predownpour sandblastings. Watch the car door when you get out," Justine said.

"Once it starts to rain the wind should drop off. Rain will settle the dust, too." Ella gazed at the dark, angry clouds overhead and heard the distant rumble of thunder. "Black Thunder's voice. My brother would say that it's a good omen. Black Thunder is the chief of all thunders and can counteract evil."

Before Justine could reply, Ella saw an elderly woman wearing a long skirt and long-sleeved blouse come to the front of the house. She waved quickly, motioning for them to come in, then ducked back inside.

Ella and Justine hurried to the porch, struggling to see with the gusts whipping their hair across their faces. They had to hold tight to the door to keep it from flying right off the hinges.

"Wind gives us all life and warns us of danger, but sometimes it's hard to see it as a friend," Mrs. Eltsosie said, waving them to the sofa. "I've made *naniscaadas*. Would you like some? Whenever I find myself missing my family, I cook something special. My husband and daughter used to put cream cheese on them. That, and a little herbal tea, always helps me to remember the good times."

Ella loved those homemade tortillas, but more than that she knew it was a way to break the ice. She accepted, then waited, watching Mrs. Eltsosie get everything ready and studying the house. It made sense for this woman, who was obviously living alone, to do things that would remind her of a time when her nest hadn't been quite so empty.

Out of respect, Ella avoided looking directly at Mrs. Eltsosie as she brought the food to them. They ate in comfortable silence for a little while, then at long last, Ella spoke.

"We understand that your husband disappeared about three years ago. We were hoping you could tell us a bit more about what happened. We know your daughter filed the report."

"I don't speak of that time," she said flatly.

Ella made a show of adjusting her medicine pouch, then leaned back in the old couch. "Back then we weren't able to help you find answers, but certain things have come to light recently. We may be able to tell you more now."

The woman wiped a tear that fell down her cheek. "I already know all I need," she said. "My daughter has turned into a *bilisaana*. That's why she doesn't understand."

Ella knew the term. It meant apple—red on the outside, white on the inside.

"What her father did, he did for us—me and her." Mrs. Eltsosie took an unsteady breath. "He knew he didn't have long, so he walked off into the desert one cold January morning. He went in the way of our people," she said, then stared down at her hands. "When my daughter found out, she blamed me and called the police. She's forgotten our ways."

Ella felt her heart go out to the elderly woman. Her husband had acted according to his highest sense of right. Their daughter, influenced by a culture that differed from her parents, had also done what she had felt was right. Two opposites could seldom coexist without friction and, even more importantly, disappointment. It was the way of the reservation these days. After growing up in a conflicted home herself, she'd seen it all.

"He was gone even before the snows came. I knew it in here," the woman said, pointing to her heart.

The sadness for what would never return, what Navajos called the *ch'ééná*, filled her voice and her expression. Yet, as it often was with their people, Mrs. Eltsosie endured and continued walking in beauty.

"I respect your beliefs and won't speak of this again. Thank you for the wonderful food, and for your time," Ella said, standing up.

"Come back next time you're in the area. I'll make more *naniscaadas*. My daughter's living back east now and the house is too quiet."

"Do you have members of your clan living close by?" Ella asked.

She shook her head. "But I see my friends at the Laundromat in town. We talk—well, gossip."

Ella nodded. Water was a precious commodity, particularly way out here, so Laundromats had become great meeting places.

"The *chaa-man* charges extra to come this far to pump out the septic tank, and too much soap, well, it clogs the pipes. So I take my truck and go to the Laundromat once a week. My friends and I meet there, talk, and go for walks while we wait for the machines to wash our clothes."

Ella smiled. Navajos always found each other, despite the distances. The connections that allowed them to walk in beauty were always there.

As they drove back to the main highway, Ella's gaze drifted over the violet lupines in the fields and the pink and white flowers of bindweed that hugged the road. "Even a little rain and runoff goes a long way out here. Look at those colors."

"Your mother's love of plants is rubbing off on you, cuz," Justine said with a smile as they turned onto the main highway in the direction of Shiprock.

"Maybe so," Ella said, then looked in the side mirror.

"Are we being tailed?" Justine asked, immediately checking the rearview mirror.

"No, but I'm going to start keeping an eye out," she said, and told her about the latest text message.

"If the calls are coming from a throwaway phone or an electronic dead drop, the messages will be nearly untraceable."

"I know, so let's play it by ear a little longer and see if there's another way to track down the sender. Maybe it's just a crank."

Ella typed the name of the man they were going to interview next into the MDT, verifying the address. "I hope we'll have better luck at our next stop. I don't think Mrs. Eltsosie's husband is one of our victims, but Emmaline Yazzie might be the female vic. The time frame matches. We'll be talking to Jake Yazzie, her husband. He didn't report Emmaline missing, but his brother, Billie, did."

"Interesting," Justine said. "What do we have on them?"

"He and his brother own a gas station off Highway 64 just on the other side of Fruitland, but both live on the Rez. They stay out of trouble and work hard, according to our sources."

The drive took them into Shiprock, then west toward Beclabito and the Arizona state line. For several miles there was not much to look at except for a few hills to the south and the river valley along the north side of the road.

"Do you think you and I should get out there more?" Justine said, breaking the silence that had settled between them.

"Out where?" Ella glanced around. It would be difficult to be any more out there than they were now.

Justine chuckled. "No, I was talking about our social life—or lack of one. Let's face it, most of our days are spent working a case, or cases. Personally, I'd like to settle down someday, but I've yet to meet anyone that's right for me."

"Yeah, and the more time slips by, the choosier we get."

After a beat, Justine asked, "I've never been engaged or even lived with a guy. Do you think I'm letting life pass me by?"

"All of a sudden you're in a rush? What's happened?"

"Marilu Draper. She passed away last week without any warning. And, Ella, she was only thirty-six, my age."

"Accident?"

"Yeah," Justine said. "She went for her usual Sunday trail ride, but the horse apparently spooked and threw her. No helmet, of course, and she hit her head on some rocks. By the time her sister found her, it was too late. Skull fracture."

"Were you two friends?"

Justine nodded. "We went to high school together and she lived less than a mile from my parents' house. A few weeks ago we went for a drink and had a great time catching up. She was working for the tribal fire department and loved her job. She and I talked about settling down, but we both agreed there was no rush."

"She served her tribe, loved her work, and from what you said, was happy. What more is there?"

"I know, but I keep thinking of how much she missed out on."

"Are you really thinking that *she* did, or are you worried that *you* might?"

Justine considered it before answering. "I love police work, but it takes its toll. It's not just the long hours either. It jades you. You start looking for the worst in people, not to mention overanalyzing everything."

Ella nodded. "As my brother would say, everything has two sides."

"What I like about Benny is that he understands all that," Justine said. "He knows our professions will always be part of who we are, and he's cool with that."

"So follow your heart."

"That's the problem. I'm not sure if it's really Benny I'm attracted to, or the idea of settling down. I want to have a baby someday, Ella, and the clock's ticking."

"I hear you. Most of us were meant to be moms. Dawn's made my life . . . more complete. After that first day when I held her in my arms and saw her little face staring back at me, nothing's been the same."

"I want that too—maybe too much."

"Have you spoken to Benny about that?"

She smiled. "Yeah, and he didn't run away screaming."

Ella laughed. "That's a good sign."

TEN

——— ✖ ✖ ✖ ———

Soon, they drove down a dirt track leading to a small stucco house with a pitched roof. Ella studied the old orange pickup parked beneath a scrawny elm, then ran the plate on the MDT. "That belongs to Jake Yazzie. The guy's clean."

"This place strikes me as the home of Modernists. Satellite TV dish antenna facing the southern sky, but no hogan," Justine said.

"I agree. Let's go see who's home," Ella said.

A moment later they stood on both sides of the front door and Ella knocked hard. The TV was blasting away with sound of revved up car engines, like an auto race, but there was no response. Ella tried again, and this time pounded on the door hard enough to bruise her knuckles.

"Hold your horses. I'm coming," a man's voice called out as the TV was turned down.

A moment later a small, round-faced Navajo man answered, half-full beer bottle in hand. He was wearing jeans and an oil-scented chambray, pinstriped work shirt that had *Jake* embroidered above the right breast pocket.

"If you're from a church, I'm not interested in joining, and I don't want any pamphlets. Go save somebody else."

Ella flashed her badge and identified herself. "Is your last name Yazzie?"

The man nodded. "What can I do for you?" he asked, his expression suddenly guarded, his tone subdued.

"We need to ask you a few questions," Ella said.

He stepped back and waved them inside. "Come on in, ladies. Sit," he added, pointing his lips toward the worn fabric couch. He sat down on a recliner angled toward the flat-screen TV. Two empty Coors beer bottles rested on a cracked glass coffee table beside an open bag of potato chips and the TV remote. "What's this all about?" he asked, placing the bottle on the floor beside his chair.

"Two years ago your wife was reported missing," Ella began.

"Yeah, that's about right," he said, his expression neutral as he stared at the stock cars flashing silently across the television screen.

"We'd like to know what happened," Ella said.

A lengthy silence followed, and Ella waited, watching a granddaddy longlegs spider crawl up the wall. Patience was an asset. Sometimes a witness just needed to know that she wouldn't be brushed off until she had answers.

Several minutes and two commercials later, he finally glanced back over at her. "My wife took off one day—no big loss if you knew her. When I mentioned it to my brother, Billy, he called you guys. Billy thought she might have been involved in an accident or something, and we needed to tell the police."

"But you thought it was a waste of time," Ella said, reading between the lines. "Why?"

"She and I hadn't been getting along. I figured she was playing a game, trying to make me jealous enough to go looking for her. When she didn't return after a few days, I started asking around. Verne Enoah told me that he'd seen her with some Navajo guy over at the Spurs Lounge in Gallup. I drove

over to see for myself and ended up getting into a fight with
the guy. Waste of time—Emmaline decided to stay with her
new boyfriend."

"You're divorced now?" Ella asked, getting bad vibes.

"And pay some lawyer? She's not here, that's enough
for me."

Ella watched him. There was a curious lack of emotion
in his voice. "Where's she now?"

"I heard she moved in with the guy."

"What's his name?" Ella pressed, still trying to read him.

"Gene Lee."

"Gene or Eugene."

"Don't know. I just heard Gene."

"Address?"

"Don't know the house address either, but I heard he
lived south of the highway, halfway between Coyote Canyon and Twin Lakes. That's all I know. If you want more,
you'll have to talk to her." He picked up his beer, took a
swig, then stood and walked to the door.

Ella strolled across the room slowly, deliberately taking
her time. Something felt off, but she couldn't put her finger
on it.

As they headed back to the car, Ella glanced at Justine.
"I've got a bad feeling about this guy, like he knows a lot
more than he's saying. He's trying too hard to play it casual."

"I agree. So what do you want to do next?"

"Get an unmarked over here and have them keep an eye
on Jake. You and I are going to pay Emmaline a visit."

As soon as they were back on the road, Ella called Blalock
and gave him an update. "I got a real bad feeling about Yazzie.
We're on our way to talk to the wife. If we find her alive and
this turns out not to be connected to the case, I'll drop it."

"Your closest backup will be in Gallup or Window Rock,
miles away. Don't cowboy up, you hear me?" Blalock said.

"Wouldn't think of it," Ella said with a tiny smile, then ended the call.

"What's that about?" Justine asked.

"Ever since Dwayne's ex-wife moved back in with him, he's become more cautious out in the field. He wants to make sure the deck's stacked in his favor before he or his partners go into a situation."

"Sensible strategy, but too much caution can lead to hesitation in the field. That could get him killed."

"He's got too much experience for that." Ella smiled. "I've gotten to know FB-Eyes pretty well over the years. What drives him these days is that he wants to be around Ruthann. He's a family man again."

While Justine drove, Ella checked their GPS. The residence was about twenty-five miles north of Gallup, close to the McKinley County line. As they continued down the road she ran a background on Gene Lee.

"Gene Lee, legal name Eugene Lee, is strictly small time—a few arrests for assault, mostly bar fights, and some DWIs," Ella told Justine. "Obviously he can get violent, so be ready."

The secondary highway east was paved, but after a few miles they turned south down a dirt track filled with holes from the runoff rain.

"Looks like Gene's not exactly a people person," Justine muttered as she slowed to a crawl and maneuvered around a pothole the size of a kitchen sink. "This road isn't exactly well traveled."

At the end of the track, butted up against the slope of a rocky hill, was a weary-looking white frame house with faded blue trim. "There's no house number, but I'm going to assume that's it," Justine said.

"It better be. It's the only thing around."

As they parked beside a new-looking Ford pickup about fifty feet from the front porch, a familiar, dangerous scent wafted toward them through the open car window. Both of them tensed up and glanced at each other.

"Ammonia," Ella said softly, pointing to the partially opened door. A big fan was on the floor, venting the interior.

"She could be cleaning," Justine said, her hand reaching down to the radio.

"No. Look at those foil-covered windows. I think we've found a meth lab," Ella said, shifting in her seat.

"I'm calling for backup," Justine said.

"Get the McKinley County Sheriff, not Window Rock. Gallup's closer," Ella said, reaching for the shotgun.

A long rifle barrel suddenly poked out the door.

"Gun!" Ella yelled, ducking below the dashboard. A fist-sized chunk of the windshield crumbled as the crack of a rifle sounded from the direction of the house.

"Crap," Justine mumbled, her head just a foot away from Ella's. "I dropped the mike."

A second blast struck the front of the car.

"Bail out—my side," Ella yelled, lifting the handle and scrambling out the door. Inching over to the front fender, she aimed her pistol at the house. The front door was now closed.

"Move! The shooter just ducked back inside," Ella urged.

Justine scrambled out, pistol in hand. She crouched behind the engine compartment and looked across the hood.

"Make the call, but keep your eyes on the left side of the house," Ella ordered.

Justine brought out her cell phone, contacted Gallup dispatch, then made a second call to the Window Rock station. "A state police officer is south of Tohatchi, about ten minutes out," she told Ella. "Deputies from Gallup are on their way, and I asked for a hazmat team as well."

"Good." Ella looked around. "I can't spot the shooter, but the pickup is their ticket out of here. If they try to climb that hill behind the house on foot, they'll be sitting ducks. Slip back toward the trunk and cover the front door."

"Did you ID the shooter?"

"Navajo man with short hair. That's all I saw," Ella said.

"So what's the plan, sit tight and wait for backup?"

Ella nodded. "Stay put and don't fire unless they come out shooting. I don't want to risk blowing up the place or exposing ourselves to those chemicals."

"Roger that."

After five minutes passed, the scent of ammonia faded somewhat. In the distance, they could hear the wail of an approaching siren.

As they waited, Ella heard the sound of a new text message coming in. "Stay sharp. I'm going to get this in case it's Blalock." As she switched on the screen, she knew instantly who it was.

DON'T GET SHOT, CLAH. It was unsigned. Ella read it to Justine. "He knows where I am."

"I never spotted a tail," Justine said.

"Me neither." Ella took a breath. "But I can't let him sidetrack us now. We've got to concentrate on the ones inside that meth lab. What do you say, we give them a chance to come out on their own?"

"Go for it."

Ella aimed the shotgun. "Tribal Police. Put down your weapons and come out slowly with your hands in the air," she yelled. "Don't turn this into a gun battle. You can't win. You're trapped in a house full of dangerous chemicals."

Two minutes went by and they could hear arguing inside the home. Then the sound of voices was drowned out by the siren of the black-and-white state police cruiser that came up the road. The vehicle pulled up to their left, angling so the engine block shielded the officer from the house.

A second later the front door opened a crack. "I'm coming out. Don't shoot," a woman yelled.

Before Ella could reply a wild-haired Navajo woman wearing a dirty yellow house dress stumbled out onto the wooden porch. She dropped to her knees and toppled over slowly, her head hitting the floor with a thud.

"Cover me," Ella told the black-and-white-uniformed state patrolman. Crouched low, he had his pump shotgun up and pointed across the hood toward the porch.

"How many suspects in there?" he asked her.

"At least two, one with a rifle. They're cooking meth," Ella said, then slipped out from behind the front fender in a crouch. She jogged to her right, approaching the porch from the side so she could see anyone coming from around the house.

She was halfway there, watching the windows, when a man came out from the rear of the house, firing his rifle. The state cop fired back, his shotgun digging out a chunk of stucco from the corner of the house.

Ella jumped to the left, screening herself with the building itself.

The state patrolman fired again and the man ducked back around, out of sight.

"Forget the woman. Hug the wall," Justine yelled at her.

Ella, her back to the building, looked over at the woman, collapsed on the ground. "If he pokes his head around the corner again—" she yelled at the patrolman.

". . . I'll take him out," the officer confirmed, his shotgun ready.

"Cover my six, Justine," Ella yelled, then inched to the corner and took a quick look. Above her head she could see the jagged hole where buckshot had ripped away a big handful of stucco, exposing the chicken wire and sheathing beneath.

Ella waited, catching her breath, then, crouching low, inched around, leading with her pistol. "Unload your rifle and slide it out on the ground," she called out. "More armed officers will arrive within a few minutes and you're already outgunned. The woman on your porch needs medical attention. If you care what happens to her, give up—now—and save two lives."

Ella waited. In the distance the sound of multiple sirens rose in the air, emphasizing her words.

"Okay, okay. I give up," he answered from somewhere behind the house.

"Stick your hands out so we can see them, then step into view—slowly," she ordered.

"I'm putting my rifle on the ground. Don't shoot, I'm unarmed."

A few seconds later a Navajo man wearing jeans and a stained white tee-shirt stepped out from behind the corner, his hands in the air. She could see the rifle on the ground.

"Don't shoot," he repeated.

Ella cuffed him as Justine ran over to check on the woman who'd collapsed. "Anyone else inside the house, Gene?" Ella asked, playing a hunch. "Any children or animals?"

"Nah, it's just us."

As Justine checked on the location of the hazmat team, Ella gave him his rights.

"Yeah, yeah, I know all that," Gene grumbled. "Will Emmaline be okay?"

"I don't know. The doctors will have to check her out. Here comes the ambulance."

"I *knew* this was a bad idea. Emma, hell, she had big plans. She wanted to sell a bunch of this crap, then leave the Rez for good. I told her it was dangerous stuff, but she said this was the only shot life was going to give us, and we'd be suckers not to take it."

"Consider yourselves lucky. You could have blown yourselves up." Ella turned Gene over to one of the newly arrived tribal police officers and saw him place the suspect in the back of one of the patrol cars.

Once the big white hazmat van arrived and the other officers took charge of the scene, Ella and Justine were free to leave. "We've been played," Ella said as they walked to their unit. "I want to go back and talk to Jake Yazzie."

Justine slipped behind the wheel. "Do you think he knew what was going on and wanted us to arrest his wife?"

"Yeah. I also want to make sure he's not dealing, too. Maybe the reason he set her up was to take out the competition."

"You're not worried about two drug rivals. You're pissed because you think he used us to get back at his wife," Justine said.

"That's part of it, sure, but I also have a bad feeling about this guy. He manipulated us, even though he knew we'd figure it out. That tells me that he has leverage of some sort, like information he hopes to trade to stay out of jail. He may see that as a way of maintaining the balance—we do something for him, he does something for us," Ella said.

"You're thinking of the murders over by Hogback," Justine said, nodding. "Drug dealing and murder go hand in hand, and the bodies we found were shot execution-style—punishment for something."

They were halfway back to Shiprock when Ella got a call on her cell phone from Ford.

"How about letting me take you out to dinner tonight?" he asked.

Ella suppressed a sigh. No wonder she was gaining weight, everyone insisted on feeding her. "I have a better idea. Join me at home for dinner. Mom's been busy cooking and she loves company."

"I need a chance to talk privately, just you and me."

"It sounds serious," Ella said.

"It is."

She and Ford, Reverend Bilford Tome to his parishioners, had been dating for a couple of years. For the most part, she was happy with the way things were. Ford and she were more than friends, but less than lovers since Ford's religion

BLACK THUNDER ✳ 125

didn't allow them to cross that line. Though there'd been many times she'd wished that were different, she'd learned to accept it.

"Come over anyway. I'll find time alone for us, I promise. We can go for a long walk after dinner."

"Good enough. See you tonight."

As Ella hung up, Justine glanced over. Although she clearly didn't want to intrude by asking, the questions were there on her face.

"He says he wants to talk to me," Ella said.

"Hmmmm. Do you know what it's about?"

"I have no idea." As she glanced at Justine, she saw her partner avoiding eye contact. "You know something, don't you, cuz?"

"No, I really don't."

"But you've *heard* something," Ella said slowly.

Justine said nothing.

"Spill it."

"Okay, but it's just gossip, and I have no idea how reliable it is."

"I'll take my chances."

"I heard some talk at church that Ford's going to be transferred."

"Any idea where?"

"To a struggling mission over in Arizona somewhere—Cow Springs, maybe."

Ella stared at her. "Pretty country, but in the middle of nowhere. How long have you known about this?"

"Since last Sunday, and before you get angry, I want you to know that this came from Bea Curtis, and half of what she says is wrong."

"Which makes her right half the time," Ella said.

"If you don't want him to leave, you might consider going over the board's head and asking the regional council not to send him. Tell them that he does a public service here by serving as a police consultant. His prior work with the FBI in intelligence gathering and cryptography has helped us break several big cases. It's the truth, and Big Ed would gladly back you up."

Ella considered it. "That'll have to depend on how Ford feels about the transfer—*if* it turns out to be true. We both have demanding jobs and he's never complained about mine, so I need to do the same for him."

"But he's in love with—"

"Drop it for now, Justine," Ella interrupted. "We're on the clock, and I need to be focusing on this case."

When they arrived at Jake Yazzie's home, they saw him out back, changing a tire on his truck. Spotting them, he stood, wiped his hands on his pants, then walked over to meet them.

"So, did you have to shoot her?" he asked, looking at Ella and Justine.

"Is that what you were hoping for?" Ella snapped back.

"You can't arrest me for wishing she were dead," he answered. "My brother and I spent the last three and a half years working our butts off, building up business at our gas station. We even built one of those garage bays ourselves. My wife did nothing but gripe nonstop from day one, but the land it sits on is deeded to her. About six months ago she threatened to shut us down unless we started paying her rent. If she'd ended up dead we would have finally had that crazy bitch off our backs."

"So you *knew* we were walking into a dangerous situation, but you failed to warn us," Ella said through clenched teeth.

"I didn't *know*, not for sure, but I'd seen her hopped up several times—her boyfriend, too. I also knew she didn't have the cash to buy that poison."

"If you had reason to suspect she was running a meth lab, you should have warned us," Ella said.

"So now you want to arrest me."

It hadn't been a question, something that didn't surprise Ella. "I can't think of any reason not to," she said.

"I can. I heard you're investigating those murders over by the Hogback. According to the TV, you're still trying to identify the victims."

Ella waited. This was his hedge. She'd been right.

"I think I know who one of the victims might be. If I give you a lead, I stay out of jail?"

Ella nodded once. The lead was worth more to her than the paperwork it would take to book him.

"The man who built most of our gas station, a Navajo named Elroy Johnson, disappeared before the job was done. My brother and I paid him the first half of the money up front. Then about three-quarters of the way through the job, he stopped coming to the site. He vanished off the face of the earth. His workers couldn't find their boss, and weren't getting paid, so they quit. We were left holding the bag, so we had to finish the job ourselves."

"When exactly did Johnson disappear?"

"Four years ago. The kids had just gotten out of school, so it must have been the last of May or early June. I remember because we ended up hiring several teenage boys to help us finish up the main building."

"Didn't you try to track down Johnson?"

"You bet. The only reason we'd been able to afford a contractor at all was because he'd agreed to give us a special deal. We were going to be trading services. In exchange for a reduced fee, we'd service his company's vehicles for one year at no cost for labor. It was a good thing for both of us, but then he just disappeared."

"If you think of anything else give me a call," Ella said, handing him her card.

As they got underway, she glanced at Justine. "I need to call Blalock and update him."

The FBI agent answered on the first ring and Ella quickly briefed him. "What I'd like to do is get everyone, Dan Nez included, over to my office. We need to compare notes, see where we are, and more importantly, figure out our next step."

"Done."

Ella put the phone away. "Pedal to the metal, partner."

ELEVEN

✖ ✖ ✖

An hour and a half later, her team, Blalock, and Detective Nez met in Ella's office. Dan and his people had been able to rule out nearly twenty possibles. Thanks to the M.E.'s descriptions, Tache and Neskahi had also been able to cross several names off their lists.

Ella started the meeting by telling everyone there about the text messages she'd been receiving. Nobody else had received anything similar. "Opinions?"

"Someone's messing with your mind," Neskahi said. "You've got a lot of enemies—the families of those you've arrested, those out on parole, and so on. Since you're in the news again, maybe one of them decided to push your buttons."

A groan went around the room.

"I think we should get a court order and hope it doesn't lead us to an electronic dead drop," Justine said. "My granddad, Judge Goodluck, may understand the problem better than most and streamline the process. Shall I talk to him?"

"Yeah, do that," Ella said. "If the text messages are untraceable, we can at least rule out the less intelligent troublemakers." Ella then filled them in on what she and Justine had been told by Yazzie. "On the way back here I did a background check on Elroy Johnson. Our four-year-old corpse fits his height and build. Johnson's business was in Farmington, out of tribal jurisdiction. He may have lived there, too. I couldn't find a home address." She looked at Dan, then Blalock. "You two will have to handle any off-Rez interviews."

"We'll get the ball rolling, then let you know what we find—if anything," Nez said. "Just give me what you have—addresses, social, driver's license numbers, etcetera."

Ella gave Justine a nod, then continued. "Progress has been slow, but at least a pattern's starting to emerge. The killer, or killers, act only once a year, and if we find out that two of those victims were Kelewood and Johnson, that'll place the time of the killings at around the end of May or early June. We need to find out what makes that time frame special. When you conduct interviews, stay on the alert for an answer to that question. It might be a drug deal, reunion, anniversary of some event—anything like that."

"Word about these murders has already spread," Tache said. "If we're right and the killer or killers like late May or early June for some reason, that'll get around fast, too, no matter how hard we try to keep a lid on it. Then we'll have an even bigger problem on our hands. People are going to start looking over their shoulders, because it's almost June now."

"The clock's ticking, so we need to nail this guy quickly," Ella said with a nod.

Blalock glanced around the room. "The fact that all the victims appear to be Navajo brings up the obvious. Maybe the murders are racially motivated, like what happened here in the seventies."

"I remember reading about that," Benny said. "Some Anglo high-school kids were rolling drunk Navajos for sport, but things got out of hand. Three men were tortured and killed in some canyon near Farmington. There was a lot of racial tension back then, especially when the killers were sent to reform school instead of prison."

"That was a long time ago," Ella said.

"The only racial tension I've heard about recently in the Four Corners centers on illegal immigrants, not Navajos," Nez said. "But it's still worth checking into. New Mexico has more than its share of anti-whatever groups."

"Those AP rounds used to kill the first victim—they penetrate most ballistic vests," Benny said. "I haven't been in the area long, but do we know of any missing police officers?"

Justine shook her head. "I thought of that, thinking the killer may have selected a cop as his first victim. According to the database Agent Blalock checked, no officers are unaccounted for. As for retired or former officers, they have to turn in their vests when they leave their agency. Besides, the victim was shot in the head, a poor use for those type rounds anyway."

"Yeah, a waste of expensive ammo, unless it was stolen, therefore free," Ella replied. "But let's not lose track of this detail when checking for suspects, people." She turned to Blalock, who nodded.

"Guys, it looks like we're in for a long night. What do you say we order in?" Blalock said.

Ella thought of Rose's banquet. "I've got a better idea. Why don't we finish this meeting at my house? My mother's cooking beats the heck out of fast food."

When everyone eagerly accepted, Ella stepped out into the hall for a moment and brought out her cell phone. "Mom could you accommodate my team, plus two others for dinner?"

"Of course," Rose replied without hesitation. "There's plenty of food, and we still have the folding chairs from when your father had his church board over for those Saturday meetings."

"We'll have to make this a working dinner, so are you also willing to set things up in the den for us? Maybe your husband could bring in one of those folding banquet tables."

"We'll get things ready right now," her mother said, her enthusiasm obvious. "I made a lot more corn stew than I'd intended, and there's plenty of fry bread, too. Your preacher friend also called a while ago. He's going to be running late, so I told him I'd save him a plate."

Ella cringed. She'd totally forgotten that she'd asked Ford over, but the situation wasn't totally unworkable.

"Okay, Mom, we're on our way."

A half hour later, they sat in Ella's den. On the old quartersawn oak sideboard that stood against the south wall, Rose had set the big cast-iron Dutch oven filled with stew on top of a warming tray, four plates heaped with fry bread, and two large pitchers of iced tea.

Since they were all hungry, no one was shy about loading up their bowls and plates. Everyone found a seat on folding chairs that had been set around the large wooden folding table.

Ella waited until everyone finished their meal, then brought their attention back to business. "Let's pick up where we left off."

Detective Nez used his laptop to access the old Farmington P.D.'s case files. "We discussed the possibility that the murders could be tied in some way to the racially motivated ones that went down in the seventies. Here are the particulars on those."

The details he read aloud were gruesome and the murders chaotic in nature. Before long, Ella held up her hand, signaling him to stop. "Those old crimes are completely unlike what we're dealing with here. They were spur-of-the-moment acts carried out in a very unorganized fashion," Ella said. "The murders we're investigating appear to be the work of an adult with a clear objective—and patience."

As they came up with new avenues of investigation, each team member contributing their thoughts, Ella glanced at Dan, who'd remained quiet. He'd folded up his laptop and was doodling on the back of his paper napkin.

"Dan, you mentioned the presence of fringe groups on the county side. We know about the ones taking antigovernment positions, with the immigration issue at the top of the agenda. Have you heard of any that might be promoting racial purity, too?"

"There's nothing specifically targeting Navajos. There are organizations that are against tribal casinos, but most of those have religious affiliations and aren't violent," he said.

"There's one group on our own side of the fence that's bound to complicate things for us—the Fierce Ones," Justine said. "If you can believe the gossip, they've already started patrolling the highway between Shiprock and Farmington."

"That's the first I've heard of that," Ella said. The Fierce Ones were a vigilante group of mostly Traditional Navajos who were as dangerous as they were unpredictable.

"It's more than rumor. It's a fact," Neskahi said. "I've seen them. There are usually three to four in a vehicle, all with rifles clearly visible."

"Tache, Neskahi, Pete, you keep working on that list of missing people, narrowing it down. Justine, you and I are going to pay the leaders of Fierce Ones a visit tomorrow and see what they have to say. We need to make sure this doesn't flare up into another 'us against them' issue."

"You might also want to do a little additional checking on Elroy Johnson," Dan said. "When I ran his background I discovered that although his business was based in Farmington, he actually lived on the Rez. His wife, Leigh, has a place here," he added, handing Ella a slip of paper with the address.

"We'll follow that up," Ella said.

Once her team left, Ella began picking up the den. Ford still hadn't shown up, but he hadn't canceled either, which meant that sooner or later he'd drop by.

As Ella went around the room collecting glasses, she remembered Dan had seemed a little distracted. More curious than anything else, she went to the trash where he'd pitched the napkin he'd been doodling on.

The one with pencil marks was near the top, so she unfolded it. As she saw the sketch, Ella smiled.

TWELVE

✖ ✖ ✖

Rose came in so softly Ella didn't hear her at first. "Your preacher friend just arrived. He's sitting at the kitchen table drinking some of my special tea," she said, and glanced down to see what Ella was holding. "That's a wonderful sketch of you! Who's the artist?"

"The new detective from county," she said, avoiding names out of respect for her mother's beliefs. Ella folded up the drawing and placed it in her shirt pocket.

Rose looked at her. "A keepsake. He interests you then?"

"His artistic talent does. The department let our composite artist go when we got a computer program that could help us translate a victim's description onto paper. But the program has its limitations. For accuracy, you need to add that touch of humanity. But that's just my opinion."

Hearing a chair being moved in the kitchen, Rose stopped picking up and glanced at Ella. "Go talk to your friend. He seemed a little anxious about something."

Ella went into the kitchen to meet Ford, and he stood as she came into the room. "With our crazy schedules, I was beginning to doubt we'd actually have a chance to talk tonight," he said.

"Why don't we go for a walk? I need to unwind a bit, and it's a beautiful evening."

With a nod, he followed her out. Moonlight from a cloudless, star-covered sky illuminated the desert floor as they walked away from the house. Ella stopped by the horse corral and, resting her foot on the metal railing of the gate, noticed Chieftain, her horse, and Wind, Dawn's faithful pony, lying in the sand, enjoying the coolness of the evening.

"My daughter and that pony were a perfect fit once. But she's growing up. Now she wants to ride Chieftain."

"She'll always be your daughter, Ella. Time can't change that."

Ella smiled at Ford. "You always see beyond my words and understand. I'm glad we're such good friends."

She saw the flicker in his eyes and the hesitation.

"What's bothering you, Ford? There's nothing you can't tell me, you know that."

He took a deep breath. "There's a mission northeast of Tuba City that's falling apart. It's in a place called Cow Springs. The preacher lost his faith, threw up his hands, and took off without any warning. The church board's in disarray, desperate to find someone who'll fill the void. The need is urgent, and I've been asked to go."

"How soon do you have to leave?"

"Next week," he said in a heavy voice. "The Cow Springs Mission is about three hours drive from here. That's a long ways, particularly for two people who work as hard as you and I do." He paused, then added, "You mean everything to me, Ella, I don't want to lose you."

"We'll find ways to see each other. Distance isn't going to destroy our friendship."

He stared at the ground, then looked back up at her. "Ella, my feelings for you . . . pose a constant temptation to me. I serve the Lord, but I'm still a man. I'd like you to be able to come out and spend time with me as often as you can, and for me to be able to join you here."

"I'd like that, too, but your parishioners aren't going to understand," she reminded gently. "The church board will throw a fit, then throw you out."

"Not if we make it right." He reached into his pocket and brought out a small diamond ring. "Will you marry me?"

Maybe she should have seen it coming, but the sudden question took her completely by surprise. Ella stared at the delicate ring with the tiny diamond at its center.

"Ford, I—"

"Ella, I've loved you for a long time, almost from the moment we met, you know that. I would have preferred our relationship to continue growing at its own pace, but circumstances are making their own demands."

At a loss for words, she stared at the ring, wondering how to keep from hurting Ford. She wasn't ready to say good-bye, but he'd put it on the line this time. Feeling trapped between wanting to protect him and the need for honesty, she took a shaky breath.

"I love being with you, Ford. Your friendship means more to me than I can say. But our relationship can never lead to marriage. There's just too much working against us."

"I wouldn't pressure either you or your daughter to join my church, if that's what you're thinking. That's something that would have to come from you two, or not at all. More importantly, I can live with whatever choice you two make."

"Live with, maybe, but you'd want more," she said, shaking her head. "You and I . . . weren't meant to be. I care deeply for you, Ford, but I'm not in love with you."

"Love in today's world is often nothing more than a rush of hormones and the desire not to be alone. What we have is stronger. It just needs time to grow."

"No. What I feel . . . isn't enough." Ella bit back tears. By hurting him, she was hurting herself.

He nodded slowly, then looked up at the stars for a moment. "All right. I had to know."

It was then that she realized his proposal had also been meant to clarify once and for all where they stood. He hadn't wanted to leave and continue hoping for something that could never be.

"I really care about you, Ford, more than I'll ever be able to put into words. If you'd allow it, I'd like to continue being your friend."

"If friendship is all we can have, then I accept your terms." He placed the ring box back into his pocket, took her hand in his, then walked with her back to his pickup.

"Good night, Ella, and thank your mother for the wonderful tea." He gave her hand a squeeze, climbed into his pickup, and drove away without another word.

Ella stood there a moment longer composing herself, then walked back into the house. Grabbing a dishcloth, she joined her mother at the kitchen sink. While Rose washed, she dried and put away the dishes.

"I'm really tired, but I'm too wound up to go to bed," Ella said. "After we finish this, is there anything else that needs to be done?"

Rose sighed softly. "He asked you to marry him, didn't he?" Seeing Ella's surprised look, she explained, "Earlier, while I was pouring the preacher some tea, I caught a glimpse of him looking at a ring."

"I said no."

Rose handed Ella the last bowl to dry, then pulled off her rubber gloves. "You did the right thing, Daughter. Marriage to a preacher isn't easy, particularly if you don't share his religion. I lived through all that with your father. No matter what they say at the beginning, they never give up trying to get you to believe as they do."

Ella gave her mom a tired smile. "I know. Even if he never spoke of it again, it would be there in his eyes. I just couldn't step into his world without giving up a lot of what I am, and that's a sacrifice I'm not willing to make, at least not for this man—at this time in my life."

"You and he . . . weren't right for each other. But you still need a husband—the right one."

Ella chuckled softly. "Do you have someone in mind?"

Rose shook her head and stood. "I wish I did. I want you to be happy."

"I *am* happy." Seeing the searching look Rose gave her, Ella reached for her mother's hand. "I like my life, Mom. I have everything I need and want right here."

Rose smiled. "Your family and your job both need you. Your heart is full."

Before she could give much thought to exactly what her mother had meant, Rose ambled down the hall and disappeared from view.

The first thing Ella heard the following morning as she struggled to come awake was the guitar-heavy twang of girl angst country music coming from Dawn's MP3 clock. Since being told she'd have to wait until Christmas for an iPod, Dawn had stopped using her headphones. Now she started each day with the external speakers cranked up high—an obvious psychological ploy.

Groaning, Ella placed the pillow over her head, but soon felt someone poking at it. As she moved it aside, she saw Two, Rose's scruffy brownish-gray mutt, looking at her.

She was scritching the old boy behind the ears when Rose appeared. "Good. You're up! Make sure you ask your daughter about her last science quiz. Brace yourself. They allowed her to retake it, so you may not want to know how she did the first time."

Before she could wake up enough to formulate a response,

Rose disappeared down the hallway. Ten minutes later, showered and presentable, Ella met her daughter, Rose, and Herman in the kitchen.

Seeing Rose busy cooking oatmeal, Ella sat at the table across from Dawn. "I understand you were allowed to retake your science quiz."

"We all did. Mr. Andrews said that almost everyone failed, so it must have been him and the quiz, not us. So we went over the material again, then retook it with new questions," Dawn said, nodding. "I got a C-minus."

Ella stared at Dawn. "So you must have bombed the first time?"

"Yeah, it was really hard. The second one wasn't that easy either."

"Earlier this year, you were bringing down A's and B's. What the heck's going on, Daughter?"

"*Nothing's* going on. I just *hate* science! Half of the time it makes no sense to me."

"If you're having problems understanding, you need to spend more time studying and ask for help. Lately, you've been putting things off until the last minute. When you were given a second chance, why didn't you pay attention and buckle down?"

"There's lots of stuff going on, Mom. School's out in a week, and Rita's going to be gone all summer. I won't see her for . . . well, months," Dawn said, referring to her current best friend. "I needed to talk to her about—" She stopped speaking abruptly and stared at her hands. "Girl stuff."

"Lately she spends most of her homework time on the telephone," Rose said quietly.

"Can't I *ever* get any privacy around here?" Dawn protested.

"Do *not* take that attitude with your *shimasání*," Ella snapped. "She wants what's best for you."

"What about what *I* want? Doesn't that count anymore?" Dawn said, then jumped up and ran out of the room.

"I'm sorry about that, Mom. I'll go talk to her right now," Ella said, standing.

"There are many things on her mind. That's why she's been . . . distracted," Herman said.

Rose and Ella both looked at him. "What do you mean?" Ella asked him first.

He shook his head. "I shouldn't have butted in. This is between you and her," he said, then hurried out of the room.

Ella walked down the hall, and as she drew close to her daughter's room, heard Dawn on the phone.

"They're always telling me what to do. They treat me like a five-year-old!"

Ella stepped into the doorway and signaled Dawn to hang up.

Dawn said a quick good-bye to the person on the other end, then sat on the edge of the bed and waited.

Ella let the silence stretch out and, as she did, saw her daughter become increasingly uncomfortable.

At long last Ella spoke. "I'm very disappointed in you, Daughter."

"You never got a C-minus in your entire life?"

"It's not the grade that worries me, it's the way you're acting. You're so involved with your friends and your gadgets that it looks like you've stopped caring about anyone but yourself. I know that's not true, but you owe your *shimasání* and her husband an apology—and the sooner the better. After that, I'll drive you to the bus stop. We can talk on the way."

Dawn picked up her red windbreaker and matching book bag. "Mom, if we don't get going, I'm going to miss the bus."

"Go apologize first."

Dawn hurried into the kitchen, but the apology Ella overheard was brief and not very sincere. Realizing it would have to do for now, Ella met Dawn outside. Soon they were in the tribal SUV on the way down the gravel road that led to the bus stop.

"If you don't bring your science grade up when you take your finals, your cell phone privileges will be restricted into the summer. I'll also limit your TV, Internet, and music hours. Those are perks, and they have to be earned, Daughter."

"But no one else I know has to earn them. They're just part of a normal life, Mom!"

"This is our family and our rules—*our* normal."

Ella dropped her daughter off then drove on to the highway. As she headed north to the station, she remembered her daughter's halting first steps and her first night on a bed instead of a crib. Like a movie unfolding in the screen of her mind, each set of images filled her with longing for what would never be again.

The tone on her cell phone signaling an incoming text message brought her back to the present. Already at the station, she parked in her usual slot, and glanced down at the screen.

YOUR DAUGHTER LOOKS GOOD IN RED.

The pleasant warmth indulging in memories had brought her vanished in an instant, and her blood turned to ice.

THIRTEEN
✖ ✖ ✖

As she rushed inside the station, cell phone in hand, Ella hit the speed-dial number that connected her to Dawn.

"Are you okay?" she asked as soon as Dawn answered.

"Yeah, Mom, I'm on the bus, halfway to school. You just saw me, what, fifteen minutes ago. What's going on?"

"Are you still wearing the red windbreaker?" Ella saw Justine standing in the hall and motioned to her.

"Yeah. Why?" Dawn asked.

"Did you notice anyone new parked around the bus stop? A car, truck, anything like that?"

Justine heard the question and gave Ella a curious look.

Ella signaled her partner to wait, holding up her hand, palm out.

"Um, no, just the regular crew," Dawn answered. "What's going on?"

"It may be nothing, sweetie, and I know that school will be out soon, but don't go off by yourself, and don't take the bus home this afternoon. Either your grandmother, her husband, or your dad will pick you up. One last thing. Don't let anyone you don't know approach you."

"You're scaring me, Mom."

"I don't mean to, but I'm serious about this. Be smart. I'm working a special case and I need to know you're okay. I'm going to call the principal and have him ask the other teachers to help keep an eye out for any strangers hanging around the campus, okay?"

As Ella hung up, Justine jumped in immediately. "Is somebody threatening Dawn?"

Ella showed her the text message and gave her the highlights. "Get me that court order."

"I'll need some info that's on your cell phone," Justine said.

"Let me make a couple more calls first."

Ella called Dawn's school. After speaking to the principal, she dialed Kevin's number. He was in court, so all she got was his voice mail. Lastly, she called home and spoke to Herman, asking him to pass the news to Rose.

"I'll handle it," Herman said. "The principal is the son of a good friend of mine. I'll make sure he has enough people available to watch the entire campus and the street in front of school."

Ella knew how well connected Herman was. Considering the manpower shortage at the station, she was glad to have him involved.

Ella closed up the phone, feeling more reassured, but it rang again before she could give it any more thought.

"Can you come by the morgue?" Carolyn asked. "I've got something that'll make it worth the trip."

"I'll be there in ten," Ella answered.

Carolyn started to say something else, but her other phone line rang, and she said a hurried good-bye instead. These days Carolyn was trying to do it all, and the workload was staggering. Though she'd tried repeatedly to get some office help, it was nearly impossible to find someone on the Navajo Rez who was willing to work at the morgue. Those who did come left just as soon as they could find something else.

After apprising Justine and giving her the cell phone information needed to request the warrant, Ella left, eager for action. Her nerves were taut and she needed something to do right now.

Once she arrived at the hospital, less than a five-minute drive, Ella headed directly to the basement. As she entered the outer office, she saw her friend eating.

Carolyn glanced up. "There's more over there on the table. It's one of my special coffee cakes—very low in calories, but tastes great."

Ella tore off a piece from the corner. "Hey, this is *good*."

"Help yourself to more if you want," she said.

Turning her head to look back at Carolyn, Ella's gaze traveled over the body on the waist-high aluminum autopsy table just past the glass partition.

Her appetite suddenly lost, Ella shook her head. "I just came from my mom's breakfast table."

"You're lucky to have her," Carolyn said, then walked over to the x-ray mounted on the lit screen. "This corresponds to the oldest victim, the one buried for at least four years. Detective Nez—Dan—left me an e-mail telling me about a Navajo man named Elroy Johnson. I checked dental records and they're a match. Johnson was the first victim, without a doubt."

"Any progress on the others?"

"Nothing yet. I'm still trying to do some comparisons on Kelewood, but at least you've got one solid ID. Good way to start the day, right?"

"You bet," Ella said, sensing that there was something else on Carolyn's mind.

Carolyn led Ella back to her office, poured herself a cup of black coffee, and brought Ella one, too. "I'd like your opinion on something."

"Go on."

"You and I are strong, independent women," Carolyn

began in a thoughtful voice. "We have demanding jobs that challenge us, and after-hours routines we enjoy. Generally, things are working right for us. Do you think we should shut the door on relationships? Our track records with men stink big time."

"That's a tough question to answer," Ella said after a long pause. "As you said, we both have the kind of jobs that make it difficult for whoever's around us. To find a guy who understands all that, and can live with it, is hard enough, but if you're hoping to find that special spark, the magic . . ." Ella shook her head. "I think you and I would have better odds playing the lottery."

Carolyn laughed. "That's what I was thinking, too," she said, then growing serious, continued. "After more years than I care to count, I'm getting asked out on dates again, but I'm not sure it's worth the trouble. I know exactly what it's like when things fall apart, and they invariably do, at least for me."

"I'm the last person you should be asking about relationships, particularly now," Ella said, and told her what had happened with Ford.

"You care about him, Ella. It's written all over your face. Are you sure you've made the right decision?"

"Yeah. I'm going to really miss him, but it's time for both of us to move on. Going solo isn't so bad," she added with a shrug.

"You live in a full house, I'm willing to bet that *solo* is something you can only achieve when you're in the bathroom."

Ella laughed. "True enough."

"Thank your lucky stars, kiddo. I get lonely sometimes," Carolyn said, then added, "Mind you, G.P. can be good company. He shares my love of food. But he's a lousy conversationalist."

Ella laughed. G.P. was Carolyn's guinea pig.

On her way to the station, Ella called Justine with the

news. With luck, Elroy Johnson would open up new investigative avenues that would break the case wide open. They could now also start looking through their list of missing persons for anyone connected to Johnson.

When Ella entered her office a short time later, she saw Justine typing at the keyboard.

"My computer's being serviced this morning and I didn't want to just sit around," she said, giving Ella an apologetic smile.

"It locked up on you again?"

Justine nodded.

"All the equipment around here is so outdated it's a wonder we can still do our jobs."

"We're lucky we have jobs at all. The tribal budget's on life support and I've heard that the department will soon be laying off nonessential personnel."

"Like who? We're down to bare bones as it is," Ella said. Standing behind Justine, she glanced at the screen. "What were you looking up?"

"Anything I can find on Elroy Johnson's widow, Leigh. All I've got so far is that she owns a flower shop in Farmington, just off Main. From what I've learned, it does a brisk business."

"Let me call Dan and Blalock. Maybe one of them can meet us there."

Dan wasn't available, but Blalock seemed to welcome the interruption. "Come by my office and I'll drive you there," he said, then hung up.

"Justine, I'm going to head over to Blalock's. But first fill me in—what else do we know about Leigh?" Ella brought out her pocket notebook and pen.

"Her shop's featured on Facebook, it's independent, not franchised, and she offers a variety of services, including a bit of garden landscaping in partnership with a nursery. That's it."

"It must have been difficult to put your life together again after that," Ella said, glancing around the shop.

"At first, getting up in the morning was all I could do, but time doesn't stay still, though grief can sometimes make you believe that. After a year, I finally accepted the fact that Elroy wasn't coming home, and I would have to figure out what to do with my life. Since my husband was missing, not legally dead, there was no hope of getting his life insurance. So I got a job, but I hated it and was barely getting by anyway. That's when I decided to take what was left of our savings and use the money to lease this space. I'd always wanted to run my own flower shop. What I didn't count on was Norman Ben breathing down my neck. He assumed that I had the company's missing funds and that's how I'd been able to start up a business. He's been out to get me ever since."

"What makes you think that?" Ella asked.

"Look out there," she said, pointing to a sedan parked just across the street from the shop with a MADD sticker on the bumper. "That's Ross Harrison, a private investigator Norman hired to find Elroy. The day I opened the flower shop, he appeared. Since then he's been coming by, off and on, watching me."

"Has Harrison actually approached you?" Ella said, catching Blalock's eyes and pointing toward Harrison, who was texting on his cell phone.

"Yeah, but the last time he came into my shop and started hassling me I threatened to call the police. After that, he's stayed on public property. If he's parked on a public street, there's nothing I can do."

"What did the P.I. say to you?" Ella asked, seeing Blalock working his BlackBerry, probably trying to get background after reading Harrison's New Mexico tags.

"The creep accused me of conspiring to defraud Norman, his client. He said that if I thought I could launder the company's money by funneling it through the flower shop I was kidding myself." She shook her head, then shrugged in resignation. "I'll never get rid of Harrison or the older guy who works for him, Bruce Talbot. I can't prove I'm innocent, not without allowing them access into my business and personal life, and I won't do that. I'll just have to get used to being watched whenever I'm off the Rez."

"They have no right to harass you," Ella said.

"I've threatened to sue all three of them, but I've sunk every dime I have into this shop. Even a hint of scandal could ruin me. This is a very conservative community."

"Clah," Blalock said, poking his head in the door.

Ella spotted Harrison, a fit, tanned man in his early forties, going over to Blalock's sedan and glancing inside.

The moment Ella hurried out of the shop with Blalock, Harrison began walking away quickly.

"FBI agent, stop right there," Blalock snapped.

Harrison did so and turned around. "Sorry. I was just curious about your ride. I've been looking to buy that same make and model."

"Save it," Blalock said.

Harrison reached into his jacket, but seeing Ella tense up and lower her hand to the butt of her weapon, immediately stopped and smiled. "Hey, relax. I'm just reaching for my ID." He pulled out his identification and handed it to Blalock.

"So you're Ross Harrison, a P.I. licensed in New Mexico," Blalock said. "Why are you staking out this flower shop?"

"Staking out? Nah, I was just hanging around and waiting to interview the proprietor when she wasn't so busy."

"You were already parked across the street when I arrived," Ella said, recalling the vehicle.

"I'm a patient man—paid by the hour."

"What business do you have with her?" Ella pressed.

"My clients ask for anonymity, but I can tell you why I'm here. A source of mine claims that Elroy Johnson's body

was one of those found over by Hogback at that secret graveyard. I wanted to ask his widow to verify it for me. But the
fact that you're here suggests my source is right. Care to
comment, Investigator Clah?"

"How do you know who I am?" Ella countered.

He gave her an ingratiating smile. "I'm a former Farmington police detective. Although we've never met, I recognize your face from both the media and the few times our
cases have overlapped."

Ella didn't remember Harrison, but she'd check him out
later.

"It'll be public knowledge soon enough, so how about
it? Was Elroy's body one of those dug up?"

"Yes," she answered. "So now where does that leave you?"

"My primary job was to find Johnson. My client needed
answers about some missing assets. Since Johnson's dead,
the second part of my job is gonna take some refiguring." He
pulled a card from his wallet and handed it to her. "When it
comes to finding missing persons, I'm the best there is. I get
things done. Keep that in mind in case the tribe ever needs
outside help. My retainer's reasonable. Call me."

Not waiting for an answer, Harrison walked away, whistling, and headed across the street to his sedan.

"That man's part weasel," Ella said. "Or cockroach."

"There *is* something smarmy about him," Blalock agreed.

"According to Leigh Johnson, Harrison's client is Norman Ben, Elroy's business partner. Let's go pay him a visit
and see what he has to say."

FOURTEEN

———— ✖ ✖ ✖ ————

They arrived at a small, flat-roofed one-story industrial center on Farmington's east side and checked the signs in front of the businesses. One in black and turquoise at the far end announced, THUNDER-BIRD CONSTRUCTION.

As they walked through the front door, they found the reception area empty, but they could hear a voice in the office beyond talking on a phone. A moment later, a round-faced, portly Navajo man wearing a bolo tie, a shirt with a yellow collar, and jeans came out.

"I'm Norman Ben. You've come to the right place if you're looking for quality *and* economy in your construction needs. How may I help you?"

Blalock brought out his ID and identified himself. Ella followed his lead. By the time the introductions were finished, the man's expression had changed from friendly to guarded.

"What can I do for you officers?" he asked.

"Your partner, Elroy Johnson, has been found—dead," Blalock said.

Ben's eyebrows rose. "Come into my office and we'll talk there," he said. "I've got nothing but time. The construction business has been pretty slow for the past two years because of the recession."

Leading the way, he took a seat in one of four leather chairs clustered around a stained oak desk and gestured for them to do the same. The thickly padded chairs were comfortable and plush, and the air-conditioning silent and effective.

"I've been following the news," Ben said. "Is his one of the bodies found over by the Hogback?" Seeing Blalock nod, he continued. "Are you one-hundred-percent sure it was Elroy?"

"Yes. A positive ID has been made," Blalock said.

"Did he happen to have a large amount of cash on him, or maybe a deposit slip or storage key among his possessions?" Norman asked.

"Nope," Blalock said.

Ella watched Ben carefully, thinking his question had sounded rehearsed. There was also no grief or regret in his tone.

"Why don't you tell us about the last time you saw your business partner," Blalock said.

He nodded slowly, as if expecting the question. "It was four years ago, but I still remember that day as if it was yesterday. From the moment Elroy walked into the office, he was pushing his new plan. With construction booming, he insisted we branch out and take on more projects, private as well as commercial, even remodels. He wanted Thunderbird Construction to be the number one construction firm in this area and was willing to do whatever was necessary to make that happen."

"And you?" Blalock asked.

"My partner was a risk taker, but that's not the way I like doing business. I didn't want to gamble on our company's future. I knew in my gut that the housing bubble wouldn't last forever and, to me, it made more sense to allow our company to grow slowly and steadily."

"Did you disagree often?" Blalock asked.

"Yeah, but if you're thinking that I had something to do with his death, you're way off base. I needed him alive—then and now. We didn't always get along, but we were a good team. I was better making the job sites work smoothly, and he excelled at bringing in new clients."

"So what happened to the company once he left?" Blalock pressed.

"My partner disappeared overnight, and a couple of business checks I'd written bounced on me a day or so later. That's when I had our company's accounts audited and discovered that the books were short by nearly one hundred thousand dollars. That was almost the exact amount of the loan we'd taken out. I hired an ex-cop P.I. to track Elroy down, but even he wasn't able to pick up the trail. It was as if Elroy had vanished from the earth—and considering what you just told me, I guess he had."

"Did you ever get any leads on the missing money?" Blalock asked.

"No," Norman answered. "That's why I was hoping the detective would haul Elroy's sorry butt back here. Dead, he's no good to me. You can't squeeze money from a dead man."

"You mentioned bringing in an auditor. Did someone else handle finances for your company—an accountant, or bookkeeper, maybe?" Ella asked, her glance taking in the office. Their business license, with both their signatures, was framed and up on the wall in a prominent location over Norman's desk.

"We used an accountant to figure our taxes, but we didn't have a secretary or office staff. Elroy and I were the only ones with access to our money. Either one of us could withdraw funds when needed."

"Do you know a Navajo man named Chester Kelewood?" Ella asked.

"The name sounds vaguely familiar. We may have employed him at one time or the other. We hire a lot of construction workers on a job-to-job basis, and sometimes we bring in consultants and subcontractors. Do you want me to check and see if he's ever worked for us?"

"Do that," Blalock said.

Norman typed the name into the computer, then after a brief wait, looked up. "No one by that name shows up. Who is he?"

"Another missing person," Blalock said.

"You think he knew Elroy?" he asked.

"We don't know," Ella answered.

Ten minutes later, as they climbed back into the Bureau's sedan, Ella glanced at Dwayne. "Norman's bitter about his situation, but I don't think he's our serial killer."

"I'll ask Nez to look a little deeper into his background and see if Norman's been in contact with anyone on our list of missing persons. It's still possible he hired someone to off Johnson, so it won't hurt to find out who he hangs around with."

"Sounds good," Ella said. "If we could figure out what triggered the killings, that alone could lead us to a suspect. That once-a-year pattern suggests this is the work of a serial killer acting out of logic, not impulse."

"*His* brand of logic," Blalock said. "What we've learned about the first victim may be the key."

"If we could put the pieces together."

"We need another brainstorming session. I'll call Nez and have him join us at my house in Bloomfield. You can call your partner and bring in the rest of your team, if they're available."

"I'll have Justine meet us, but Ralph, Benny, and Joe

need to keep working on that missing person's list. I'll also have Justine run a check on Ross Harrison."

Blalock drove directly to his house outside Bloomfield and forty-plus miles east of Shiprock. As he pulled into the driveway Ella was struck by how much work had been done in the garden. "It's beautiful, and the flowers look like they've been there for years. Everything's flourishing."

"They're all drought-resistant varieties. Ruthann looked into all that. She loves working outside."

They went inside and Ruthann called out a hello from a room down the hall.

"She's probably painting," Blalock said.

Ella followed Dwayne down the hall but stopped at the doorway of what was Ruthann's artist's studio. The wall was lined with colorful, realistic watercolor paintings of flowers and plants.

"You do beautiful work," Ella said, greeting the short, stocky, blue-eyed blonde. Ruthann looked comfortable wearing jeans and a faded yellow tee-shirt. "I love that one," Ella added, stepping through the doorway and pointing to one of a native plant with bright green leaves and red berries.

"Come and take a closer look." Ruthann invited Ella in with an engaging smile. "I've retired from teaching, but art's still my passion. I do watercolors as a way of relaxing."

Ella studied the paintings, mostly of desert wildflowers she'd seen since childhood. She immediately recognized the blue and purple asters with their bright yellow centers.

"Do you plan to sell any of these?" Ella asked, knowing Rose would probably love to have one.

"No. If I do that, then it becomes work, and I'd rather keep it strictly a hobby. I'm always running out of room, so I give most of them away to people I think will appreciate them. Would you like one?" she said, waving her hand around the collection.

Ella glanced back at the first one that had caught her eye.

She remembered seeing that plant somewhere before. Though she couldn't name the variety, the image brought back pleasant memories of family outings in the Chuska Mountains. "I'd love that one. Do you know the name of the plant?"

Ruthann shook her head. "No, I'm afraid not. I just thought it was pretty. There's one growing out back."

"Mom will be able to tell me what it is."

"Is your mom familiar with the local native plants? If she is, I'd love to talk to her. I'd like to know more about what I'm painting."

Ella told Ruthann about the Plant Watchers. "Their knowledge is generally passed on from one generation to the next, but these days our younger people are too busy trying to make a living, or have other interests. The Plant Watchers membership is dwindling."

"Back when I was teaching grade school, we'd often have people from the community come talk to the kids and give presentations. Your mom and I could do something like that here if she has the time. I could discuss my painting and she could talk about the plants themselves. Do you think she'd be interested in something like that?"

Although she had a feeling Rose would jump at the chance, Ella had been raised never to speak for another. "I'll bring it up when I show her your painting and have her give you a call," Ella said, still admiring the watercolor. "This is just beautiful, Thank you, from both of us."

"You're very welcome."

Blalock came in, brushed a kiss on his wife's forehead, then smiled at Ella. "Hey, Clah, we gonna work, or are you gonna spend all day chatting?"

There was no anger in his voice so Ella smiled. "I'm ready whenever the others arrive."

"Nez and Justine showed up while you two were plant-talking," he said, turning to wink at Ruthann.

As they walked into the massive den, Ella sighed with

envy. This wasn't that fake laminated wood paneling; the material here was the real thing.

"This must have been the room that sold you on the house," Ella said, nodding at Dan and Justine, who were already seated.

"I admit that I've always wanted a study like this, and when I saw this room it blew me away. But to answer your question, no, this isn't why I bought the house. Remember the big windows in the studio? I knew that room would be perfect for Ruthann."

Ella smiled. There was no mistaking the love in his voice when he spoke of his wife. For a fleeting moment she wondered if she would ever again find that kind of relationship, a love she had shared only briefly, just out of high school, with her late husband Eugene. Then she brushed the thought aside. She had a wonderful family and a great job. That was enough.

As Ella took a seat next to Justine on a leather sofa, a sturdy-looking bulldog ambled in, snorting and sniffing the air noisily.

"Hey, Cat," Blalock said, scratching the dog behind the ears before stepping across to a big blue recliner.

"You know the first time I heard that, I figured it was just a cute name—a dog named Cat," Ella said.

Dan looked at her, then at Blalock. "It isn't?"

"No, the dog belongs to my son Andy, a Marine captain. Cat comes from category nine, Marine speak for ultra stupid, he says. I'm taking care of the beast while Andy's deployed."

Dan laughed as he reached down to pet the dog, who was sniffing curiously at his new, brown Tony Lama Boots.

As the dog wandered off with a snort, he brought out his BlackBerry and glanced around the room. "Why don't I start?" Dan said, then seeing the nods, began. "I've been digging through everything our department managed to get on Elroy Johnson. According to sources interviewed at the time he disappeared, Johnson was an honest man with big dreams. Those who knew him flat-out refused to believe he'd embezzle from his own company and then just walk away—much less leave his wife."

"What about his personal finances? Do you have anything on that?" Ella asked.

"Our records show that he was overextended, but if he stole that money he also hid it extremely well. There's no record of it anywhere and his wife never showed any sign of coming into a large sum of money."

Ella shared what Blalock and she had learned. "His business partner, Norman Ben, hired a P.I., so I doubt Ben knows where that money is."

"So it makes sense he'd want to keep a close eye on Johnson's wife," Dan said. "But the fact that there's missing money doesn't clear him. Let's say Ben and Johnson had a fight and, during the course of that, Johnson ended up dead. Ben wants his money back, but with Johnson gone, his only shot at recovering it is via Johnson's wife. So he focuses on her, hoping she'll lead him, or Harrison, to it somehow."

Ella nodded. "Yeah, it sounds plausible, but what possible link could Ben have to the other three victims?"

"They may have been attempts to cover up the first murder—getting rid of people who knew too much, maybe," Dan said, then shook his head. "No, never mind. The killings were a year apart and the acts themselves were cold-blooded assassinations. My theory doesn't add up right."

"What'd you get on Harrison?" Ella asked Justine.

"The man is ex-FPD, served in the department for nine years, rising to detective, then resigned four and a half years ago and got his P.I. license. He has no criminal record except for a few speeding tickets," Justine said, looking at her Black-Berry.

"Why'd he resign?" Blalock asked.

"Personal reasons, according to what I could get. Death of his fiancée. He's never been married," Justine added.

"He have a concealed carry permit?" Ella asked.

"Yeah, a Glock 30—a forty-five. Right company, wrong caliber for the killer," Justine added.

"Glocks are popular. Anything that might suggest a motive?" Dan asked.

Justine shook her head. "Nothing that jumps out at you. He didn't have an aggressive reputation, any known prejudices, no flags on his personnel files—at least according to those I spoke to. He's a dead end right now."

"He's a pain in the butt. Too bad," Ella said. "Let's move on."

After another half hour of brainstorming, Ella and Justine headed back to the reservation. The watercolor painting Ruthann had given Ella was lying flat on the rear seat.

"Mrs. FB-Eyes is a talented artist," Justine said.

"Yeah, she is, but you know what? Even if she couldn't draw a figure eight, Dwayne would think she's brilliant," Ella said with a smile. "The guy's in love all over again."

"Yeah, you're right," Justine said. "I'm jealous. I've never had a guy look at me the way he does her."

"Maybe you aren't looking in the right direction," Ella said.

"You don't mean Benny, do you?" she asked, giving Ella an incredulous look.

"Okay, he's not exactly the longing-looks type," Ella said, "but he really seems to care about you. It's there in the way he acts."

Justine smiled, but said nothing, keeping her eyes on the road.

Ella glanced out the window. To find a perfect someone who fit all your needs, someone whose life you could also complete, that was the stuff of romance novels. In her experience, relationships were seldom that simple or clear cut.

Her musings came to a stop only a few miles out of Shiprock when her phone rang. Hearing Neskahi's voice, she put it on speaker.

"Whatcha got?" Ella asked.

"I managed to cross another person off my list. That particular man was eventually found by a neighbor and taken back home. He's got dementia and wanders off sometimes. The family never notified the authorities." He paused for a long time.

Ella had a feeling that he wasn't finished, so she waited.

"There's something else I thought you'd want to know," he said at last. "On my way back to town, heading along the ditch road just south of Cudei, I saw a group of teens playing on one of those big sandbars out in the river. One of them was Dawn. Isn't she supposed to be at school today?"

"Yeah. So where exactly did you see my kid?" Ella asked immediately.

"About six miles northwest of the old bridge."

"Thanks," Ella said, ending the call. She turned to Justine. "You get the gist of that?"

Her partner nodded, but didn't comment.

"Find the place," Ella said, giving her directions. Torn between concentrating on the case and her personal life, she felt the tension building inside her. But she couldn't let this go.

"Has Dawn ever skipped school before?" Justine asked after a few minutes.

"Not that I know of. She's always enjoyed school."

"What's changed?"

"I don't know, and that's what worries me." She ran a hand through her hair. "Maybe this is my fault. I get so busy with my cases, I may have missed something going on right in front of me."

"Don't go there. She's a kid and bound to get in trouble at times, especially this close to the end of the school year.

I'm sure you broke the rules once in a while when you were her age. I ditched the last day of school more than once."

"There's still a week left in this school year, cuz," Ella said, trying to reach Dawn on her cell phone but unable to get a connection.

After reaching Shiprock's west side, Justine turned down the road paralleling the river, and they headed into the *bosque*.

"Just ahead," Ella said, gesturing to an approaching pickup whose cab was filled with teens. "Pull them over."

Justine turned on the lights and the sirens, then stopped diagonally, blocking the ditch road. The truck slowed and came to a stop.

Ella walked up to the passenger-side door, while Justine went to the driver's side to ask the boy at the wheel for his license.

As she drew near, Ella heard Dawn's voice. "I'm DOA," she whispered.

Ella opened the door, automatically sniffing the air and looking for alcohol containers. "Let my daughter out, please," she said to the two girls seated closest to the window. As they moved out of the way, she focused her gaze on Dawn, who was beside the driver. "Get out of the truck."

"Mom," Dawn said in a strangled voice as she scooted toward the door. "I can explain."

"Not here, not now, Dawn. Let's go."

Rather than have a full-blown confrontation in front of her daughter's companions, Ella led her back to the SUV and stopped beside the front passenger door.

Ella crossed her hands across her chest, then stared into Dawn's eyes. "You cut school."

Dawn looked down at the ground. "Just the last two periods, Mom. Mostly it was just a long study hall. Leonard had his dad's pickup for the day so we thought we'd go out and wade across the channel to the sandbar. We wanted to unwind."

"Those kids aren't from your school," Ella said. "Nobody middle-school age can legally operate that truck."

"Leonard's sixteen. He's from Shiprock High," Dawn said in a hushed whisper.

"Get in the backseat. I'm taking you home right now."

"Let me say good-bye to Leonard first?"

"No."

Dawn started to protest, but seeing the look in her mother's eyes, ducked her head to hide her anger and climbed into the SUV. Ella closed the door as her daughter fastened the seat belt. There were no handles in the back of the unit—used to transport those under arrest—so Dawn wouldn't be able to get back out until someone opened the door from the outside.

Ella headed back to the pickup, intending to speak to the boy behind the wheel, but Justine intercepted her. "You're way too pissed off. Let it go for now. The boy has a legal operator's license and proof of insurance, and there's no sign anyone has been drinking. I instructed him to drop the other girls off, then head home."

"Who is he?"

"Leonard Skeet, the son of one of our patrolmen. I know the family. They're basically good people, but Leonard's become a magnet for trouble, or so I hear. There was a shoplifting incident in Farmington in March, and he was caught driving away from the Quick Mart last month without paying for gas. His father made it good, promised it wouldn't happen again, and the complaint was dropped."

"And, of course, that's the boy my twelve-year-old daughter's interested in," Ella muttered.

"The bad boy . . . ," Justine said with a shrug, turning off the flashing lights, then backing up to their right so the pickup could pass.

Ella watched in the side mirror as the truck pulled away. This wasn't over, not by a long shot.

A tense silence followed as Justine drove southeast toward the highway, but that was soon interrupted by the call coming in on Ella's cell phone.

The ring tone told Ella that it was Kevin even before she flipped it open and answered.

"I just got out of a court hearing and was on my way home when Dawn's school called. Dawn's missing. She never made it to class this afternoon. A campus search is underway."

"Call it off. She's in the car with me," Ella said, giving him a quick update. "When did the school report her missing from class?"

"She wasn't there for science class after lunch, so they sent an administrator and security to search the building and grounds."

As Kevin hung up to call the school, Ella gave her daughter a lethal glare.

Dawn avoided eye contact and shrunk down even farther into the seat.

As Ella considered how to best handle the situation with Dawn, she heard a call coming over the radio. A shooting victim had been found several miles east of the reservation line, and the sheriff's department was requesting her presence at the scene. From their current location, approaching the main highway west of the bridge, taking Dawn home first would cost them at least a half hour.

Ella asked Justine to pull over, then called Kevin back. "Is there any chance you can meet us at the junction just east of the high school and take our daughter home?" she asked him. "I just got an urgent call from dispatch."

"I'm coming down off the mesa now, and I can meet you there in less than five. Park by the gas station. I'll take her over to my place and she and I will have a long talk there."

"Good idea."

As Justine headed to the location, Dawn fidgeted, wiping off a shade of lipstick that wasn't on her permitted list.

"Mom, we're meeting Dad *now*?"

"Yes," Ella replied curtly. "He's happy for the chance to speak to you face-to-face."

"But you'll be too busy to be there, too?"

The words stung, but Ella knew her kid was using the tactic as a diversion. Her daughter was bright and knew which buttons to push. "I wasn't too busy to come looking for you, was I?"

"Mom, I can explain everything. Really. Can't you and I talk right now, just for five minutes?"

"No. I've got to calm down first. I'm too ashamed of you at the moment. I trusted you, and you really let me down this time. You knew that I was especially worried about you today—that you might be in danger. Yet you took off like this anyway."

"But I wasn't alone, I was with people the whole time. Besides, nobody could have found us," Dawn argued.

"I did," Ella retorted.

Kevin pulled up behind them as they turned into the business parking lot. By the time Ella opened the back door and let Dawn out, Kevin was already out of his car.

"Get inside," he snapped.

Dawn burst into tears and practically ran to Kevin's sedan.

"The boy's sixteen," Ella said, filling him in as they stood by the SUV.

"Who's the kid?"

"Leonard Skeet."

"He's bad news. Dawn and I are going to have a talk she isn't likely to forget. And that boy—he's history. He won't be getting anywhere near our kid again."

"How can you be so sure?"

"You've met his stepmom, Mona Todea, now Skeet, my legal assistant. In fact, that's how Dawn and Leonard met, in my office," Kevin said, then shook his head at Ella's raised eyebrows. "Don't say a word."

Ella climbed back inside the tribal SUV and nodded to Justine. "Let's roll." She'd just finished fastening her seat belt when her phone rang again.

This time it was Blalock. "Dan and I are going to meet up at the county crime scene. Are you on the way?"

"Yeah. Did you get any specifics? All I know is that the vic was shot to death," Ella said.

"I've asked that details be kept off police frequencies. Too many reporters are monitoring calls," Blalock said. "But to answer your question, the vic was found about a mile west of Kirtland High School, within sight of the bridge. He'd been shot in the head. That's the only similarity so far to the Hogback cases. This guy was found inside his car, fully clothed, and the shooting took place only a few hours ago."

"Okay. I'll be there shortly," Ella said, already wondering if the killer was changing his M.O. or if this would turn out to be an unrelated incident.

FIFTEEN

✖ ✖ ✖

When Ella arrived on the scene, she immediately spotted Nez and Blalock. They were standing about twenty feet back from where the county crime scene team was processing a blue, older-model sedan with a muddied license plate. The car was parked under a low-hanging cottonwood, in the shade.

As she walked up, techs were carefully easing the body out of the car, guided by one of the county's deputy medical investigators. The victim appeared to be a Hispanic male. He'd been shot in the upper left temple and in the neck.

"That's not our killer's M.O.," Justine said. "This was an in-your-face–style shooting."

"There are a couple of empty beer cans on the floor on the passenger's side," one of the techs said into a throat mike as he continued to examine the interior of the car. "Three other empties are on the backseat and two unopened cans were sitting on the seat beside him. Tire tracks indicate he pulled off the road and parked before the shooting. Blood splatter indicates he was killed in the car. Blood smears on the seats and the position of the body when discovered suggest the deceased was manhandled. He was pushed over onto the passenger seat, maybe to allow the shooter or another party to remove the vic's wallet. The fade pattern—outline of a wallet—is still present in the vic's jeans, but the wallet hasn't been located."

"Road rage incident leading to murder and robbery?" Ella suggested to Blalock and Nez.

"The commonality between M.O.'s so far is that this vic was also shot twice. The other hit was in the neck, which could mean the killer's aim was a bit off this time, the victim tried to duck, or we're dealing with someone else entirely," Dan said.

"This is a well-traveled area, close to a lot of school traffic. Maybe the killer struck, but something happened that kept him from repeating his usual M.O.," Justine said. "The victim might have resisted, or a potential witness could have forced him to hightail it out of here."

"There's another possibility we haven't discussed before," Nez said. "We could be dealing with a professional hit man—a hired gun who has been working right under our noses for a while. That would explain how unrelated victims ended up dumped in the same area. And now that the original burial site has been compromised, he's had to change his game plan and M.O."

"By leaving the vic in the open like this, he also might be sending a message to any interested parties—including us. 'Screw with me and you're dead,'" Justine said.

"A pro . . . that could make things even more difficult," Ella observed. "The killer wouldn't need a motive except serving his client. But that theory still doesn't fit in with that once-a-year pattern."

As Nez and Blalock voiced other possible scenarios, Ella heard her cell phone's distinctive beep signaling a text message. Moving away from them, she flipped open the phone.

This time the message was succinct: THOSE IN MY WAY DIE.

Justine, who'd watched Ella's reaction, came over and

looked down at the text message. "We've got the court order. You can ask for a trace," she said.

Ella called her cell phone carrier and requested the message be traced.

After a wait, an administrator answered. "The call came from a prepaid device, Investigator Clah. That means that the only thing I was able to get for you is the location of the closest cell phone tower at the time he sent the message. It's in Farmington at the west end of Apache Street."

Blalock came over. "What's up, Clah?"

Ella showed him the message. "He's trying to keep me off balance, maybe to slow down my work. I'm sure that's why he chose to mention my kid in the last message. He's playing head games with me."

"Keep us posted," Blalock said. "In the meantime, the possibility of a hit man is worth following up, if only to rule out that theory. Nez and I will do the legwork here on the county side. This vic still has fingerprints and a face, so we should have more on him soon, unless he's an illegal."

As he spoke, the head of the county's crime scene unit came over. "Here's what we know," she said. "The vic was shot in the temple and neck. There's one nine-millimeter slug embedded in the headrest, the other is still in the vic. His wallet's gone but we got a quick hit on his prints. His name is Ignacio Candelaria, he's got a green card, and he works at a business called Eddy's Garage just this side of the Farmington city limits. Candelaria had several DWI arrests, but nothing else."

"This is looking more and more like a road rage incident, or maybe even an attempted carjacking," Ella said. "County should check out the locals, beginning with the high school students. I realize this would have happened while class was in session, but kids come and go. Maybe one of them saw something, or worse, was the perp."

Blalock nodded. "These days it's not that unusual for kids to take guns to school or ride around with them in their cars. In my day, we used to settle things with a fistfight behind the gym."

"Or the student parking lot," Dan said.

"Local deputies can handle questioning at the school," Ella said. "Meanwhile, Dwayne, can you check your databases and see if we've got any professional criminals working the area?"

They returned to his sedan and Blalock typed in the information. "We've got a couple of names here from a RMIN report," he said, speaking of the Rocky Mountain Information Network. "Gilbert Romero and Jimmy Bowman, both Navajos in their early twenties, are wanted fugitives who were last spotted in eastern Arizona. They've been linked to a carjacking early in May and the murder of a motorist in Tuba City. The victim was shot twice at close range. Bowman lived in Waterflow as a teen, so it's possible they've moved into our area."

"I can update our team and see if we can get any leads on them," Justine said. "Some of our officers might know the pair."

"Head back there and see what you can do," Ella told Justine.

"I'll leave the SUV with you. I'll catch a ride with someone from county."

"Let me see what I can get on Eddy's Garage," Dan said, then went to his vehicle. He returned moments later. "Our burglary unit has the victim's employer, Eddy Pounds, on their short list for suspected auto theft. They've paid Eddy several visits in the past but got nowhere. It's possible, even likely, that the vic was involved in a chop shop operation."

Ella looked at Dan, then back at Blalock. "This is out of my jurisdiction, but that also means I'm less likely to be recognized as a cop. If I go in alone posing as a customer, I can look around and ask some questions. There's no telling what I might see."

"Let's switch vehicles. You take my pickup," Dan said, tossing her the keys. "Even an unmarked is likely to send up flags since departments tend to favor the same models."

Ella nodded. "Good thinking. I'll keep my cell phone on so you can hear what's going down, too. If I see anything connected to the chop shop, you can move in."

"Sounds like a plan," Blalock said. "We'll close off the perimeter, cover the rear, and wait for Clah's signal."

Twenty minutes later, Ella pulled up beside an old cinder-block, flat-roofed former filling station on the outskirts of Farmington. The pumps were gone, but the island remained, a weed-landscaped chunk of concrete. The black-and-white metal sign in its center advertised EDDY'S GARAGE and offered discount tune-ups and brake jobs. Two five-foot-high stacks of old tires rested against a side wall.

Ella parked near the front doors, noting through a dirty upper row of windows that fluorescent lights were on inside. Both doors of the two-bay garage were closed despite the heat, and the height of the windows hid everything but the ceiling from view. Ella dialed Blalock, pressed the speaker button, then slipped the phone into her shirt pocket.

As she climbed out of the pickup, she could hear the machine-gun rattle of an air impact wrench. Ella went inside the small front office and looked around. There was a small TV on the counter, a stack of girlie magazines, and a dirty-looking coffeemaker, but no cash register. Three beat-up wooden chairs rested against the wall below the outside window, and on the opposite side was a taped-up business license and a three-year-old pinup calendar depicting Miss October.

"Anybody home?" she yelled, pushing the wooden door leading into the garage. It was locked on the inside.

"Hey, I think my engine is overheating. Anyone here work for a living?"

"Keep your shirt on, lady. I'm coming," a man's voice yelled from inside the garage. She heard a clank, then the sound of a lock opening.

An Anglo man in his fifties wearing a stocking cap and dirty gray shirt poked his head out a crack in the door. "Hey," he said, giving her a quick once-over, pausing at her breasts. "I'm Eddy. Sorry to keep you waiting, sweetie. You got a problem with your ride?"

He stepped halfway out, then looked through the dirty window at Nez's tan truck. "Nice looking 150. What's the problem?"

She looked past him into the bay, where a dark green Mercedes was parked, minus the hood and right front fender. No one else seemed to be around.

Ella stepped closer to him and brushed aside her light jacket revealing her badge and firearm. "I'm a police officer, Mr. Pounds, and I'd like to speak to you about one of your employees."

"Crap!"

The man jumped back and tried to pull the door shut, but Ella managed to get her boot in the way. As she pushed it open, he turned and ran.

The guy raced around the Mercedes and disappeared from view. To her left, Ella could see another exit.

"Watch the back door," Ella shouted to Blalock and who-ever else could hear.

Ella pulled out her Glock and ducked down, glancing beneath the car, trying to spot feet on the other side. Unable to do so, she ran to her left, expecting him to have circled the Mercedes. Then, out of the corner of her eye, she caught a glimpse of something flying through the air.

Ella ducked and the object flashed by, brushing her left ear before hitting the bay door with a metallic clank.

Hearing running footsteps on the concrete floor, she whirled just as the man raced out from behind the engine compartment and headed for the front.

"Stop!" she yelled, raising her pistol. She wouldn't have shot him, but he didn't know that.

The guy grabbed the doorknob, but it suddenly flew open with a thump, catching him full force in the chin and chest. Eddy flew back, falling flat onto the hard floor like a stepped-on spider, legs and arms splayed out.

Ella raced over, joining Blalock, who'd been responsible for the stop. Nez came in next, weapon drawn.

"Nice backhand, Dwayne," Ella said, putting her foot next to the groaning man's head. "Roll over, slowly, Mr. Pounds, and keep your hands where I can see them."

"I'm Agent Blalock of the FBI," Dwayne said, as Ella and Dan hauled him to his feet. "What's your name?"

"Edward M. Pounds," he grumbled.

"I'm not really that interested in you, so relax, Mr. Pounds," Blalock said. "I need information about one of your employees. Give me some answers and I'll get out of your face."

"No problem, man," he muttered, rubbing his bruised chin. "What do you need to know?"

"Everything you can tell me about Ignacio Candelaria," Blalock said.

"He's one of my mechanics and he's late for work today. What's he done, robbed a bank or something?"

"As far as we know, he's done nothing except get shot in the head," Blalock said.

"Dead?" he asked, his color turning one shade paler.

"Yeah, that's what usually happens when a bullet blows out a chunk of your skull."

"I had nothing to do with that," Pounds said quickly. "Ignacio was just a guy who worked for me, a loner if there ever was one."

"Do you have his home address?"

"You're practically looking at it. He lives—lived—in the back of the shop. There's a cot in the storeroom along with some of his stuff. It's my place, so poke through whatever you want."

"Anyone ever come by to see him? A friend, male or female? A family member?" Blalock pressed.

"No, man, it's like I told you. He was always alone. Iggy liked to argue, and could get people really pissed off. No way he had friends. First thing he did after work was get in his car and head for the liquor store. From what I could tell, all he did off the clock was drink and get into fights. I'd be here late sometimes, working on the books, and see him come in, dragging, and bloodied up."

"Bar fights?" Blalock asked.

"Or on the road." Eddy wiped a greasy hand on his baggy gray slacks. "One night he was in a car accident and ended up in a fight with the other driver. There was one thing about Iggy you could count on: He didn't like being told he made a mistake, or worse, that he was wrong. And if he was drunk at the time, there'd be hell to pay."

Nez, Blalock, and Ella left Eddy's Garage shortly afterwards and met by Blalock's sedan, which had been parked to block the exit of Eddy's business truck.

Ella and Dan exchanged vehicle keys. "Your tribal SUV is over there," Nez said, pointing down the road a hundred yards.

Ella nodded. "Bowman and Romero are looking like our best bets for the Candelaria murder. We should also check and see if Elroy Johnson ever had an encounter with that pair, one that could have led to a deadly second meeting. If they were the ones who killed Elroy, it's possible they each took a shot, sharing the kill, and making sure neither would rat out the other. I admit it doesn't address what else we know about the snake-eyes murders, but those two characters might have done some work-for-hire killings."

Dan nodded. "I'll look into that from my end and let you know if it goes anywhere."

Ella soon set out for Shiprock. She was less than five miles east of town when she noticed a white sedan about a hundred yards behind her. It seemed to be keeping pace with her unit, never speeding up or closing in, even when she altered her speed.

Since this was the only road leading directly into Shiprock, the first thing she needed to do was make sure she wasn't overreacting. Finding a side road, Ella slowed, signaled, then turned up a lane leading to a farmhouse. When she looked back in the rearview mirror, she saw the vehicle continue along the main highway toward town.

More at ease, Ella returned to the main highway and was on Shiprock's outskirts when she saw the white sedan again. It was parked beside a convenience store. Moments later, the vehicle pulled out into traffic, caught up to within a few hundred yards, then took up its position behind her again.

Ella picked up the radio, got Officer Talk's location from dispatch, then switched to a tactical frequency.

"I'm not far from your location," Marianna said. "I just grabbed a coffee at the Totah Café. I'm still in the parking lot."

"Stand by. I'll be passing you in three minutes. After I do, watch for a white sedan, a Ford Taurus. Pull out behind him, then close in. We'll box him in between us and force him to pull over."

"On it."

Ella slowed to thirty as she passed the Totah Café. The white car was behind her about six car lengths when Marianna pulled out behind it.

"Hit your siren," Ella told her.

Ella cut her speed sharply and braced for a possible collision, but the Taurus driver suddenly cut a hard left, jumped the median, then raced back east. After nearly colliding with an oncoming pickup, the driver ran the light, then raced north.

"I'm going after him." Marianna whipped her cruiser around in a turning lane, then roared after the suspect, racing past Ella.

"Don't lose him," Ella said, taking the next turning lane, reversing directions, then hurrying back in pursuit.

Reaching the intersection where the highway split, Ella used her lights and siren, checked to see if it was clear, then ran the light, racing north uphill. She saw Marianna's unit stopped just ahead behind two cars that were blocking the road.

"Lost him," Marianna said, using the car-to-car frequency. "He ran the light and caused a T.A."

"Crap. Anyone hurt?"

"Looks minor," Marianna said.

Ella pulled up behind Marianna's unit. A pickup was blocking the road diagonally, half of its load of hay scattered across both lanes. Another vehicle, a small compact, was resting against the pickup's right fender, its steering wheel lodged just south of the bumper.

"He's probably halfway to the state line, but I'll see if we have any units between here and Colorado," Ella said as she joined Marianna on the scene. "You get a read on the plate?"

"No luck. It was one of those state centennial jobs, yellow on turquoise. Hard as hell to make out unless you're right on them," Marianna replied.

"Tell me about it." After making the call, Ella stayed in the intersection, holding back traffic until the truck driver and three volunteers moved enough bales to clear a lane. Marianna tended the driver of the compact, who'd suffered cuts and bruises. Once the paramedics arrived on scene, Ella left Marianna in charge and headed back to the station.

News of what had happened spread quickly. Not long

after Ella reached her desk and began to write up a report, Blalock came in, followed a few steps behind by Dan Nez.

"We heard," Blalock said. "Do you have any evidence that would prove the text messages and this tail you picked up are connected to our case? You've been shot twice already, Clah, now this. It's starting to look like you're the next target."

Ella's eyes narrowed. "If you're considering trying to get me pulled off this case, don't go there. This jerk's just messing with me. I may not know why yet, but I will."

As Nez and Blalock took a seat, Justine came in. "I've gone over everything we have on Elroy Johnson. His driving record's clean and we have no reports that he was involved in any traffic incidents or physical confrontations. Even his personal relationships were solid."

"Same on the county side," Dan said.

"That doesn't mean that there wasn't an altercation," Blalock said. "A lot of crimes and disturbances go unreported."

"We need to dig deeper. I think we should pay his wife another visit," Ella said. "It's almost six, but I remember her telling me that she often stayed till eight working on her books."

"Good thinking. While you're there, Detective Nez and I'll go put a little more pressure on Norman Ben and see what we get," Blalock said. "Okay with you, Nez?"

Dan nodded. "I've got a home address."

Justine was at the wheel as they drove to the flower shop, but when they got there they found no sign of Leigh Johnson.

The young Anglo woman who ran the small deli a few doors down was in the process of locking up when she saw them standing by the front window. "She closed up early. You'll have to come back tomorrow," she called out.

Ella went over to talk to her and identified herself. "Leigh's normally here till late, isn't she?"

"Yeah, but when I delivered her dinner earlier she mentioned she was going to lock up for the day. She looked really tired. I think it's all the pressure. Starting up a new business is really tough, particularly these days. My deli takes fourteen-hour days, sometimes more."

The deli owner obviously didn't know that Leigh had just learned of her husband's death, and Ella didn't enlighten her. Thanking the woman for her help, she walked back to the SUV with Justine.

"Get Leigh Johnson's home address, partner."

"It's on the Rez," Justine answered after typing it in. "Maybe a half hour to forty minutes away."

"Let's go," Ella said.

Justine glanced at Ella then back at the road. "I can handle the interview on my own if you'd like to call it quits and head home. I know you want to talk to Dawn," Justine said.

Ella shook her head. "Thanks, but no. Dawn's with her dad, and although I hate to admit it, it's the best place for her right now. She sees him as larger than life, and if anyone can, he'll be able to get through to her." Ella stared ahead. "I keep thinking that if I'd been a better mother I would have seen this coming months ago."

"Don't be so hard on yourself," Justine said. "The kid screwed up, that's all."

"But police work's such a huge part of my day, my personal life sometimes takes a big hit."

"It's the same for all of us, but we do our best, and things work out."

Ella thought of Dawn. She'd raised her to know right from wrong, and hopefully that would define the woman her daughter would become someday. Until then, all she could do was take things one day at a time.

SIXTEEN
——— ✖ ✖ ✖ ———

As they drove into a rural area north of Shiprock, it was easy to guess which houses belonged to the Traditionalist families. Those were usually farther back from the highway down unpaved roads, and had wood and coal stoves instead of bottled gas, and were missing the usual TV antennas or satellite dishes. Traditionalists also tended to have hogans in the back, along with corrals for livestock—mostly sheep and goats.

Justine turned east down a wide gravel road and slowed to a crawl when they discovered a flock of sheep moving through an arroyo close to the road. After about three miles, they arrived at their destination.

Leigh's home was a rectangular pitched-roof double-wide nestled against a low hill. Around fifty yards away in a field was what appeared to be a neighborhood dump containing an old stove, miscellaneous construction debris, black plastic trash bags, and a twenty-year-old car with flat tires and a missing hood. The absence of trash services contributed to the ugliness of many tribal neighborhoods, and people in these neighborhoods tended to ignore outward appearances.

Seeing a dusty minivan with Leigh's business sign on

its door, Justine parked, then walked with Ella to the front door.

Leigh took a few minutes to answer, and seemed surprised to see them, but invited them inside. She looked tired, and was barefooted, wearing a multicolored ankle-length house dress.

"We won't take long," Ella said, noting from her wrinkled clothing that it looked like she'd been in bed.

"It's all right, I was just trying to wind down a little. Have a seat. May I get you something cold to drink?" she asked.

"No, thanks," Ella said. "We just need to ask you an important question, then we'll get out of your way."

Leigh nodded and sat down on her sofa, tucking her legs under her.

"I need you to think back hard, Leigh. Did your husband *ever* have a problem with another driver on the road? Maybe something along the lines of an incident he didn't bother reporting to the police, but told you about?"

Leigh stared at the floor, her eyebrows knitted together. "I can't remember him mentioning anything like that," she said, looking up. "My husband wasn't the kind to get into fights with other drivers. He preferred to avoid trouble out on the road. He always said that too many crazies had driver's licenses."

"I was hoping you might remember something, even something minor," Ella prodded gently.

Leigh stared at the floor again, lost in thought. "There is something, but I don't think it's what you're looking for. My husband came home late one night, mad as could be. He'd been driving extra slow because of some trouble with one of his tires, and got pulled over by the police. They'd given him one of those field sobriety tests—walking heel to toe, and having him count backwards."

"Did your husband ever drink to excess?" Ella asked her.

"No, in fact it was just the opposite. He often stopped at

the Silver Nugget after work for a beer before coming home, but he *never* had more than one. He was methodical about things like that. He'd also have some snack food, chips or pretzels, along with it. His father was an alcoholic, and my husband took pride in being able to know when to stop."

"You said methodical . . . ," Ella said. "Does that mean that he kept to schedules and routines? For example, did he always take the same route home and at around the same time?"

She nodded. "He liked routines. He'd stop at the Nugget, then come home at around seven, but as I said, always sober."

"If you think of anything else, give us a call," Ella said, rising. "We'll let you get some rest now."

"You know, it never fails. Every time I come home early wanting nothing except to crawl into bed, I get visitors. Norman Ben came by less than thirty minutes ago," she said with obvious distaste.

"I gather you didn't invite him over?" Ella asked.

"Hardly. He has all but accused me and my husband of being thieves. Now that he knows Elroy is dead, he suddenly wants to be friends?" she said, grimacing. "I don't trust him one bit."

"What do you mean, friends?" Ella asked her.

"Norman hasn't been here in years, but he suddenly showed up at my doorstep offering condolences and telling me that he wanted to invest in my flower shop. He said he'd provide the capital I needed to finally get things on solid ground."

"What did you tell him?" Ella asked.

"I turned him down. The whole thing made no sense. My shop's doing okay, but I certainly can't guarantee that an investor would make a decent profit—now or ever. I told him that point blank, too, and asked him to explain his sudden interest."

"What did he say?" Justine asked, prodding Leigh after she lapsed into a thoughtful silence.

"At first, all I got from him was b.s. about how sorry he was about the way he'd treated me, but I kept pushing him for a straight answer. Finally he told me that in exchange for his financial help, he would be making one small request."

Ella's eyes narrowed.

"No, he didn't want me to sleep with him—like I ever would. He wanted me to stop talking to the police. He said that endless discussions about Elroy's disappearance were going to hurt his company, and maybe mine as well. He even offered to make sure I had an attorney on call in case you came back with more questions."

"We're talking now, so I gather you didn't take his offer?" Ella asked.

"No way, but after he left I saw that one of his private eyes, Bruce Talbot, was still snooping around."

Hearing angry shouts outside, Leigh muttered something under her breath and went to the window. "Talbot's probably out there again, taking photos," she said. "Yep, there he is."

Ella came up behind her and looked out. A brown-haired man in his late fifties, wearing a windbreaker and ball cap, was aiming a camera at an elderly couple coming out of a medicine hogan. Traditionalists, particularly the older ones, hated to have photos of themselves taken by strangers. They believed the images might be used to witch them.

"I'll take care of this," Ella said, and gestured to Justine.

As they hurried out, the man directed his camera at Leigh's house and took shots of Justine and her.

Ella strode up to him. "What do you think you're doing?"

"Taking photos isn't illegal, ma'am. I'm on a public road, not private property."

"You're standing on property that belongs to the Navajo

tribe," Ella clipped and flashed her badge. "Here, non-Navajos go by our rules and need permission to take photographs, so I'll need your camera. Our Traditionalists find personal photos threatening."

"I meant no offense. Let's compromise, officer." Talbot, who looked liked retired military with his haircut, grooming, and posture, showed her the monitor. As she watched, he deleted the photos he'd just taken. "Happy now?"

"Exactly why *are* you taking photos?" she asked.

"I'm Bruce Talbot," he said, flashing his driver's license. "I work for Ross Harrison's agency. Mrs. Johnson's friends and visitors are of interest to us."

Ella glared at him. "From now on, you are to stop harassing our people. In fact, I want you to stay well away from our residents unless you're invited to approach." She stopped, and emphasizing every syllable, continued. "If you choose to ignore this, I'll make sure the tribe declares you unwelcome on our land. If that happens, we can detain you the moment you enter our borders and subject you to legal action. Clear?"

"Abundantly." Talbot got back into his vehicle, a green pickup, and drove off west toward the highway.

A half hour later, having learned nothing more from Leigh Johnson, Ella and Justine climbed back into their SUV.

Ella glanced down at her watch. "We're going to be running out of daylight pretty soon. What do you say we go back to the . . ." Before Ella could finish, her phone rang. It was Carolyn.

"We have a confirmed DNA match on a second victim. Your earlier hunch paid off. The remains are what's left of Chester Kelewood."

"Thanks for the heads-up, Carolyn."

They'd traveled about a mile when sheep on the dirt road ahead forced Justine to slow down again. "We'll have to get out and chase them off, unless you want me to try and go around."

"The ground on either side looks pretty soft. If we get stuck, we could be here for hours," Ella said, taking a look out the window.

"I don't see a herder around, but I hear a bell. If we can get the leader moving along, the rest should follow, right?"

"Beats me," Ella said. "Clifford and my mom are the ones who know about sheep and goats. Sheep generally do their best to annoy me. They bleat once or twice, then keep right on doing whatever they want."

Justine laughed. "I like them a lot better than turkeys. My cousin had about thirty of those suckers, and they're mean. I was sent in to feed them one time, and they jumped me. I dropped the bucket and ran straight out of the pen." She opened her door. "You ready?"

"Yeah," Ella grumbled. "The one with the bell is on your side of the road. Go over and see if you can get it moving. I'll try to moosh the rest."

"Moosh? Is that shepherd talk?" Justine said, looking among the flock, trying to find the one with the clanking bell.

"It is now."

They were right in the middle of a dozen or so dusty sheep, pushing gently and shooing them along, when a shot rang out.

"What the hell?" Ella whirled around, trying to see the shooter among the deepening shadows.

The sheep began to panic, bleating and scattering in every direction.

Then a second bang sounded, and Ella heard the thud behind them, somewhere near the SUV.

Ella stumbled against a big ewe. Reaching out to break her fall, she grabbed a fistful of wool just as the sheep jumped away from her. Ella fell flat, barely avoiding a sharp hoof.

"Sounds like a rifle. Where's the shooter?" Justine yelled from somewhere across the road.

"North," Ella yelled, scrambling to one knee and drawing her weapon.

"I hear a hiss. Did we just lose our radiator?"

Ella turned her head. The SUV was sagging on the passenger-side front end. "No. The tire took a slug."

"No sheep are down. Maybe he was aiming at the car, not us."

"Stay down anyway and keep looking. He's out there somewhere, probably well out of pistol range."

The sheep, following their leader, the one with the wildly clanking bell, were now racing across level ground to the left, bunching together as they ran. The scent of dust, sheep manure, and sage mingled together, but there were no more gunshots.

Ella waited, watching the ground to the north where there was a gentle ridge.

"Hear that?" Justine said.

Ella held her breath. A car engine was racing away, and the sound of tires on gravel was fading off into the distance.

"Cover me." Ella raced to her right, weaving through the sagebrush and angling toward the rise. Within fifteen seconds she reached the ridge. Off to the east, she could see dust rising from the road where it curved back toward the highway.

"He's gone. All I could see of his vehicle was the gleam of chrome and taillights," Ella said, walking back to the SUV. "It's just too dark and dusty. I couldn't even say if it was a car or pickup."

"I called it in, but without a vehicle description . . ."

"Yeah, I know," Ella muttered.

As they were examining the right front tire and looking for traces of the bullet, Ella's phone rang. The special ring tone told her it was no ordinary call.

Ella answered and heard Big Ed's voice at the other end. "Shorty, I've sent some officers to help you search for evidence. What can you tell me?"

Ella gave him the highlights.

"Do you think it was some crackpot, or are Harrison or Talbot after you now?"

"Despite the timing, I can't say for sure."

"I'm going to report this to Sheriff Taylor and Sheriff Gonzales from McKinley County. I talked to both of them just a while ago and some of their deputies have heard talk. The meth lab you shut down has made you some enemies in these parts. Your bust put a dent in current distribution over the Four Corners."

"Noted. I'll watch my back," Ella said.

"What's next on your agenda?" Big Ed asked.

"Now that we've got a positive ID on Chester Kelewood, I'll be digging a lot deeper into his life. I want to know if there's any connection between him and Elroy Johnson."

"Let's hope you find one."

Justine had searched all around the vehicle by the time Ella put the phone away.

"Did I hear you say that you want to find out more about Kelewood?" she asked, moving toward the back of the vehicle.

Ella nodded, and reaching the tailgate first, opened the back so they could access the tire jack and tools.

"Back when Dan was pushing to see if Curley's identity theft crime included homicide, I dug into Kelewood's background. I was searching for a connection between the two men." She began moving tools aside to access the spare tire.

"Was there anything noteworthy there?" Ella asked, helping Justine lift the heavy spare out of the SUV.

"Kelewood was single and lived on the Rez with his sister, Martha Jim, and her daughter. In fact, she was the one who reported him missing. He'd stopped for a beer after work, but he never made it home. The next morning she reported him missing."

"The M.O. fits—stopping for a drink after work, then driving back to Shiprock on the same highway," Ella said, helping Justine put on the spare.

"There was something else, too. . . . He was scheduled to inspect a mine here on the Rez, but I can't remember the details."

They continued working on the tire, and before long saw the lights of the crime scene van approaching, a tribal cruiser behind it.

"Our team's here," Ella said. "Let's hope this guy left something besides footprints."

SEVENTEEN
✖ ✖ ✖

They were able to recover the badly deformed high-caliber rifle slug that had flattened their tire. After passing through the steel belts, the round had flattened against a sandstone boulder beside the road. The other bullet, however, had apparently ricocheted away, trajectory unknown. All they were able to find was a streak of metal on a rock.

After estimating the shooter's position based on the path of the bullets, they found where he'd lain on the ground atop the ridge using a boulder to brace his weapon. He'd made his escape across hard, dry ground leaving scuffs but no defined shoe or boot impressions. Even the tire prints of the vehicle he'd used were indistinct.

After another hour, Ella glanced at her watch. Although they'd powered up the generator battery, lanterns and flashlights were more useful outside the immediate circle of light. Finally it was clear there was nothing left to find.

"It's time to wrap it up, guys," she said at last.

After everything was put away, the crime scene van headed back to the highway.

Ella and Justine followed in the SUV, the spare tire now

in place. "If you want, you can access my computer at work from here and see what I've got on Kelewood," Justine said.

Ella shook her head. "I'll wait until tomorrow for that. Right now I've got to meet my kid at her father's. Give me a ride there, okay?"

"Yeah, no problem," she said. "Once I drop you off, I'll see if I can come up with something on the slug we recovered. I'm also going to try and find out where Bruce Talbot and Ross Harrison were at the time of the incident. Talbot left only about a half hour before we did. He would have had plenty of time to set up the ambush, or if he's innocent, he might have seen the shooter coming our way."

Ella nodded. "We have to check it out, but I don't think either of them would have been stupid enough to do something like this. The motive's not there."

A half hour later, Justine dropped Ella off at Kevin's, a relatively new home southwest of Shiprock. "You want me to wait and give you two a ride home?" she asked.

"No, Kevin can do that. It'll give us all a little extra time together."

Justine was driving off when Kevin came to the door. "Good timing. Our daughter just finished three slices of day-old pizza for dinner. I offered her steak and salad, but she wanted the pizza and iced tea. I figured I'd do better picking my battles."

Ella followed him inside, noting that he seemed tired. "It's quiet," she said, noting the absence of Dawn's favorite music.

"She's in the spare bedroom doing her homework, a term paper she put off to the very last minute," he said, then took Ella to his study and closed the door.

"I gather things haven't gone well," Ella said with a sigh.

He ran a hand through his hair. "I spoke to her and she knows she messed up big time. She swore she would never do that again."

"Do you believe her?"

"She knows that she let us both down, and I think she regrets what she did. But I'm not sure of anything else."

Ella exhaled loudly. "Me neither."

"I also spoke to her science teacher on the phone. He told me that it's not that she's incapable of doing the work. The real problem is that she's not taking any notes or paying attention."

"And ditching school . . . That's all going to cost her. She'll have to forget going to any end-of-the-year parties or get-togethers."

"That's a good plan. We both have to clamp down hard on her."

Five minutes later, they were all in Kevin's car. Dawn fidgeted in the rear seat. "I'm really, really sorry," she said in a teary voice.

"I'm sure you are, but don't expect either of us to instantly trust you again," Ella answered. "Once trust is lost, it has to be earned back, and that might take some time."

"Are you both going to stay mad at me *forever*?"

"We're not mad. You let us down, and we're sad and disappointed," Kevin said.

A thick, tense silence stretched out in the car after that. Ella knew that their battle was just beginning. Teenage angst and hormones were a powerful force, and those were lurking just around the corner.

Ella was up early the next morning, eager to get started with her day. It was Saturday and Rose was outside gardening. Dawn was in her room, her phone privileges suspended and Internet severely curtailed. The last time Ella had checked on her, Dawn had been working on her term paper, which was due on Monday. So far, so good.

Justine came into the kitchen shortly after seven-thirty carrying the watercolor Ella had inadvertently left inside the tribal SUV the evening before. "You forgot this."

"Thanks for bringing it in," Ella said. As she looked outside, she saw Rose was still busy. "I'll leave it on Mom's favorite chair. It'll be a nice surprise."

"There's some interesting news on the slug. There were some scrapes along the base, which fortunately wasn't deformed like the tip, and it looks like a reload," Justine said.

"So the shooter owns reloading gear. That narrows it down to what, several thousand New Mexico residents?" Ella responded. "Do you think we might be able to match the marks to a particular reloading press?"

Justine shook her head. "No, just a particular spent case, which the shooter took with him. And once he reloads it again . . ."

"We lose any chance of making a connection. Good work, anyway—the fact that he reloads may help us once we get a suspect. Anything else?"

Justine nodded. "I've also brought you a printout of everything I have on Chester Kelewood. Turns out he was the crucial player in a controversy that involved one of the local coal mines. Kelewood had inspected some heavy machinery, drag lines, and ore trucks, and concluded that they didn't meet the required safety standards. He reported that the company mechanics were signing off on maintenance work that wasn't being done. That could have led to a total shutdown of operations for a while, and a lot of jobs were on the line."

"How did the company running the operation take that?"

"They were urging the state to give them the all-clear on their equipment. They claimed that the irregularities were all a matter of improperly filled forms—clerical errors, nothing more, and that any shutdowns would only hurt worker salaries and the economy. Kelewood told the company that he was coming back for a second inspection of their operating equipment. He was putting them on the line."

"But Kelewood disappeared before that reinspection could take place?" Ella asked, taking the papers.

"Yeah, and here's the interesting thing. With Kelewood gone, the company mechanics had an extra week to work on the equipment. When Kelewood's replacement finally came in, he found no violations. A potential fine, which would have been upward of a quarter of a million, was never issued."

"So, as far as the company goes, his disappearance couldn't have come at a better time."

"That's the way Martha looked at it. She believed that her brother had been taken out of the picture because he refused to look the other way. The problem was, there was no evidence to support that claim with Kelewood gone. Chester's car was found in a grocery store parking lot just outside Farmington a few days later, the keys still in it. There was no sign of foul play."

They arrived at Martha Jim's home twenty minutes later. She lived near the high school in a residential section populated by Modernists, judging from their homes. Justine parked in the narrow concrete-slab driveway, and Ella led the way to the door.

Martha came to the door before they even had a chance to knock. "I saw you coming up. Is something wrong, officers?" she asked, looking down at the badge on Ella's belt.

Ella identified herself and Justine. "Can we come in for a moment?"

"Sure. I've got some freshly brewed coffee. Would you like some?" she asked, leading the way to the kitchen.

"That would be great," Ella said. Familiar routines often helped people relax, and she had bad news to deliver.

"We're here about your brother," Ella announced after Martha had set the steaming cups down on the table.

"I'm surprised the police are finally taking an interest," she said, sitting down. "Did you find Chester? Is he okay?"

"I'm afraid not," Ella said gently, giving her an overall report that left out the details.

Tears spilled down her cheeks and she wiped them away with her hand. "Who killed him, those people from the coal mine? I need to know."

Ella heard the anger in her voice and knew that emotion would help keep Martha from falling apart. She'd seen this before more times than she cared to remember. "We have no suspects or answers yet. We're still gathering information. That's why I was hoping you could tell us more about your brother."

"Chester was a good man," she said in a heavy voice. "When my husband was killed overseas, Chester moved in with my daughter and me. He told me it was because he didn't like living alone, but the truth is, he came to help me. He shared his paychecks with us and made sure we had everything we needed."

"And he was happy with his life?" Ella asked.

Martha nodded. "He never married or lived with anyone, though he dated sometimes, mostly Anglo women. He had a fondness for blondes, but there aren't many of those on the Rez."

Ella glanced down at the printout she was carrying to double-check her memory. "You reported him missing. Is that correct?"

She nodded, took a sip of her coffee with a shaky hand, then continued. "When he didn't come home at eight, his usual time, I figured that he'd probably met up with friends and gone out for a drink at some off-Rez bar. But when I woke up the next morning, I realized he'd never come home at all. That's when I got scared. I thought maybe he'd been in an accident. I'd often warned him about drinking and driving."

"Did he drink to excess?" Ella asked.

"When he went out, he had a tendency to have one too many, but if he thought he couldn't drive, he'd sleep it off in the car. By morning he was always home."

"Do you know if he'd been having problems, personally or at work?"

"I don't know all the details, but my brother was having problems with Stepson Inc. They're the Anglo company from Wyoming that runs local mining operations here on the Rez. Some of their equipment needed a second inspection because things weren't right. From what my brother said, they weren't happy at all about that. At first I thought they had something to do with my brother's disappearance, so I told the police. They checked it out and found nothing. Looking back now, I wish I'd pressured the police to keep looking."

"We'll be investigating all his contacts, including his business with Stepson," Ella said. "But we also need to find out more about your brother. Do you know if he ever had any trouble with another bar patron, or maybe a motorist on the road? Any major or minor incident," Ella added, "it wouldn't have to have been a fight."

"No, there was nothing like that. If there had been, he would have mentioned it to me. People who got in his face really pissed Chester off, and when he was angry he'd prowl around the house like a caged tiger. He wasn't the kind to hold stuff like that in."

They soon left, and on their way back to the station, Ella reviewed what they knew. "Now that we've narrowed down a time line, we should try to cross off John Curley as Kelewood's killer, if at all possible. I doubt he's going to remember his exact whereabouts every day of late May and early June of last year, but ask him anyway."

"I'll take care of it and let you know," Justine said.

Ella was about to say more when Big Ed called her on the cell. "I need to see you ASAP," he said, a sense of urgency in his tone. "How soon can you be here?"

"Ten minutes, maybe less. What's going on, Chief?"

"I'll tell you in person," he said, and ended the call.

Ella glanced at Justine and told her what he'd said. "Step on it, partner."

They arrived at the station within five minutes. While Justine went to the holding cells to interview Curley again, Ella hurried down the hall to Big Ed's office. As she approached, she could hear Sheriff Taylor's voice inside.

Ella stopped by the open door, knocked, then stepped into the office. "I'm here, Chief." She nodded to Sheriff Paul Taylor, whom she'd known and worked with off and on for years.

"We've got a problem," Big Ed said, and slid a copy of the Farmington daily paper toward her from across his desk. The headline was clear: "Snake-eyes Killer Baffles Police."

"Snake-eyes killer? That throwaway line came from one of the county techs," Ella said. "The dice is another matter altogether and had nothing to do with the killings. That was part of a police report, and no specifics about what was found at or around the scene were given out to the press."

"That's not all they know," Sheriff Taylor said through a clenched jaw. "The article also mentions that all the vics at the Hogback site were Navajos killed execution style—two shots to the back of the head. This added credibility to the dice found at the scene—according to the reporter."

"None of that information was supposed to be released," Ella said, "not the dice, nor the number of wounds. We met as a group at the site and instructions were clear to everyone present."

"The reporter, Don Cardwell, only cites an 'unnamed source,'" Taylor said. "But other news services have picked up the story, too, so now it's on the AP, Reuters, and even the Internet."

"The story also hints that Romero and Bowman may be responsible and are in this area," Big Ed added.

"Our job just got a lot tougher," Ella said.

Big Ed looked at Taylor. "I will personally vouch for my people. The leak didn't come from this department. In a later report I filed here, I clarified where the dice had come from—the Bitsillie boy, not the killer."

"Cardwell quotes this unnamed source as saying that the police are keeping the details of the case under wraps to the detriment of public safety." Taylor cracked his knuckles. "The source insists he's acting solely on the public's behalf. That strikes me as coming from a politician wannabe."

"You've got someone in mind, don't you?" Ella observed.

"Yeah, an individual in our department who's already posturing to run in the next election cycle. Unfortunately, I've got no way of proving it," Taylor said. "Putting pressure on Cardwell, the reporter, won't work either, I've met the guy. If anyone tried to get the name of his source, *that* would be the focus of his next article."

"If we don't plug this leak it could compromise the entire investigation," Ella said.

"We know," Big Ed said. "That's why we spoke to Agent Blalock. He's agreed that we should alter our normal procedures. Neither you nor Nez will submit any written reports to us until the case is closed. The ones your team members file will go directly to you two, with a cc to Blalock. If the higher-ups scream, Blalock says he'll threaten to use his Bureau jurisdiction and split the case up, leaving county twisting in the wind with no cooperation whatsoever."

"Sounds like the old FB-Eyes is back. I'll get my team together for a briefing. Does Detective Nez already know about this?" Ella asked.

"He does, and he should be arriving to talk to you at any moment," Sheriff Taylor said, glancing down at his watch.

When Ella returned to her office, she saw Dan standing at the far end by the window facing the mesa. He turned around as she walked in. "Before you ask, I don't know who the leak is. If he or she is part of county's on-site team, rest assured that person's days in the department are numbered. But I have a question for you. How sure are you of the people on *your* team?"

"I've worked with them for a long time and I'll go to the wall to back them up," Ella said, reminding him about the dice. "That leak didn't come from the tribal P.D. Everything we release to the press goes through Chief Atcitty first."

He nodded slowly. "For what it's worth, I tend to think that the leak's on my side, too, but I haven't been with the department long enough to know who can't be trusted. Time will tell. In the meantime, what's your plan?"

"Let's wait until my people are here, Dan, then we'll go through it."

The rest of her team soon came into her office, and Ella asked everyone to pull up a chair. First, she briefed them on what had happened, including the fact that the bullet used to take out the SUV tire was a reload, then updated them on their new orders regarding the leak to the press. "We're on our own, people, but the press will be dogging our footsteps. Watch what you say, text, or e-mail, and don't discuss anything pertaining to this case over our radio network."

She paused as she looked around the room. "Now let's move on. Where do we stand right now?"

"At the time our tire was shot out, Ross Harrison was in civil court," Justine said. "His employee, Bruce Talbot, works for him part-time only. He has a clean record and, unlike Harrison, doesn't have a concealed-carry permit, although he does own several weapons, including a Glock nine-millimeter. Talbot hunts deer and ducks in season, and belongs to a gun club. Talbot appears to be just a leg man. Logically, he would have been on route to Farmington when the shooting went down, but I can't confirm that. He has no alibi."

"Nothing seems to add up right here," Ella said. "The only suspects we have, Romero and Bowman, are in-your-face gunmen who act and react on impulse. They're not snipers."

"Then let's focus on our victims," Dan said. "We now know that two of the four were killed on the same month, years apart. We may, or may not, have Ignacio Candelaria to take into account, too, though he wasn't killed on the Rez."

"The M.O. on that murder is too different. From a standpoint of logic alone, I'd say Candelaria's death is unrelated to our case," Ella said.

"Not necessarily. Candelaria was shot twice, in or near the head, and June—killing season for our suspect—is only days away. Those details fit in," Dan said.

"But everything else is off," Ella said. "The four victims were killed, literally, in their Hogback graves. They may have even been forced to dig them."

Benny spoke next. "Anything new from the Bitsillie family? Has the boy remembered anything else about the guy in the white car?"

Ella looked over at Dan.

"We're sharing officers with Farmington P.D. and trading off watching the family, but I haven't heard about any new revelations," Dan said, then looked back at Ella.

She shook her head. "Me neither. I think the shooter was initially worried that the boy had seen his license plate. Once we didn't show up at his door, he knew he was safe and that he'd overreacted. I doubt the Bitsillies have anything else to worry about—but keep providing the protection for now."

"Will do," Dan said. "County will also continue following up on the Candelaria shooting. All we know so far is that the victim was legally drunk at the time of his death—that's according to the tox screen from the lab."

"Anything new on Romero and Bowman?" Ella asked, glancing around.

"Arizona highway patrol reported a white pickup stolen from a campground near the Grand Canyon by two Navajo men about three days ago," Justine said. "The description was too generic to be of any help."

"A man fitting Romero's description was seen buying gas for a white Ford pickup at a Farmington station just this morning," Nez said. "Our off-duty officer started to tail him but lost the suspect when he got cut off by a carload of drunk teens. There's an ATL out on the pickup's driver and the vehicle."

"Unfortunately, we're no closer to finding a motive for the murders over at Hogback. There's got to be some commonality between these victims, people," Ella said, looking around the room.

"Johnson and Kelewood went to the same high school for two years," Neskahi said. "It's possible they were friends back then, and very likely that they knew each other. That's the only connection I've been able to find between them."

"That would make it random," Benny answered with a nod.

"Keep digging. Run down former classmates, teachers, and neighbors at the time," Ella said.

"What about road rage, as with Romero and his pal, only someone else completely?" Joe asked. "From what we know so far, the victim's vehicles were moved. If they were driving home or to some other Rez destination and cut some sicko off, maybe somebody who'd just been in an accident, he might have retaliated. And after the first incident, he went looking for trouble, deciding to make examples of poor drivers. There are plenty of them in New Mexico, that's for sure."

"He chose the Rez for his victims because there are a lot

fewer cops around, maybe?" Benny added. "And it's not about money or killing for their cars. It's personal, in a disturbed way."

"Serial killers have had stranger motives. Let's keep it in mind, anyway, guys. Moving on—has anyone here heard of anything shady going on at Stepson, Inc.?" she said, then explained what she'd learned about Chester Kelewood.

"They have an office in Farmington and another here in town, up on the mesa among the tribal offices," Justine said.

"I say we tackle this from both sides of the line and see if we get some answers," Dan said.

"I like your approach. Let's do it," Ella said. "Justine, you're with me. The rest of you, continue with the interviews. We need to ID the other two vics."

EIGHTEEN

————— ✗ ✗ ✗ —————

Justine slipped behind the wheel as Ella fastened her seat belt. "Stepson's offices are right across the street from Kevin's. The tribe must have rented them some space," she said.

As Justine drove, Ella logged into her office computer remotely.

"What are you looking for?"

"Kelewood was investigating safety issues at the mine on behalf of the state of New Mexico, but our tribe has its own systems in place, too. You can bet someone here was also looking into the problem. I want to know who that was."

"Those kinds of investigations always have political undertones. It's even more so when there's reason to believe safety regulations are being compromised and there might be a cover-up. Why don't you check with the special investigator to the tribal president?"

"Logan Bitterwater," Ella said with a nod. "I remember when the president first hired him as an executive bodyguard. It was after that mob scene outside the council chambers a few years ago. He saved the president's life, if you can believe the stories."

"Bitterwater was at the right place at the right time all the way down the line. After the tribal casinos started operations, there was a lot of flak about possible law enforcement corruption with all the money that was floating around. So all of a sudden our president created a new position for his favorite warrior—executive special investigator," Justine said. "Nice work if you can get it."

"What still bugs me is that Bitterwater has no law enforcement training whatsoever."

"Loyalty's good, but I think the president's gratitude went a little too far. I hear Bitterwater pulls down close to six figures," Justine said.

"That really pissed off Big Ed. He wanted to see the job go to someone from the tribal police—or at least a Navajo with a law enforcement background. Near as I can figure, Bitterwater has never taken part in any investigation—before or since."

"That we know about," Justine said.

"Either way, he's kept his post, so he must be doing something right," Ella said. "Let's go talk to Joe Preston, the local head of Stepson, Inc., then we can track down Bitterwater."

On the way, Ella typed Bitterwater's name into the tribe's database, and searched under "executive special investigator," but nothing came up. "He's not listed. Maybe he's already out of a job."

"Try the tribal president's staff."

"Nothing," Ella replied after a moment. "I've never heard of any tribal employee this far below the radar. Maybe the position was cut during the latest belt-tightening."

"Or maybe he's meant to stay under wraps," Justine replied, then after a long silence, added, "Try using the key words 'special category president's staff.' "

The screen changed and Ella saw Logan Bitterwater's name listed along with his title, but there was no telephone number or address there. "Interesting. I guess we'll have to go through the office of the president to contact him. His job sounds more like a political payoff than anything else. He probably sits behind a desk drinking lattes all day long."

"Jealous?"

Ella laughed. "You bet. You know what the coffee's like at the station."

They topped the slope leading up the mesa on Shiprock's north side. Ahead at the stoplight they could see what appeared to be an accident. Several cars were logjammed around it. Justine switched on the emergency lights and siren and they drove past the line of vehicles by using the shoulder of the road.

As they drew closer, Ella spotted a subcompact car on its side, pinned to the road by the front end of a large pickup.

"Stop. I think someone's trapped inside the car. See those men? They're pulling away the windshield," Ella said. "Call it in."

As she jumped out, Ella smelled gasoline and saw liquid on the asphalt. She glanced at Justine.

"Clear as many vehicles as you can from the intersection," she said as Justine racked the mike. "If something sparks that gas, we're all toast."

Ella grabbed their vehicle's fire extinguisher from underneath the dashboard and headed to the accident. "Get back," she yelled at the excited onlookers as she ran up.

One man remained by the overturned car, pulling windshield glass away despite the cuts on his hands. "The driver's trapped inside," he said as she came up.

Ella took a closer look at the crushed car. Both doors were inaccessible—one was pinned against the highway, and the other beneath the big wheels of the truck. "Where's the pickup's driver?"

"Right here," the man with the cut hands replied, not

looking away from his work. "I tried to back up and get the truck off the car, but I can't get it into reverse. My transmission locked up."

Hearing the sound of a really big engine approaching the scene, Ella turned her head. A man in a blue western-cut suit was driving a yellow backhoe right toward them. Across the road, she could see an empty tractor trailer parked beside a mound of gravel at a construction site.

"Good thinking!" Ella yelled at the guy in the suit, then turned to two onlookers who'd slipped past Justine. "Help the officer and keep everyone away. The backhoe will need more room to work."

Ella ran over to meet the impromptu backhoe operator, who'd stopped several feet from the car, engine idling. She held up her badge. "Police officer. This your machine?"

"No. I couldn't find the operator, but I can handle this baby. I paid my way through college working construction," the man yelled back.

"Are you thinking of using this to pull the pickup off the car? If so, we're going to need that," she said, pointing to the cable and hook wrapped around a bracket on the side of the backhoe.

The Navajo man looked down at her, still shouting to be heard over the roar of the backhoe. "No towing. Too much gasoline's spilled. Yanking the pickup off the car might create sparks. Maybe I can lift it up just enough to free the driver."

"You could still get sparks if there's any slippage," Ella yelled back.

He looked back over at the construction site. "Maybe we can insulate the scoop with that tarp." He pointed.

"I'll get it." Ella raced over to the trailer, which had been used to transport the backhoe to the off-road site. The big cloth was made of rubber or vinyl-coated canvas and weighed a lot more than she'd expected. She picked it up, then raced back as fast as she could manage carrying an extra fifty pounds.

With the help of the pickup driver, Ella unfolded the big cover and placed it, three and four layers thick, over the scoop at the front of the backhoe.

Standing close, her boots in gasoline now, Ella directed the man at the backhoe controls, motioning and pointing as he placed the big scoop just below the pickup's front axle.

The backhoe drooped in front as it took on the load, but the volunteer operator manipulated the controls and extended the digging arm at the rear, shifting back the center of gravity. The tactic worked. With a creak, the scoop began to raise the front end of the pickup a few inches at a time. Once it cleared the car by about a foot, the man stopped the motion and held everything in place.

Ella reached in through what was left of the windshield and pulled away the deflated air bag, freeing the obstruction so the pickup driver could reach the victim. With Ella directing, the driver grasped the injured woman below the arms. Then he lifted her up and out as Ella steered her hips and legs through the mass of jagged glass and metal. The woman was unconscious, but Ella could see she was breathing—a good sign.

As they moved her away from the wreckage, Ella heard the creak of straining metal and looked back at the man working the controls of the backhoe.

"Hurry," he yelled.

Once the woman was taken to dry ground and placed on a blanket, Ella hurried back to the wreck.

"Okay, ease it back down," she called out to the man on the backhoe. In the distance, she could hear horn blasts and sirens.

The Navajo man in the suit eased the pickup down again, backed the machine a hundred feet off the highway, then turned off the engine. As he jumped down, a fire truck pulled up beside the construction vehicle. Within seconds, firemen were emptying bags of ground corncob sorbent on the gasoline, soaking it up and stopping the flow.

Ella walked over to the accident victim but, by then, paramedics were busy working on her. A police cruiser soon pulled up and Ella, greeting the officer, turned the scene over to him.

As she joined Justine at the SUV, Ella looked around for the man who'd driven the backhoe, intending to thank him, but he was nowhere in sight.

"The patrol officer can take care of things here. Let's go pay the Stepson office a visit," Ella said.

Ten minutes later, after being forced to take a circular route to get around the clogged intersection, Ella and Justine walked into the offices of Stepson, Inc. "I'm looking for Joe Preston," Ella said, showing her badge to the young, attractive, Navajo receptionist behind the desk.

"Mr. Preston's in a meeting right now, Investigator Clah. Would you like to wait? He should be available soon," she said, motioning toward several chairs across the room.

"Thanks," Ella said, she and Justine choosing seats where they could watch the front entrance and still see the closed office door behind the assistant's desk. Years ago, while an FBI agent, Ella had picked up the habit of never having her back to a door, and Justine had quickly followed suit.

A few minutes later, the same Navajo man who'd operated the backhoe came out of the office, followed by a tall Anglo man wearing a tan shirt and a gaudy turquoise and silver tie.

"If there's a problem with what you've told me, I'll be back here tomorrow morning first thing."

"There won't be," the Anglo answered.

Seeing Ella, the Navajo man gave her a nod, then walked out before she could speak. There was no time to go after him, but before she left here today, someone would tell her who he was. He deserved an official thanks from the department.

The Anglo man exchanged a few quick words with his assistant, then turned to Ella. "Investigator Clah, I'm Joe Preston," he greeted, not offering to shake hands. "Must be my day to be investigated."

"Say again?"

"First, Investigator Bitterwater, now two tribal police officers."

Ella forced herself not to react. She had a lot of questions for Bitterwater once they officially met, including his reason for being here—today.

Focusing on the present, Ella introduced Justine, then said, "We're investigating the death of a state mine inspector, Chester Kelewood."

"Let's go into my office and we can talk there," Preston said, nodding to Justine.

Once they were inside the cool, spacious office, he closed the door behind them and walked to his desk. "Have a seat, officers. I'm afraid I know very little about Mr. Kelewood. All I can tell you is that he conducted periodic inspections of our equipment. I'd accompany him on those visits as a courtesy whenever I could. About a year ago, just before a scheduled inspection, he went missing."

"He's been found—murdered," Ella said.

"That's a shame. I'm sorry to hear it," he said. "How can I help you?"

"Tell me more about that safety problem Mr. Kelewood was investigating. I understood there was some controversy involved."

"It was a mistake, that's all. Mr. Kelewood got the idea from badly worded maintenance paperwork that some of our ore haulers and draglines didn't meet the minimum safety requirements. He was supposed to come back with his crew to check further, but he never showed up. The state then sent in another inspector and team and they confirmed that all of our vehicles and equipment met or exceeded industry standards."

"Yes, but there was a delay of more than a week before that second inspection. Some say that delay gave Stepson time to correct the problems and avoid a monumental fine," Ella said, watching his reaction.

"If you're suggesting that we had something to do with that man's death, you're way off base. Should I call our attorneys?"

"No need, Mr. Preston. It's a question that needed to be raised, and you've answered it," Ella said. "Did Mr. Kelewood have any enemies that you know about, maybe a Stepson employee who felt threatened by the inspections?"

"I can't think of anyone in particular. Our employees support what the safety inspectors do. Their lives are on the line every day and they want to feel safe."

Ella and Justine left the office, then walked down the long sidewalk toward the street-side parking lot. "We need to talk to Bitterwater. I want to know who or what he's investigating, and if it's connected to Kelewood."

"He must have an office somewhere. So how do we find him?" Justine said, thinking out loud.

"You might try looking behind you," a man answered. "I was wondering if I'd be seeing you again, soon. Investigator Clah, isn't it? Do you want to talk out here, or do you prefer someplace away from Stepson's people?"

Ella turned around, surprised by how quietly Bitterwater had moved. "Away from here would be better. Do you have a suggestion, Investigator?"

"How about the Totah Café, officers? I'm hungry."

"We'll follow you there," Ella said.

The Totah, down in the valley beside the main highway, was less than five minutes from their location. On the way,

Ella called Big Ed and gave him the morning's highlights. "Is there anything you can tell me about Logan Bitterwater?"

"I tried to look him up at one time, but his records, at the request of the tribal president, are sealed. So I did things the old way—asking around. I found out that he's from the Arizona side of the Rez. He's a New Traditionalist, and served in the Army but his work there was classified. In the tribal president's office he's known as *Naalzheehí*, The Hunter."

They arrived at the Totah Café shortly afterwards. It was a bit past one and the decades-old restaurant—the most popular sit-down eatery in the community—was bustling with activity.

As they walked inside Justine slowed down and spoke into Ella's ear. "You might get more from him one to one. I can have lunch at the counter."

Ella considered it, then nodded.

Logan, already inside, stood as Ella approached the small table he'd chosen, well in the back and by the kitchen.

"There's room for your partner," Logan said, gesturing to the third chair.

"Officer Goodluck has a friend working behind the counter," Ella said, telling the truth but avoiding the issue. "I'm Ella Clah, as you've already guessed. Do you know why I wanted to talk to you?"

"I assume you're investigating Kelewood's murder."

Ella noted that he knew the ID had been made. "You've accessed our files?"

"The nature of my job gives me the necessary clearance."

"So I assume you're looking into his death, too?"

As the waitress came over, they turned their attention to their menus. Ella ordered a stuffed sopaipilla, her favorite fare here. He ordered their Wild West burger, a new addition with enough hot green chile to melt an iceberg.

Once the waitress left, he leaned back and answered.

"The murder is police business. I'm interested in Stepson's operations. I want to make sure they're not cutting corners and endangering lives."

"Is there anything you can tell me? I'd be particularly interested in anything that might tie in with Kelewood's murder."

"I can't tell you if Kelewood's disappearance is linked to Stepson or not. I've just started my investigation. Rumors that the company's cutting corners have persisted, and with word of Kelewood's murder reaching my boss's desk, I've been ordered to find out if there's any truth to the stories."

Ella realized that the tribal president was trying to protect his own political career as well as the tribe's reputation. "Have you heard anything that might suggest Stepson tried to pay off Kelewood or pressure him into calling off or delaying his inspection?"

"Not a thing, but as I said, I've just begun, and have only read a few files so far. But if that turns out to be the case, I'd put my money on Preston. His head would have been the first one on the chopping block at corporate."

"If you come up with anything, will you let us know?"

He remained quiet for a beat. "I'm not a cop, nor do I work in a way the department would necessarily sanction," he said at last. "My job is to get answers for the tribal president, particularly in matters that threaten our tribe. Before I can share information with anyone outside his office, I'll need his permission."

"All right, but let me know either way."

"You got it."

Ella had just taken her last bite when Justine hurried over. "We just got a ten–twenty-nine call. Time to roll."

Ella reached for her wallet, but Bitterwater shook his head. "Go, you can get it next time."

"Thanks."

Ella hurried out with Justine, wondering which fugitive had been spotted. "Who's the suspect?"

"One of Emily Marquez's informants reported seeing someone they believe to be Gilbert Romero over at the C.O. Jones bar and grill in Kirtland."

The mention of the name of the bar made Ella's stomach sink—she'd had a bad experience there—but before she could reply, Emily contacted them on the State car-to-car channel. "It's Romero, all right. I just got a cell phone photo from my informant. Romero and Bowman were leaving the place at the time. They're now heading south toward the old highway. They're in a dirty white Ford pickup with New Mexico plates."

"Ten-four. We've got it on this end," Ella said, ending the call. "That white Ford matches earlier reports."

Switching frequencies, she coordinated other units to cover the secondary roads leading in and out of Shiprock.

Justine gave Ella a mirthless half smile. "We've got them now."

Ella said nothing. She'd learned the hard way never to count on anything. There were few sure things in police work.

NINETEEN
✖ ✖ ✖

There were two paved roads leading into Shiprock, but the southern route was round-about and less traveled and could be covered by the same unit watching the Gallup highway. All things considered, the road Justine and she were on seemed the more likely choice.

"We've got two options," Justine said. "We can pull over by the westbound lane and pick up Bowman and Romero as they pass, or stay eastbound and wait for them to approach from that direction."

"Continue east," Ella said.

As they kept watch, Ella quickly briefed Justine on the conversation with Bitterwater. They both agreed that the man's loyalty to the tribal president might get in the way of any help he could provide. On the plus side, Bitterwater had access where they didn't, and he represented an extra set of eyes out there that might stumble across the killer's identity. Hopefully, he would share.

Soon a white Ford pickup passed them, its only visible occupant, the driver. It was followed only a few seconds later by a cream-colored truck, also a Ford, with at least two people in the cab.

Justine slowed, approaching the next pass-over on the median. "Which one do we target, the first truck or the second?" she asked.

Ella quickly contacted Sergeant Marquez. "Are you sure the pickup was white and not cream?"

"It was white—an older-model Ford with a damaged tailgate. It has to be on Navajo land by now."

"Ten-four." Ella glanced at Justine. "It's the first truck. Catch up to him. They must have been watching for patrol units and the passenger ducked down as they went past us."

"Should I go silent?" Justine asked, crossing the median and taking advantage of a gap in traffic to enter into the flow quickly.

"Yeah. We don't want to force a high-speed chase through Shiprock if we can help it."

Justine accelerated, and, as they passed the cream pickup, Ella got a closer look at the driver, a woman in her sixties. Two younger women were beside her, probably a daughter and granddaughter, based on their looks.

Ella strained to get a clearer look at the white pickup ahead. The road leading into Shiprock curved back toward the southwest and tall poplars just a few feet off the shoulder partially blocked her view.

Justine slowed down to thirty miles per hour as they entered the small town. "They're not ahead of us anymore," she said, looking down the virtually straight highway. "Maybe they turned off."

Ella studied their surroundings with a careful, practiced eye as they passed the post office and a few small businesses.

"There, to your left," Ella said.

Justine slowed again to twenty-five miles per hour and cruised past a side street that lay between an old forties-era wooden home and a cinder-block grocery store. While passing through the intersection they spotted the white pickup moving down the road perpendicular to them.

Justine waited for a break in traffic, did a one-eighty turn, then headed down Chamisa Lane. The white Ford with the crumpled tailgate was now parked at the curb next to an old welded-pipe corral. Two heads were clearly visible in the cab through the rear window.

Justine was already calling for backup as Ella reached for her pistol.

"Let's take them down, Justine."

Justine slowed the SUV and hit the siren.

Almost instantly the passenger reached out, pistol in his left hand, and aimed straight at them.

"Gun!" Justine yelled, whipping the wheel to the left just as the man fired.

Ella heard the bullet thud somewhere behind her as she was thrown to the side by the violent maneuver. A cloud of dust and flying gravel struck the front of their vehicle as the pickup's driver suddenly hit the gas.

"Get around and cut him off." Ella was reluctant to return fire here. There were homes all around them. The only thing she could do was try to take out a tire, but she needed a clear sight picture to do that.

Ella held on to the door with her left hand, aimed with her right, and fired just as the pickup jinked to the left. Dust kicked up just to the right of the tire she'd aimed at.

When the pickup faked left then cut right at the next intersection, Ella brought her weapon back inside. There were single- and double-wide trailers on both sides of the road and their walls were paper thin. She couldn't risk a shot.

Justine pulled up almost even with the rear bumper of the pickup, cutting off the shooter's angle. The pickup's driver instantly swerved left, then right, fishtailing all over the road.

Ella cringed as the left end of the tailgate slammed into

the fender of their SUV. There was a thud, and their vehicle shook, but Justine stayed in control. She touched the brake, kept the SUV in line, and backed off a few feet.

The pickup's driver faked a right turn, then cut to the left at the next intersection, racing down a narrow, unpaved street lined with more mobile homes. An alarmed woman looked up from her clothesline a few seconds before a cloud of dust engulfed her.

Nearly a half block ahead now, the pickup suddenly slid to a stop. The passenger jumped out and fired a wild shot in their direction as he took off down the street, leaping over a low fence.

"I'll take the runner," Ella said, jumping out while the SUV was still skidding to a stop. Using the extra motion, she exploded forward at nearly sprint speed.

As Justine raced off after the pickup, Ella ran down the street, watching her right flank and looking into the residential yards for a potential ambush.

There was a long, high fence about a hundred feet beyond the row of mobile homes. Ella figured the passenger had made his way over there and was running parallel to her, out of sight, beyond the trailers.

A moment later her suspicions proved right. As she reached the next corner, the man raced out into the middle of the street. His eyes on her, he never saw the oncoming car.

"Look out!" she yelled.

Leaning on his horn, the driver swerved hard, but it was too late. The car struck the man with a sickening thud, scooping him into the air and across the hood.

Ella had to keep running or get hit herself as the car spun sideways, throwing gravel everywhere. Once across the road, she stopped and looked back.

People rushed outside to see what had happened. The thick dust was now beginning to settle, and the results of the collision were there for all to see. An old Navajo woman was standing on the front steps of her trailer, not fifty feet from the street, her hands over her mouth as if stifling a scream.

Trying to get her own breathing under control so she could speak clearly, Ella reached for her cell phone and hurried toward the body. On the way, she picked up the .45 Colt autoloader the fugitive had lost, careful to handle the weapon only by the trigger guard and slipped it into her pocket.

A moment later she reached the body. It was nothing more than a bloody heap of flesh lying next to the post of a mailbox. Ella nearly gagged, barely recognizing Bowman.

Ella swallowed hard as she knelt beside Bowman, speaking softly to him. "The EMTs will be here soon. Hold on."

"Tell . . . family . . . never killed anyone. It was . . . Romero," he said, then began choking on his own blood.

"*Who* did Romero kill?" she asked quickly, but even as he looked at her, his eyes went blank, then faded.

Ella glanced over at the elderly Navajo driver whose sedan had struck Bowman. He sat frozen behind the wheel of his car. As she hurried over to speak to him, she noticed that he looked familiar, but she couldn't place him.

"Sir, are you all right?" she asked, but got no response. The man continued to stare blankly ahead. He was in shock.

"Sir, this wasn't your fault. There are plenty of witnesses, including me, who can testify to that," she said gently, noting the death grip he had on the steering wheel.

The paramedics arrived, and soon after that pronounced Bowman dead. As they covered the body, the elderly driver looked at her, his eyes clouding with pain. Gasping, he suddenly leaned forward, clutching his chest.

"I need help here. This man is having a heart attack," Ella yelled.

The EMTs ran over. Brushing her aside, they removed him from the car and worked to stabilize him.

Several minutes later as the EMTs lifted the stretcher off

the ground, ready to transport, the man motioned to Ella. She came over and kept pace with the paramedics as they hurried to the awaiting ambulance.

"You're the sister of the *hataalii*?" Seeing her nod, he continued in a weakened voice. "Need Enemy Way. Tell him *'Atsidii* needs him."

Ella knew that the nickname. It meant "Smithy" and she suddenly realized why he'd seemed so familiar. Although he didn't shoe her horses, his son did. Smithy was her brother Clifford's farrier and a well-known Traditionalist. The poor man was undoubtedly afraid of Bowman's *chindi*.

Ella called Clifford and quickly told him what had happened.

"I'll get my things ready. An Enemy Way takes several days and a lot of preparation, but a short purification rite will put his mind at ease for now."

"The accident wasn't his fault, but I'm not sure he realizes that."

"I'll get a medicine bag ready and speak to him as soon as possible. Tell him I'll meet him at the hospital."

Ella had just told the man that Clifford was on his way when Justine drove up in the department SUV. From what Ella could see, her partner had no prisoner, so Romero must have eluded her.

"I heard the call. You okay?" Justine asked, giving her a quick once-over.

"Yeah, but Bowman was killed when he ran out in front of that car," Ella said, gesturing toward the scene. "The driver who hit him probably suffered a heart attack. What happened with Romero?"

"I was closing in, but he went through a red light and got away. Two trucks nearly collided trying to avoid hitting him, and ended up blocking both lanes. By the time I was able to get through, I'd lost sight of him. I put a BOLO out on his pickup. All four major roads leading out of town will be covered."

"Good," she said, then filled Justine in on the rest of her situation.

As she finished speaking, one of the EMTs came over. "We're transporting now. A second unit will come for the body."

"We'll stay here until they do," Ella said.

"Should I call off backup and get the crime scene team here?" Justine asked her as the EMT moved away.

"Yeah. There won't be much evidence, but shots were fired, and we'll want to follow up on that," Ella said. "We'll also need photos of the truck's tire imprints and statements from witnesses."

They spent the next two and a half hours at the scene. As temperatures rose into the low nineties, Ella was reminded of what lay ahead in July and August, notoriously the hottest months. No matter how rough working in the sun was now, it would be far worse then. Consoling herself with that thought, she finished talking to the last of the witnesses, then went to meet Justine by the SUV.

"No bullets fired into the neighborhood could be traced, but Neskahi found a pistol round wedged in the plastic interior door panel of our SUV. It entered at an extreme angle and never made it completely through. I'm sure it'll be a ballistic match to the forty-five Bowman had on him," Justine said, pointing out the hole in their rear passenger door.

"Remember to write up a report while it's still fresh in your mind, but don't file it. Until we can figure out who is leaking our reports to the press, and how much access he's got to our system, we need to cover our butts."

"I hear you," Justine said somberly. "But what about Dan Nez? Should I update him verbally?"

"I'll do that right now."

Ella made the call, but Dan was the first to speak. "I just heard from our dispatch that you had an encounter with Romero and Bowman, and that the latter is now deceased. Did you get anything from him?"

"Not much," she said, repeating the very short exchange she'd had with Bowman regarding his partner.

"Bowman's forty-five doesn't match the snake-eye killer's weapon of choice. He used a nine-millimeter. So maybe Bowman told you the truth. What we really need to know now is what Romero's packing," Dan said.

"To get answers we need to catch Romero."

"I'm involved in the search for him off the Rez," he said. "We've got every available unit on the lookout, and FPD has active patrols inside the city limits. Blalock's here, too, coordinating all the interagency efforts."

Back at the station sometime later, Ella went directly to her office and shut the door. A lot had happened in the past few hours and she needed a few moments alone to process everything.

Ella filled out a report, hoping to organize her thoughts. She wouldn't be filing it, but the process of getting things down sometimes helped her see details she'd overlooked. She took her time sorting through the information, but nothing new came to her.

At long last, Ella sat back, rubbing her temples. Lately it felt as if she were being pulled in all directions at once. She still hadn't figured out exactly what to do about Dawn; Rose wouldn't discuss what was bothering her; and here at work, the pressure to find answers was constant. The anniversary of the Kelewood and Johnson murders was coming up and the snake-eyes killer could strike again very soon.

She took a deep breath, forcing herself to take things one step at a time. She'd just started to type again when she heard a knock at her door. Annoyed, she blew her breath out in a hiss. "Come in, dammit."

To her surprise, her brother Clifford walked inside. Although his movements were fluid, she could tell from the way he held himself that something was wrong.

"Sorry about my reaction, Brother. Did the patient get your help?"

Clifford nodded, then adjusted the medicine pouch on his belt as he sat down. "I bring news."

She noticed the absence of the words good or bad and braced herself. That meant whatever he had to say was open to interpretation.

"I had a visit earlier today from the leaders of the Fierce Ones."

Ella's muscles tightened. She and Justine had been meaning to pay the Fierce Ones a visit, but more pressing business had forced them to postpone a meeting.

"Who came to see you?" she asked, though she knew her brother hated using proper names.

"Their new leader, his right-hand man, and his cousin."

Without using names, Clifford had managed to give her the information she'd wanted. The new leader of the Fierce Ones was Delbert John. He was in his mid-thirties and worked construction. The membership had ousted their former leader, a man in his late fifties, and Delbert had ushered in a new, more militant stance. With members eager to assert their power, the group often acted as judge and jury. Many in the tribe were afraid to speak out against them, fearing retaliation.

Delbert's right-hand man was Peter Joe, a fireplug of a man barely five feet tall, with a brawler's reputation. Peter's cousin, Robert Largo, was quiet, at least on the outside, and his eyes never revealed anything. To date, Ella hadn't been able to figure out if his brain was as vacant as the look he gave everyone, or if his poker face was by design.

"What did they want from you?" she asked.

"They asked me to arrange a meeting with you."

"Tell them to come to the station," Ella said.

"I realize that this is a power play of sorts. They're pushing to see if you'll meet them on their own turf. Normally I'd advise you to ignore a request like that, but this feels different to me."

"How so?"

"They've heard all about the snake-eyes killer and have decided to help protect the tribe—in their usual, heavy-handed way, of course. They've started advising Navajos—me included—to carry firearms whenever they're out on the road."

"Crap. Too many people around here already carry guns in their cars or trucks. If everyone is expecting the worst from the driver next to them, that could turn our highways into war zones, road rage times two."

"Maybe you can redirect their . . . enthusiasm . . . by enlisting their help. Have them keep their eyes and ears open but convince them to report to you. Remind them what happened in the past when they used intimidation to assert control."

"The *Diné* eventually stood up to them," Ella said, nodding. "But I have to run this past Big Ed. He would need to okay a meeting of this kind."

When Clifford remained seated, Ella studied his face. "There's more, isn't there?"

"They already know I'm here. I saw their truck parked about a quarter of a mile away at the gas station. They're probably waiting for me to leave. They'll want to know what your answer was. I'll have to make sure they catch up to me long before I turn off the highway and head home. I don't want them anywhere near my family."

"I agree, so let me go talk to Big Ed and see what he says." Ella called Big Ed's office and got his secretary, who informed her that he was in a meeting.

"We'll have to wait a little longer," Ella told Clifford.

"No problem," he said, sitting back.

"Have you spoken to Mom lately?" Ella asked.

He nodded. "Something's bothering her, but whatever it is, she's not ready to talk to me about it."

"We're in the same boat. I really want to help her, but I don't know how."

"You know Mom. Give her some time," Clifford said. "When you pressure her, she pulls away even more."

Ella started to answer when Big Ed appeared at her door. "My secretary said you were looking for me. What's going on, Shorty?"

Big Ed nodded to Clifford, then came in and took a seat. Ella laid out what Clifford had told her about the Fierce Ones.

Big Ed considered it for a long while. "Dictate the terms—time and place," he said at last. "Choose open country so you'll know exactly who's there. Also take backup, but not Justine. She was forced to shoot one of the Fierce Ones a few years ago, and her presence might heighten tensions. Take Sergeant Neskahi and make sure you're both wearing vests."

"Copy." Ella looked at her brother. "Can you suggest a meeting place?"

"How about one of the oil company's service roads northeast of Beclabito? I know of one spot that's pretty flat. I think there used to be a big stock pond there at one time."

"The place Mom likes to go pick herbs for her tea," she said with a nod. "That's a good idea. Let's set it up for two hours from now. That'll give me time to round up the sergeant. Now to the more immediate problem. How are you going to make sure they contact you while you're well away from your house?"

"If they're still where I saw them last, I'll pull over to the shoulder of the road and walk right up to them."

"Want me to get someone to cover you?" Ella said.

"No, it's a public place and they're not interested in trouble. Pulling something now would be counterintuitive."

As Clifford walked out, Big Ed looked at Ella. "What's the latest on Bowman's partner, Gilbert Romero?"

"No news. He's either on the run or gone to ground."

"Off the record, what's your take on what Bowman told you, Shorty?"

"My gut tells me that they're not the snake-eyes killer, Chief. But Romero's one dangerous Navajo and he's still out there—armed. We need to find him."

"Get it done."

TWENTY

——— ✖ ✖ ✖ ———

Ella and Neskahi parked at the end of the oil company's service road, then climbed out of the tribal SUV. The rhythmic mechanical swoosh of the massive pump stood in stark contrast to the dry grasses and juniper covered hills northeast of Beclabito.

The closest dwelling was at least a mile south, closer to Highway 64 and nearly hidden by the terrain. Ella turned to Neskahi, who was checking his shotgun, and adjusted her highly visible vest. Her handgun was holstered at her side within easy reach. They weren't looking for trouble, but if it came, they'd meet it head-on.

"There's the sheep trail," Joe said, pointing to the dirt track leading up a shallow arroyo.

"They're supposed to meet us there just around a bend in the arroyo. You ready?"

Joe nodded. "Want me to take point?"

"No. They expect to see me first so let's play it out. But let's go along the top instead of walking through the arroyo. You take the right flank, and I'll cover the left."

Ella walked along the top, checking the dry wash for anyone hiding below. She could see the imprints of small, pointed sheep and goat hooves. Judging from the color of the unearthed sand, now dried out and the same color as the surface, she guessed the flock had come through earlier today.

They continued along the arroyo, which deepened as they moved upslope. Reaching a fork in the wash, they saw three men standing below, one at the junction, and the other two several feet away, in opposite channels.

Ella braced for trouble, but Delbert John, who saw her first, didn't appear armed. Instead, he waved, then turned to nod at Joe, letting him know he'd been seen, too.

"Don't bother looking for weapons," he said as they approached. "This isn't a confrontation. We asked for a meet because we're both interested in keeping the *Diné* safe."

Ella nodded but didn't comment.

"But this meeting is intended to be private. No recording devices," he said, climbing out of the arroyo at a spot where the bank had caved in.

"As a gesture of good will, we'll turn them off," she said. Glancing at Neskahi, Ella nodded, and he switched off the mike attached to his uniform at the shoulder epaulet. Then she looked back at Delbert. "Don't make us regret it."

"If we'd wanted a fight, you would never have gotten this close." He waved at Peter and Robert, then Neskahi, to approach him and Ella.

Once they were all together in a loose circle not far from the arroyo, Delbert sat down on a flat rock. The others crouched down on their knees, except for Neskahi, who continued to stand, shotgun at quarter arms.

"We have a theory about the snake-eyes shooter," Delbert said, looking solely at Ella. "Our sources have said that you believe Romero and Bowman are the ones behind this, but you're wrong. Those two are more like rabid dogs—they strike without thought or reason. The snake-eyes killer stalks his victims like a mountain lion, using patience and planning."

Delbert's sources were wrong, which was actually good news. She and Detective Nez had pretty much ruled out the pair as the snake-eyes killer. She knew now that whoever had been in contact with the Fierce Ones *wasn't* in the inner circle of their investigation. Her team, and the county people working with Dan, had kept security.

Still, there might be information she could use. "Do you have any idea where Romero might be hiding right now?"

Delbert let his breath out in a hiss. "So it's true. The other one's dead?"

Ella nodded, knowing he'd find out soon enough on the news.

Delbert frowned. "The one that's left will be more dangerous than ever now. He'll want revenge for the loss of his friend and will be eager to force a confrontation."

"We'll bring him in," Ella said. "We've dealt with this before."

"Maybe so, but that will only solve one of your problems. You have no idea who the real snake-eyes killer is, or why he's striking out at the *Diné*. We'd like to help. I'm told he stalks people who've been drinking in bars. We can get some of our men to ride solo, make it look like they've had one too many, and draw them in. Then you can make the arrest."

"We can't have civilians taking on these kinds of risks, or operating outside the law. I repeat—this is *our* job. We'll handle it," Ella said.

Delbert stared at the ground, then after several moments looked back up. "Don't count on our cooperation. Things will get ugly in a hurry if any other member of our tribe is killed."

"It's possible that not all the victims were Navajo," Ella said. "One death happened outside our borders."

"You mean the Mexican national," Delbert said, proving that the Fierce Ones had a reliable source, at least at some level.

Ella shrugged.

Faced with her silence, Delbert finally continued. "That man wasn't killed the same way. It may not have anything to do with us. Either way, that's county's problem."

"In case you're interested, the detective leading that investigation is Navajo."

"You mean Nez?" Delbert spat out an oath. "He's worthless—an apple—red on the outside, white on the inside."

"Detective Nez's personal philosophy isn't an issue as far as I'm concerned," Ella said, recalling that she'd been painted with that same brush years ago when she returned to the Navajo Nation—as an FBI agent. "He's a good detective who won't stop until he gets answers. That's enough for me."

"So just to make sure we're on the same track. What you're telling me is that you'd rather join forces with Anglo agencies than accept our help?" He glared at her, then after a beat, shrugged. "Know that if we get to the killer first, the county will be spared the expense of a trial."

Ella had never reacted well to threats, and it was no different now. She took a half step toward him, then stopped. She couldn't let him get to her now. She'd lose control of the situation.

After a long pause, she finally answered. "If you really want to help the *Diné*, then contact me if you get a lead—a name, a witness, anything. Vigilante justice won't restore harmony."

"We can restore order more effectively than you can."

"No, evil doesn't neutralize evil. At best, it just allows one evil to defeat another."

"Weakness can never defeat strength."

"Refusing to become part of the evil you're fighting isn't weakness. Until you can understand that, you won't be able to help the *Diné*."

"We're done here," Delbert said, then signaled his men with a cock of his head. The trio walked away.

"For a while there, I was sure you were going to deck him," Joe said, crossing the arroyo to join her. "Rearrange-the-face-of-evil type of thing."

Ella chuckled softly. "I thought about it, believe me."

Joe and she were inside the tribal unit on the way back when Dan called her on the cell phone.

"We found Romero's white pickup about forty miles away from where you last saw him. It was abandoned in a parking lot in Aztec, where another vehicle was just reported stolen."

"Is Romero's truck in impound yet?"

"Just arrived. Our crime scene unit is processing it now. They've already found Romero's and Bowman's prints all over it—no surprise—but nothing that ties them to the murders in Hogback."

"What's Romero driving now?"

"A blue, heavy-duty Ford SUV."

"Did you put an ATL on it?"

"Yeah, and every agency in the Four Corners area will see the bulletin."

By the time they reached Shiprock again, the sun was setting. "Drop me off at my house," Ella told Neskahi. "And please pick me up tomorrow on your way to the station. Justine's got lab work so she'll probably be going in early."

"No problem," Neskahi said. "By the way, she's kind of annoyed that you chose me instead of her as your backup today," Joe said as he turned south onto Highway 491.

"I know, but it was the right call. And thanks for having my back out there. I noticed you bringing the shotgun to your shoulder when I got in Delbert's face."

Neskahi chuckled. "So did they."

After he dropped her off, Ella stood at the end of the driveway, watching the bright kitchen lights and hearing her family's voices coming from inside. No matter how crazy things got, her family kept her grounded. Each of them held a special place in her heart and helped her stay on track.

Ella walked up and as she reached for the screen door handle, Rose came out and gave Ella a hug. "I love the painting. Thank you, Daughter."

Happy to see Rose in such a good mood, Ella followed her inside. "It's good to see you smile again, Mom. We've been worried about you."

"I have some things I need to work out for myself, Daughter, but nothing's wrong."

Although it wasn't easy, Ella nodded and forced herself to respect her mother's privacy.

"I saw the name at the bottom corner of the painting," Rose said. "I didn't know FB-Eyes' wife was an artist. She must like to hike, too. The bearberry plant makes its home on the mountain slopes."

"She likes being outdoors, but I think she mentioned that this was actually growing in her backyard."

"Someone had to have dug it up, brought it down to the valley, and managed to keep it alive. Did you remember that particular plant? Is that why you brought the painting to me?"

"It caught my eye, but I'm not sure why," Ella said, following her to the living room.

"When you were young, our family would sometimes go up into the mountains and pick the leaves for your dad. Once dried, they could be mixed with store-bought tobacco and smoked. Your father would use that as a way of cutting back on expenses. Later, I discovered the leaves had medicinal uses, too. Bearberry could be used as a disinfectant, and also to reduce inflammation."

Rose led Ella into the short hallway that linked the recent edition to the kitchen and showed her where she'd hung the painting. "Every time I pass by it'll bring back happy memories," Rose said.

"I think FB-Eyes' wife would love to know more about the plants she's been painting. You two should get together. She'd really enjoy meeting you, Mom."

As they were talking, Dawn went into the kitchen. Seeing Ella down the hall, she quickly ducked out of sight by the refrigerator.

"How's she been acting today?" Ella whispered.

"She's stayed in her room despite not having a phone. She's still got an Internet connection, but her father did something to her computer so she can't use e-mail or chat. When she found out she got terribly upset and called him using the house phone. She couldn't get him to change his mind, so she locked herself in her room," Rose said. "He spoke to me afterward and said that he'd tell you about it later."

"I think he made the right decision. She has to learn that breaking the rules carries consequences."

"I just hate to see her so upset. I know she really cares about that boy, or thinks she does, but he's much too old for her." Rose glanced back toward the kitchen. "I set out a bowl of corn stew for you. It's on the counter. All you have to do is put it in the microwave."

"I'm starving. I'll eat first, then talk to my daughter."

Ella returned to the kitchen, and by then Dawn was gone. Ella savored every bite of the large bowl of stew, then holding a cup of her mother's herbal tea in one hand, went down the hall. Dawn was sitting cross-legged on the bed, an open book before her.

"How are you doing?" Ella asked her in a soft voice.

She shrugged. "I sure wish you and Dad would see that I'm not a kid anymore."

"You're not a little girl, and you're not an adult, but you're still our daughter. And, kiddo, you messed up big time."

"You make mistakes, too, Mom."

"Yes, I do, but I face the consequences and try not to let

it happen again. Rules help us maintain balance and harmony. Adults as well as kids need them to walk in beauty."

"I won't skip school again, Mom. I promise," Dawn said in a whisper-soft voice. "And I've only got five more days of class, so I'm going to be hitting the books real hard."

Ella gave her a hug, then walked to her own room. Home—this is what gave meaning to everything else she did.

TWENTY-ONE

———— ✖ ✖ ✖ ————

Ella's cell phone rang at 5:00
A.M., according to the display. Suddenly wide awake, she
picked it up quickly, glad she always left it on while charg-
ing and within arm's reach on the night stand.

"Investigator Clah? Sorry for the timing. This is FPD Officer Nadine Kelly. I'm providing security for the Bitsillie
family," the woman said. "They're gone. I thought you should
know."

"What do you mean, *gone*? They just drove away? How
long ago was this?"

"About ten minutes ago. Their cousin, Earl Sells, said
that someone had placed a note inside Mrs. Bitsillie's car
while she was at work. It scared her so much that she got
Mr. Sells' help and gave me the slip. While he was distract-
ing me out front with questions about their security, she
slipped out a side window with the kids and took Mr. Sells'
car, which was parked one street over."

"Crap. Anything else?"

"Yes. Once they were gone, Sells felt guilty and told me
what was going on. The family's headed to Albuquerque to
stay with another cousin in Alameda, on the city's north
side. That cousin thinks she can help Lois track down a job,

234 ** AIMÉE & DAVID THURLO

something he says is nearly impossible on the Reservation right now. Mr. Sells was still worried about their safety so he gave me the address and telephone number of the cousin. I've e-mailed it to your dispatcher already—which is where I got your cell number."

"Good. Did you see the note?"

"Mr. Sells kept it for us, and I have it now. It reads, 'If you love your children get out of town and stop talking to the cops. Next time I won't miss.' "

"He tracked her down at work . . . ," Ella muttered. "It's my fault. I should have seen this coming. Lois was wearing her work uniform the day her family was attacked, and the shooter also got a look at her vehicle. He must have gone to every Burger Haven in the county to find her."

"I've already called the State Police and Sandoval County deputies. They'll try to locate the vehicle en route, then follow at a distance. My sergeant also notified Bernalillo County Sheriff's Department and APD. Whoever has jurisdiction will have an undercover officer watching the house. The Bitsillies don't have to know. I'm going to have the note dusted for fingerprints and if we get anything other than what we expect, our techs will let you know," Officer Kelly added. "Sorry about the screwup. It was my responsibility."

"A lesson to be learned, but I appreciate your honesty, Officer Kelly. I'll follow up on this." Ella ended the call, then flopped back down on the pillow.

The killer's actions revealed far more than he'd intended. If she was right, this last play had been just another attempt to divert her focus. The good news was that it wouldn't work.

After she woke up again a few hours later, Ella called in to verify that the Bitsillie family had made the trip safely and was now being protected. Assured that all was well, she finished breakfast and caught a ride to the station with Joe.

As she walked past Justine's lab, Ella heard Benny's voice. Something in his tone seemed odd and caught her attention, so she glanced inside. Benny was standing in front of her partner holding a terra-cotta pot that held a small sunflower.

"That isn't just an ordinary sunflower. I grew it myself," Benny said. "All you have to do is transplant it outside and add water. As it grows, the flower will get heavy and become a big head of seeds, which you can eat."

Ella smiled, recalling that Justine had a black thumb and that the sunflower wasn't likely to make it to harvest time without the help of her roommate. Unnoticed, Ella continued on to her office.

She'd just taken a seat when she heard approaching footsteps. As Ella glanced up she saw Ford at her doorway. He was wearing a short-sleeved tropical-print shirt, windbreaker, and jeans rather than his normal Sunday suit and tie.

"Hey," Ella greeted. "What have you been up to, surfing?"

He smiled. "Sounds like fun, but actually I went up into the Chuskas on a personal retreat. I needed some time alone. While I was climbing around on one of the eastern slopes I spotted a Navajo man setting up camp. What caught my attention is that he'd chosen to stay in an old, abandoned hogan that had a hole punched on the side. Obviously, he doesn't believe in the *chindi*, but even the ones who say they don't usually avoid places where a death has occurred."

"Did you get a chance to talk to him?"

He shook his head. "I went closer, intending to offer a prayer and share some of my supplies, but I saw he was armed. It's not hunting season, but he had a rifle propped up against a tree and a pistol stuck in his belt."

"Did you ever get a look at his face?" Ella asked quickly.

"Yeah, and I'm glad I did. I had my binoculars and confirmed it was Gilbert Romero. I knew you'd been looking for him, so I hurried to my camp, got my stuff, and drove straight here."

"How do you know Romero?"

"His older sister died of cancer a few years ago and I regularly met with the family, trying to help them out. Gilbert was out on parole and he struck me as very unstable. From what I've heard here and there, he's even more so now."

"Do you think he saw you?" Ella asked.

"No. He would have reacted if he had," Ford said. "It was very early in the morning and he was gathering kindling off the ground so his head was mostly pointed down. I chose my approach carefully, too, coming in with the sun behind my back, but there's really not much to hide behind up there. The hogan is just over a small, windswept ridge, tucked up against the mountainside. From there he can see down into the valley for miles."

"Good location for him, not so much for us," Ella muttered.

He nodded. "I was lucky enough to be farther along the ridge when I smelled his campfire and came up more or less from the west. If you intend to go up after him, you're going to need some careful strategy. If he bolts, he'll head right into a canyon and lose you in that rugged country. There are a lot of old mines in the area, and not all of them show up on maps."

"So you didn't see a vehicle?" Ella asked.

"No, he probably hid it down the mountain among the trees, then walked up."

"Makes sense," Ella said. "Can you stick around for a bit and help me trace the route you took on a map or an aerial photo?"

"Yes, but I'm not sure it'll help. I can find it again for you on foot, though, and show you the best way in."

"So you think he's still there?" she asked.

"He had food and firepower, and had gathered enough firewood to last a couple of days at least. I'd guess he plans to hole up there until the heat's off."

Ella assembled her team, then hearing Blalock's voice down the hall, invited him to join them also. Once everyone was seated, she repeated what Ford had told her and called up an aerial photo map of the area on her computer. "We have to go after him, but we need to come up with a solid tactical approach."

"Helicopter after dark, approaching low and over this ridge," Blalock said, pointing at the image. "It'll put us in the vicinity quickly, providing there's a viable landing site within striking distance." He looked over at Ford.

The preacher shook his head. "Either you rappel down into the trees here"—he moved the mouse cursor across the image to indicate the location—"or you spend a lot of time trying to work your way up this cliff. In the dark, under ideal conditions, those options would still be problematic."

Justine checked her BlackBerry, then shook her head. "High winds are forecast for later this afternoon and evening, so a helicopter assault would be risky."

"It'll take a few hours, but your best option is to let me lead you to him from around the mountain," Ford said. "I can retrace the route I took earlier. I'd say just follow my tracks, but it stormed up there yesterday afternoon and I'd expect a repeat of that today."

"Are you sure you want to do this? You'll be the only one who's unarmed," Ella said.

He nodded. "I've got all the protection I need," he said, gesturing to the simple crucifix around his neck.

"You'll also have to wear a vest—nonnegotiable," she added.

"No problem," Ford said.

"Okay. Stick around. I'm going to need the chief's permission for this op."

Ella went directly to Big Ed's office and detailed her plan, bringing up the same aerial images on his computer monitor. "Romero has good instincts, so I doubt he'll stay long at any one location. I think we need to make our move tonight. I'll take point and Ford can direct me while Blalock covers his back."

"Get it set up, and between now and then have your team gather all the intel possible on that area," Big Ed ordered.

"We'll come up with at least two takedown plans and work out the bugs over tactical channels while in transit," she replied. "I'll also have Justine download the latest photos and topo maps. Joe and Benny can assemble any special climbing gear Ford thinks we'll need."

Ella returned to her office and briefed the others quickly, instructing them to return in two hours with the necessary equipment, ready to go.

Everyone filed out and seconds later Ella's phone rang. The caller ID told her it was Detective Nez.

"I've tracked the tech who processed Kelewood's car after it was found in that Farmington supermarket's parking lot," Dan said. "I wanted to know more, but the tech quit shortly afterwards to join another department. He's now back home and waiting for an opening locally. I'm scheduled to meet him in twenty minutes at his place on Farmington's west side. I thought you might want to come along."

Staying in contact via radio, she met Dan by the highway, then followed his vehicle up to a white stucco home with bright blue trim. The garage door was open and they could hear someone vacuuming out the interior of a car.

"Jerry Reed?" Dan called out. When he didn't react, Dan touched him on the shoulder.

The man jumped, then relaxed the moment he saw Dan's badge. "Sorry. I didn't hear you." He glanced at Ella and noted the badge and sidearm at her belt. "How can I help you officers?"

"I'd like to ask you a few questions about a vehicle you processed a year ago," Dan said.

Jerry invited them inside the house and led the way to a mostly empty living room. He sat on one of the wooden folding chairs, and motioned for them to take the couch. "I've processed a lot of cars," he warned, "and you want me to remember one in particular? I sure hope it was memorable in some way."

"I've got a copy of the file in my handheld. Take a look and see if helps you recall something that may not have made it into the report," Dan said. "Anything left in the car, even if it didn't seem out of the ordinary, for instance?"

He glanced at what Dan handed him. "I remember this guy. He was that state mine inspector who just vanished. There's one thing that's not spelled out in my report. The key chain he left behind held a custom-made, handcrafted silver bucking bronco. What that told me is that whoever came after him wasn't interested in the car, or in a simple robbery. If he had been, that chunk of silver would have disappeared, too, you get me?"

"Thanks. If you remember anything else, call me," Dan said.

As they went back to their cars, Dan spoke first. "So what made him a target? It's not robbery. We know that now for sure. The fact that he'd had a drink—or too many?"

"Good question," Ella said. "By the way, I think you should know that a tribal investigator—not connected with our department—is also checking into Kelewood's activities. You might run into him."

"Logan Bitterwater?" Seeing her nod, he continued. "He came by and talked to me just before I called you. He's trying to retrace Kelewood's steps following the report of safety violations at the Stepson mine. He mentioned he'd spoken to you and was planning on sharing information with your department."

"He answers only to the tribal president and has his own way of working. Maybe he'll be able to turn up something new," Ella said, then checked her watch. "I better be heading back to the station. There's something going down in a few hours." She briefed him on the upcoming operation. "I'll let you know if and when we have Romero in custody. I'm sure you'll want to be there when we question him."

"You bet I do," he said. "If you can use one more officer, give me an hour lead time and I can join you."

"No, in this case the fewer the better. We're going in low profile," she said, describing the terrain.

On her way back to the Rez, Ella's cell phone rang. It was Carolyn.

"I've got more toxicology results back. The female vic has been dead about two years and had chemical residue in her system that's consistent with chemotherapy and cancer tissue. Those types of medical records are sealed, so you'll have to look into it from your end."

"That's a great lead. Thanks for letting me know ASAP."

Ella called Justine. "We have new information that'll help us narrow down the list of missing females. See which of the women were undergoing chemo about two years ago this June."

"I'll start a computer search on that right now."

Ella returned to her office ten minutes later and shortly thereafter gave Benny the revised list. As their newest team member, he was given the assignment of continuing to narrow down names. If at all possible, Ella wanted to ID the female victim by the end of the day. Although clearly disappointed not to be taking part in the Romero takedown, Benny accepted the job without complaint.

The team reviewed their proposed tactics and went over

all the details of the terrain Ford could remember. Neskahi had also borrowed special gear from SWAT and they all had to work to familiarize themselves with the equipment.

It was late afternoon by the time Ford, Blalock, Justine, Neskahi, and Ella set out in two community-college SUVs on loan from the tribal motor pool. If Romero was keeping watch from higher ground he'd see a group dressed in civilian clothes driving vehicles consistent with a field trip or special project. All weapons and special gear would be kept out of sight until dark.

They arrived at Ford's former campsite west of Todacheene Lake in the Chuska Mountains just after sunset. They quickly set up a cover campsite with two tents. Then as soon as it grew dark, they changed into dark gray-green camouflage uniforms and caps.

Although Ford wore the required pants and jacket, he declined the night vision goggles, saying they would throw off his visual images of the route. Once everyone had been given GPS equipped handheld field radios, they set out.

The three-mile hike was difficult because they were constantly climbing uphill on rough, unfamiliar terrain and trying to move quietly. They went single file, keeping within sight of each other. Ella took point, while Ford stayed between her and Blalock. Neskahi and Justine hung back, covering the rear.

Moving as quickly as the terrain allowed, they soon entered a narrow canyon. A small creek flowed swiftly down its center and the faint bubbling of water over rocks helped cover their progress.

Ella glanced back at Ford, who was five feet behind her. She hated the surreal effect the night vision glasses created. Everything was an unearthly shade of green. "We've gone just about as far as we can. Are you sure you remember the location?"

Ford nodded. "Just before you reach that stunted pine,

we start up the side of the canyon. There's practically no cover up there so stop before you risk exposing yourself to anyone on the other slope. Just short of the summit you should be able to see the hogan clearly in the moonlight," he whispered. "But that means he'll be able to spot us, too."

"We'll be in the background of the ridge behind us, so he shouldn't be able to see us clearly unless he's right on top," Ella said. "And even then, we'll be in shadow."

"Unless he has night vision, he won't know us from mule deer," Blalock said, coming up from behind Ford.

"It's time for us to split up," Ella said. "We have to stay about fifty feet apart, so there'll be virtually no chance he could wipe us all out at once."

"So we go with Plan A?" Blalock asked.

"Yeah. Tell Justine and Joe to advance to this spot then wait for us to begin our ascent before they start their own climb up the ridge. Have them stop ten feet from the top, watch for my signal, then we'll all top the ridge at once and flatten. They'll know what to do after that."

"Roger that," Blalock said, then went to join the others.

Two minutes later, Ella started the climb. It was steep and rocky, and she had to grab on to dry, scratchy oak shrubs more than once to pull and position her way around or across sheets of smooth bedrock.

Halfway up she looked back down at Ford and gave him an encouraging smile. As he met her gaze, she suddenly understood why he'd insisted on coming with them. Ford knew this was the last chance they'd have to be together before he left.

Ella took a breath and continued the climb. She'd make sure nothing happened to either of them. Their memories of this experience should be uplifting, not bittersweet.

Ten minutes later, she neared the summit of the barren ridge, starlit sky behind it. Here, the ground held only short tufts of grass, and no cover at all. She crouched down, and Ford soon came up beside her.

"The hogan is on the other side, down the ridge maybe a hundred feet, and to the right," he whispered.

Blalock came up, breathing hard. "What's it like on the other side, going down. Any cover?"

Ford shook his head. "Not for the first thirty feet or so, then some big boulders, if I remember right. It's pretty much like it is on this side, but with more boulders and not as steep."

"Let's hope he's inside the hogan," Ella said.

"It's about ten-thirty now," Blalock said, checking his watch. "Maybe he's asleep."

Ford shook his head. "Don't count on it. If I were on the run, I'd be sleeping in the daytime and watching at night. . . ."

"For people like us," Blalock finished. "The plan is to move in on him slowly and carefully, cut off his access to the old road on the east side, then rush the last fifty feet unless we're spotted farther out."

Ella looked along the ridge for the others. "They're even with us. Time to go." She brought out her penlight and signaled.

Seconds later she and the others were at the top. Lying on her belly Ella looked down at the hogan. From this angle, it looked like a log pillbox in a scooped-out natural amphitheater. There was a door instead of a blanket at the entrance, but it was open.

She looked to her right. Justine and Neskahi were in position, waiting and watching. She motioned with her hand, then rose to a crouch and headed toward the reverse side of the ridge, her eyes on the cabin.

She'd only traveled a few yards when she saw a flash and heard a roar. A bullet whistled over her head as she dropped to the ground. Ford froze in a crouch.

"Get down!" she yelled just as Blalock returned fire.

244 ❋ AIMÉE & DAVID THURLO

Seeing Ford hesitate, Ella jumped over, shoved him flat, then rolled and fired blind toward the hogan. "Wait here and stay down!"

Justine and Neskahi also began to fire from the ridge, giving Ella some cover as she and Blalock moved downslope, veering to their left to cut off the easiest escape route.

"Where is he?" Ella asked, trying to find their target.

"Behind the hogan, I think," Blalock called out, his M16 weaving back and forth, looking for a sight picture. "From what I can tell he's moved twice already."

"These night goggles are a pain in the ass," Ella said, trying to reposition hers. They had slipped when she'd hit the ground.

"Cover fire," she yelled, going with the emergency tactics discussed earlier. One team would pin down the target while the other advanced, then they'd reverse roles.

Something bright flashed down by the hogan, and she was suddenly blinded. "What the? . . ."

"Fire bomb!" Blalock called. "Forget the night vision."

Ella yanked off her night goggles and jammed the device into her jacket pocket. A stand of trees about twenty feet from the hogan had erupted in flames, and the brush around it was catching as well.

"Plan B," Ella yelled, calling for a flanking movement. She and Blalock would continue around from the left while Justine and Neskahi remained in position and provided cover fire.

Ella followed Blalock down the ridge, half running, half sliding. The scent of gasoline now joined the glow of the spreading flames, which gave them all the light they needed.

Within two minutes they all met among the burning trees and searched the ground for tracks. Romero had disappeared—vanished beyond the flames—and unless he was up a tree, there was little chance of finding him now.

"Call the tribal forest service," Ella yelled to Justine,

who'd come around from behind the hogan. "We've got to get this fire out before everything between here and Narbona Pass goes up in smoke."

"What about Romero?" Ford asked as he turned slowly in a circle, taking in the site.

Ella looked at Blalock, who shook his head. "No way that man's still around," she answered. "He created a diversion and split, but I'll sweep the perimeter and look for vehicle tracks."

"Take Justine with you. Joe, Ford, and I will see if we can do anything to slow down this fire," Blalock said.

Justine came out of the hogan. "There's a shovel and an axe in here."

"I'll take the axe," Neskahi said.

"I'll take the shovel," Ford said. "I can dig a hole and move dirt with the best of them."

"I'll clear branches and debris away from the path of fire," Blalock added. "Let's get busy."

Fortunately, since fire season was well underway, a forestry team was already stationed at an Owl Spring base camp. Men arrived in a brush truck within half an hour, driving up the dirt track on the east that led almost all the way up the mountain to the hogan.

By that time, Ella and her team were hot, tired, and dusty. Their eyes burned from the smoke, and they'd done their share of coughing, but they'd managed to keep the fire from getting out of hand.

They were happy to see the professionals arrive, with water to suppress hot spots and plenty of tools to share. Combining their numbers and working under the guidance of the firefighters, they managed to contain the blaze to about a half acre. Since the flames had gone up the ridge, and there was little vegetation there, the danger of a big fire never materialized.

246 ✻ AIMÉE & DAVID THURLO

It didn't take long for the forestry workers to find the fire's origin, an open can of camp stove fuel tossed into some brush, then ignited. The ranger in charge of the forestry group took photos for the report he'd be filing later in the day.

Although Ella made a call to Big Ed to update him on the situation, there was still hope in locating Romero. As soon as they could, they renewed the search while the fire crew took care of any glowing embers and cleaned up the scene. They already knew, from discussion during their firefighting, that the forestry crew hadn't encountered a vehicle or seen fresh tire tracks, ruling out the eastern route. Ella's team had to look elsewhere.

While searching for tracks along the narrow passageway next to the mountainside, Ella spotted a mine shaft opening. It had been concealed by brush and was located at the back of the small amphitheater.

"He came this way," Ella called out, motioning to get Blalock's attention.

She pulled the clump of brush away with her left hand, keeping her pistol in her right just in case. The air coming up from the shaft, what was basically a hole leading into the mountainside, was surprisingly fresh.

"Feel that breeze? My guess is that there's either another opening somewhere on the other side of this mountain, or a ventilation shaft," Ella said.

Blalock aimed his rifle into the darkness as Ella unclipped the flashlight from her belt and illuminated the opening.

"It appears to follow a seam of coal and goes back quite a ways," she said, noting the dark surface of one rock face, basically stripped clean of coal.

"Aim your light on those boot prints again. I thought I saw spots, maybe drops of blood," Blalock said.

Ella did as he asked. "Yeah, that's dried blood. He must have taken a hit during the exchange of gunfire."

"I don't recall seeing any mine shafts listed on our maps," Blalock said, bringing out his own flashlight, a powerful LED model.

"That's not unusual. A lot of smaller mines never got on the charts. Navajo crews would dig out all the coal they could find, then just walk away. After the easily reached coal dwindled, the small mining companies went belly-up and their records disappeared along with them," Ella said, and peered down into the hole. After a moment she looked back up at Blalock. "I wonder where this tunnel ends up, and do you suppose Romero's still in there?"

"We have to find out," Blalock replied.

"Let's get everyone together. Big Ed has given me a free hand on this, and I'm going to push this search as long as we have a chance to catch up to him again."

Working to a quickly devised plan, Justine, Ford, and Joe circled the mountainside searching for other openings into the mine. While they did that, Blalock and Ella went inside the shaft and followed the suspect's trail, working their way in a crouched position most of the distance.

They all found the exit shaft about the same time. When Ella and Blalock emerged, stiff-legged, they saw the others shake their heads. Maintaining silence, Ella took point as they followed Romero's footprints down the mountain for about a mile. There, on the dirt road ahead, they found a clear set of vehicle tracks that led southwest through a narrow pass.

"He's long gone." Blalock aimed his flashlight at the area next to the tire tracks where the trail of blood suddenly ended. "Also note that his bleeding has slowed to just a few drops here and there now. Unless his clothes are soaked, he didn't suffer a critical hit, not bad enough to slow him down that much."

"There's an ATL out in four states, and roadblocks on all major routes," Ella said. "We've done all we can for now."

"Maybe Benny's uncovered a lead on the woman vic-tim," Justine said as they circled around the mountain, then took the forestry road east.

"Yeah, maybe, but that'll wait till tomorrow—well, later today," Ella said, aware that it was a bit after 3:00 A.M. "Drop me off at home and we'll get back to work after we've grabbed some sleep."

Justine stifled a yawn. "No problem. I'm beat."

They made good progress, most of the route was down-hill, and reached their vehicles in less than an hour.

Ella glanced at Ford, then reached for his hand. "Ride back with us. All our cars are at the motor pool anyway."

He hesitated, then shook his head. "I'll go with Blalock and Neskahi."

Curious as to why he'd decided not to ride with them, Ella allowed the others to get ahead, then voiced the ques-tion on her mind. "Did you change your mind about us re-maining friends?"

He shook his head. "We *are* friends, but riding with you after working a case will bring back too many memories for me. It'll make me think of what might have been, instead of what is."

Ella nodded and didn't comment. Although what he'd said was true, it saddened her to acknowledge that part of her life was over.

Once back at camp, Ella checked their vehicles, making sure nothing had been tampered with and everything was as they'd left it. She then helped the others take down and stow away the tents. In five minutes they were finished.

"Time to roll," Blalock said. "We've got everyone look-ing for Romero and when he surfaces we'll know—day or night."

"Let's meet in the morning at the station and see where we're at then. Say nine-thirty or a quarter to ten?" Ella sug-gested. "That'll give us a few hours of sack time."

"Done."

As Blalock walked off to join Joe and Ford, Ella's gaze shifted to Ford and remained on him a moment longer.

"You ready to leave?" Justine asked, interrupting her thoughts.

Ella nodded. Ford was right. Even though it hurt like crazy, it was time for both of them to move on.

TWENTY-TWO
✖ ✖ ✖

Ella was up at nine. It was Monday, and her thoughts were on Dawn, so she couldn't sleep any longer. According to Rose, who'd woken up and met her in the kitchen when she'd returned home, Dawn had been studying hard for her remaining finals. Hearing that her kid was finally back on the right track had helped her get a few hours of sleep.

Kevin had also left voice mail, assuring her that Leonard wouldn't get anywhere near Dawn again. The highschool boy, it seemed, had already moved on to another girl closer to his age. Perhaps, Kevin joked, it was the in-his-face reminder that Dawn had a protective mother who carried a pistol and had already proved she could track him down.

As Ella poured herself some coffee, she couldn't help but notice that her mother was in a far better frame of mind than she'd been in weeks.

"Your daughter finished her term paper, and seemed in a good mood when my husband drove her to the bus stop. I'll be gone most of the morning," Rose said. "I'm meeting the artist for coffee at her home."

It took Ella a minute to figure out who her mother was talking about. "You mean FB-Eyes' wife?"

Rose nodded. "I called to tell her how much I loved her painting and one thing led to another. Now we're getting together to talk about presentations we'd like to give at the schools this coming fall. We could teach kids about native plants, particularly the rare varieties. She'd do watercolor representations based on my photos and descriptions, and I'd tell the kids about their uses."

"That's a terrific idea, Mom. It works for everyone, particularly the children. They need to know as much as possible about their culture—and nature."

"Her idea helped me remember one of the most important lessons the Plant People teach us. Nothing ever stays the same, no matter how much we may want that. Those who can't embrace the new get left behind."

Aware that at long last Rose was confiding in her, Ella said nothing, afraid to ruin the moment.

"My life has always been filled with purpose. I was needed here at home and my work with plants was important to the tribe. Then one morning I looked around and everything had changed. My job was gone and my granddaughter didn't need me anymore. You had your own life and my husband spent most of his free time working in the garage. No one seemed to value what I had to offer anymore and that made me feel useless." She took a deep breath, then let it out slowly. "Finding a new direction, one that would fit me as well as the old one did, hasn't been easy."

Ella gave Rose a hug. "I need you, Mom, and so does your husband. My daughter does, too, though I realize that at the moment she wants to think she doesn't need anyone at all."

"You were that way, too, at her age," Rose said. She smiled, then stood and walked over to pour herself another cup of coffee. "It'll make you crazy now, but when time passes, and it will, you'll find you miss these days more than you can imagine."

252 * AIMÉE & DAVID THURLO

Before Ella could say anything, she heard Justine's honk. "I've got to go, Mom. We all got to sleep in a little this morning, but now I have a meeting."

"Take care of yourself, Daughter."

"You, too, Mom."

At the station, twenty minutes later, Ella entered her office and saw that the rest of team, including Blalock, were already there.

Ella took a seat, and as she did, Dan appeared at her door, visitor's tag around his neck.

"I came to get an update on last night," he said, nodding to the other seated officers.

"Perfect timing," she said, waving him to the only empty chair.

Ella briefed Dan and Benny on the attempt to bring in Romero the night before, then gave Benny a nod. "Tell us about the female vic."

"I've narrowed the possibilities down to two women. One was unmarried and living with her mother, but I haven't been able to contact anyone at that house. The other lived alone. I tried to track down members of her family, but haven't had any luck so far. I thought I'd start knocking on doors this morning."

"What about the vehicles that belonged to the missing women? Were those ever found?" Justine asked.

"One was left at the Farmington bus station. The other never turned up, or if it did, it's not in the system."

"Keep digging," Ella said.

"I'll be spearheading the search for Romero and coordinating the interdepartmental effort," Blalock said. "I placed an alert with the medical community last night, but no gunshot victims have turned up."

"Here's what I'd like to do," Ella said, then looked at Dan. "Why don't you and I pay Norman Ben another visit? I'm certain he knows more than he's telling us."

"Good idea," Dan said.

They soon got underway in Detective Nez's sheriff's department vehicle, a similar model to her unmarked unit but
in much better shape. It still had that new-car smell, Ella
noted with envy. Seated on the passenger side, she shifted
to look at him. "I think we need to push Ben a lot harder—
put him on the defensive and keep the pressure up."

"If he's involved, then the missing money's the key,"
Dan said. "In every hassle between business partners it's
always about the money."

"I don't think we're going to get a simple answer on this
one. If Ben had been trying to get the stolen money back, he
wouldn't have killed the person he thought had it," Ella replied.

"What if he'd already gotten the money back and has
been covering so he doesn't look guilty of murder? Or maybe
he never borrowed the money at all—he stole it and killed
his partner because he found out."

"Then why turn around and hire Ross Harrison?" she
countered.

"To muddy up the trail? Naw, never mind. That theory
just doesn't fly," Dan said. "Nothing adds up in this case."

"That's the biggest problem we've got. Answers seem to
stay just out of our reach," Ella said. "It would help if we
had a motive, something besides random road rage."

"This is a tough case, but you've got the worst of it."

"What do you mean?"

"The pressure's constant at work, and for you it doesn't
let up after hours."

Ella looked at him, trying to figure out how much Dan
knew about her. She had a hard time believing that Justine
had spoken to him about Rose or Dawn.

"In case you're wondering, I've gone out a few times
with a woman from Reverend Tome's church," he said. "I
understand you and he have been an item for months. Now

the church is sending him to Arizona. Long-distance relationships can be complicated."

Ella didn't answer right away. She usually didn't talk about her personal life. Yet getting to know the ones who'd have your back was always a good idea and confidences generally worked both ways.

"He and I were close for a while, but it was a deep friendship, nothing more."

He said nothing for several moments, then finally spoke. "He was in love with you, but you just wanted friendship. Was that it?"

Dan was perceptive. Maybe that's what made him such a good artist. "Pretty much," she answered at last.

"That's tough—on him for obvious reasons, and on you, too. You knew all along that once he realized the relationship had limits the connection would fade. I've been there."

"Which side?"

"I had a very close friendship with a woman who wanted more than that—a husband. It ended badly."

"You miss her?"

"More than I expected—a lot more, actually. You know how closed cops are. When we find a friend outside work we can be open with, that means a lot."

Ella nodded slowly. That was exactly how she felt about Ford. Losing him would hurt, and letting go wouldn't be easy, but it was the right thing to do.

"If you ever need to just talk, I'm a good listener," Dan said, "and whatever you say will stay with me."

The offer touched her. She didn't think it would happen, but it was still good to know.

"We share the same duties, but not in the same department," he added. "That's what makes it workable. Friendship, I mean."

Ella suddenly realized something else. The offer wasn't altogether altruistic. Like many officers, he was lonely.

"I hear you," she said, not committing to anything.

They arrived at Norman Ben's east Farmington business—Thunderbird Construction—about twenty-five minutes later.

Having seen them pull up and park in the open parking slot just outside his front door, Norman stepped out to greet them. "Come in and have a seat." He waved his hand toward two chairs along the wall. "Business is at a standstill these days, as you can see from all the empty parking slots and for-rent signs in the windows. I stick around the office, hoping something will come in, but time can sure drag. I spend most of my time making cold calls, which I hate. If this economy doesn't pick up soon, a lot more businesses are going to be history."

"Do you have a backup plan?" Dan asked.

"Nah. Even if I wanted, I'm too broke to start a new business and too old to retrain and get hired. I'll stick it out and hope for things to turn around," Norman said, taking a seat behind his desk.

"You've said that you've spent the past four years trying to find Johnson, is that correct?" Dan asked, getting down to business.

"Yeah, off and on. My slimeball partner took money I could have been using for advertising, promotion, and a better location."

"Taking your best guess, what do you think happened to that money?" Ella pressed.

"I've thought a lot about that. Elroy really wasn't the kind to take the money and run. His attitude in business and life was that if something was wrong you fixed it, but you left what was working alone. Ross Harrison, the P.I., suggested Elroy might have taken our money to invest, hoping for a quick score that could grow the company. Maybe Elroy lost his shirt on the deal and bailed rather than face up to me. Ross tried hard to track Elroy and the money. He got several leads, too, but in the end they all fizzled out."

"What kind of information did Harrison actually turn up for you?" Dan asked. "Other than theories and speculation, that is."

"For one, he was able to retrace Elroy's movements after he left this office the day he disappeared. Elroy had told me he was going to his lodge meeting, but I never could verify that. Those fraternal orders are closed to nonmembers. Harrison found a way around their rules and confirmed that Elroy had actually been there that day after work. There'd been nothing unusual about the way he acted then, according to members Harrison interviewed. Elroy left later to pick up his jacket at the dry cleaners in Farmington. Before you ask—the jacket *was* picked up. After that, poof."

"Which lodge are we talking about?" Dan asked him.

"The Hickory Lodge, originally formed by woodworkers and craftsmen, according to their pamphlets. It used to be some kind of guild, back in the seventeen-hundreds, but these days it's a service organization. They donate time to community building projects, and that kind of networking is good for drumming up business. I was up for membership, but I backed out. I'm not a joiner. When I finish for the day all I want is a cold one and a big-screen TV with every sports channel known to man."

Ella made it a point not to glance down at his gut. A little community work might have done wonders for him.

"Do you think you'll ever find my money?" he asked.

"The money isn't our priority," Ella said, "but if it turns up during our investigation, we'll let you know."

As they walked back outside, Dan glanced at her. "You don't like the guy, do you?"

"No. It's his attitude," she said as he switched on the ignition. "His partner may have taken some badly needed funds, but instead of sucking up the loss, Ben spends even more on a P.I. He complains how poor he is, but instead of going out to job sites, builders, and whatnot hustling for business, he sits beneath an air conditioner while his company slowly tanks."

"In situations like these, a lot of businessmen lose focus and let knee-jerk reactions overrule their common sense. It's human nature to try and screw whoever screwed you."

She nodded slowly. "Not the best side of human nature but, yeah, good point."

"I know where the Hickory Lodge is. Do you want to see if anyone's there now?"

"Yeah. If they have any retired members, someone's likely to be around. But having anyone remember who they saw four years ago . . . Our chances are slim."

"Maybe not. I had a friend who was a member of one of these groups, and I went to a meeting with him once. You have to sign in before you can go into the club section. Maybe they won't mind giving us a look, particularly since we're trying to find out what happened to one of their members."

"Have you ever thought of joining one of these brotherhood lodges?" Ella asked him.

"No way. When I'm on my own time I don't like being cooped up indoors—or in any kind of structured environment, for that matter. I'm in a gun club, and a member of the police association, but that's it. How about you? Some of these lodges have female branches."

"That's not for me. I spend whatever free time I have with my family. What do you do in your off hours besides practicing at the shooting range?"

"If it's spring or summer I'm usually off hiking or backpacking. In winter, I don't tend to go very far because the weather's more uncertain."

"You go alone?"

He nodded. "But I use common sense. I've got a GPS

with me and a phone in case of emergencies. Of course out here cell phones are unreliable."

Ella heard what he'd left unsaid. Being without immediate family around was hard, not to mention lonely. She knew eventually that day would come for her, too, but it was hard to even imagine her household without Rose, Herman, and Dawn.

Soon he drove into the parking lot that surrounded an old but beautifully constructed wood and stone building. There was a large carpenter's brace and handsaw emblem carved into the heavy oak door.

"Let's see what we can get from these people," Dan said, his tone all business again.

They went inside a small lobby, but found no one at the outer desk. Along the cherrywood paneling were rows of photos in metal frames, most of them depicting lodge members at outings and public service events over many years, judging from clothing style changes. Hearing voices just past the closed door, Dan knocked loudly and identified himself.

A panel in the door opened and a face appeared. Ella was suddenly reminded of old movies about Prohibition.

"How can I help you, Detective?" the man asked through the peep hole.

"We need to talk to someone who can show us membership sign-in records going back four years."

"I have that authority—for legal, legitimate purposes. I'm Lodge Grand Master," he said, coming out into the lobby and closing the door behind him. "I'm Larry Clement." He offered his hand.

Dan, used to the Anglo greeting, shook the man's hand, as did Ella.

"We're investigating the death of one of your members, a Navajo man, Elroy Johnson," Dan said. "We understand he came by here the evening he disappeared."

"I remember Mr. Johnson—we only have a few Navajo members. I just read that his body was found and that he'd been murdered."

"That's why we want to look at the actual sign-in sheet for that night—June first. We'd like to see who else was here that evening and compare those names to anyone who might be part of our investigation."

The man led them down a wood-paneled hallway lined with shelves containing trophies and public service plaques, then down to a small office. He opened a well-worn file cabinet, brought out several large clothbound notebooks, and set them on a glass-topped desk. "You're probably used to computer files but, here, we still keep our records as our forefathers did, pen to paper."

He found the book that corresponded to the proper year and month, then turned the pages until he reached the right date. "Here we are, June first. I don't see Elroy's name," he said, scanning the page. "Wait, here it is. It's at the very bottom."

"Would you mind if we took a closer look?" Ella asked.

"Not at all," he said, turning the notebook around, then sliding it toward them across the desk.

Ella studied the signature. It wasn't the same one she'd seen on the company's license that hung on Norman Ben's office wall—not even close.

"Has anyone else asked to examine this book?" Ella asked him.

He thought about it for a moment, then nodded. "Yeah, now that you mention it. I was Grand Master back then as well, and not long after Elroy disappeared, a private investigator showed up. He said Mrs. Johnson had hired him to find her husband, so I let him take a look. It's okay because we're not a secret organization, though we don't make our members' names public or describe our rituals."

"Was he alone with the book at any time?" Dan asked.

"I can't say. The only reason I remember it at all is because he was the first private investigator I'd ever met."

"Could you make a copy of this page for us? It would be for official use only," Dan said.

"If that's the case, then yes, indeed. Our lodge always cooperates with law enforcement officers. One of our missions is public service."

He took a copy using a stand-alone machine against the wall, then handed Dan the page. "If there's anything else we can do, officers, let us know. Elroy was one of our lodge members, and I know he would have wanted his killer taken off the streets."

"Thanks," Dan said, then walked out with Ella.

"You saw what I did, didn't you?" Ella asked him. "That's not Elroy's signature."

"I know. Elroy's signature slants to the left, so he's probably left-handed. I was wondering if maybe Harrison added it himself so he'd have something to report. Keep the client on the payroll?" Dan added.

"That's what I was thinking, too, but we're going to need to compare it to Harrison's handwriting," Ella said.

"His signature is probably on his P.I. license application."

"Good thinking. That's a state agency, so you'll probably have easier access. Once you get a look, will you let me know?" Ella said.

Dan nodded. "You ready to head back to the Rez now?"

"Yeah, you don't need me for a follow-up, and I've got work waiting."

"Even if the signatures match, it still won't mean Harrison's guilty of anything except keeping a client on the hook with dubious evidence," Dan said. "I usually hate checking up on an ex-cop, but I ran a background on Ross, and from what I saw, he has a good track record finding missing people."

"In this case he hasn't done much for his client except take the money," Ella replied.

Twenty minutes later, Dan dropped her off at the Shiprock station. As he drove off, her cell phone rang, and she noticed that it was Logan Bitterwater, the tribal president's investigator.

"I've got some information to share. Do you have a moment?" Logan said.

"I just pulled into the station. If you're in the area . . ."

"Actually, I'm in Window Rock, but I have something I wanted to pass along. I leaned on Joe Preston, the Stepson operations manager, and it paid off. Here's what I got. After Stepson failed to pass muster with the state mining inspector, Preston knew they were in trouble. There was no way the company could fix the problems in the two days Kelewood had given them. So Preston met up with Kelewood at a bar in Kirtland that evening and offered Kelewood a small financial incentive to postpone the inspection. Kelewood refused and left."

"I was never told about that."

"There's more. Preston then made some calls to unnamed superiors at the company and got permission to up the ante. Hoping the additional money would buy him a few days extra at least, he decided to try and catch up to Kelewood before he got home. When Preston finally spotted Kelewood's pickup, it was on the shoulder, having just been pulled over by a sheriff's department cruiser. Preston said he knew stopping would be a mistake under those circumstances, so he decided to wait down the road and intercept Kelewood as he passed by later. But the car never showed up, so Preston finally went home and the second offer was never made."

"Didn't Preston realize that he was establishing himself as a suspect by admitting all that?" Ella asked, trying to come up with a way of connecting the dots. It still didn't add up. If Joe Preston had killed Kelewood, then what about the other victims?

"I'm not a cop. I don't arrest people. That gives me some leeway. But if you ask him about this yourself, he'll probably deny the whole thing."

"So the bottom line is that once Kelewood disappeared, Stepson Inc. got the time they needed to bring their equipment and machinery up to par."

"Joe Preston had reason to want Kelewood out of the way, but he's not your killer. That's what my gut tells me," Logan said. "That's all I've got. Hope it helps."

Before she could thank him, Logan ended the call. Ella put away the phone, trying to process the new information, and wondering how it might fit with what they already knew. Before she could gather her thoughts Justine came outside.

"Perfect timing, partner. We've got a positive ID on the female vic, and I've located her next of kin. Wanna go with?"

"You bet," Ella said. "Fill me in on the way."

TWENTY-THREE
—— ✕ ✕ ✕ ——

As they headed out to a neighborhood in southwest Shiprock, Justine updated Ella on her findings. "The vic's name is Alice Pahe. She was thirty-four years old, Navajo, and taught here at the college. When she disappeared two years ago she'd been undergoing cancer treatment. The day after she was reported missing her car was the one found at the bus station parking lot in Farmington."

"Who are we going to see?" Ella asked.

"Her mother, Nadine Pahe. Nadine teaches at one of our middle schools."

"Has she been given the news?"

"Yes," Justine answered. "I spoke to her on the phone just before I called you. She's waited a long time for closure."

"Who interviewed her back when her daughter disappeared?"

"One of our uniforms took the report. I checked, but that officer since resigned and now works for the Bernalillo County Sheriff's Department."

They soon entered a Modernist's residential area, passing the middle school campus only a few blocks west of the highway. The houses, constructed in the seventies, were nearly identical and separated by low cinder-block walls.

As they pulled up, Ella saw Ford's old Dodge pickup parked in the driveway. That truck had sure seen a lot of miles.

"Looks like she's one of Reverend Tome's parishioners," Justine said.

"I'm glad he's here. He'll help the mother stay calm. I've seen Ford work miracles with people fighting their way through grief."

"This is going to be a rough one, I can tell you that. Nadine gave me some details already. Alice was her only daughter and was fighting hard to stay alive. The chemo and radiation treatments were only keeping her cancer at bay. Some of her Traditionalist relatives thought she'd gone off to die somewhere, but Nadine flat out refused to believe it. She never gave up hope that she'd see her daughter again."

Ella felt her heart go out to the woman. The loss of a child, particularly under those circumstances, would have been unbearable.

Ford showed them into the house, and Ella saw Nadine Pahe just beyond them on the sofa, staring blankly at the wall.

"We need to talk to her," Ella told Ford.

"I know. When she called and asked me to come, she could barely speak. Just don't push too hard."

"Understood," Ella said.

As Ella drew near, Nadine Pahe glanced up at her.

"I'm so very sorry," Ella said.

"We all are," Justine added gently.

"I know you from church—all the Goodlucks," Nadine said. "That's why your voice was so familiar."

"We'll be praying for you," Justine assured softly.

"Her daughter's in a far better place now and Nadine knows that. Jesus Christ promised that those who do His will, rise again," Ford said. "Alice is at peace now, and watching over her family. She wouldn't want anyone, particularly her mother, to be sad."

Nadine wiped the tears from her face. "She always said that worry and sadness were a terrible waste of the time we're given."

Ella sat down across from her. "Tell me more about Alice."

"She was a wonderful daughter and had more courage than anyone I've ever known. Even the cancer couldn't defeat her spirit. After the Army, she got her degree at the University of New Mexico, then came home. She worked at the community college as an assistant professor of anthropology and her students just loved her. She'd already signed a contract to go back in the fall," Nadine said, looking at the photo on the table beside her.

"Is that her?" Ella asked, seeing a young woman with waist-length ebony hair smiling at the camera.

Nadine nodded. "She loved her hair. She kept it as long as allowed while serving in the Army, though she'd tie it back in a bun. When the chemo made it fall out by the handfuls, I thought she'd be heartbroken, but she said that no one should sweat the little things. She even refused to wear a wig."

"Her car was found in Farmington beside the bus station. Do you know where she was going when she disappeared?" Ella asked.

"I don't know how the car got there. My daughter was on her way home after chemotherapy at the medical center in Farmington. They were all evening sessions. The clinic wasn't far, so she insisted on driving herself there and back. I would have gladly taken her, but there was no arguing once her mind was set." When Nadine looked up, her eyes were vacant. Sorrow had blasted a hole right through her heart. "Then one night, June first, two years ago, she never made it home. The police checked with the bus company after her car was found there, but she never got on any bus. She was just . . . gone."

Nadine's last words were nothing more than a whisper that faded into the air.

Ella felt the woman's pain and wished she could back off, but she had a job to do. "So you reported her missing right away?"

"Yes, I did, but except for her car, the police had no luck," she said in a hard voice. "So I hired an investigator to find her."

"Who?" Ella asked her.

"A man by the name of Harrison. He came around about a month after Alice's disappearance and asked me if I needed help. He said that the police don't always have the time or manpower to find missing people, but that was all his agency did. If anyone could track her down, he could—but he never did."

"When did he finally stop working for you?"

"He didn't. Every year at this time I hire him to go out and check through all the records just in case something new has turned up, or we missed something." She took a shallow, shuddering breath. "But now I know my daughter's in heaven, so I guess I won't need him anymore. I should call him. . . ."

"I'll speak to him for you," Ford said.

Nadine looked at Ella, then Justine. "Find whoever murdered my daughter. She fought for every moment she had left on earth, and he robbed her of whatever time might have been hers. He had no right. . . ." Her voice broke and Ford went to her side instantly.

"We'll find him. We won't stop until we do," Ella assured her.

Once outside, Ella took a shaky breath. Justine's hands were also unsteady as she reached for her keys.

"When snake-eyes killed Alice, he also took a vital piece of her mother," Justine said.

"If there's a hell on earth, it's a parent outliving their child," Ella said in a heavy voice.

As they got back into the car, dispatch came over the radio. "I've got a Priority call. There's a standoff between motorists about two miles west of Hogback. Shots have been fired. Officers are on route, but the closest unit is twenty minutes away. Can you respond, SI One?"

"Ten-four. ETA, ten minutes," Ella said into the mike as Justine started the engine. "Anything else you can tell me, dispatch?"

"The cell phone caller said some armed Navajos have forced a non-Navajo driver off the road. That's when the shooting started."

"The Fierce Ones," Justine muttered. "As if our day wasn't crappy enough."

"We're approaching from the west," Ella told dispatch, then racked the mike. "Lights and sirens—go," she told Justine as she adjusted her vest.

"Do you suppose the Fierce Ones found the snake-eyes killer?" Justine yelled over the wail of the siren.

"I doubt it, but they wouldn't risk jail time by pulling over every Anglo male coming down the highway," Ella answered. "Something got their attention."

Soon they approached the curve in the highway at the south end of the Hogback. Up ahead Ella saw a big gray pickup off the westbound highway beside a ditch, blocked at the west end by a green truck that had obviously cut it off. A second vehicle, an old boat of a Chevy sedan, had come in behind the gray truck from the east, trapping it in place.

As Justine whipped past the old Chevy, Ella saw two armed men crouched low beside the front and rear driver's side tires, their shotguns aimed at the trapped pickup.

"That's Delbert John on the right," Justine said, cutting across the median, then braking to a stop at an angle and turning off the siren.

"Keep watch for the gray pickup's driver," Ella said, opening her door and jumping out. She kept out of view, knowing the door itself wasn't really that much protection.

"What's the story, Delbert?" Ella called out. She unsnapped the holster strap but didn't draw her weapon.

"Anglo with a pistol. One of our people saw it on his seat when he stopped for gas in Waterflow. He was heading into the Rez," Delbert shouted, not taking his eyes off the gray pickup.

"So your crew decided to pull him over. What did you do, go alongside and show your guns?" Ella asked.

There was a long pause. "Yeah, pretty much."

"So what did you expect? He started shooting when you forced him off the road, right?"

"Yeah. But we've got him trapped now."

"Anyone get shot yet?" she asked.

"Don't think so."

"These guys pulled over the wrong man," Justine said, coming up behind Ella and speaking just loud enough for her to hear. "Look at the shirt hanging up by the gray pickup's rear window."

Ella studied it for a moment. "It's a uniform shirt. That patch on his sleeve . . . he's a security guard."

"Which explains the weapon," Justine said.

"You get a visual on him?" Ella asked.

"He's by the front passenger-side fender, using the engine block for protection."

"I see a foot. Sir—you, in the gray truck, I'm a police officer," Ella yelled, then stood, holding up her badge. "I know you're a security guard and that you were attacked first. We're in charge of the scene now, so please put your weapon down and stand up. Place your hands on the hood of your truck so we can see them."

Ella turned to Delbert. "Order your people to put down their weapons and stand, hands visible. We'll handle this."

Delbert gave the order. Someone grumbled, but after a pause, everyone stood. Ella stepped around her open door and moved to the right. She was now visible from the pickup. "Cover me," she told Justine.

"Come on out, sir," Ella called, walking toward the pickup slowly, holding her empty hands at breast level.

"Okay, I'm moving in your direction." A tall, red-haired Anglo man with a southern accent walked slowly down the north edge of the road toward the back of his pickup. "I'm a security guard at the Four Corners Power Plant. My shift is over and I was on my way to see my girlfriend in Shiprock. These armed men tried to hijack me. I have the right to defend myself, ma'am."

Ella closed the distance slowly and glared at the two vigilantes standing to her left at the front of the big car. As she reached the tailgate of the pickup both men showed their hands.

"Are you okay?" she asked the guard at last.

He nodded. "I'm going to reach for my ID, okay?"

"Go ahead," Ella said.

The man's ID's, both his company name tag and New Mexico operator's license, identified him as Jesse Pritchard of Farmington. "Things up and down this valley have been tense as of late, so that's why I kept my gun handy," he said. "My red hair, well, it makes me stick out around here."

Ella had to admit he had a point. She'd never seen a brighter shade of natural red. "Stay here, Mr. Pritchard."

Ella walked back and showed Justine the ID. "Run it."

Justine came back moments later. "Jesse Pritchard has lived in this area for about eighteen months. He's ex-military and was stationed at Eglin Air Force Base in Florida for two years before that. He's not our guy."

Ella nodded. "Tell Delbert to move the vehicles over to the side of the road up by that mileage marker, then have his crew wait there until I tell them otherwise. We'll need their names, telephone numbers, and addresses."

A few minutes later, after the Fierce Ones had moved their vehicles, Ella joined Jesse. "You're free to go now, Mr. Pritchard. We've got things here now. Would you like to check your pickup for damage?"

"No ma'am, not necessary. We never actually collided. I'm just glad you showed up when you did."

As the security guard drove off, Delbert walked over to where she was standing.

"Why do I bother even trying to reason with your kind? You just can't listen to anyone's voice but your own," Ella said, crossing her arms and glaring at him.

"Face it, the police are getting nowhere. You need more eyes and ears out on the highway."

Ella swallowed back an angry retort and forced her tone to stay even. "Had that man been injured, you and the others would have been facing felony charges. Or you could have gotten yourselves shot."

"You should be grateful for our help. We're doing what the police can't do."

Ella took a deep breath. "You're vigilantes, Delbert, working illegally and without a lick of common sense. I should throw you all in jail. Get a clue. This is New Mexico, and over there," she pointed west, "is Arizona. Combining that state with ours, you're looking at hundreds of thousands of gun owners. There are plenty of long stretches of open road, so a lot of people who travel alone carry weapons. When word of this gets around, rest assured that even more will be putting their pistols under the seat or their rifles on the rack. You can't go around attacking every lone Anglo traveler you see."

"Armed ones, yes."

"No. You're not paying attention. Most of them will be innocent people exercising their second amendment rights— something you clearly believe in or *you* wouldn't be packing.

This is the West, and you're not a cop. You have no authority to stop anyone just because they have a firearm and light skin. What's worse, someone—you guys included—could die trying."

"We're willing to take that risk to keep the tribe safe."

"There's something else you might want to keep in mind. You have better odds of looking like a fool than a dead hero. Is that the way you want Anglos to see the *Diné,* or identify the Fierce Ones—as a joke?"

Wordlessly, Delbert strode off and joined the others. As the trio cleared out, Ella went to join Justine. "Let's get out of here."

"Where to?" Justine asked.

"The community college. I want to talk to people who worked with Alice Pahe. We need to find out if she had any enemies, and if so, who they were."

It was midafternoon by the time they arrived on campus. Ella had called ahead and received directions to the office of the head of the Anthropology Department and an assurance that he'd be there.

As they walked down the hallway of the large building, they passed several large classrooms, most in session. The department office was situated about midway down the hall, and they headed there.

Verifying the name on the closed door, they knocked. A Navajo man came to open it, glanced at the badges on their belts, then waved them inside. "Come in, officers, and close the door behind you so we won't be disturbed. My listed office hours are over so I can give you as much time as you need. I'm Paul Becenti, the department chair. I was told to expect you."

Ella leaned back. "We're here to ask you about Assistant Professor Alice Pahe, whose body was recently identified. I need to get a clearer picture of the victim. What can you tell me about her?"

He leaned back in his chair and took a deep breath. "Alice loved her work. Even after she started chemotherapy and radiation treatments she gave everything to the job. That dedication earned her the admiration of our staff and her students."

"Can you think of any reason someone might have wanted her dead?" Ella asked.

"No. But if someone had wanted that, all it would have taken was a little patience. It was no secret she didn't have long to live. I think that was why she made every minute count. She tutored free of charge and was always there for the students who needed her. Her absence has been felt."

"Did she ever teach a student by the name of Gilbert Romero?" Ella asked, trying hard to find a tie-in.

"I'll have to check," he said, moving over to his computer. A few minutes later, he looked up. "I couldn't find anyone by that name in her old class rosters."

Ella bit back a frustrated sigh. "Did Alice ever have a problem with another teacher or maybe a student?"

"I generally don't hear about things like that, but her former grad assistant might know. His name is Vincent Charlie." He glanced at his computer again and typed in something. "He's here now, just down the hall. He's been working for Professor Benallyson."

"We'll find him," Ella said, standing up. "Thank you for your time."

Justine fell into step beside Ella as they went down the hall. "Maybe the grad assistant will be able to give us something more."

"You never jumped in with questions back there. How come?"

"I was watching him, trying to read his body language. He was listening to you, Ella, really listening. You got all the information he had to give," Justine answered. "Keep in mind that it's in his best interests to have the case closed. That's the only way everyone in his department will finally be in the clear."

"Good point," Ella answered. She knocked on the open office door. "We're looking for Vincent Charlie."

"You've found him, but give me a sec," the young Navajo man said without glancing away from his computer screen. A minute later, he finally turned around. "Sorry— ladies. I'm entering term paper grades and I wanted to finish up before saving. What can I do for you?" His wide, toothy grin would have lit up a stadium.

Ella introduced herself and Justine, and as she did, saw the young man's gaze linger on her partner a moment longer than was necessary. Ella forced herself not to smile. Though Justine was probably at least ten years his senior, her partner still looked as if she were in her mid-twenties.

"We need to learn more about Alice Pahe, and the department chair suggested we talk to you," Ella said.

He nodded slowly, his expression now sober. "I probably knew her better than anyone else," he said. "It's been a long time but I still miss her."

"Were you two involved?" Ella asked.

"No, it wasn't like that," he said quickly. "I was her assistant and friend, that's all."

"Did she have any enemies that you know about?" Ella asked him.

"Who doesn't? Dr. Pahe's major fault, if one could call it that, was that she spoke her mind even when she shouldn't have."

"Give me an example," Ella asked.

"I remember a time in class. One of the students said that our people show real courage when they step outside Anglo laws and force others to act right—like the Fierce Ones do. Although she knew that the Fierce Ones have a lot of support and it's risky to say anything against them, Dr. Pahe didn't hold back. She told him in no uncertain terms that anyone who takes the law in their own hands creates chaos."

"How did the student react?" Justine asked.

"Not well, until Dr. Pahe told us what had happened to her a few days before when another driver out on the highway took it upon himself to play judge and jury. She'd been feeling more fatigued than usual after chemotherapy and pulled out into the highway too slow for some guy coming up in a pickup. She'd made up her mind to pull over at the gas station up ahead, but the other driver went a little crazy. He pulled up beside her and cursed her out, calling her a bleeping drunk."

"Did she call for help?"

"She couldn't. Her cell phone was in her purse on the passenger-side floor and she couldn't reach it without letting go of the steering wheel. The other driver passed her, then slowed to a crawl, speeding up every time she tried to get around him. Finally she swerved onto the power plant highway and headed for their main gate. The other driver broke off the chase. To Dr. Pahe, that was a prime example of the harm created by citizens who take it upon themselves to threaten and harass others for an imagined offense."

"Perfect road rage scenario. Did she report the incident?" Justine asked him.

The question told Ella that Justine hadn't found anything on record and was as curious as she was.

"I have no idea."

"Thanks for your time," Ella said, standing.

"I'll be around if you have any more questions," the young man said as they left the office.

As they walked out of the main building, Ella looked over at Justine. "Try to narrow down the date of the incident by relating it to her chemo sessions. Then see if it coincides with Romero's whereabouts. That road-rage thing has his mark all over it."

TWENTY-FOUR

————— ✖ ✖ ✖ —————

On their way back to the station, Benny called with important news. "We've got a positive ID on the fourth body. Arthur Nih—another Navajo—disappeared three years ago and had been on Highway 64 on the way to his girlfriend's house. When he didn't show up, she called it in. She figured he'd gone out drinking again and got into an accident. According to our records, that was on June first, same as the other victims. I called Dr. Roanhorse earlier and gave her the name. It didn't take her long to match Nih's Army dental records to those of the deceased."

"What about his vehicle?" Ella asked.

"It was found over in the Bisti area, wrecked, about a week later. No evidence of trauma was detected in the car. It was the opinion of the investigating officer that the vehicle had been pushed over the edge of the ravine and that nobody had been inside at the time."

"Next of kin?" Ella asked.

"No one came forward. All we know is that he'd divorced an Anglo woman from Albuquerque six years prior, and at the time of his death, Nih lived alone. The Gallup police investigated, and so did one of our officers, but no one found any leads. The girlfriend had an airtight alibi, so eventually the case was filed away with the other open cases."

After Ella slipped the phone back into her pocket, she gave Justine all the details. "Let's go over the facts on this case and see what common ground we have for all four killings."

"The two kill shots, in combination with the other facts, suggest two people were involved and took turns with the same weapon. Two perps would have also made it easier to grab the victim, transport him or her, dig the grave, and get rid of the victim's car," Justine said. "That means Bowman and Romero are still in contention."

"I don't buy it. Jimmy Bowman told me he hadn't killed anyone. In fact, he insisted on it. Why lie when he knew he was dying?" Ella asked.

"Doesn't make much sense, does it?" Justine answered.

"There's also something I got from Logan Bitterwater I haven't had time to share," Ella said and gave her the highlights of Preston's meeting with Kelewood.

"If Kelewood got ticketed, there should be a record of it," Justine said.

"We have to follow that up," Ella said. "There's also that one name that keeps popping up in this investigation—Ross Harrison."

"Yeah, but it stands to reason that it would. He's in the business of finding missing people, and since he's a former cop, he probably has friends in law enforcement who keep him informed."

"Check him out again anyway. You got us some general background on him earlier, and Dan's working it from his end, but we need to find out if he's been in contact with any of our officers. I also want to know if he's involved with the friends or families of the two other victims."

"If I recall correctly, FPD officers carry nine-millimeter handguns, and have for years. So Harrison probably carried one when he was on the force," Justine said.

"And had access to AP rounds, like with the first victim. The time frame is right," Ella replied. "Talbot owns a nine-millimeter handgun, according to background-check records. Harrison could have borrowed his weapon to throw off a trace."

Once they reached the station, Ella let word out that she was interested in talking to anyone who was regularly in contact with Ross Harrison. Time passed and when no one came to her office, she decided to take a walk to the front desk and speak to the sergeant there. He was usually well informed.

As she arrived in the front office, she ran into Harrison himself, who was standing at the counter, texting on his cell phone. Seeing him there caught her off guard momentarily, but she covered it well. "What brings you down to our station? Are you working for a client?" she asked him.

"Nah, Investigator Clah. Just paying a speeding ticket," he said, putting away his phone.

"Since you're here, maybe you can answer a few questions for me. Your name seems to turn up every time we dig into the backgrounds of our murder victims."

"I could say the same thing about yours," he shot back. "It's true that I'm always drumming up business, but I do that by following up missing persons reports. I don't kill people so I can contact their relatives, if that's what you're suggesting."

"I'm not suggesting anything," Ella said coldly.

"Just so we're clear then—when I started searching for the ones who turned out to be the snake-eyes killer's victims, they were just missing people no one was busting their butts to find. I wasn't obstructing your department's efforts either, because nobody here had any leads. Tell me I'm wrong."

Harrison's in-your-face attitude pissed her off. It was as if he were daring her to make something of it. She had a feeling that he was enjoying the game, too. "But now they're active investigations, and if you get in our way, I'll throw your butt in jail."

Without giving him a chance to respond, she headed back down the hall to her office. As she stepped through her door, she found Justine waiting.

"I've checked on Romero's whereabouts around the time of Alice Pahe's disappearance, but there's nothing on record," Justine said. "And he hasn't been in a classroom since dropping out of high school at seventeen."

"So he'll have to remain a suspect for now, since we can't conclusively rule him out," Ella said, then glanced up at the clock. It was already five in the afternoon. "I'm going to stop by the house and check on Dawn. We'll be working late tonight for sure, so I want to touch base with her. Consider it my dinner break," she said.

"Go. I'll call you if anything new comes to light."

On her way home, just after she'd turned off the main highway, Dan called. "The signature on the Hickory Lodge roster was a phony. It appears to have common points with Harrison's writing."

"He was doing whatever was necessary to keep his client writing those checks," Ella said, slowing down as she hit a washboard section of dirt road.

"Yeah, that's what I think, too. I'm going to keep digging into this guy's background. We know he's cheating his clients, so let's see what else he's doing on the side."

"That's a good idea. Keep me—" She heard a thump. Glancing into the rearview mirror, she saw a bullet hole in the window and almost simultaneously, she heard the distinctive crack of a small-caliber high-velocity rifle.

Ella dropped the phone and swerved hard to the left, raising a cloud of dust before driving off the side of the road into the shallow drainage ditch. Nearly at a stop, she cut back to the right at the last second, placing the SUV between her and the direction of the shooter.

"Clah, you okay?" Ella could hear Dan yelling.

Ella grabbed the phone off the passenger seat, then jumped out, ducking and using the engine block as a shield. "Someone just shot through my rear car window. I'm on the road to my house less than two hundred yards west of Highway 491. Call my station for backup."

TWENTY-FIVE

————— ✖ ✖ ✖ —————

Ella slipped the phone into her pocket and brought out her pistol. She moved toward the front of the SUV, but avoided looking across the hood, not wanting to present a shooting-gallery target. Crouched low, she looked out from headlight level, taking only a three-second glance before pulling back. To her left, the north, the terrain between her and the road was relatively flat. If the shooter was over there, they only had brush for cover.

Slipping to her right, she moved to the rear of the SUV and looked out from bumper level. There was no sign of the sniper along the long low ridge that ran parallel to the highway south of the dirt road. An expert at this game would have patience, waiting for her to show herself long enough to get another shot.

She inched back down the length of the vehicle, then took another look, this time longer and below the front bumper. Again, she couldn't see anything between her and the highway, and all she saw moving among the waist-high brush were a few pieces of traffic litter blown from the highway.

Not anxious to stay in one spot long enough to present a target, she rose up to take a quick glance along the SUV. She couldn't see an exit hole anywhere, not in the windshield or side windows, so either the bullet had ricocheted off the glass, or it was stuck in the interior someplace.

With more time to look at the small, circular hole in the rear window, she guessed the bullet had come from a .22 rifle. Such weapons were used for hunting small game or plinking. Had she been in any other profession she might have assumed it was an errant shot from somebody shooting at beer bottles or cottontails.

Ella waited, but everything around her remained quiet. The only sound she could hear was the ticking of the engine metal as it cooled, and the distant hum of traffic going down the main highway. It was possible the shooter had left—or not. She'd play it smart and stay put for a bit longer. Even a small bullet could kill if aimed carefully enough.

Ella called Justine, all the time scanning the terrain to the north and south. She'd become vulnerable again if the shooter came up on either flank. "I want whatever cruisers are in the area to take the road a few miles north of the turn-off and circle around to my house, making sure my brother is okay when they pass by. My family . . ."

"Got it," Justine said immediately. "Nez didn't give any details when he called our dispatch. What direction did the shot come from?"

"Somewhere behind me, east toward the highway, and just north or south of the road—probably south because there's more cover. I can't get a handle on the trajectory except that the round struck my rear window. If he'd fired from an extreme angle, the bullet would have probably ricocheted off the glass, so maybe he was all the way back at the highway. That was about a hundred and fifty yards away at the time the shot was fired. Anything beyond that would have been too far of a reach for someone with such a small caliber weapon."

"Did you see any vehicles by the road when you turned off the highway?" Justine asked.

"No, but I could have been followed, or maybe seen by someone coming from the south. All they'd have had to do was pull over and take a shot from inside their vehicle," Ella said. "Stay on the line while I take a better look around."

Ella flattened, looking from beneath the vehicle and beside a tire, knowing that she was in shade and difficult to spot as long as she stayed still. There was enough cover out here to conceal a prone sniper, but she saw no movement except for the natural sway of the brush and grasses.

"I think that was it for him, partner," Ella said, rising to her knees.

Ella poked her head up high enough, beside a window pillar, and checked the interior of the SUV. She quickly found the location of the missing bullet. There was a tear in the back of the passenger's side headrest, but no exit hole. The round was still in there someplace. The fact that she'd been moving in a straight line instead of turning may have saved her life.

"Justine," Ella said, bringing the phone to her ear again, "set up a checkpoint between here and Shiprock. If he headed north and stuck to the highway, we might get lucky. Be sure to have the officer in charge ID every driver who passes by within the next twenty minutes. We're looking for someone with a rimfire rifle and probably a scope."

"You'll be heading back this way in case he tries to turn around?" Justine asked.

"Exactly, but if he drove south after the shot, we're screwed," Ella said. "There are lots of places to turn off between here and Gallup."

Justine called back five minutes later. "I've got a unit in place. The officer is going to be checking licenses and writing down names. Same with the Gallup police."

"What about Ross Harrison?" Ella asked. "I spoke to him just before I left. Is he still at the station?"

"I passed him in the lobby on my way out—just a few minutes before you called. He was hitting on Mavis Zahnie, and I had to stay and watch him crash and burn."

Ella knew Big Ed's secretary, a buxom woman in her late forties. She was interesting-looking and highly intelligent, but not at all friendly to the male officers—or the women either, for that matter. "Interesting that he'd choose her. Cathy, at the desk, seems more his type."

"Mavis told him to come back when she was ten years younger and he was twice as good-looking. She said that in front of half the staff," Justine said, chuckling. "Were you thinking he might have been responsible for taking the shot at you?"

"Yeah, he and I butted heads just before I left," Ella said. "But if you left the station before he did, there was no way he could have been the shooter. Make a note to check on Talbot, his associate."

"Copy that," Justine said. "Some of our team is on the way to your location, but the crime scene van is in the shop at the moment. Think we need it?"

"Not just to search for the shooter's tracks and a spent cartridge."

"That's what I thought. I put a metal detector in my car to help in the search. Also, since we'll have to impound the SUV, we're bringing you another set of wheels."

"ETA?"

"Less than ten minutes—make that five now."

While she waited, Ella inspected the SUV, verifying the bullet, about the size of a .22 long rifle, was lodged in the headrest as she suspected. She'd intended to dig it out, but just then her phone rang.

"I asked FPD to send an officer to Harrison's office and look for Talbot. We'll get a call within ten minutes," Justine said.

"Where are you now?"

"I'm cresting the hill, and I can see the turnoff now," Justine said.

Less than two minutes later Justine pulled up on the opposite side of the road and parked. Ella was walking across to her partner's cruiser when her phone rang.

"I just got a call from Detective Nez," Blalock said. "The officer he assigned to watch Norman Ben observed the subject, suitcase in hand, chartering an airplane to Tucson with connections to Mexico City. Nez had the officer detain Ben at the Aztec airport. I'm heading over there now."

"I'll let Justine take over here and join you shortly. The sniper is long gone by now."

"Roger that. We'll wait to question Ben until you arrive."

Ella reached the small airfield west of the county seat—Aztec—forty minutes later. The facility was small and she didn't have to search long to find Nez and Blalock. They were standing at the other end of the main counter in front of a closed door.

"I'm here, guys," she said, hurrying across the tile floor to join them. "What's the deal with Ben?"

"He was instructed not to leave town without notifying the police, but he chose to run," Dan said. "Now we have to find out why."

"What else do we know?" Ella asked. It was often easier to extract information from a suspect when you already knew at least some of the answers.

"He closed his business and personal bank accounts earlier today and withdrew all the funds in cash," Blalock said. "I don't have the exact amounts because what I got was off the record. Without a court order, I can't get any more than that."

"That still doesn't mean he's the killer, or one of them," Ella said. "What we need to find out is why he's running, and from who or what?"

As they went into the room Norman Ben raised his head to look at them, a total lack of expression on his face.

Blalock advised him of his rights.

"I have nothing to say until my attorney arrives," he said stiffly.

"Mr. Ben, we understand you've cleaned out your bank accounts and now you're heading out of the country? What's the story?" Blalock asked, sitting across from him.

"All the money I've taken is mine. It's not a crime to convert all your funds into cash."

"But you *are* running," Ella insisted in a soft voice. "Why fly out of the area from Aztec when you live so much closer to the Farmington airport? It's like you're trying to slip away, unnoticed."

"I was on my way to visit my Mexican girlfriend. That's all I've got to say. I have the right to remain silent and I'm exercising that right."

Ella tried pressing him for more answers, but he refused to even look in her direction. After a few minutes, she stood and looked at Blalock.

"Play it your way," Blalock told Ben. "We'll turn you over to the Aztec Police for now and have you locked up as a material witness. Later, after you've spoken to your attorney, you and I can have another talk."

"You're looking for a murderer and that's not me," Ben said in a barely audible voice. "Elroy and I had plenty of disagreements, that's for sure, but I never did anything to him. I was as surprised as everyone else when his body turned up over at Hogback."

"Can you remember where you were on June first, four years ago?" Ella asked.

"That was a *long* time ago," he said. "Is that when Elroy was killed?" No one said anything, and at length he continued. "Normally I wouldn't be able to cover a date that far back, but every June I go to Mexico for a month—and that, by the way, is where I was going now. I include my old desk calendars with my tax papers and those'll back me up. I've also got receipts for the flights and other expenses like restaurants and hotels."

"It's not June yet," Blalock said, "and do you always empty your accounts before you go? Will that show up in your old records?"

Ben didn't answer.

Two City of Aztec police officers appeared at the door moments later. Ella and Blalock stepped out of the way as Norman Ben was taken into custody.

Once they were alone, Nez looked at Blalock, then at Ella. "How did you narrow all the murders down to June first?" he asked.

She answered him, filling him in on the details. "I don't know for sure that all four victims were killed on the first, but it seems a good bet."

"The bad news is that if the pattern holds, on June first another Navajo will be murdered. That's a little over a week away, so we should keep that detail to ourselves. We don't want to start a panic," Blalock said.

"Norman Ben isn't in the clear yet, guys," Nez pointed out. "Being out of the country is a great alibi, but that doesn't mean he wasn't involved. Ben could have hired a hit man, one who had targeted the other victims already. One man— one common burial ground."

"Without more evidence, substantiating that theory is going to be tough," Blalock said. "Who hired the assassination of the other three victims, for instance?"

"And why the same day every year?" Nez asked. "I see your point."

"Let's go to my Shiprock office," Blalock said. "I've got access to most law enforcement and regional news databases there. If we dig hard enough, maybe we can find out what's special about June first. That's got to be connected to the motives in some way."

Ella glanced at Dan, who nodded. "Let's go then," she said.

They arrived at Blalock's office on Shiprock's north mesa within the hour. Blalock led the way inside the one-story office building he shared with several tribal agencies. "I work better from home these days, but the Bureau still wants me to keep office hours when I'm not out in the field. I wish they'd at least let me relocate to Farmington. It would make it a shorter drive at the end of the day."

Once again, Ella found herself envying Dwayne. He'd found, or at least rediscovered, his soul mate. She wasn't sure she'd ever find someone who understood the demands of the job, and who'd value the work she did even when it required her to pay a price.

FB-Eyes unlocked his office door, then took a seat by his old oak desk, which looked to be older than any of them.

"When are you going to get another resident agent?" Ella asked, seeing Dan looking at the wall photos of previous agents who'd worked the Four Corners area.

"With budget cuts and the fact that the Albuquerque field office is low priority, probably not anytime soon. But working alone poses fewer complications."

Ella sat down in front of one computer, Nez by a laptop, and Blalock at his desk. "Ella, you take the local papers and media, including the cable channels. Nez, you take regional and networks, and do an Internet check. I'll check agency databases."

Minutes passed by slowly, then Blalock glanced up at them. "Here's something. Five years ago on June first, a year prior to the death of our first victim, a young woman named Rosemary Archuleta and her unborn child were killed on Highway 64 near Hogback. The accident was caused by a drunk Navajo driver, Ambrose Todacheene. He was driving his pickup on the wrong side of the road, according to the report. He survived with cuts and bruises."

"Let me cross-check with the tribal and Farmington papers and see if I can get something more," Ella said. A moment later she let out a low whistle. "You'll never guess who Rosemary Archuleta's fiancé was."

TWENTY-SIX
——— ✖ ✖ ✖ ———

Blalock and Dan both came to look over Ella's shoulder. "Whatcha got, Ella?" Blalock asked, looking at the screen.

"A newspaper story on the accident that identifies Farmington police officer Ross Harrison as her fiancé." She scrolled up the screen to show a photo of the accident scene.

"*Our* Ross Harrison, the P.I.?" Dan asked, looking from Ella to Blalock.

"One and the same," she answered. "But we've known for days that his fiancée had died in an accident. Just no details."

"Did the drunk who killed the woman serve time?" Dan asked.

"I'll check," she replied, doing a search using the accident victim's name on the newspaper database.

"Here it is. He was convicted of DWI and involuntary manslaughter but only served six months of a two-year sentence. A week after his release, he died in a one car rollover accident," Ella said. "Toxicology reports indicated that Todacheene had been well over the legal limit."

"And Harrison resigned from the FPD not long after that. Anyone believe this is all just a coincidence?" Dan asked. "That road rage theory Sergeant Neskahi came up with may be coming back to haunt us."

Ella sat back, her eyes still on the computer screen. "Harrison might have caused that accident. He was still on the force and had access to Todacheene's address."

"If Ross is our guy, we're going to need a lot more than timing to put him away," Blalock said, moving back to his desk.

Ella's cell phone rang and she picked it up.

"It's Marianna," the officer said, identifying herself.

"Go ahead, Officer Talk," Ella answered.

"After you put out the BOLO on Romero, I remembered hearing that his cousin, Hoskie Romero, lived next door to Herbert Lee. Herbert's a former officer with our department, so I asked him to keep an eye on the place in case Gilbert showed up," Marianna said.

"And it paid off," Ella said, reading her tone of voice correctly.

"Yes. Herbert just called," Marianna said. "He'd gone out to check on his horse when he saw two people over at Hoskie's place. Gilbert's there. Herbert's certain of the ID because he arrested Gilbert a few times for fighting over by Window Rock. Herbert thinks Gilbert drove up at night on the opposite side of the river, then waded across. When he took a look around, Herbert saw a blue Ford SUV hidden in the brush across the river."

"Good job, Marianna. Thinking outside the box was exactly what was needed," Ella said.

"Do you want me to meet you there?"

"What's the location?" Ella got an address, then thought about it for a moment. "Let's join up at the post office parking lot, which is on the way. We'll get more facts and come up with a plan there. Our ETA is ten minutes."

As she updated the others, Blalock grabbed an assault rifle and ammunition clips from the closet gun safe.

Dan looked at Ella. "It's outside my jurisdiction, but I want in."

"Done. Call Sergeant Marquez and have her set up road-blocks on all county routes leading east off the Rez," Ella said with a nod.

"Roger," he said.

On the drive east through Shiprock, Ella called Justine at the station. "Bring the team and come well armed. I have a feeling this isn't going to go down easy."

"We'll give you plenty of backup," Justine said. "Tache's here and so's Neskahi. Benny's around someplace, too. I'll also send a unit up the south side of the river to cover escape routes. We don't want Gilbert giving us the slip this time."

As she raced down the highway, Ella knew danger lay ahead. Her badger fetish felt warm against her skin, a sign she'd learned to trust.

Soon they met at the post office parking lot and everyone gathered beside Ella's SUV. Marianna briefed them on the layout around Hoskie's place, and Ella drew up a tactical plan.

"Let's go, people," Ella said at last.

Hoskie Romero's home was typical for the Rez—a simple rectangular wood frame with a gray stucco scratch coat and a tan fiberglass shingle roof. Since rifle bullets could penetrate those walls and expose officers on opposite sides of the building to friendly fire, Ella instructed everyone to use handguns and shotguns only.

Blalock and Benny approached along the river's northern bank, covering the narrow margin between the house and the waterway itself. Marianna and Dan covered the road and open area on the north side. She and Justine approached from the Shiprock side while Tache and Neskahi came in from the east. All had voice communications via their handhelds.

They advanced steadily, closing in on the house, using whatever cover was available. With all escape routes covered, Gilbert would have two choices—surrender, or shoot it out. Considering the guy's track record, Ella braced herself for the worst.

With Justine covering her, Ella took a position behind Hoskie's old orange-and-white pickup, which was parked fifty feet from the front entrance. The truck was locked, so she jammed a sliver of wood into the mechanism and broke it off. It would slow down anyone with a key.

Ella unsnapped the bullhorn she'd attached to her belt earlier. "Police. You're surrounded. Hoskie and Gilbert Romero come out now, unarmed, with your hands in the air."

Less than a minute went by, then the front door opened, and a man came out with his hands over his head. It wasn't Gilbert, she'd seen his photo.

"Don't shoot!" he yelled out, seeing Ella aiming her pistol straight at him. "I'm not armed."

The fact that he was shirtless, barefoot, and wearing snug jeans made that easy to verify at a glance. Ella studied the front door of the house, then the two facing windows, wary of an ambush.

Marianna Talk spoke over the radio. "That's Hoskie. I recognize him from Herbert's description," she said.

"Come over here, behind the pickup," Ella shouted. "And keep your hands where I can see them."

As Hoskie approached, Ella reached out and pulled him behind cover, forcing him to lay down face-first. She handcuffed, then frisked him while Justine kept watch on the house. "Who else is in there?" she asked.

"Gilbert, my cousin, and he's freakin' crazy! He showed up this morning while it was still dark, dripping wet after wading the river. When I saw the gun and a bloody bandage on his arm, I told him to take off. But he wouldn't leave. He's been eating my food, listening to the news, and watching out the windows. He finally dozed off, but then you guys showed up and he told me to get out. He wants to fight and die with a gun in his hand. Like I said—he's crazy."

"What kind of weapons does he have?" Ella asked him.

"That pistol I told you about, a nine-millimeter of some kind. He called it a Car. It's an automatic with a clip, not a cowboy gun."

"A Kahr, no doubt. What about ammo, what's he got?" Ella asked him.

"Just what's in the gun," Hoskie answered. "He bitched for an hour about not switching to a full clip. He said he dropped the other one in the river and couldn't find it. I don't own any guns or bullets, but he looked around in case I was lying."

Ella conveyed the information to her team, then sent Hoskie over to Justine. She handcuffed him to a tree, safely out of sight.

"If he wants a fight, we shouldn't wait till dark, Ella," Blalock said over the radio. "I've got some tear gas in my unit. I say we force him out—now."

"If we do that, he's going to come out shooting. He's decided on suicide by cop," Ella said.

"Not good," Neskahi said over the radio.

"He's only got whatever rounds are in his pistol," Justine reminded them, having taken up her covering position again. "Most Kahr autoloaders have seven-round magazines, so even with one in the chamber, he can't have more than seven shots. He'll come out blasting, but if we keep him firing blind until his ammo is spent, we can take him down with Tasers."

"Tasers and tear gas then," Ella said. "But use lethal force if there's no other option."

Five minutes later they were ready to make their move. Ella fired a tear gas grenade through the front window, and seconds later, Romero rushed out the front door, yelling, and firing blind. He'd already expended four rounds, and was still screaming like a banshee when he decided to make a run for the pickup.

Ella slipped down the length of the vehicle, keeping as much metal between her and Gilbert Romero as possible.

As Gilbert reached the driver's-side pickup door and yanked on the locked handle, he saw Ella. Cursing and groping in his pocket for the keys, he snapped a shot, forcing Ella to duck behind the tailgate. The bullet went wide, whistling into the *bosque*.

"He's out," Justine yelled, seeing Gilbert staring at the pistol's open slide.

Ella holstered her pistol and fired her Taser at Gilbert, but only one probe hit the mark. The other bounced off his weapon and ended up striking the pickup's side mirror.

Gilbert yelled, then threw his pistol at Ella. As she ducked, he sprinted down the road. Then he saw Marianna and Dan rise up from the brush where they been hiding. Romero swerved to the right. Racing east now, he headed straight toward Ralph Tache.

Ella knew that Ralph's injuries made him vulnerable and he was likely to be seriously injured in a hand-to-hand battle.

"Taser him, Ralph," she yelled.

Instead of taking action, Ralph just stood there, frozen, staring at the device in his hand.

Nez, who'd quickly closed in from the north, fired his Taser on the run.

The probes made contact and Gilbert fell to the ground, his body twitching.

"Turning it off," Dan yelled as Ella came up to the groaning man on the ground.

Ella rolled Gilbert facedown, then cuffed him before he could recover. She still wasn't sure why Tache hadn't fired, but she'd look into that later.

Ella pulled away the Taser leads, then Neskahi, with his wrestler build, hauled Gilbert to his feet.

Gilbert shot Ella a look of pure hatred. "You think I killed all those people over at the Hogback, don't you? But it wasn't me, no matter what anyone says. Ya hear?" he yelled out as Neskahi led him to his cruiser.

Ella was walking back to retrieve her discarded Taser when Blalock joined her. "What do you think? Is he our man?" he asked as she stowed away the wire leads and reloaded the device.

"No. I stand by my original theory. Romero doesn't have the personality to carry out carefully planned murders. His style is exactly what we just saw—rush out with guns blazing. Simple road rage murders, yes, but not the crimes we're investigating. He and Jimmy Bowman got caught up in our manhunt mostly because they were in the area at the right time."

"I agree," Dan said, coming up to join them.

"So that leaves us with Ross Harrison. We need to find out more about his business and take a real close look at his alibi," Ella said, placing the Taser back into her pocket. "I'd like county to stake him out for a day or two. Let's see where he goes and who he meets. I also want to know a lot more about Talbot. How did those two ever find each other?"

"I can place Harrison and Talbot under surveillance," Dan said. "If we get anything, I'll contact you. Either way, we'll keep a close eye on their whereabouts and a tally of everyone they meet."

After Dan left, Ella and Blalock returned to his office. Tossing her a cold drink, he went to his chair and leaned back.

"If Harrison's responsible for these murders, he's got brass balls and isn't likely to break under questioning," Blalock said, sitting behind his desk and gazing at her. "We'll need hard evidence to put that man away, and the

296 ✖ AIMÉE & DAVID THURLO

only thing we've got are those recovered nine-millimeter bullets. We have to find a way to link them to a weapon in his possession."

"If it's his, he's probably ditched the gun already, and the highly incriminating armor-piercing rounds. If he borrowed it from Talbot, we'd have to find a way to tie it back to him convincingly. Let's check the police files, government files, and whatever else you can access from here," she said.

Blalock logged on, and after a few minutes read her what he had on screen. "Talbot's retired Army. Currently, he works part time as a security guard over at the Four Corners Power Plant. I'm going to call and see what they have on file for him."

Blalock used his Bureau credentials, and soon was promised that a copy of Talbot's file would be forwarded to him via e-mail. As they waited, Dwayne sat back, stretching out his long legs. "Their background checks are usually pretty extensive, so this should be interesting."

"The revenge motive is there for Harrison—his fiancée was killed—but that's not evidence, it's just a reason. The only evidence we have to support our theory is the matching date—June first—and that's clearly circumstantial. And does Talbot play into this at all, or is he just Harrison's employee?" Ella said, mostly thinking out loud.

Moments later the file came in. As Blalock called it up, Ella came over and stood behind his chair, looking at the screen.

"Talbot was Rosemary Archuleta's biological father. Talbot married someone else, but when Rosemary's single mother died, he and his wife stepped up and took the two-year-old. They raised her as their own," Blalock said, skimming the information. "When Talbot filled out these forms, Rosemary was still living in a *casita* on the back of their property."

"So there's our tie-in between Harrison and Talbot—

Rosemary. They both have a strong motive. Someone they love was killed. They could be taking it out on what they believe to be Navajo drunk drivers."

"It's still not evidence—not by itself," Blalock said, beginning a new search on Talbot. "But here's something that might mean something. Talbot has two vehicles, and one matches the make and model of the police cruisers in this area."

"If we're to believe Joe Preston, Kelewood was stopped by a deputy on the night he disappeared," Ella said.

"You're suggesting that a fake county vehicle pulls over the victims?" Seeing her nod, he continued. "You might have something there. Around here it's more than just an urban legend. We've had actual cases in this area where predators posing as cops have pulled people over, though they've usually targeted women."

"That would explain how Harrison and Talbot were able to secure their victims without a struggle," Ella said. "And I bet I know how the Bitsillie kids fit in, too. Harrison's and Talbot's game plan was working just fine until two kids from a homeless family spotted one of them in the phoney cop car scouting their burial site. When the fence crew found the graves, they panicked, thinking the boy might have led them there. Worse—Del had been close enough to maybe see a face. They tried to take him out that same afternoon, but I got in the way. Knowing the boy was guarded, they found another way to get him out of the area without taking any more risks. That note they left in his mom's car was enough."

"Good theory, Clah. It all ties together and explains why, even in daytime, we weren't able to find the sniper who tried to kill the kid. He was driving a car tricked out to look like a sheriff's department cruiser. The shooter blended in as part of the hunt, and nobody looked twice. Slick. But how do we *prove* any of this?"

"I'm not sure, but we better figure it out fast. Those text

messages they sent me were meant to mess with my mind. It was probably Harrison, I've seen him texting a couple of times, right in front of me. The guy is arrogant. The shooting incidents were designed to misdirect and slow us down. The only reason I can think of for them to actively try and divert our investigation is if they're planning on striking down another DWI Navajo on June first. We're about out of time."

Blalock studied the information on screen. "Bruce Talbot and and his wife Emily divorced three years ago, but she's still living in Farmington. I say we go talk to her. Maybe we can get a read on what's inside Talbot's head."

"Good idea," Ella said with a nod. "Ex-wives, more often than not, will give you the dirt on their old man. But I may get farther if I go in alone. I can keep it low key and tell her I'm updating the information in her husband's file for the power plant."

"Okay, sounds like a plan. I'll drive, and you can go in alone. I doubt she's involved in the killings, but just in case, I want to be close by—CYA."

"I appreciate that. Where does she work, anyway?"

"According to what I read, Emily Talbot has been the receptionist at a small interior design firm off Main Street for nearly five years."

The Farmington business was located in a one-story brick building across from a huge building supply warehouse on east Main Street. As Ella walked in, she saw a woman in her fifties with reddish auburn hair sitting at the front desk.

"Hi. I'm Emily. Can I help you?"

Ella smiled back. "Mrs. Talbot? I'm Ella Clah. I work for the tribe and I'm doing an update on Bruce Talbot's power plant personnel file."

"You guys must really be behind. Bruce and I have been

divorced for three years. I don't even remember the last time I saw him, so I'm not sure how much help I'll be. Our lives and finances are pretty much separate now."

Ella gave her a weary smile. "Look, Mrs. Talbot—Emily? I have a list of standard questions I'm required to ask. Some of them are just 'yes' or 'no.' So how about it? If a client comes in, I can sit back, wait, and appreciate the air-conditioning."

"All right. My boss is on vacation anyway, so all I'm doing is keeping the office doors open and collecting my paycheck."

"I know all about the importance of a paycheck," Ella said. "I'm a single mom."

The woman's expression clouded over. "Consider yourself lucky. Bruce and I had a daughter, but a drunk driver took her away from us a week before her wedding," she said, her voice wavering.

"I'm so sorry. You must have been devastated."

"After Rosemary died everything changed," she managed in a dry-throated whisper. "It was the beginning of the end for my marriage, too. Bruce and I kept drifting apart until there was nothing left. He was bitter and angry and kept it all inside. I needed to talk, to share the pain, but he shut me out."

Ella nodded, thinking how often that turned out to be the case. During times of crisis when a couple needed each other most, they sometimes went in opposite directions and never found their way back.

Emily took a slow, deep breath. "The drunk who killed Rosemary died several months later in another accident. At least no one else was hurt that time. I thought I'd be happy knowing that justice was served, but all I felt was . . . empty."

"How did your husband and your daughter's fiancé take that news?"

She considered it. "My husband started shaking when we read that Rosemary's killer was dead, then he just got up from the table and walked away. I think he wanted to put things behind him, but the pain just stayed and stayed. I never saw Ross, my daughter's fiancé, show any emotion, ever, except during Rosemary's funeral. I guess he spent too many years as a cop."

"I've met a private investigator named Ross Harrison," Ella said casually. "Is that the same man?"

"Yeah, small world," Emily said. "Strangely enough, my daughter's passing strengthened the friendship between Bruce and Ross. Last I heard, Ross had hired Bruce to help him on some of his cases. Bruce has always been a police buff, so it was a perfect chance for him to play cop. He even bought an ex-sheriff department's vehicle at auction, and in the months following my daughter's death, he and Ross spent hours restoring it. They even refinished the official paint scheme."

"To keep it authentic, I guess."

She shrugged. "Those two found comfort working with cars and collecting police memorabilia. It kept them distracted and I envied them that. Me, I've never been able to get away from the pain. It's always there, like my shadow."

Ella asked her a few rote questions, then after a bit, stood, and thanked her. "You've been through a lot, Emily, but time will help you."

"So they say." Emily walked with her to the door, then excused herself to answer the desk phone.

Ella met Blalock back at the car. He was standing outside in the shade of an elm, sipping bottled water. As they drove away, she told him what she'd learned. "Here's how I think it might have gone down. Bruce took on the role of ride-along while Ross posed as a deputy and pulled the victims over, selecting someone who appeared to be male and driving drunk. Next, Ross incapacitated the individuals, maybe with a Taser, and with Bruce's help put the person in the trunk of their 'squad' car. Ross drove the cruiser while Bruce took the vic's car. They met at the Hogback site, then finished the job."

"They might have even dug the grave the night before and hidden it with brush or tumbleweeds. That would have saved them a lot of time," Blalock said. "It would have also lessened the risk of getting discovered there."

Ella nodded. "They were probably monitoring police calls with a scanner in case someone called in a report. Harrison could have supplied them with what was needed before he left the department."

"Yeah, and once the body was in the ground, they ditched the vic's car at one of their preplanned locations and destroyed their victim's clothing, maybe burning everything, or just tossing it in a Dumpster thirty miles away."

"With Kelewood, they screwed up. They somehow missed his wallet, or maybe Chester managed to ditch it, hoping he could be traced," Ella said.

"It's also possible they decided to move fast after Joe Preston drove by and checked them out. In their rush, they never even saw it," Blalock said.

"Later, maybe weeks after the body was buried, they returned at night to make sure the site looked as natural as possible. They moved around some plants growing close by, and restored the terrain," Ella said.

"Sounds like a lot of work, but I guess they were motivated. Every act was another well-planned blow against their image of an injustice."

"Ross also muddied up the trail while pretending to look for the victims," Ella said. "He'd pick up information on the status of the official investigation, and get some extra bucks from the vics' families in the process. The irony of it all must have been very satisfying for them."

"Okay. Now we have a probable scenario—something

we never had with Romero and Bowman—but we still don't have anything conclusive. It appears that the only living witnesses to the crimes are the killers themselves," Blalock said.

"At least we can cross another suspect off the list— Norman Ben. There was no hesitancy in his tone when he offered up his alibi, but let me check with Benny and see where that stands," Ella said. After a moment she got her answer. "Norman's alibi checked out."

"If we're right about Harrison and Talbot, we'll need to nail them before June first. I bet we could find damning evidence at their homes, and I'd sure like to check out that car, too, but we'd need a warrant for all that."

"If we try to get one, we'll tip them off for sure," Ella said. "Harrison has contacts at the county courthouse, and maybe even at the district attorney's office. The second they get wind of it they'll get busy sanitizing their places and walk away clean."

When Ella's cell phone rang, she saw it was Dan and picked it up before the second ring.

"I was staking out Harrison and had one of my detectives covering Talbot. I didn't think I'd been spotted, but something obviously spooked Harrison. I think he must have been the one who called in a phony bomb threat on the house next door to his. When the fire department and the Farmington police showed up, I ended up losing him in the chaos. Then I got a call from the deputy who'd been watching Bruce Talbot over at Kirtland. The guy managed to get the drop on my man with a Taser. He took the deputy's weapon and keys, then tied him up and split. That was at least fifteen minutes ago."

The next sound she heard over the phone was an explosion, filtered by the phone but unmistakable. Then there was a confusing thud.

"Dan, you there? Detective Nez? You okay?" Ella called, looking at Blalock, who was clearly confused.

"What's going on?" Blalock asked her quickly. "Is Nez in trouble?"

There was a rustling sound, then Dan came back on the line.

"Sorry, the blast knocked me down and I dropped the phone. Harrison blew up his own house," Nez said, obviously shaken. "It *wasn't* a phony bomb threat, just the wrong address. Fortunately, nobody was close. The firemen had just pulled away but they're deploying again now."

"Harrison and Talbot are destroying evidence. Quick, call the deputy at Talbot's place. Warn him!" Ella said.

"I'll call you back."

Moments later, her phone rang again. "It's Dan. Talbot's place is still standing, and my officer is clear of the structure and evacuating the neighbors. The fire department is sending another unit there, and I'm responding as well."

"Blalock and I will meet you there. Do you have any idea what Ross is driving now?"

"His sedan is still here, but I got the plates off a truck I saw leaving the area. It's the only vehicle that went by my position, so I think that was him. I'll verify, then put out an ATL."

As they ran to Blalock's car, Blalock's phone rang, and he listened while climbing inside. "Hang on," he said, then turned to Ella, who was fastening her seat belt.

"It's county dispatch," he said. "Their bomb squad and the Farmington unit have their hands full at Harrison's residence. They want to borrow Ralph Tache as first responder over at Talbot's place. Is he up to it?"

Ella hesitated. She knew why Blalock was asking. When they'd made their move to take down Romero, Tache had dropped the ball at a critical time, hesitating to use his Taser.

She'd been tempted to pull him from active duty right then, but just hadn't had time to make it happen.

"I don't know," Ella finally said. "Maybe his Taser malfunctioned at the takedown," she said, yet even as she spoke, she knew in her gut that wasn't what had really happened.

"Dispatch needs an answer *now*. Do you think Tache's stable enough to search out and diffuse a bomb?" Blalock pressed.

"I'll call and talk to him. If Ralph gives me bad vibes, county will have to find someone else."

Five minutes later, as they were racing to Talbot's home, Ella finally reached Ralph Tache.

"I'll go," Ralph said without hesitation after she briefed him.

"Are you sure about this?"

"Yeah. I blew it with Romero. If I can't come through now, it's time for me to turn in my badge."

Ella hung up, then told Blalock what Tache had said. "After all these years I've come to one conclusion—police work either makes you stronger, or breaks you."

"The badge is part of him, Ella. He doesn't want to walk away from the job," Blalock said. "And that's what will see him through this. Police work gets under your skin. It isn't just what you do—it's who you are. I remember a time when being a Bureau agent meant everything to me. As far as I was concerned nothing stacked up against it."

"But not now?" Ella asked, following up on what he'd left unsaid.

"These days, it's just one part of my life. What matters to me most is no longer connected to my badge. Half of my future is at home painting watercolor flowers, and the other half is deployed overseas—in harm's way."

Ella noticed that when Dwayne referred to his wife and his son Andy, his voice gentled. He was a new man.

"I love my family more than I can ever put into words,

but the job I do for the tribe has a piece of my heart, too," Ella said. "I need both to feel complete."

"Nothing's wrong with that. You make it work."

"I've had to, so I did." She was a mother, a daughter, and a cop. Each of those facets came with challenges at almost every turn, but in her heart she knew she was exactly where she belonged.

TWENTY-SEVEN

——— ✖ ✖ ✖ ———

As Ella got out of Blalock's car, Nez came over to meet them. "We haven't searched Talbot's house yet, but his landlord has given us access. Talbot's also got a detached garage out back. One of his neighbors said that Talbot keeps one of his cars in there."

"Which house is Talbot's?" Ella asked, looking ahead.

"The one directly in the middle of the cul-de-sac," Dan answered.

"We need to keep everyone away until Tache arrives," Ella said.

"Someone call my name?"

Ella turned her head and saw Ralph step out of the bomb squad van. One of the department's mechanics was behind the wheel, giving Tache time to get ready en route. He was suited up in his protective gear, but had the helmet visor flipped up. Ella filled him in. "Will you need backup as you search, or if there's a bomb to diffuse?"

"I might. I don't know yet," Tache said.

"Use your headset to stay in touch and let me know," she said. "I'll be as close as you allow."

Tache walked toward Talbot's front door slowly, his gaze on the ground, searching, perhaps, for trip wires. His visor was down now and she couldn't see his expression, but Ella could almost feel the war going on inside him. He'd fought so hard to stay alive. After all those months of recovering from nearly fatal injuries, would duty demand that he lay his life down today?

Ella thought of calling him back. There were other jobs within the P.D. and Ralph had paid his dues many times over. There was no reason to demand so much from one officer. She brought her handheld radio up to her mouth, then stopped and lowered it to her waist again. This was his call—and his monster to face.

"There's no one else who could do the job, at least not for the next few hours," Blalock said, reading her correctly. "What's inside may crack this case and he knows it as well as we do. Let Officer Tache do what he signed on for. He needs this just as much as we do."

Ella saw Tache step onto the front porch gingerly despite the fact it was a concrete slab. Then he studied the door and trim, his body perfectly immobile and his hands at his sides.

"Bomb," came the verdict over the headset. "It's crude, but effective. There's fishing line fastened to a piece of wood that's keeping two electrical contacts apart. The door isn't quite shut, and if I'd have pulled it open, the line would have yanked out the wood, the circuit would have closed, and . . . boom."

Ella moved closer then stopped. "Do you need help?"

"No, I'm going to check the back door. If it's clear, I'll enter and deactivate the bomb from the inside," he said.

He turned toward the firemen and his driver, who were standing by the road. "Make sure no one comes near the porch until I disconnect the bomb and give the all-clear."

Hanging back, Ella followed Ralph around to the rear door, which looked solid. Ralph examined the mechanism carefully, looked all the way around the trim, then reached up and turned the knob.

"Unlocked. I should have thought of it sooner. This is how Talbot got out, of course," he said speaking into the headset. "Stay back, just in case." Ralph opened the door very slowly.

Ella heard footsteps and saw Nez and Blalock behind her, waiting.

Five minutes later, Ralph emerged carrying a big cardboard box, his visor flipped up. "It's deactivated." As Ralph looked at the detached garage, he added, "Let me check that building too before anyone moves in."

Ella, Blalock, Nez watched Tache examine the overhead garage door. After a few minutes, he walked around to the side wall, then checked a metal access door. He brought out a lock pick set, and thirty seconds later was inside.

The ensuing silence made Ella nervous. Ralph was on his own. She knew he'd come through . . . but at what cost?

An eternity later the big overhead door opened, revealing a sedan-sized vehicle covered by a big blue tarp. Tache walked out holding a flashlight and carrying a can of Coleman Fuel in his gloved hand. He set the fuel down about twenty feet from the building, then flipped up his visor.

"All clear," he said. "We got here just in time. There was an electric heater turned on high and aimed at this camp stove fuel. I unplugged the heater, so we're okay now. Just don't mess with the fuel for a while, the can's still a little warm. I'm going to get some water to pour over the thing, just to be safe."

As Ralph passed Ella, he stopped for a second. "Thanks for giving me a second chance."

"You're welcome," she said.

As Ralph continued to his van, Ella glanced at Dan and Blalock. "House first?"

"Sounds good to me," Blalock said, and Dan nodded.

Ella leading the way, they went inside through the back door. The house, a small two-bedroom rental with a combination kitchen–dining room and living room, had an empty, soulless feel. There were no photos on the wall and the scant furniture seemed utilitarian and completely impersonal. The living room furnishings consisted of two chairs placed in front of a particleboard stand that held a portable TV with rabbit ears.

"Anyone know how long he lived here?" she asked Nez and Blalock.

"Almost three years," Dan said after checking his Black-Berry.

"This looks like a crash pad—just a place to sleep," Ella said, thinking out loud.

"Maybe that's exactly what it is," Dan said. "I've had apartments that looked like this."

His words made Ella remember what it had been like for her a lifetime ago when she'd worked as a Bureau agent. "Come to think of it, I've had my share of crash pads, too. The younger you are, the less it matters, I think, but Talbot's not a young man. The transition from family life to this must have been rough."

"Come look at all this reloading equipment," Blalock said, calling their attention to the second bedroom. One wall held a sturdy wooden workbench equipped with an expensive-looking progressive reloading press, dies, powder measures, and all the rest, including an electronic scale. Plastic ammo boxes and bins on wooden shelves held brass, bullets, and other components, including gunpowder.

"Hey Ella, I think I know who was sending you those text messages. Your name and cell phone number are written on a desk calendar," Blalock said. "And mine, too. Where the hell did he get this?"

"Harrison and his police contacts," Dan suggested. "I guess I'm not important enough to make his list."

"No, yours is on the next page, Nez," Blalock added. "Along with every other agency I can think of."

Ella saw an empty Taser box on the bench. "Any fire-arms?"

"Not that I've seen," Dan said, still looking around. "But there's a nine-millimeter pistol die still in the press."

Ella went to the bedroom and opened the closet door. "We've got a county deputy's uniform here," she said. "Looks real."

"It supports your theory, Ella," Blalock said, coming up. "They played cop and pulled the vics over."

"I bet they added authentic-looking squad car markings along with everything else," Nez said.

They went to the garage next. Working together, they pulled the tarp back and revealed what looked like an older model unmarked county deputy's cruiser. A red emergency light was resting on the dashboard, the power cord dangling down.

Peering into the backseat, Ella could see two vehicle-sized county gold stars, serial numbers, and unit numbers. "Magnetic stick-on signs, easily applied, easily removed. They could drive around without gathering attention, or pass as the real deal in a hurry. Unless you looked real close, you'd never know the difference."

"We need to move fast if we're going to catch these guys," Dan said. "Officers also need to know that there's a chance that the two are armed with AP rounds. Conventional vests won't provide much protection."

"Good idea. As for tracking, maybe we can call in a state police helicopter to patrol state road 170? Five-fifty north is already covered, so the La Plata route is the only road leading to Colorado from this area," Ella said. "They won't be able to avoid our east–west roadblocks, and the routes south have already been put on alert."

"I'll do that now," Blalock said. "I'll also update the ATL, and advise all the agencies to use tactical channels in case the suspects have a scanner."

They reentered the house and helped the crime-scene
team as they waited for news. While they were working,
Blalock received a call on his radio.

He put it on speaker so Ella and Dan could hear the helicopter crew's report. "We've got a pickup under surveillance on an oil field access road. It fits the make and model
you gave us, and there appear to be two individuals inside.
We ran the license plate, and the vehicle belongs to Talbot."

Acting on the news, Ella and Blalock climbed into his
sedan, and within seconds were racing north, monitoring
updates from the helicopter. Nez followed in his sheriff's
department unit.

"Set up roadblocks just inside the Colorado state line,
north of La Plata," Blalock told her, his eyes on the road.
"Act on my authority."

"They might have been in Colorado by now if they
hadn't taken the back roads," Ella said. "Guess they picked
up the initial ATL on their scanner and were hoping to
avoid the roadblocks. Think we can beat them to La Plata,
Dwayne?"

"Find out everything you can on the conditions of those
unpaved county roads. They get a lot more rain up there this
time of year than we do."

Ella made two quick calls, then hung up. "According to the
state police, the public roads have been poorly maintained
this season—budget cuts again. There haven't been any road
closings, but it's slow going, and the roads will be even worse
on the stretch east toward the La Plata highway."

"Hastily laid plans. I would have gone south on the dirt
roads instead and tried to get lost in the Albuquerque area,"
Blalock commented.

They rode in silence, cruising quickly along flat stretches
of highway, then onto the mesas west of the La Plata River.
Three miles south of the New Mexico community of La
Plata, the road divided and Blalock took the westernmost

route on the advice of the helicopter observer. Other units coming in behind them could cover the road if the two suspects reversed direction.

"Unless they change course they'll reach the highway you're on within five minutes," the helicopter observer said. "You just passed that junction."

Ella looked back down the highway. "They'll be coming out behind us. So we've managed to get ahead of them."

"We made good time. And with units following them on the back roads, they have no place to go—at least by vehicle."

"The GPS shows a cutoff just ahead where they could turn east. How about if we set up a roadblock this side of the intersection, just around the curve ahead?" Ella said, pointing.

"Good choice," he said. "We'll block the highway past that culvert. The ditch will keep them from going east or west."

Seconds later, they stood, armed, behind Blalock's vehicle, now parked sideways across the narrow highway. Ella had a shotgun and Blalock's M16 was propped against the car. All they had to do now was wait.

Seven minutes later, Blalock got a call on his cell. He listened intently for a few minutes, then answered, "Okay, keep circling the area. We'll continue north and keep them from going into town."

"Hop in," he said, handing Ella his M16 as soon as she tossed her shotgun onto the back. "Keep it handy. Our subjects spotted the chopper and drove off-road into the tall brush. Officers in the pursuit vehicles followed and found the pickup empty except for a twenty-two rifle. Harrison and Talbot took off on foot, heading north into the tree line."

"Do you think they'll circle to the east and try to reach the road that way?" Ella asked as Blalock spun the vehicle back around, accelerating north again.

"Naw, it's open ground and the helicopter would pick them up in a nanosecond once they reach the clearing," Blalock said.

"We should have Nez and his deputies cover the road behind us anyway. Should I make the call?" Ella asked, and reached for the mike as he nodded.

"Meanwhile we'll drive into La Plata, then cut west and try to intercept them. They'll have to come out of cover sooner or later if they hope to find another vehicle. If they hoof it west, they'll enter the Ute Mountain Rez, which is pretty desolate. There are almost no roads in that particular section, so they'll have a hard time finding new transportation."

They entered the western outskirts of the small, semirural village of La Plata within a few minutes, and quickly reached a dead end. About a half mile ahead, to the west, they could see a white farmhouse surrounded by dark green fields of alfalfa.

Ella pointed to a spec in the sky. "There's the helicopter."

A call came in over the radio. "Suspects located. They're running east toward a small farmhouse about a mile west of the main highway," the state police observer said. "They're carrying a rifle and a big duffle bag."

"Roger that," Blalock answered. "We're approaching the farm road just to the southeast. Keep the suspects in sight."

The drive was bumpy, and they bounced around so much Ella had to grab on to the door handle.

A minute later, Blalock pulled up to a closed metal gate that blocked the driveway. They were about a hundred feet from the front door of the wood-frame house, which was surrounded by a four-foot-high wire fence. Between them and the structure were several tall pines, with a narrow footpath leading through a wooden gate to the porch. An old station wagon and a relatively new, big Ford pickup were parked to the side underneath a metal-roofed carport.

"The suspects climbed the fence and just entered the

building through the rear," the voice on the radio reported. "Looks like they kicked in the door."

"Crap. Another thirty seconds was all we would have needed," Blalock said, turning off the engine. "Keep your head down, Clah," he said, opening the door and slipping out.

"Dwayne," Ella called out, reaching across the seat and handing him the M16 butt-first. "You've got more experience than I do with this." She grabbed her shotgun and stepped out.

As they started toward the trees, several shots rang out, whistling past or thudding into the wood. Blalock flattened on the hard ground, and Ella, to his right, did the same, using the trees to screen herself from view.

"We've got hostages," Harrison shouted from somewhere inside. "Back off!"

Ella got Harrison's cell phone number from the card he'd given her days earlier and called him directly, looking back and forth at the windows facing the road. There was a small window in the door as well, but it was covered by a stained-glass image.

"Ross," Ella said, identifying herself, "you're not going anywhere. Give up now before someone you *don't* want dead gets hurt."

"We've got two hostages. If you try to rush the place, you're going to need more body bags than you counted on."

"You don't want to do that. The drunks you killed might have ended up hurting someone else out on the road. I get that. They were accidents waiting to happen and you took them out to protect others. But the ones with you now are innocents."

"Then don't do anything stupid," Harrison answered. "Their lives are in your hands. We won't kill anyone—unless you or your people try to get any closer."

Ella heard weariness and resignation in his voice. "Ross,

are you planning to come out?" Ella asked, still trying to get a handle on Harrison's game plan.

"Yeah, but not yet."

"When, Ross?"

"I'll let you know."

"Don't wait too long. Officers from several agencies are surrounding the area, and before long someone else will be making the decisions, Ross," she said, using his name once again. The police training manual said that fostered intimacy and sometimes got a suspect to lower his guard. However, she seldom had occasion to use the technique. That mostly worked with Anglos, but not so much with the *Diné*, for obvious reasons.

Ella looked at Dwayne. "He's got a plan in mind, but I'm not getting a read on it."

"So you want to just sit here?"

"Actually, unless I hear shots, I think that's our best option," Ella said.

"Okay. Officially, I'm in charge, but you seem to have a handle on things. Since the tribe has suffered the most from these loose cannons, you should continue speaking for us here."

The next forty minutes taxed everyone's patience to the limit. Justine and Neskahi had arrived, and more than two dozen officers from state and county were also present behind their parked vehicles, or hiding in the surrounding fields and forest. The perimeter around the farmhouse was all but impregnable now.

Ella considered calling Harrison and initiating another dialog when her phone rang. "You're going to wait us out, aren't you?" Ross asked.

"Yes," Ella said. "You were a police officer, so you know the drill, Ross. We already have SWAT from two agencies, complete with sniper teams, assault rifles, tear gas, flash bangs, an armored car, overhead capability, night vision—frankly the whole nine yards. Hell, I've even got the FBI breathing down my neck. This is already above my pay grade, so by the time it gets dark, some hard-ass former Marine is going to be running the show. Count on it. Take the easy way out while there's still a chance to settle this peacefully."

"Okay, okay," Harrison said after a long silence. "I'm sending the hostages out—but there are conditions."

"I'm listening."

"They walk all the way out, hands up, and meet you behind the police line. *Nobody* comes up to grab them. We'll have them in our sights. If you move in, rush the house, or try any diversion whatsoever, we'll know, and the hostages will die. Clear?"

Ella looked at Blalock, who nodded. "Deal. And you'll come out after that, unarmed. Right?" She wanted to push Harrison a little. Maybe they could end the standoff without any blood being spilled.

"Yeah. We'll come out. We've done what we set out to do—get the public's attention. We made a video and have just uploaded it to YouTube. Our defense, our message, is now there for all to see. We got drunks off the road—permanently. We stopped them before they could take other lives."

"You didn't just get drunks off the road, Ross," she said. "The woman you killed hadn't been drinking at all—she was a cancer victim barely able to drive home after chemotherapy. Her name was Alice Pahe, and she was fighting for her life."

There was a long silence at the other end. "I know. We discovered that too late, but she was dying anyway, so maybe we did her a favor. Suffering pets can be put to sleep—humans have to die an inch at a time. How humane is that?"

"Something's happening," Blalock whispered, pointing toward the front door, which was opening slowly. A tall, gray-haired man in his mid-sixties wearing jeans and a sleeveless white tee-shirt stepped out. Beside him was a frightened-looking woman in a long, shapeless house dress. Both were barefoot.

"Hold your positions," Ella called out over the radio net. "They have to come to us." Glancing over at Blalock, she added, "Dwayne, use your scope and check them for explosives."

"If they're hiding anything, it's got to be pretty small," Blalock said after a beat. "I'm guessing they're clean."

The older couple soon passed through the gate, closed it, and hurried toward two white sheriff's department vehicles parked in the drive. When they reached safety, Ella and Blalock were there to meet them.

"Are you hurt?" she asked, urging them behind the engine block of a sheriff's department SUV.

The man shook his head as he tried to catch his breath. "No. Those men weren't really interested in us. They kicked down the back door, came in, showed their guns, then had us lay facedown on the floor. After they tied us up, they didn't pay much attention to us at all. They were too busy with a small computer, then some other stuff from inside their duffle bag."

"They told us that if we stayed quiet, they'd let us go," the woman said. "Eventually, they untied us and told us to walk as fast as we could from the house—but not to run. If we did, they'd shoot us."

"They also ordered us to close the gate after we got through, then come straight here and get behind cover," the man added.

"Why 'cover'?" Blalock said, quickly stepping out to look at the house.

"What was in their duffle bag?" Ella asked the couple, then reached up to touch her badger fetish. It was hot, too hot.

TWENTY-EIGHT
───── ✗ ✗ ✗ ─────

The farmhouse suddenly blew apart. A massive shock wave of hot air slammed against them, followed by an enormous ball of fire and smoke. An ear-shattering boom shook the ground and rocked them off their feet.

"No!" the woman screamed. Her husband held her tightly against him as high-speed debris flew everywhere, rattling off glass and metal and whistling across the ground.

Officers crouched and covered their heads as pieces of wood, metal, glass, and roofing material slowly rained down, like a thunderstorm right out of hell.

At long last Ella looked over the edge of the SUV's hood, shielding her eyes from the glare. There was nothing but raging chaos where the ranch house had stood just seconds before. "Everyone, stay alert. This could be a diversion," she yelled.

The radio crackled. "No one came out," the helicopter observer informed her as the aircraft circled to avoid the billowing cloud of black smoke.

Ella walked a little closer to the inferno, then stopped, and shook her head slowly. As Blalock came up she turned to look at him. "Did I cause this? Was it because I forced them to see what they'd become?"

"No way, Clah. They planned this. That's why they brought those explosives and had the video ready to upload. They wanted to go out this way—martyrs for the cause. A shoot-out would have taken away their credibility—at least in their eyes."

Ella took a shaky breath. "They stole time from a woman fighting for every minute she could get and, now, laid down their own lives in payment. Balance is restored."

The next morning, Ella walked into the kitchen, suppressing a yawn as she groped, half asleep, for her coffee cup.

"There are some tortilla wraps in the fridge, Daughter, but they'll taste better if you warm them up first." Rose was seated at the kitchen table, notes spread everywhere.

"It's good to see you happy again and doing something you love, Mom."

"We all have to redefine ourselves from time to time, Daughter," Rose said.

As Ella transferred the tortilla wrap into the microwave, she caught a glimpse of Dawn standing in the doorway. "You're right, Mom. What we are isn't always what we'd like to be, but by changing ourselves we grow and find our own place in life."

Grabbing the tortilla wrap from the microwave, Ella went outside. It felt good to linger on such a beautiful morning. Now that the case was closed, she didn't need to rush in to the station.

"Mom?"

Ella smiled at Dawn, who'd followed her outside. "Good morning, Daughter."

"I heard what you just told *Shimasání* about finding our

own places in life," she said. "I'm not really sure who 'me' is yet, but until I am, I don't want to close any doors."

Ella waited, wondering where this was going.

"Mom, have you ever regretted not having a *kinaaldá*?"

"Sometimes," Ella admitted slowly. "Back then, it meant very little to me—I had my own issues to deal with—but time changes us in ways we never expect."

"I know. We . . . outgrow things. Like my old computer. It was just right a year ago, but now . . ."

"Are you lobbying for a new one?" Ella asked, laughing.

"No, well, yes. But what I'm trying to say is that I want to have my *kinaaldá*. I've read about it in some of *Shimasání*'s old books, and it sounds really—well, cool. You know I love to run, and during the ceremony, I know I'm supposed to race twice each day, beginning before dawn—if you'll pardon the pun." She grinned. "There's a whole lot more to it than that, of course, and I'd like to do the four-day ceremony, if that's okay. Can we still put one together?"

Ella looked at her daughter and smiled. "Of course. What do you say we go visit your uncle later this morning and see what his plans are for next week?"

Rose opened the back door and stepped out. Ella knew she'd heard them through the open kitchen window.

Rose's eyes filled with tears as she looked at Dawn. "Your coming-of-age ceremony is something you'll never forget, Granddaughter."

As Ella watched them go back inside, arm in arm, she couldn't help but notice the love that drew her mother and daughter together. Dawn was no longer a child, but that very fact was fostering a new closeness between them.

Time. It was slipping right through their fingertips, but with its passing came the whispers of new beginnings.